Frenzied Love

Book Ten

Salvaggio's Light

An Epic Contemporary Romance Serial
By C. L. Cattano

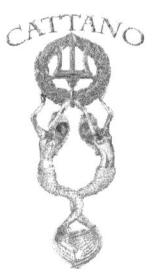

VAGARY PUBLISHING

Frenzied Love
Book Ten
Salvaggio's Light
A Vagary Publishing Book
Copyright © 2018 by C. L. Cattano

Cover Art, Title Page Art and Typesetting Copyright © 2018 by Chynsia Hinesley

Published by:

VAGARY PUBLISHING

www.vagarypublishing.com
inquiry@vagarypublishing.com

Rogena Mitchell-Jones, Independent Literary Editor
RMJ Manuscript Services LLC *www.rogenamitchell.com*

ISBN: 978-1-947852-11-2
First Edition

WARNING

It is suggested readers of this story be adults over the age of eighteen.

This dramatic romance series has many scenes describing sex as well as intense emotional scenes and acts of violence.

This is a serial story with themes flowing from one book into another with lots of twists and turns. Reading this series from the beginning is highly suggested, or the reader may not be able to follow all the storylines.

Go to the Salvaggio's Light Facebook page to join other readers who are talking about the series. www.facebook.com/SalvaggiosLight/

Join the C L Cattano mailing list and check out my website at www.clcattano.com

Acknowledgments

THANK YOU TO everyone who followed until the end. This is it! The journey is over! It has been a crazy time, and though I'm happy to give you the conclusion, it's also a bit depressing that my time with these characters is over. They will forever live in my mind and heart, and I hope they have been in some way meaningful to you, reader. My thanks also go out to my Editor, Rogena, for putting up with my long-windedness and OCD tendencies. Last, but never least, I must thank Marie for all the strange discussions about all my Salvaggio's Light friends... late at night, at dinner, during commercial breaks, on car rides everywhere, and in many other possibly inappropriate places and times. I am a willing victim of your love, and my heart appreciates your gentle handling – even when I'm going on incessantly about imaginary people.

I've been asked if there will be more... the short answer is—never say never...

Dedication

For Marie — may our story never end.

Salvaggio's Light

An Epic Contemporary Romance Serial

Shattered Paradise
Blue Inferno
Sowers of Discord
Wildling's Claim
Sowers of Discord
Fire of Wrath
Confronting Darkness
Traditorè
Cyprian the Fair
Frenzied Love

Cyprian the fair sent down her rays of frenzied love...
I saw my lady more beautiful,
and just as, in a flame, a spark is seen...
— Dante Alighieri, *The Divine Comedy*

1

Less than an hour later...

ROLLING SMOOTHLY DOWN the pathway within the grounds of the villa settled in the outskirts of Florence, Italy, Rafe Salvaggio pulled the motorcycle up to her cottage. Cutting the engine, she got off the bike and headed for the door. As she stepped inside the cottage, she put her helmet, gloves, and jacket on a chair, then headed to the bedroom to get out of her dusty clothes and to take a shower.

After showering, Rafe dressed, then went to the nightstand by her bed and opened the drawer. Reaching inside, she pulled out her pill pack for the night. She wanted to take them now because she did not know how late she would be out. Pills in hand, she headed to the kitchen where she tore open the pack and took the pills with a glass of water.

It had been her routine for the past six months—white pill pack of vitamins in the morning, blue pack with meds to help balance brain chemicals in the evening. If things got too bad at night, Gabri had pills to help her sleep. Rafe knew Gabri hated giving her the sleeping pills, but sometimes they were the only thing to help her shut down her mind and rest. For a while, she saw her doctor, who would come to the villa every day, not only to have sessions but also to administer medications. Then she started going to the therapist's office along with Gabri, who made sure she kept her appointments. After reducing her medication and sessions gradually, trips to the doctor happened only twice a month now, unless she needed additional help. Rafe's nightmares still haunted her, but they weren't as intense or as often since a lot of the major stressors were now removed. It had been tough, but she was doing better. She was finally getting out and living again.

Until the day Eden showed up carrying Rafe's old school bag, Rafe hadn't taken a sleeping pill for a couple of months. Then yesterday, after her conversation with Julia, she needed the relief the pills could give once more. Julia had confirmed all Rafe's worse fears. Eden and Julia were sleeping with each other and planning a life together. Rafe took it hard. The decision to see Eden again had not been easy. Seeing Julia ensconced in Eden's hotel room, and knowing they now slept in the same bed, had been heartbreaking.

Rafe sat down at her little kitchen table, recalling her day with Eden. She hoped she did the right thing in telling Eden the secret she kept from everyone for so long. On the table, she noticed the piece of paper with Eden's information. *I forgot to remind her to keep the secret.* The thought worried her until she had to take action.

She went across the room and picked up her jacket. Pulling out her mobile phone, she tossed the jacket aside again, and then went back to the table. Checking the phone number on the paper, she dialed, then put the phone to her ear.

"Hello," Eden's voice came over the phone.

"Eden, this is Rafe."

"Rafe, is everything okay?" she asked with surprise in her voice.

"Yes," said Rafe and hesitated. "I just wanted to remind you to keep the secret," she said softly.

"I will." Eden went silent.

"Okay, well, I have to go," said Rafe. "Bye."

"Bye."

Rafe disconnected the call and stared at her phone for a moment. As her mind went over the day, she remembered she had left the school bag in the saddlebag on the bike. Tossing the phone down, she went outside and got the bag, then took it into her bedroom. She looked around, frustrated there were no good hiding places.

Who builds a house and does not include hiding places, she thought in irritation.

She lifted the mattress on the bed and shoved the bag under it. It was the hiding place she had used before and would have to make do until she could figure out something else. She would have left it with Eden but was afraid she would start using it again.

There could be no hint her mother knew anything about Maria or even that she had ever existed. This included a school bag, stolen when she was twelve, suddenly showing up and leading to questions.

She lay down on the bed and looked up at the ceiling for a moment, and then closed her eyes. Images flashed behind her lids of disjointed memories from her childhood mixed with thoughts about the troubles she went through when she was back home and the things happening now.

A wave of dizziness crashed over her. She sat up quickly and caught her breath in panic. She held her hand to her head and felt the fear and regret of telling Eden her secret sear her mind. She sprang out of bed and raced for the bathroom where she made it just in time as she vomited into the toilet.

"Fuck!" she said as she saw the medication mixed with the bile as she wiped her mouth just before gagging again as her stomach turned.

Trembling slightly, she got up and rinsed her mouth out and wiped her watering eyes. She grabbed her toothbrush and the toothpaste and brushed her teeth quickly. She looked up into the mirror at herself.

"You are fucked," she said softly. "There's no way you can stay here now." She closed her eyes and hung her head down.

She didn't know how she could face Gabri again since now someone else knew the secret. Once she realized her father knew her secret, she lived in fear for years that he would tell Gabri. So many times, her father had hinted he knew and would tell. So many times, he subtly used it against her.

Now Eden knew.

I should have thought things through better, thought Rafe. *Eden said she wouldn't use my secrets to hurt me, but she might use it to get what she wants. She could hold it over my head and threaten me. Like my father. The things he had done were to remind her of what she had done, of what he had lost—his wife, her mother.*

Rafe looked up into the mirror again. "Think," she told herself, her eyes still haunted with guilt after all these years.

She had to find a way to control things so Eden couldn't use the secret, and so Gabri would never find out. She had to take control of the matter and make sure it didn't turn into a life-ruining mistake. She couldn't lose Gabri. He was all she had left.

"Think!" she screamed at herself in the mirror.

She walked back into the bedroom and over to the bed. Lifting the mattress, she grabbed the canvas school bag.

"Have to get rid of the bag," she mumbled as she took it to the kitchen and threw it on the table.

At the kitchen counter, she grabbed a knife from the block, then turned to the table and sat down. Picking up the bag, she removed the tools, drawing pad and lighter, and then unclipped the shoulder strap.

Using the sharp knife Rafe carefully cut the strap into small pieces. Satisfied with her work on the strap, Rafe opened the bag and cut out the area at the top where her mother had written, 'R. Salvaggio.' After chopping the piece of fabric into even smaller pieces, she added them to the pile with the pieces of the shoulder strap.

"Ashes," she said under her breath. Gathering up the small pieces carefully, she cradled them as she picked up the lighter. A few steps later, she was outside in front of the stone bowl where she had burned the pages from her drawing pad.

She put the pieces in the stone bowl and used the lighter to start a small flame. "Shit!" Rafe hissed as the pieces caught fire but went out abruptly.

Hurrying back into the house, she looked around the kitchen, quickly finding the old drawing pad. She grabbed it off the table, taking it back outside where she tore out pages. Wadding them up, she filled the bowl, then picked up a few twigs and sticks from the ground beside the house. Finally, she put the scraps of canvas on top of everything in the bowl.

After lighting the paper in several places, Rafe ripped out more paper from the pad and collected more twigs to keep the fire going. She fed the fire until it finally consumed the entire drawing pad and the canvas had charred and burned. There was not enough fuel to make a fire big enough to burn the rest of the school bag. She would have to find another way to make sure it never came back to haunt her again.

She made another swift trip into the house, grabbed the canvas bag, and took it back out to the stone bowl. Scooping the ashes from the bowl into the bag, Rafe's hands were now covered in blackened soot. When satisfied all the ash was in the bag, she looked around the outside cottage. Finding several heavy stones, she put them inside the canvas bag, then fastened the buckles to keep it closed.

Carrying the bag to the motorcycle, she put it inside the saddlebag. She stood back to look at what she had done.

"Good," she said nodding to herself.

She turned on her heal and went back into the house. Inside, she looked down at her hands blackened with soot. Ash was on her shirt and pants, too. *"Merda!"* She rushed to the kitchen sink and began washing her hands.

Amid covering her tracks, the phone rang. Grabbing a towel to dry her hands, Rafe picked up the phone and answered.

"Pronto,"[1] she said shakily.

"Rafaella, where are you?" asked Gabri through the phone. "Are you still out? What have you been doing? We are performing in less than an hour. We thought you would be here by now."

"I..." stammered Rafe, "I'm at home. I was sick again," she said rapidly leaving out the fact she threw up her meds.

"Sick again?"

"I'm fine," Rafe said quickly in response to the worry she heard in his voice. "I'm just going to get cleaned up. I'll be on my way as soon as I can."

---

[1] Hello

"Are you sure you're okay? Should I send a car back?" asked Gabri.

"No, I'm fine," said Rafe. "I'll take the motorcycle. I need to go," she said. "I'll see you soon."

"Please, be careful," he said, his voice still full of worry.

"Okay," she said ending the call.

Rafe tossed the phone back onto the table then looked down at herself and the dark streaks on her clothes. Rushing to the bedroom, she frantically stripped out of her dirty clothes and put on clean.

"Time to go," she said to herself, grabbing her jacket, gloves, and helmet. In her rush, she forgot her phone and about the pills.

Rafe rode away from the cottage and off the villa grounds. She made it onto the streets of Florence where she pushed her way through the traffic on the main thoroughfares until she turned off onto one of the many side streets and made her way over to *Via Maggio*.

She followed the street until she came to *Ponte Santa Trinita*. Pulling over to the side of the bridge, she cut the engine and got off the bike. At the back of the bike, she carefully took the school bag, now heavy with stones and stained with ashes, out of the saddle bag and carried it to the side of the bridge.

She remembered when she was young and she, along with Gabri and Brettito, watched people throw things off bridges. She didn't understand then why they would do such a thing.

Now she understood.

The river *Arno* was muddy and dark. Anything thrown in would be lost in the muck at the bottom forever if it was heavy enough.

Now she understood how some things needed to be lost forever.

She hefted the stone-filled bag up onto the side of the bridge. In the distance, she could see *Ponte Vecchio* where everything started with Maria so long ago. She would have gone there if it weren't for all the people and lights. She leaned over the bridge, looking down at the water below, seeing very little except blackness.

Perfect, she thought and pushed the bag over the edge. Seconds later, she heard the splash. She closed her eyes and felt relief, the reminder and evidence of her betrayal was now gone forever.

She brushed her gloved hands together and then scrubbed the ash off her leather jacket. Satisfied with her work she turned and got back on the motorcycle, making her way to *Piazza Massimo D'Azeglio* where Gabri and Nora were waiting.

2

PARKING THE motorcycle next to the curb, Rafe Salvaggio removed her helmet and gloves. After dismounting, she stowed her helmet, jacket, and gloves in the saddlebags. Putting the keys in her pocket, she turned and made her way into the crowded plaza toward the main stage area. The crowd was enjoying the soulful singing of a performer on a smaller stage while the main stage looked like it was almost ready. Rafe was glad she hadn't missed the duo set for Gabri and Nora. As she made it to the main stage, she heard her name called.

Nora walked toward Rafe as the crowd gave way to the very pregnant woman. "Rafe!" Nora called grabbing Rafe's arm as soon as she got close. "Gabri is beside himself with worry. You have to come talk with him. Are you all right? You missed my set."

"I'm fine," said Rafe, putting her arm around Nora as they walked back to the stage. "I'm sorry I missed you, but I'm here for the duo."

"Rafe!" Gabri yelled as he rushed to her. "There you are! Are you feeling better?"

"I'm fine," she said again, smiling to prove her words. "Are you ready to go on? Do you need my help?"

Gabri was concerned but didn't pressure Rafe about how she was feeling. He could see she didn't want the fuss. It was probably because Nora was there.

"I need you to look after Nora and help her up and down the stage stairs. Then I need you to be my wild dancer," he announced excitedly.

Rafe laughed just enough to reassure him. "Okay, I think I can handle those jobs."

They made their way backstage where chairs were set up for the performers and stage crew. Rafe and Nora found seats, and Gabri ran to help Stefano and to make sure their equipment was set up and their set would begin on time.

"What did you do today?" Nora asked as they watched all the activity. "We've been wondering where you went, especially when we had to leave the house and you weren't back yet."

"I was taking your advice," said Rafe then gave her a smile and a wink. "I went to see Eden and spent some time with her."

"Oh, my god," she exclaimed happily. "This is so great! Tell me everything. Did the day go well?"

Rafe nodded. "It was good." She leaned back in her chair. "We saw Carisa and her bees. Then we came back to the city and mostly walked around. We had lunch and then gelato," she recounted, purposely leaving out their visit to the cemetery. "Then I took her back to the hotel. Bronte was asleep, so I didn't get to visit her. I visited a little with Eden and Julia, and then I went home."

Nora could tell Rafe was just giving her the basics. She let it go because she was happy Rafe was taking the risk and spending time with Eden. "Gabri said you were sick again," she whispered so no one else would hear. "What happened?"

"I don't know," said Rafe and shrugged offhandedly. "Maybe it was something I ate." She didn't want to tell her she was sick because of how she felt about telling Eden her secret. "I'm better now," she assured her.

"Good," said Nora, rubbing Rafe's arm. "Is Eden coming to see Gabri?"

"She mentioned it," said Rafe with a nod.

"She—" Nora shook her head. "Rafe, you should have made sure she was coming. We could all go out together after the performance and visit."

"I wasn't sure what I'd have to help with, and I didn't want to be rude if she came and I couldn't spend time with her," said Rafe knowing it was not much of an excuse.

"Rafe," Nora admonished, "what am I going to do with you?" She gave Rafe a stern look and sighed. "Let's just hope she comes despite your lack of effort."

The drummer on stage played a warmup of kicks, crashes, and booms, letting everyone know the performance was about to begin. Several other instruments did a quick tune check, and the MC took the microphone to introduce Gabri and the band.

"I should get you up on stage," said Rafe, helping Nora up.

"Just remember, I don't want to stay up there for the full set. So come and get me after my last song," she instructed Rafe as she helped her up the stairs. Nora smiled at the fact Rafe and Gabri thought she needed the help, but she took their over protectiveness with as much grace as she could muster.

"I'll remember," said Rafe. She then went back down the stairs to get a chair for Nora. After she brought the chair up, she made sure Nora was settled then got off the stage.

The *Angelo di Firenze* was introduced by the MC, and the music began to the shouts and applause of the crowd. Rafe made her way to the front of the stage and into the crowd to enjoy the performance. Gabri and Stefano were playing guitar, and other musicians were filling in the sound with percussion and wind instruments. They even had a quartet of strings for a few songs. Above it all was Gabri's voice, the final instrument, making everything complete.

Pushing the stroller through the plaza, Eden glimpsed Rafe through the crowd and couldn't help her smile. She pointed her out to Julia and started toward her. The crowd got thicker as they made it closer to the stage. Eden stopped and picked Bronte up out of the stroller. While Eden sought out Rafe to let her know they were at the concert, Julia took the stroller and went to find a more convenient place for them to sit down.

Eden watched for a moment as Rafe clapped and danced happily with the rest of the crowd. It was still amazing she was once again looking at Rafe, and it was real. Bronte spotted Rafe and reached toward her excitedly. So Eden moved closer and let Bronte down so she could run to her mama.

Rafe felt small arms wrap around her leg. She looked down smiling at the sight of Bronte. Leaning over, she picked her up and spun around as Bronte giggled. Looking around, Rafe spotted Eden and carried Bronte to her.

"I think you lost something," Rafe said with a grin, leaning close so Eden could hear over the music. "I found this little girl wanting to dance," she said and kissed the baby.

"Let's dance!" shouted Bronte, bouncing with excitement.

"She's very happy to see you," said Eden, a rush of feelings surging through her at the scent and brush of Rafe's hair against her face. "So am I."

A sharp mix of emotions sliced through Rafe. She tried not to regret telling Eden her secret about Maria or worry she would use it against her. Her heart ignored her mind and quickened its beat, creating a rush of warmth to run through her. She knew, undeniably, the feeling was love. A little fear dusted the feeling, though—the consequence of being hurt so many times. Just like the hurt that she felt that Eden and Bronte would be leaving soon to go back to life with Julia.

"I'm happy to see you both, too," she said with a forced grin. Because Gabri and Nora were watching, Rafe was determined to take what she could get and just be happy tonight. "Let's go see Gabri," she said to Bronte.

"*Corri, Gabri!*" Bronte called out excitedly.

"Right!" Rafe laughed. "*Corri!*" she repeated and pretended to run. She carried Bronte closer to the stage and pointed out Gabri and waved to him. He smiled at them and waved back as he sang. "*Balliamo,*" Rafe said to Bronte and danced to the music with her until the song was over. Gabri introduced Nora for their first duet, and Rafe carried Bronte back over to Eden. "Here's your little dancer," she said handing her the baby.

"Did you have fun with Mama?" Eden asked the baby as she took her.

"Yeah, I wanna do it again," she said. "You can dance too, Mommy!"

Eden laughed and turned to Rafe. "Julia is saving us a seat over there," she pointed. "Do you want to go sit down?"

"I have to be backstage after the next song," said Rafe, not wanting to deal with Julia. "Why don't you and Bronte come with me, and we can sit there."

"Well," Eden hesitated, "what about Julia?"

"You can tell her to come." Rafe gave a shrug, disappointed Julia had even come and unhappy she had to watch Eden worry about her. "I'll take Bronte and see you there," she said, reaching for the baby who went to her happily.

"Oh, okay," said Eden. She watched Rafe walk away as Bronte talked and jiggled in her arms. When they were lost in the crowd, Eden went to find Julia.

Rafe carried Bronte happily toward the stage as Nora and Gabri started their second duet, which had a fast, danceable tempo. The crowd was in a frenzy of dancing and singing. They loved the new song, and it looked like it might just be a hit for Gabri, at least in Italy. They were still working on the English version in the studio.

On stage, Gabri was really getting into the song and dancing around as he sang. When they were next to the stage, Bronte saw him, and she yelled out, "*Corri, Gabri!*" He heard her and started running in place, and Rafe laughed with Bronte.

Rafe put Bronte down, and they ran in place together to the beat of the music then Bronte started running around in circles and laughing happily as Rafe chased after her. The song ended, and Rafe scooped Bronte up, and they went backstage to help Nora.

Rafe ran up the stage stairs with Bronte in her arms. "We've come to help you as promised," she said, a bit breathless.

"It looks like you've brought extra help," Nora said, happy to see the little girl. "Hello, Bronte," she said, running her hand over the little girl's sweet cherub face affectionately.

"You two sounded great," said Rafe. "Even Bronte loved dancing to the song."

Nora laughed unable to hide her pride in the music they created. "I saw her! Let's get off this stage before Gabri thinks I need to stay," she teased.

"I'm not sure how I can help you and carry the B Girl," said Rafe. She looked around, but there was no sign of Eden. "I'll just set her down here." She put the wiggling girl down on the stage, and Bronte immediately ran out to Gabri and hugged his leg.

Gabri looked down and tried not to laugh while he was singing. He bent down, scooped her up, and began singing the song to her.

Nora laughed at Gabri's situation. "Uh, oh, I may have some competition for stage time!"

Rafe caught Gabri's wink, letting her know it was okay. "Let me get you down the stairs, then I'll rescue B Girl," she said with a chuckle. She took Nora down the stairs, delivering her to her chair. She quickly got Nora a bottle of water then ran back up onto the stage to get Bronte.

Gabri finished his song and began speaking to the crowd. *"Salutami la bella, Bronte Salvaggio!"*[2] He spoke to Bronte. *"Grazie per cantare con me. Vuoi parlare nel microfono?"*[3] he asked and put the mic near her mouth.

Bronte grabbed the microphone and put her mouth to it to say the only Italian she knew well, *"Ti voglio bene! Corri, Gabri!"*[4] She pushed the mic away with a proud smile.

---

[2] Say hello to the beautiful, Bronte Salvaggio
[3] Thanks for singing with me. Would you speak into the microphone?
[4] I love you! Run, Gabri!

Gabri laughed into the mic. *"Che può essere un ottimo consiglio!"*[5] The crowd laughed with him. He saw Rafe had come back, so he put her down. *"Andare al mama,* go to mama," he told her and pointed her in the direction of Rafe.

Rafe held her hands out, and Bronte ran to her. When she made it over, Rafe picked her up and kissed her. "You're a star now!" She quickly took her off the stage and over to Nora. "Your competition has the crowd in the palm of her hand," she said, sitting next to her. "I'm not sure where Eden is. She was supposed to be getting Julia then coming back here."

"I'll be fine here if you want to go look for her. Gabri has two or three songs after this one," said Nora then sipped her water.

Rafe scanned the area to make sure Eden hadn't already found her way there but was unable to find her in the crowd. "Maybe she got lost in the crowd or something," she said with a frown, trying to figure out the reason for her not being there. "Okay, I'll go look. I should be back soon."

Carrying Bronte around the stage, Rafe walked back to where she first met Eden but still didn't see her. She made her way through the crowd in the general direction Eden had pointed when showing where Julia was supposed to have gone.

It wasn't hard to pick Julia and Eden out of the crowd with their light hair, especially Julia's long silver hair. Rafe couldn't hear them but could see they were talking. Julia was very animated and looking vexed. Thinking they had just let their conversation delay them, Rafe walked up close enough to hear their discussion.

---

[5] That may be good advice!

"I'm telling you, Eden, you can't keep putting up with her shit," said Julia over the noise of the crowd. "You have to start thinking about yourself and Bronte."

"I am thinking about us," said Eden tensely.

"Really?" scoffed Julia. "Have you even told her why you're here yet? Why are you letting her do this to you? You asked her if she was going to be here tonight and what does she do? She tells you she doesn't know if she'll make it when clearly, she knew she'd be here. Then you get here, and she barely talks to you but takes Bronte off somewhere. I saw the whole thing! She's still treating you in the fucked-up way she was in the States, and you just keep taking it. She sends notes, had huge Italian men demanding things of you, and you just jump at her command. She's put a fucking buffer of people and places between you, and all of us, and she expects us to just go along with it. And you are! You sit up in the hotel room just waiting for notes or calls, or you walk around looking for her on the streets. It's fucked up! If she really cared about you, she'd be treating you better."

"Look," said Eden with a sigh of frustration, "she's waiting for us. Are you coming or not?" she asked and tried to walk away.

"Don't ignore me, Eden," said Julia taking Eden's arm and pulling her back. "You know I care about you. I just want what's best for you. You need to think about what we talked about. You need to move out of her house, stop waiting for her permission to live and start thinking about yourself more. Everyone at home, especially me, is worried about you. We want to help you get a fresh start. Rafe's obviously not thinking about you. You didn't come here to wait in a hotel room for her to call. She's not interested in going home. She's purposely avoiding you. It's painfully obvious she's not leaving the new life she has here. You need to stop letting her abuse you emotionally. We should just enjoy our last few days then get back home so we can get on with our lives."

Rafe had heard enough. "Hey," she said, interrupting them. She kissed Bronte and handed her to Eden.

"Hi," said Eden looking at Rafe with guilt as she took Bronte.

"Hello," said Julia coolly.

Rafe stared at Julia menacingly until she looked away. "If you felt so strongly, why the fuck did you let her come here?" Julia glared back but did not reply. "It's good to know I have less to go home for than I thought." She turned to Eden who was looking back with wide shifting eyes. "I have to get back to..." Rafe was not sure of what or where. "I hope you and Bronte enjoy the rest of your time in Italy." She set a dark gaze on Julia again. "I don't even know what to say to you. Fuck off, I guess." She turned on her heal and walked away.

"Rafe, wait!" Eden called, but Rafe was already lost in the crowd. "Dang it, Julia!" she cried out in frustration.

"I'm sorry," said Julia throwing her hands up. "I didn't know she was there."

Eden put Bronte in the stroller and strapped her in. "I need to find her," she said angrily. "I have to fix this!" She made her way through the crowd, leaving Julia behind shaking her head at the whole situation.

Eden was unsure exactly where to look for Rafe but knew she was helping Nora and Gabri. She pushed the stroller around the stage and found Nora sitting next to some other people, but she didn't see Rafe.

Nora smiled when she turned and saw Eden. She wanted to make sure Eden was invited to go out with them tonight. She thought it might take the pressure off Rafe and give them a chance to just be in a fun, positive atmosphere together. "Eden," Nora called, "Rafe went looking for you," she said then saw Bronte in the stroller. Looking past Eden, she did not see Rafe. "Where's Rafe?"

"I don't know," said Eden anxiously. "She said she had to get back somewhere, so I thought she meant here."

"What happened?" Nora asked in surprise. "She was supposed to find you, so we could all go out."

Eden sat down next to Nora in distress. "She's upset," she said then took a calming breath. "Julia said some things, and Rafe overheard her. Now she's angry, and I don't blame her."

"What kind of things?" Nora asked with concern.

"Julia is angry with her," Eden explained with a sigh. "She thinks Rafe is purposely avoiding me, and she's not happy with how she thinks Rafe is treating me."

Nora furrowed her brow in confusion. "How she's treating you? Who does she think she is, her judge and jury?" Just thinking about the torment that she knew Rafe had been going through lit Nora's temper. "What does this Julia woman expect? Neither of you has any idea the torment you've caused her!" Clenching her jaw tightly, Nora fought the urge to angrily inform Eden what it had been like over the last two days with Rafe. Knowing both Rafe and Gabri would be upset if she mentioned anything stopped her.

After watching Rafe spiral, and agonizing over the decision, Gabri had finally given Rafe one of the pills prescribed to make her sleep. It had been a long time since she needed them. They were warned to be careful giving them to Rafe so she wouldn't become addicted. For months, Gabri worried she would be on them too long and become dependent. Though the pills were a risk, they really seemed to allow her the rest she needed to function. Now Gabri had to give them to her two nights in a row, and Nora hoped tonight would not be the third night.

Nora unclenched her jaw. "You know, maybe I made a mistake trying to help you."

No, please," Eden said fearfully. "I don't agree with Julia. I don't agree at all. I know it's hard for Rafe." She could feel panic trying to ease through her as her heart beat painfully hard. She took a breath to control and calm herself. When she gained control of her anxiety, she looked up at Nora and couldn't stop herself. "I love Rafe," she blurted nervously. "I came here to tell her. I'll do anything to get her back," Eden proclaimed desperately. She felt like Nora had been so helpful and nice, and Eden felt compelled to tell her the things she wanted to tell Rafe. She thought maybe if Nora knew what she had to say, she might help her talk with Rafe and convince Gabri to let her come home. She had to find Rafe and fix the damage Julia had caused too, and she needed help. "Bronte and I need her to be with us and have a family again. It's more, really. I'm in love with her, and I don't want to live without her in my life. Even if she decides she's not in love with me, I want her in our life somehow."

Nora furrowed her brows in contemplation, taking in everything it seemed Eden had spilled uncontrollably. "Wow," Nora said, surprised and unable to help her laugh of relief. "I'm sorry. I'm just glad you're here because you love her and not to break her heart. I know she loves you too, even if she hasn't told you she does."

"She said she loves us," said Eden, relieved Nora seemed to be open to listening to her. "She told me she didn't think I should wait for her to get better. She's getting better, though, and I want to help her if I can. Maybe she'll let me if I can just make her understand I'll be there for her."

"She has been getting better," said Nora seeing Eden seemed sincere, "but Gabri says she still has a hard time sometimes." Nora hesitated because she didn't want to do the wrong thing. She knew Rafe had a lot of issues and worries, and just because Eden said she loved her didn't mean those things would be worked out. She sighed because it seemed like Gabri and his opinions and doubts were rubbing off on her. "Rafe is doing her best with this whole thing," she said gently. "You have to understand. You've shown up unannounced when Rafe was unprepared. You can't expect her to welcome you with open arms and not have some concerns. She told me she hadn't even started thinking about your relationship yet when you got here."

"I know she has concerns. I don't blame her," Eden assured her. "But right now, I just need to tell Rafe I don't agree with Julia. I need to tell her again that I love her. I do want what's best for her, and I need your help to fix this. I love her," she repeated, desperately hoping Nora could see she was telling the truth.

Even though she knew Gabri would be unhappy, Nora felt the right thing to do was to help Eden, but with caution. In her heart, she knew it was what Rafe needed. If Eden were telling the truth, then Gabri would have no reason to be angry.

"I think you should tell me exactly what's been happening. You have to convince me that helping you fix things is the right thing to do. I have to know everything before I can even think about talking to Gabri."

3

PUSHING HER WAY through the crowd, Julia Hawthorn made it out of the plaza and down the street toward the hotel. She was angry they had come all this way, and it seemed to be for nothing. She wanted to argue with Rafe and tell her how she had done everything she could think of to convince Eden not to make this trip. It was something she knew she couldn't do in front of Eden, though, because it would lead to revealing her own feelings and hopes. She knew the time wasn't right for that conversation.

What made her even angrier was that this wasn't the first time Rafe had done something like this—just taking off and leaving everyone behind and expecting everyone to be fine with it. It seemed like a pattern with Rafe where she had to take off and be unreachable. She thought Rafe was finished with all her craziness and unruly behavior. She knew Rafe had some problems and needed medical help, but Julia was also sure those problems were only part of the reason Rafe left everyone behind.

She felt like Rafe could have found help at home, better help— the best help in the world. There was no reason to run away to another country unless Rafe was regressing back into the person she had been before Eden. It was painful, but after thinking everything through, Julia finally had to admit Abby was right about Rafe. Admitting Abby was right about anything pissed Julia off even more.

The only positive thing to come of the matter was the possibility Eden would finally give up on Rafe. Then she and Eden could start their own relationship. If it happened, and Eden came to work with her and her father, then Rafe and her so-called friend Gabri could fuck off. Julia didn't care how much money Rafe might remove from her father's firm.

In Julia's opinion, Rafe and the people she allowed to run her life were inconsiderate and completely heartless. She especially did not like Gabri. Julia was sure he was behind the way Rafe was treating Eden, and the visit by his wife was proof. Even Gabri's wife couldn't control his influence over Rafe. She did not understand how Rafe could let *that man* take over her life and control everything.

Julia wished she could make Eden see she was fighting a losing battle. Rafe was going to do whatever she wanted to do, and it was probably what Gabri wanted her to do. She could see Gabri wanted to keep Rafe here, and it was probably for more reasons than to help Rafe get better. He had access to her money and everything, so Julia was certain he was convincing her to help pay for the ostentatious villa Eden told her about.

She knew there was no way Gabri could afford to keep up an estate on what a musician made unless he was making millions. She was sure that wasn't the case because she had never heard of the guy or his music. He probably talked Rafe into paying for everything in exchange for him bringing her to Italy and taking care of everything for her.

Eden had revealed Gabri wouldn't even let Rafe live in the main house, and she was living in a little shack on the estate. It was horrendous. Julia thought Rafe should have made her or her father power of attorney because Rafe had been her friend for half her life. At least then Rafe could have stayed in America, and they could have taken care of her money. They could have taken care of everything.

Julia finally made it to the hotel, ready for a hot shower. Afterward, she would make some calls to her father and their friends. Walking into the lobby, she noticed Rafe sitting in the lounge.

Rafe noticed Julia too. She walked over quickly to confront her. "Where's Eden?" Rafe asked gruffly.

Julia couldn't believe her gall. "She's still at the concert. Probably running around in a hopeless effort to find you," she said, crossing her arms defensively. "What are you doing here?"

Rafe just glared because Julia knew why she was there. "Fuck off. You're not my friend, remember," she said angrily and walked out of the hotel.

Julia followed her out and caught up with her. "I am your friend! You're the one who's not being a friend!" Rafe ignored her and kept walking. "Yes, all right! Walk away without a word like you always do!"

Rafe stopped and turned on her heal to face Julia. "What the hell are you talking about?"

"I'm talking about you skipping out on everyone all the time and disappearing for undetermined amounts of time," she said angrily.

"What? Skipping out?" Rafe scoffed not understanding.

"Yes, skipping out," said Julia hotly, "skipping out on most of your girlfriends, or friends, like me, and the others back in California. Now you're doing the same thing to Eden and the baby you convinced her to have for you!"

"What?" Rafe said affronted. "I have never—" She seethed then controlled her anger. "I have never skipped out on anyone! I've especially never skipped out on Eden and the baby! I've made sure they would have everything they need!"

"Oh, right," said Julia sarcastically, "throwing money at the problem. I thought you hated it when people accused you of doing such a thing, but now I see you just hated the fact it was the truth!"

"Fuck you," Rafe rumbled evenly as she turned to walk away.

"Go ahead, walk away again," Julia called. "It's okay, I'm used to it," she said as she followed her. "Now I guess you're going walk away from Eden again, too! Maybe someday she'll get used to it!"

"I have no idea what you're talking about," she muttered and kept walking.

Julia was not going to let her get away with walking away again and caught up to her. "Oh, you know exactly what I'm talking about!" she argued.

Rafe stopped abruptly, turning on Julia angrily. "I thought this is what you wanted! You should be happy! You get to go home and keep fucking my girlfriend who you're so in love with now. Isn't this what you wanted to happen? Well, you got it!" she fumed then stalked away.

"This has nothing to do with Eden and me! You don't get to go there! You were the one who left," Julia shouted as she followed Rafe. "This time you're fucking up two people's lives, Eden and Bronte!" She was not about to discuss her lack of physical relationship with Eden. As far as Julia was concerned, who Eden slept with, or did not sleep with, was none of Rafe's business anymore. At this moment, she had other things she wanted to say to Rafe. "This has to do with you and how you treat everyone!" she said heatedly.

Julia's anger built as Rafe just kept walking away and ignoring her.

"Now you're doing it to Eden! The difference is Eden has come all the way here looking for you! Do you know why she's here? It's not because I didn't try to talk her out of it! It's because she's still so naïve she doesn't believe you would walk away from her if she came and talked to you in person. She thinks you might still have something more to your relationship than co-parenting and you shoving money at her! She thinks, no matter what, you'll be in their lives, even if you're not together. You and I know better, though, don't we?"

Rafe stopped next to her motorcycle and turned to Julia. "Don't push me, Julia," she said evenly. "You've never had any idea what went on with me or my relationship with Eden." Rafe eyed her intently and thought about what Julia had said. "You're right. This isn't about Eden, is it? This is about you." She chuckled. "You're still jealous, aren't you?"

"Fuck you!" said Julia angrily. "I am not and never have been jealous of you!"

"No," said Rafe knowingly, "you're just jealous of Eden and probably all the others. I thought we were through all the jealousy stuff from high school. Can't you make up your mind who you want to fuck?" She laughed condescendingly.

"This isn't about what I want or who I want to fuck!" said Julia defensively. "This is about you taking the easy way out of every relationship you've ever been in."

"Oh, really," Rafe said with disdain. "You know nothing about any of my relationships. What makes you so sure any of them were easy for me to end?"

"I know plenty," Julia said scornfully. "I was there every time one of those girls came looking for you!"

"Right." Rafe sighed and shook her head. "And you were there to try and take my place." She remembered when Julia would try to date the girls she broke up with, and it never worked out. She was always trying to be a knight in shining armor but could never figure out the girls didn't need or even want to be rescued.

"I wasn't trying to take your place!" Julia snapped. "At least I cared about them! I can only remember a handful of people you've ever taken the time to say a proper goodbye to in all the time I've known you. Then you have the nerve to be angry when someone does it to you!"

Rafe shook her head because she had no idea what Julia was talking about. "I've never left anyone without telling them goodbye or letting them know I was going."

"Are you kidding? You walk away from everyone! You even did it to girls you dated in school! You'd just disappear with no explanation all the time, or vanish for the summer, and those girls would come looking for you, not knowing you left town, or the country or you were off on some mysterious adventure. You walked away from my house with barely a word and left the country! You did the same thing in college and when you moved to California! I've been treated the same way, and I'm supposed to be your friend!"

"So you *are* talking about high school." Rafe shook her head. "It was so long ago. Any of those girls who came looking for me, I wasn't even dating whenever I had to leave. I ended things with them well before summer if I knew I was traveling, and you know it. You always knew when I was going for the summer unless my father sprang it on me last minute, but I still called you."

Oh, yeah?" she said, challenging Rafe. "What about when you were shipped off to Italy the last time? You barely said anything to me, and afterward, you couldn't find the time for me until I was in England and then only when a party or long weekend was involved."

"Julia," said Rafe still not understanding why they were having this conversation, "I spent the entire day before I had to leave with you. Don't you remember? We met in the park and hung out with Hannah and her school friends?"

"I remember," she said sullenly. "It was one day out of almost four weeks you were out of school! And the ballet girl was hanging all over you the whole time. Then you just dropped me off at home said 'ciao' then walked off with the girl pulling you along as fast as she could."

"Well," said Rafe with a shrug, "she wanted some one-on-one time."

"Is Hannah the striking black woman you had your one-on-one time with when you were in New York?" she asked, making quote signs with her fingers along with the accusation. "The realtor woman, Lauren Street, said you met with her after a show and went out for drinks."

Rafe scowled threateningly and wanted to punch her. "No," she said evenly. "If you make anyone, and I mean anyone, think I'd—" She stopped. She wanted to say she would kill her but knew it would get her into trouble. "You'll regret it," she said finally. "I didn't have an affair with anyone in New York."

Julia could see the murder in Rafe's eyes. She knew she was on shaky ground because she couldn't prove anything. "Fine," she said relenting. "But it doesn't change the fact you skipped out on everyone."

"I didn't skip out on anyone," said Rafe crossly. "Stop saying I did! I'll always take care of Eden and Bronte no matter what happens." Rafe fought to calm herself. "What is it you want from me, Julia?" asked Rafe in frustration, running her hand through her hair. "What's your point with all this?"

"My point is, I'm pissed off at you!" she said angrily. "How could you just let *that man* take you away and give him power over everything? I was there for all your adventures in school and when you moved to California! I was there when Eden left you! I was your confidant and helped you through things, and this is how you treat me?"

Rafe stared in disbelief. What giving Gabri her power of attorney had to do with skipping out she had no idea. "Gabri is my closest friend," said Rafe evenly. "He knows more about me than anyone. He did what he thought was right to help me."

"But why him?" she asked in frustration. "I'm your best friend!"

Rafe let out a laugh of disbelief at what Julia was saying. She didn't feel like Julia was her friend at all anymore. "You mean you *were* my best friend," she said cynically.

"It's your choice, I suppose," said Julia haughtily. "I could have helped you. You could have let me or my father help you. I was trying to convince Eden to let me get you admitted into the best hospital to help you! She wouldn't let me help because she wouldn't do anything unless you agreed first. I'm your best friend! If I'd have had your power of attorney, I could have got you help sooner! But now you are letting some man control you and your life!"

Finally, Rafe understood why Julia was so angry with her. It had nothing to do with skipping out or jealousy over girlfriends. It was jealousy of Gabri. "Gabri is the closest I have to a family left," said Rafe wondering how Julia could still call herself her best friend after the things she had said and what she was doing behind her back with Eden. "He's more than a friend to me. We went through a lot together. We survived things you just can't understand," she said watching Julia roll her eyes. She ignored Julia's disregard for the truth. She continued, knowing Julia wouldn't really hear her. "I trust him with my life, not just in some figurative concept, but literally. It's why I turned to him. I knew, since we had been through so much, he was really the only person I could turn to when things were getting bad for me."

"But I could have helped you," insisted Julia. "You could have told me everything, and I would have been able to help and keep you home."

"No," said Rafe shaking her head. "I couldn't tell you or anyone." She was not surprised to see Julia was still not satisfied. "If you and your parents knew even a fraction of what had happened, do you really think they would have let us hang out or would have treated me the same? The answer is no. Your mother would have made sure you stayed far away from me, and your father would have just felt sorry for me. I needed a friend, not sympathy or exclusion."

"But my father loves you like a daughter," said Julia in frustration. "He would do anything for you."

"Yeah, because now he knows me," said Rafe. "But the first time I came to your house, your mother and father made a bunch of calls to make sure I was worthy of being your friend." She laughed bitterly. "Do you think I would have been worthy if they found out I'd been sick? I know the answer—it's no. We would never have become friends if anyone knew."

"You could have told me when we were in college," she insisted in vexation, "or when you moved to California!"

Rafe shook her head because Julia would never understand. "No," she said sadly, "I couldn't, and really, I didn't want to tell you. I didn't want to tell anyone. I actually really wish you still didn't know," she said and looked down at the ground.

"What about Eden?" Julia asked softly. "It all affects her and the baby. Are you going to leave her in the dark about everything and make her fend for herself while you're trying to get better?" Julia waited for an answer and saw one wasn't coming. "You're a very hard person to love sometimes, but apparently, she was willing to put up with you for a long time." *And so was I*, she thought. "She loved you and look what you're doing to her," said Julia, displeasure dripping from her voice. "She's been very hard on herself for the last six months. When you left, she was sick for months with her anxiety difficulties and," she paused, "and heartbreak. I care for her, and I don't want her to go through it all again. You need to stop giving her hope where we both know there is none. It makes me angry the way you and Gabri are treating her so horribly."

Rafe stiffened at Julia's accusation that Eden was being treated badly. "I don't know why you all treat her like she's some sort of victim, and I'm the bad guy," said Rafe defensively. "She's the one who showed up unannounced. She caused a lot of her own problems. She's the one who's responsible for most of the things that happened to me too."

Rafe fought to control her anger at Julia and the others back home.

"See, this is why I don't know if I even want to go back to California. You all decided Eden needs to be protected or something, and you just don't give a shit about me. Maybe getting away from you and the others really was best for me. You want me to treat you like you're my best friend, but you're not here for me! You're here for Eden! I heard what you said to her. You think Eden getting away from me is what's best for her! You're just here because you're going to get something out of the situation for yourself! You're just here because you think you're in love with her! You want to rescue her and be her hero, then make sure you can keep her under your thumb! I'm sure she'll like it just as much as Andi," she said scathingly.

"You're so full of shit!" said Julia angrily. "Andrea left for a new job, not because of anything I did!" Hearing Andrea's name and being reminded she left, sent shockwaves of old heartache through her. She thought Andrea was the one. Julia had thoughts of marriage and a life together before Andrea left. "You have no right to bring Andrea into this!"

"Really?" scoffed Rafe. "I think I have the right to do whatever I want!"

"Have you forgotten what you did to Andrea?"

"What I did to her?" asked Rafe with a questioning laugh. "Andi was my friend. You manipulated her and tried to pretend you were the victim! You did everything you could to make sure she felt trapped and had nothing so she couldn't leave you! So, there's the real reason she left! Whatever you do, don't try the same thing with Eden or you'll have a repeat performance!"

"Fuck you! You don't know what you're talking about! Andrea left because of a job offer in France. She chose her career over me!" fumed Julia.

Rafe laughed and shook her head making Julia angrier. "See, this is all just the game you play. If you can't have me, you date my ex-girlfriends. Just like with Andi," Rafe said disdainfully. Julia tried her knight-in-shining-armor game with Andi. It turned out Julia's idea of rescuing ended up not being anything Andi wanted boxed into, so she found a good job and left her. "Now you're going after Eden even though you know how I feel about her."

"Right, like you felt about Andrea," scoffed Julia. "You left the country and broke up with her over the phone!

"For your information, Andi knew things weren't working out, and we parted on good terms.

"I wonder," Julia said menacingly. "You didn't seem too broken up about her leaving town."

Rafe shrugged. "As you made it perfectly clear, all the time, she wasn't my girlfriend anymore. She didn't leave the country to get away from *me*," she said hoping the little dig would shut her up.

Julia laughed condescendingly. "Don't try to switch things so the conversation is about my relationships. This is about you! You're just mad because you're not the center of attention! You're acting just like the entitled troublemaker you were in school and before you met Eden!"

"Really?" Rafe scoffed. "I don't seem to remember you having a problem hanging around me. I guess it's because my so-called entitled troublemaking benefited you, too. You did try to date most of my exes, including Andi. You were even invited to all those parties because of me. I guess, since I'm not around anymore, you've turned back into the boring boarding school prude you were when I met you. Now you can just go find someone else to follow around like a puppy," she said with contempt.

"Fuck you!" Julia snapped angrily. "You're such a fucking asshole!"

"This is why I'm glad I have Gabri," said Rafe with a laugh at Julia's pathetic come back. "At least I have someone who thinks about me and actually wants to be on my side and help me. You and the others only think about Eden, or really, you only think about yourselves."

"Oh, really?" Julia challenged. "You think Gabri is thinking about you? He's taken you away from your home and your friends! He's making you live in a shack behind his villa! He's probably even using your money to supplement his income so he can sit around strumming a guitar! He even took you away from Eden and your child! How's that been helping you?"

"You have no idea what you're talking about," said Rafe evenly. She got on her motorcycle and put on her helmet. "I don't know what I was thinking, coming here to apologize and invite Eden out. Thanks for clearing things up for me. I hope Eden appreciates how you look out for her. Have a great fucking life together!" She started the engine on the bike so she couldn't hear Julia's harsh words. She gave Julia the finger and drove away.

"Oh, fuck!" Julia admonished herself and stomped her foot as Rafe sped down the street. She knew when Eden found out Rafe was here, and she ran her off, Eden would be upset. If Rafe weren't so hard headed, they wouldn't even be in this position.

4

WALKING QUICKLY INTO the hotel, Julia Hawthorn knew she had to try to calm down before Eden got back. It was maddening dealing with either one of them. Rafe was secretive and aloof, and Eden was hell-bent on the impossible feat of getting Rafe to come home. Then they had to deal with Gabri and his hold over Rafe. Julia still couldn't believe he had Rafe hidden away in some tiny guest house, and Rafe was apparently okay with it. She didn't understand why Rafe was living with him in the first place. Rafe could afford to buy her own villa or a modern apartment in the city. The only reason she could comprehend for the living arrangements was Rafe planned to eventually go home to California, someday—or worse, take off again.

In her room, Julia calmed herself by taking a shower. Dressed in her pajamas and robe, she looked through some of her shopping bags to see what she might wear the next day. Since she had been either out alone or just with Bronte the last few days, she had taken up shopping for clothes, jewelry, and shoes. She also had a list from her friends at home of things to bring back and managed to check off everything quickly. As she reorganized her purchases, she heard the elevator gate open and went to see if Eden was finally back.

"Are you okay," Julia asked as Eden unlocked the door to her room.

Eden shook her head sadly and sighed. "I'm fine," she said quietly because Bronte was asleep in the stroller. "I wasn't able to find Rafe. I waited with Nora for a while, and she tried calling, but Rafe didn't answer."

"I'm sorry," said Julia keeping her expression impassive. "Can I come over so we can talk?"

"Sure," said Eden wanting to get any criticism Julia had to dish out over with. "We need to be quiet, though." She went into the room, and Julia followed. "Let me get her into bed," she said lifting Bronte out of the stroller.

As Eden took Bronte to the bedroom, Julia went over to the kitchenette. She put the electric kettle on for tea and got out the tea and cups. By the time Eden came out of the bedroom and closed the door, the tea was steeping, and Julia had placed it on the coffee table in front of the couch. Julia could see the disappointment Eden was feeling in her demeanor.

"Sit down and relax for a bit," said Julia gently.

Eden flopped onto the couch feeling exhausted. She had been so excited about the possibility of seeing Rafe tonight. When she actually saw her at the concert, she was so sure they would have a good evening with everyone gathered together. Exhausted from the frustration and anger caused by Julia, Eden's anxiety had peaked from worrying about where Rafe had gone and what she might be thinking. Now there was also the possibility she had lost an ally in Nora.

"I don't know what to do now," Eden said softly as Julia handed her a cup of tea. "Rafe's angry, and I had to work hard to convince Nora not to feel like all we do is upset Rafe." She took a small sip of tea and set it down on the saucer. "I don't blame her," she said then looked over at Julia. "Why couldn't you wait to complain until after we got back home? You know," Eden said in frustration, "she wasn't ignoring me and taking Bronte. I sent Bronte to her, and they were playing. Do you want to know what makes me most angry? It isn't the fact you messed up a night that I could have spent with Rafe. It's that you messed it up for Bronte. She really misses Rafe and wants to see her, and I know Rafe feels the same way."

"I'm sorry," Julia repeated. "I was upset and angry about how they were treating you. I still am." She looked down into her cup.

Eden sighed as she picked up her teacup. "I'm going to have to call her or Gabri tomorrow. I'm running out of time, and I've barely had a chance to really talk with her." She set her cup back down and leaned back in the chair. She couldn't believe Julia. She wanted to throttle her for ruining the night.

Julia knew she had to tell Eden that Rafe had been at the hotel, so she prepared herself for more of Eden's anger. "She was here," she said wanting to get it over with.

"What?" Eden asked not understanding.

"Rafe," Julia paused, "she was here waiting when I got to the hotel."

Eden just stared at Julia for a moment, taking in what she had said, and then she sat up as adrenaline shot through her. "She was? Did she leave a message? Did she say why she was here?"

"She didn't leave a message," said Julia hesitantly. "She just said she was here to apologize and ask you to go out with them."

"Well," Eden said confused, "did you tell her I was still at the concert?"

"I told her," she said, but Julia couldn't look into Eden's eyes. "I told her you've been thinking about her the whole time she's been gone and…" she hesitated. She hoped knowing she told Rafe those words would help, but she knew she had to tell Eden the rest.

Eden noted Julia's hesitation, and it was clear something was wrong. "And? What happened?" she asked. "What else did you say to her?"

"We had an argument," Julia confessed.

"Great!" Eden sighed in frustration. "Why did you have to argue with her? It just makes things harder for me. I'm beginning to wonder if you even want me and Rafe to get back together."

"What? What's that supposed to mean?" Julia stammered trying not to look guilty. Julia was angry about how Rafe was treating Eden. She was trying to help, and this was the thanks she got? Eden was once again letting Rafe get away with everything.

Eden knew she wouldn't have a chance at getting anywhere with Rafe if Julia was constantly picking fights and taking her anger out on Rafe. "I need you to either back off Rafe or, if you don't think you can, just go home. You're the one who keeps pointing out I'm running out of time, and now you've managed to make me lose even more time."

Hurt by Eden's words and at the suggestion she go home Julia pressed her. "Who will help with Bronte? What if they do something horrid again like sending the car for Bronte or something? Who will be here to help you if I leave?"

"I'll just have to figure out a way to help myself," said Eden firmly. "I may never get another chance, and I can't risk anything, or anyone, ruining things for me with Rafe."

Eden remembered when Rafe had been asking her to make everyone leave them alone and now she could see why. She knew understanding Rafe's point of view better was the reason she found it easier to be so firm with Julia. She wished it wasn't so hard to be the same way with Gabri.

Julia saw the determination on Eden's face. She knew if she were to have a chance with Eden, she was going to have to stay and help her see this through. She knew, from her conversation with Rafe, the chances of them getting back together were slim, and Eden would need her.

"You know I'll help you," she said softly. "I'm your friend, and seeing what you've gone through has been difficult. I know Rafe and her history. I just don't want to see you hurt again."

"I know," said Eden with a sigh. "I really do appreciate everything you've done, but I have to do this, and I have to do it now, even if it hurts me." She thought about all the things happening and the secret Rafe had told her. She still had the letter Rafe's mother wrote in her pocket. "Can I ask you a question... about Rafe?"

"Sure." Julia shrugged and took a sip of her tea.

"Abby said Rafe changed when her father gave her his car. Do you think she changed then, too?"

Julia scrunched her face in annoyance and shook her head. "Abby has no idea what she's talking about," she said with exasperation. "Why would a car make Rafe change her behavior? No," she insisted, "Rafe changed when she met you, for the better too." She set her teacup down. "The only thing Abby might be right about is Rafe is going back to her old behaviors."

"Old behaviors," Eden repeated. "Right, the wildling thing," she said thoughtfully. "I guess I still really don't get it."

Julia arched her brow. "Really, well then, I guess the great Salvaggio has lost her touch."

"No," Eden said with a smile, "I get the bedroom part. Just not the other things you all talk about."

Julia rolled her eyes. "Probably because of the rose-colored glasses you see her through." Julia wanted the dreamy smile on Eden's face to be from bedroom thoughts about her—not Rafe.

5

THE NIGHT OF music had been a successful and proud event for Gabri De Angelis and his wife, Nora. Their new music had been very well received, and at the after party, they networked with a few other performers. They had shared drinks and good food, and hopefully, they would see them again when on tour.

Gabri noticed all through the evening that Nora had been distracted about something, and he worried about her being tired or uncomfortable. He asked if she wanted to leave several times, but she told him no, and he was to enjoy their triumph. Now they were in the car being driven back to the villa where more music and festivities were taking place.

"You don't have to join in the party tonight," said Gabri as he held Nora close. "I can see you're tired."

"I'm fine," said Nora softly. She had been thinking about how to tell Gabri about Rafe since Eden left to go back to her hotel. She knew if she told him Rafe was angry when she left, he would have wanted to go check on her right away. She also knew, though, Rafe wouldn't want her situation to mess up anything Gabri was doing for his music. She turned to Gabri. "When we get home, you should check in on Rafe."

"I will," said Gabri. "I want to know why she left. I wanted her to be there with us tonight."

"I know why she left," Nora said hesitantly.

"You do? Why?" he asked with a frown.

"One of her American friends, Julia, was talking to Eden. Rafe overheard the conversation. Things she overheard upset her," she told him. "Eden is upset with Julia too. I'm beginning to think you were right all along, and we should have done things differently for Rafe."

Gabri unclenched his fist trying to calm himself. He remembered Julia from California when he took Rafe away to get her help. He also remembered all the upsetting emails Julia sent to Rafe and the things he had learned about her. She was one of the reasons the doctor told Rafe to stop reading the emails. He couldn't believe Rafe counted her as a friend. She seemed like an angry spoiled child with no concern for anyone but herself.

"They will not see Rafe again," he said evenly.

"It's not Eden's fault," said Nora feeling how upset Gabri had become when his body tensed.

"Eden brought her here," he pointed out with a low growl in his voice, "so she is responsible."

"I don't think Eden had a lot of choices," said Nora. "Julia helped arrange and pay for the trip."

"If Eden had called us, she wouldn't have needed Julia," Gabri argued. "Rafe would have paid for her and the baby to come."

"But would you have let her come?" Nora asked, knowing he wouldn't have right now because he had denied her before. "I know you wouldn't have. I can't fault you for wanting to protect Rafe, but Eden does seem sincere, even if her friend isn't acting much like a friend to either of them."

"So, what are you saying? I need to protect them both?" he asked sarcastically.

"No, don't be so dramatic," said Nora, rolling her eyes. "I don't think either of them needs your protection. What they need is exactly what Rafe came here for, time to heal. They need it without other people picking at the scabs and making it harder to heal."

"That's a disgusting metaphor," said Gabri with a chuckle, "but it does get the point across."

Nora smiled but stopped herself from laughing because the situation was serious. "I wonder if something happened and was the reason Rafe got sick before she came to the concert," mused Nora as she noticed the car was turning onto the property. She was glad to be home.

"I'm worried too," said Gabri his mood changing to match that of his wife. "It's been a long time since she's been so sick. Actually, it's been since we made her stop reading those emails." He leaned his head back against the seat, and his mind went to thoughts of Rafe. "She'd been doing so well." He groaned in frustration at the situation. "Now they are here, and Rafe is sick again. I thought she'd be well enough that she would be okay when we left to go on tour. Now, I don't know what we're going to do."

"I think we should be thankful this happened while we were here," said Nora as the car came to a stop. "Who knows what would have gone down if we had already left," she said, disturbed by the thought.

"Please, I don't even want to think about it," said Gabri as he opened the car door to get out. He went around and helped Nora out of the car and onto the golf cart. "Drive her up to the house," he told Fausto. He turned to Nora. "I'm going to check on Rafe then I'll make the rounds at the tents. I won't be up too late, I hope."

Nora gripped Gabri's hand. "Wait," she said then hesitated. She knew Gabri would not like what she had to say. "I think you should take her a sleeping pill, just in case."

Gabri cocked his head to the side and frowned. "Why?"

"I know it will be the third night in a row but..."

"But we don't know how bad today was," Gabri finished for her.

Nora nodded in answer.

Gabri followed Nora into the house to retrieve Rafe's sleeping pill. After kissing Nora good night, he made his way to the garden path and to Rafe's cottage.

Music filled the midnight air along with the sweet scent of the night flowers from the gardens. Gabri loved this time of year and bringing all his friends together to play music and talk shop. The event had grown over the years and turned into a small festival on its own. Some musicians came as a vacation and others came to create and use the studio. Still others came to work and experiment or to find others to form groups and bands. The fact his event coincided with the bigger festival in town made it a two for one hit for those who got to play in the festival.

Sometimes, Gabri couldn't believe the wonderful life he had where he could focus on his music and live in a beautiful and inspiring place. He attributed a huge part of his luck to Ettore and Rafe who, when he needed money, a job, and a place to live, provided it and much more. When Ettore first gave him a part-time job helping with the orchards, Gabri had no idea he would be running the entire operation for six estates. Ettore put him through some very unusual intensive business sessions, but Gabri now knew his reasons.

The objects of the lessons were not to teach him to run a business but to run the people who ran all the businesses the estate land supported so they, in turn, would pay for the estates and allow them to eventually turn a profit. Gabri was able to use the education to try different things on the estates and was able to find an interesting mix of tenants and uses for all the land. He had built a staff to handle the day-to-day work, so he was able to pursue his music while still working the estates. It was a win-win for everyone involved.

As Gabri approached the cottage, he could see there were no lights on, and it was black inside. He wondered if Rafe was even there, and then he saw her motorcycle. He knew now she was home but didn't know if she was inside or up in one of the tents. He knocked on the door, and there was no answer, so he tried the door handle. He found the door unlocked, which was unusual for Rafe except when something was wrong. He opened the door with dread washing over him.

"Rafe," he called and turned on a light. The mess he found shocked him. "Rafe," he called again and went directly back to her bedroom and flipped on the light. "Damn it," he said under his breath as he saw Rafe facing the wall, curled up in her bed and rocking herself. Stepping around all the pill packets strewn on the floor along with torn up drawings and other debris, he sat down on the bed. "Rafe," he said again and put his hand on her shoulder gently. "What happened here," he said softly as Rafe turned her body to face him.

Rafe squinted up at Gabri as she got her eyes used to the light. "Squirrels," she said innocently but with a shaky voice.

Gabri tried not to smile. Since they were young, they had blamed things on the gray squirrels. They read about them in their school books. They learned that gray squirrels were invading Italy. An American ambassador brought four baby gray squirrels to Italy in 1948, and they escaped. Their offspring had since grown into a huge population that was destroying the ecosystem and carrying a virus responsible for killing red Italian squirrels. It had since become a very large problem in Italy the government still had not fully dealt with.

When he and Rafe played, they imagined the squirrels were an American rodent invasion created in a lab to reproduce in order to spy and transmit information to their American headquarters. They avoided the gray squirrel whenever possible and blamed it for all the unusual things they saw happening, and sometimes, for things they had done, but didn't want to admit to doing.

"Gray ones?" Gabri asked with a frown and watched Rafe nod. "I may have to call the Mayor. Sit up," he said, helping her up. "Tell me everything, Eroina. *Mi sembri un'anima in pena.*"[6]

Rafe sat up and wrapped her arms around her knees then rested her head on them. She felt like a soul in torment. "They still think I had an affair in New York," she said softly. "They think it was with Hannah."

---

[6] You look like a soul in torment.

"Hannah?" Gabri repeated with a frown. "Who is Hannah?"

"The dancer," she said softly looking up at Gabri with red-rimmed eyes. "She was a girl I dated a while before I came to Italy for school. Remember, I met her while I was taking classes to prepare for my test to get into prep-school. I saw her at times when I went home, and in France."

"Ah," he said as he remembered Rafe mentioning something about a dancer when she came back for school. He also recalled the woman, Lauren Street, and what she said happened in New York. "I don't think so."

"You said she was one of the people Lauren and I went out with," she reminded him as she held her hand to her head. "Plus, she's stunning... and she's black," she revealed with a shrug. "Maybe I saw her before then. I can't remember."

"No," said Gabri, "Lauren said they were surprised to see you, and she dropped you off at the apartment alone. Also, they had to go back to pack for their trip." He watched Rafe look at him with doubt on her face. "I can search for her troupe to find out where they are performing now and see if I can talk to her. Though I'm sure she will tell you nothing happened."

"Then why is Julia accusing me? Eden said they went to New York, and she believes I didn't have an affair with Lauren. Maybe she believes I had one with Hannah."

"Did Eden talk about her?"

"No."

Gabri ran his hands over his face in frustration. He didn't understand why they would come here and hurt Rafe more. "Well, I know it's important you know the truth," he said firmly, "so I will find out the truth. Do you remember the name of her troupe and her full name?"

"Hannah Pierce. I don't know the name of her troupe. I remember she was in one called Apple City Dance Company a long time ago. I don't know if it will help, though."

"I'll figure it out," he promised. He would look up dance troupes that had performed in New York when Rafe was there and follow up with any traveling to France. "I'm sorry they're still accusing you. I will tell them they are wrong."

Rafe looked up at him and fear crossed her face. "You don't have to talk to them. Just send them a note or something," she said quickly. "I–I–" she stammered, "I think we should just stay away from them. They'll be going home soon–and then everything will go back to the way it was. Eden may be doing what Julia says and moving out of the house."

Gabri shook his head. "No," he said, "Nora won't let me. She says Eden is sincere, and the other woman is causing you both problems." He could see Rafe still wasn't happy. "I trust Nora, do you?"

"Yes," Rafe whispered. She thought about the secret she told Eden and felt sick. "I have to tell you something," she said shakily.

"Tell me, *Eroina*," he said gently seeing she was in distress.

I–" she hesitated, "I'm afraid Eden will lie to you about me." She wiped her sweaty palms on her pajama pants. She hated lying to him, but she had to make sure, if Eden ever tried to use her secret against her, he wouldn't believe her.

Gabri frowned in confusion, "Why would she lie about you?"

Rafe tried to think of a reasonable reason he would believe. "Well," she said and swallowed hard, "to get what she wants, or to hurt me, maybe to make you want me to leave Italy. Or maybe, maybe to make you hate me."

"She could never make me hate you, *Eroina*," he assured her, "and she could never convince me to want you to leave, either."

"But she might try," she said wiping the back of her neck nervously. "I didn't tell you this before because I didn't think it would matter. Plus, I might be wrong... maybe she won't do it. I hope I'm wrong. Julia's been telling Eden things about me, but the things she's telling her aren't true. Now Eden is saying I told her things too when I was sick. The things she's saying I said must have been a hallucination or my mind not working right. I've been thinking and thinking about what she said, and I know those things never happened and aren't true. If they were true, you would hate me. I would never knowingly do anything to make you hate me."

"Of course, you wouldn't, *Eroina*," said Gabri. He worried Rafe was on the verge of having another break. He knew, even when taking her medication regularly, when subjected to so many stressors, they could cause issues. The fact was, even considering giving Rafe a sleeping pill for the third night in a row made rage cut through him at what those Americans had done to her. They were stealing her life, and it made him beyond angry. "What is it she's saying you told her?"

"I can't tell you," she said horrified at having to tell him anything he might confront Eden with. "I don't want you to know what she said and have it in your mind when you look at me. Plus, like I said, I hope I'm wrong and that she would never tell you those lies. I told her none of it was true, but I'm worried Julia is making her have doubts about me."

"Julia?" Gabri repeated her name with distaste as Rafe nodded. The woman Nora said had upset Rafe and made her leave tonight and may have upset Eden too. Remembering her emails, he didn't understand what was wrong with the woman and why she was treating her friend so badly.

Rafe stopped talking, feeling like she had said too much and he would know if she was rambling and making things up. She should have thought about things more before she talked to him. She just felt like she had to make sure she wouldn't lose him.

"Just," she hesitated, her eyes filled with desperation, "if she tells you I said or did something, and you think it might not be true, ask her for proof, hard proof, before you believe her. Everything she says I told her, or Julia told her, can't be proven because it's not true. If it were true, there would be some sort of proof, like photos, or notes, or objects, something. If she can't supply proof, you'll know it's not true. Okay?"

Gabri examined her quietly for a moment, and it was all he could do to hold back the tears he could feel building. Nora always said he was too sensitive when it came to Rafe, but she had never really seen Rafe both when she was severely sick and when she was completely well and full of life. All Nora had seen was this place in between where Rafe was teetering on the edge. This state was always the hardest for Gabri because the fear she would get sick again and the hope she would be herself again were churning and crashing against each other constantly.

"I will make sure she proves her words," he promised her gently. "Nothing will make me hate you. I will do my best to make sure no one hurts you or uses you badly."

"Okay," said Rafe in relief, "okay, thank you. I can't live without you in my life. I can't lose you."

"You'll never lose me," he promised and pulled her close. "You are my *Eroina,* and we have many more adventures waiting for us."

Rafe nodded then pulled away and looked around the room. "I guess I should clean up this squirrel mess," she said with a small smile.

She had been so angry at Julia about the things she said, by the time she got home, she felt like pieces of her world were crumbling again, and she took it out on the house. It was like someone else was doing it and she could only watch.

"Come," said Gabri as he helped her out of bed. "I'll help you. When we're finished, we can go listen to some healing music."

They got the cottage cleaned up quickly, and Rafe changed out of her pajamas into some jeans and a shirt. Rafe walked into the kitchen where Gabri was waiting and sat down across from him at the table.

"Can I tell you something else?" she asked hesitantly.

"Of course," said Gabri taking her hand.

"Julia accused me of skipping out on Eden and Bronte," she said and felt Gabri tense in anger. "Are you still sending her money?"

"Yes, every month just like you said."

"Maybe we should send her more," she suggested. "Maybe, because she's alone, she could use more to help her with everything."

"We can do whatever you want to do," he assured her. "Should I ask her about her finances while she's here?" he asked, and Rafe nodded.

"I just don't want her to think she's a problem that I'm throwing money at," she said softly and saw Gabri look at her in confusion. "She's not a problem. I want her to have everything she needs for herself and for Bronte."

"I don't understand," said Gabri. "Why would she say or think she's a problem for you?"

"Julia said it," said Rafe. "Eden said it once too, but I think she was just dealing with her anxiety back then. I think Julia is using Eden's words against me. I don't know why."

"These Americans are very confusing," said Gabri trying to control his irritation. "They come saying they want to help but all they do is hurt."

"I think Julia is jealous of you," said Rafe as she tore at a small missed piece of paper she found on the table.

"What?" Gabri exclaimed in disbelief.

"Yes, because I gave you my power of attorney." She pressed her lips together and nodded. "She also thinks you're mismanaging me and my money."

Gabri sat up offended. "I would never," he started but was choked by anger.

"Don't worry," Rafe said quickly. "I know you aren't. She doesn't know what she's talking about, as usual." She tore the paper again and sighed. "She's mad because I didn't give her, or her father, power of attorney. It was my decision, and I'm positive it's probably the only good decision I made at the time." She looked up into his eyes. "You saved my life again," she said softly. "Thank you."

Emotions of love and pride welled up in Gabri, and he couldn't stop the tear those emotions caused. He wiped the tear away quickly. "I love you deeply, so there was nothing less I could do for you," he said and smiled. "I will always be here for you, and now you have Nora, too." He got up from the table and held his hand out to Rafe. "Let's go listen to some music and think only of beautiful things."

There was no doubt that tonight if the music did not soothe her, he would once again be giving Rafe the sleeping pill in his pocket. He would be glad when Rafe's American friends went back home.

6

MORNING LIGHT FILTERED into the bedroom, chasing away the shadows covering Rafe Salvaggio as she lay awake in bed. She had not slept for the last two nights. Gabri had offered a sleeping pill each night, but Rafe did not want to wake up in a fog and lose track of time again. Instead, she lay in bed hoping to finally doze off. Unfortunately, too much was running through her mind. Conversations with Nora mingled with the things Eden had said, all tainted by the argument with Julia. The imminent concern about Gabri and Nora having to leave in a few months snuck into the mix too. Waves of fear and worry pounded through her head about what the consequences might be since now Eden knew her secret about Maria. It all dragged her away from a peaceful slumber.

So many challenges had come on her so fast that Rafe felt like she was stumbling along, desperately trying to keep up with everyone who already knew which way the path led. She didn't know if the path they were following was the one she should take.

Since Eden's arrival, Rafe's dreams had become filled with visions of her. She saw herself chasing after Eden through the streets of Florence but unable to catch up. She dreamed of making love to Eden, only to have her pulled away by Jake, or Julia, or some unseen person. It was heart-wrenching. Rafe would wake up in a cold sweat after hearing Jake's words echo through her mind, warning that Eden would never really come back to her. Rafe knew the reason was that she was still betraying Eden. Gabri thought the pills would help, but Rafe knew they were only a temporary fix. Good but temporary.

The last six months in Italy, Rafe had spent her time working on getting better. She also worked on trying to build up barriers. Barriers to protect herself once she eventually went home. She had no illusions her relationship with Eden was intact. She tried to prepare herself for the fact Eden would move on with her life. Hearing Julia's declarations of love the other night had proven those barriers needed to be reinforced. It was plain from the first moment she saw Eden was in Italy that those barriers were about as strong as cardboard in a fire.

Rafe could still feel the pain caused by the knowledge Eden was with Julia. Before Julia slipped the knife in her back, Rafe had felt a glimmer of hope. She even talked directly to Katheryn about the possibility of Eden moving to Italy. Kathryn was surprised Gabri wasn't involved in the call but seemed cautiously optimistic about the possibility.

But now, Rafe still felt the crash vibrating through her body, nearly making her crumble during the conversation with Julia when she found out she was right—they were together. The memory of Eden's words and the kiss in the vineyard tormented and confused her. It all felt so good when it was happening. It was like a balm over her pain for a brief moment. Then the confusion set in again. She knew Eden's words and affection were false. Eden hadn't denied Julia was in love with her, nor that they were together. Instead, it seemed, even when Rafe made it clear she knew Julia was in love with her, Eden just evaded the subject.

Rafe truly didn't know what to do about any of it. She didn't know if there was anything she could do about it. The confusion and anger surrounding everything from the past, and the events happening here and now, would surge through Rafe and push all those good feelings back down into the dark. Her immediate solution was to tell Gabri she wanted Julia and Eden to go away. She intended to cancel everything Katheryn was doing too.

Rafe threw off her sheet and slid out of bed. She had to find a way to stop her thoughts from taking her down into a dark mood. Grabbing a pill packet from the drawer, she blundered into the kitchen. She took her vitamins with a sip of water before beginning the calming process of making her espresso.

As Rafe was about to dump the previous day's used grounds into the trash, she saw her mobile phone on the table. It was dead. She had left it untouched since the concert and argument with Julia. She dumped the grounds quickly, then put the espresso-maker funnel down and went to get her charger. Plugging in the phone to charge, she went back to the stove. Rafe filled the lower chamber with cold water just below the valve, put the funnel in, and filled it with espresso. After screwing the upper part of the pot on to the base, she put it on the stove to boil.

As Rafe waited for the familiar gurgling sound, she got out the brioche someone brought to the cottage and put it on the table. Nora always thoughtfully sent things down to make sure Rafe had all the basics. Then she didn't have to walk to the villa for meals. It was especially nice now since there were so many people filling up the villa for the festival.

The gurgling stopped, and Rafe removed the espresso maker from the stove. After taking the top off, she stirred the coffee to mix all the layers. She poured herself a cup, took it to the table, and then sat down for her small breakfast.

Her thoughts went back to Eden as she drank her espresso and ate her breakfast. She couldn't help thinking about her. Looking over at her drawing pad, she reached out and opened it. Inside was filled with drawings of Eden. No matter the status of their relationship, Rafe couldn't help thinking about Eden. She picked up her pencil and began to draw Eden's face, adding it to the others. Rafe knew she would never stop loving Eden. This time, though, the loss would be much worse than before with Jake. This time, Eden would leave to be with someone she knew—Julia. *I could take her away from Julia*, Rafe thought. *Eden said she loves me so I could seduce her away just like I did with Jake. Stop!* Rafe cleared her head of those thoughts. She was still sick. She couldn't give Eden what she needed... and she was still betraying her.

Rafe saw her phone was alive again and found there was a voicemail from yesterday. She opened the phone and didn't recognize the number. Thinking it might be a volunteer wanting to know when to show up, she pressed play to hear the message.

Eden's voice came through the phone's speaker. "Rafe," she paused, "it's Eden. I just wanted to tell you I'm sorry for what you overheard Julia say. She told me you came to the hotel and she argued with you. I'm sorry for that, too. She doesn't speak for me. She's just worried, and it makes her upset, and she lashes out. You know how she is. I understand if you don't want to see her." There was silence for a moment. "I'm glad you tried to come see me, and invite me out. I'd really like to see you again. We have a lot to talk about. I have to leave in three days, two if you don't count the one when we have to fly out. Bronte wants to see you and Gabri again. She's been asking for you both. Please, call me. I'm going to call Nora and Gabri a little later, too. I love you," she said softly and hesitated. "Bye."

Rafe dropped the phone back on to the table, wondering how Eden had got her number. Then she realized she had called Eden to remind her to keep the secret about Maria. Pushing her chair back, she got up and went back into her room, throwing herself on the bed.

"Two days," she said into her pillow. She had already lost one of those days she realized despite not taking the sleeping pills. Eden would fly home tomorrow. "Stop saying you love me!" she said, punching the pillow.

It seemed like Eden must not have slept much lately, either, since she had called so early yesterday morning.

Rafe turned over onto her back and ran her hands over her face with a heavy sigh. She didn't understand why Eden kept saying she loved her when she was with Julia. Rafe wondered what Julia thought, or if she even knew.

7

CLOSING HER EYES, Rafe Salvaggio could see Eden's face in her mind's eye and how she looked in the morning. It had been a long time since she'd been with Eden when she woke up. Rafe had been hiding so many nightmares. In California, Rafe couldn't sleep with Eden, or she would have known. Once, Rafe forgot to lock the bedroom door, and her nightmare took her out of her room. Eden was there for it, and Rafe knew it terrified her. She never wanted to see the look of fear along with the pity in Eden's eyes again. She had to get better so there was no reason for Eden or anyone else to look at her in such a way again.

Rafe shook the image of Eden's face from her mind and opened her eyes. It was clear keeping her mind off Eden was not going to happen. She got up and went back into the kitchen, picked up her phone and the charger, and took them to the bedroom. After plugging the charger into the wall, she laid back down in bed with the phone. She opened the messages and listened to Eden's voice mail again. She pressed the call back icon and put the phone to her ear. After two rings, she hung up.

"What am I doing?" Rafe asked herself. She was about to put the phone down when it rang. She could see it was the number she had just called. Eden.

"*Pronto*," she said answering the call, "um, hello."

"Rafe?" came Eden's voice. "Is everything okay?"

"Yes, everything's fine," she answered, beating herself up for calling her.

"I'm glad you called."

Rafe held her breath and searched her mind for a reasonable reply. "I, um," she hesitated, letting the air in her lungs out, "I got your message. Did I wake you? I'm sorry," she said softly.

"No, no, you didn't wake me." Eden sighed into the phone and into Rafe's ear, "I couldn't sleep. Why are you awake so early?"

"I couldn't sleep, either," she confessed. "Actually, I was thinking about you."

"Really?" said Eden. Rafe could feel her smile through the phone. "What were you thinking?"

Rafe bit her lip and smiled. "I was thinking about how you look in the morning."

There was silence on the phone for a moment. "Do you want me to send you a picture?"

"I don't need a picture." Rafe chuckled because it seemed like Eden wanted to play. It made it feel like all their worries were forgotten for the moment.

"Oh, yeah?" Eden breathed into the phone.

"Yeah," she answered. "Tell me what you're wearing."

"What?" Eden laughed, and Rafe's heart warmed to the sound.

"What are you wearing? Tell the truth," she purred.

"Uh, well," Eden said playfully, "I'm wearing your pajamas."

"My pajamas? But my pajamas are here with me," Rafe teased.

"No, I'm wearing the ones you gave me."

"I would never give you my pajamas," said Rafe as she smiled.

"Oh, but you did," said Eden smoothly, "don't you remember?"

Rafe searched her memory and remembered when Eden was hurt, and she told her she could keep the pajamas she was wearing. "Oh, yeah," she said with a frown. "I wasn't thinking clearly back then. You should give them back."

"Sure," said Eden in a smoky voice. "You put them on me, so you can come and take them off me."

Rafe laughed and felt the old spark run through her for Eden. "Hmm, I must be talking to Bossy Eden. Where's my sweet and sexy Eden? I think I want her right now."

"You're going to have to take what you can get," teased Eden.

"Is that what you want, Bossy Eden? You want me to take you?"

There was silence on the phone again. "You know you're killing me right now, don't you?" Eden chuckled. "Yes," she said softly, "I want you to take me."

Rafe felt her heart beat hard, and her body react to Eden's words. "*Dimmi come*," she said then again in English, "Tell me how," she whispered, "rough and dirty or sweet and tender."

"I think I'll take sweet and tender," she said with a small laugh. "I didn't like it last time when you were rough. It hurt."

Rafe frowned and tried to think about the last time she was with Eden. It was right before the party at the Conservatory and just before she left for Mexico. "I was never rough with you. I would never hurt you."

"You were rough," Eden assured her. "Remember, it was the night you fell in the pool."

"Fell in the pool?" Rafe repeated confused. "I never fell in the pool." She laughed thinking Eden was playing and she didn't understand the game. "What are you talking about?"

Eden's breathing could be heard on the line, but she was silent for a while. "You don't remember falling into the pool?"

"If the pool was you, then yes," quipped Rafe, still playing and wondering where Eden was leading her.

"Rafe," said Eden then was quiet again, "I love you," she said finally but very quietly.

It was Rafe's turn to be silent. She was wondering if something was wrong because of the change in tone of Eden's voice. "Are you okay?" she asked with concern. "Is Julia there?"

"No, Julia's in the other room," she said quickly. "I'm fine."

Hearing the forced reassurance in Eden's voice, Rafe frowned. "Are you sure? Is something wrong?" she asked, worry suddenly wanting to surface again. The image of Eden sleeping next to Julia while wearing her pajamas flashed in her mind. She was not sure if she should feel good about it or angry. Wearing her pajamas was like Eden sleeping with her, but the thought of Julia taking them off Eden was infuriating.

"Yes," said Eden softly, "there's something wrong. You're not here next to me."

"Oh, yeah?" said Rafe relieved by Eden's words as she stretched out in the bed. She was glad the game was back on. "What would you do with me if I were there?"

"Right now, I'd probably just hold you and sleep," she said and then yawned. "I'm so tired, but I can't shut my mind off."

"I don't think I could let you sleep if I were there right now," said Rafe. "I'd have to do things to make you forget about everything else, including sleep."

"Promises, promises," Eden teased with a throaty laugh. They listened to each other breathe for a while. "Will we get to see you today?" she asked tentatively.

"I don't know," said Rafe realizing the game was over now. She didn't know if she could take seeing her in person again. "I have to help Nora today. Gabri will be working in the studio with some musicians, so he won't be able to help with all the guests and other things going on. Any other time, Nora probably wouldn't need my help, but being pregnant limits her a lot."

"I understand," said Eden trying not to show her disappointment. "When is she due?"

"Sometime in the next week or so," said Rafe happily. "I wish you were staying longer so Bronte could meet the baby." A sharp breath came through the phone.

"Me too," said Eden very softly.

"You'll have to come back before they leave on tour. I'll tell Gabri, and he can buy your tickets. Then you and Bronte can stay here if you want."

"That, uh," Eden sighed, "sounds nice."

"Yeah, and don't bring Julia," Rafe said not able to hide the unhappiness in her voice.

"I'm sorry about the things she said, and the argument she had with you. Like I told you in the message, she's really worried and angry about everything."

"I know," said Rafe evenly. She thought the only thing Julia worried about was herself. "She needs to stay out of my business. She thinks because she's known me since we were young that she should know everything, but I don't want her to know. If I wanted it, I would have told her a long time ago. I don't know why she can't go back to just sitting on the sidelines. It was one of the reasons I liked her as my friend. No hard questions, no knowledge of my problems, no real interest in them. Just someone oblivious, who I could have fun with, and not talk about or think about..." she hesitated, "dark things."

"Oblivious," Eden repeated, unable to hide the confusion in her voice. There was a long pause. "She was only oblivious because you chose not to tell her things. I think it's another reason she's upset. You purposely kept something so big from her. It feels, to her, like you didn't trust her."

"I didn't," said Rafe flatly, not liking how Eden defended Julia. Rafe wished she could tell Eden that Julia was no longer her friend. She would only share that information after Eden got back home. "I didn't trust anyone. My father told me I couldn't trust anyone. In her case, I think he was right. She and everyone else found out things from Letty, who I still have no idea how she found out anything, and they did nothing but make my life miserable," she said trying to contain her anger, but it crept out in her words. "They pushed when I asked them not to, they turned you against me, and they stopped being my friends and became part of the problem."

"Well," said Eden calmly, "it didn't happen."

"What?"

"I haven't turned against you."

"Oh," said Rafe, then thought about how she must have sounded. "I'm sorry." She rubbed her face and sighed.

"Why?"

"I probably sound like an ingrate," she answered, frustrated at herself. She knew Eden wouldn't see things the same as she saw them. Eden always thought the best of everyone and made excuses for them. Plus, Eden was with Julia now, and Rafe had to stay silent about her feelings just like she had to with Jake. "Julia and everyone else helped you, and I'm glad they did," said Rafe. "It's just hard being so exposed and feeling like everyone's suddenly putting me under a microscope or trying to shut me away somewhere," she said truthfully but leaving out all the other things she felt.

"I understand," said Eden, "but you're better now, and really, they were all just trying their best. They love you. Sometimes, it's really hard when you don't know what to do when someone you love is hurting."

"Maybe," said Rafe feeling a bit disgruntled but, at the same time, ashamed because Eden was probably right.

"You know what? Let's not think about everyone else right now," said Eden in a forced upbeat voice. "We need to make a plan for us. When can we come to see you? Bronte has been talking non-stop about you and Gabri. And we need to talk some more."

Rafe closed her eyes and ran her hand over her face. She had no idea if she even wanted to see her or if she wanted to hear what she had to say. She wanted to see Bronte, though, and it most likely meant she would have no choice but to see Eden, especially if Nora had anything to say about it.

She desperately wanted to be part of Bronte's life and hated the fact she was once again missing her grow up. The last time she missed out on Bronte's life was because of Eden and Jake. This time it was her own fault because she felt she had to stay in Italy to get better.

She wanted so much for Bronte. She could see Bronte was at the perfect age to learn languages, and in just the short amount of time since she's been in Italy, she had picked up a few Italian words. It was amazing to hear her talking so much and how smart she was. If she could spend more time with Bronte, she could teach her even more Italian.

Rafe didn't know when she would be finished helping Nora and didn't want to make a promise and then have to break it. She did not want to break promises to Bronte... or Eden.

"I'm not sure," she finally said. "Let me find out what all is happening today. I'll call you back as soon as I know how the day will go if I can."

"Sure," said Eden and then was quiet for a while. "Rafe?"

"Yeah."

"Thank you for calling me."

"You called me," Rafe reminded her and chuckled.

"No, you called me. I just didn't answer fast enough," said Eden lightly, "so I called you back. I love hearing your voice."

"Me too," said Rafe softly. "I guess we should stop so you can get some sleep."

"I guess," Eden yawned. "I love you, Rafe."

Rafe was quiet for a moment, listening to Eden breathing, wondering again why she was saying those words to her when she was in a relationship with Julia who was in the next room. "I can't wait to see you and Bronte again. I love you both," she said quickly before she talked herself out of saying it. "Sweet dreams."

"Bye," said Eden softly, and the call disconnected.

Rafe put the phone on the table beside her, forced herself out of bed, and got ready for the day. She cleaned up the kitchen and about walked out the door before remembering her phone. She headed back to the bedroom, got the phone, and then made her way out of the house and up to the villa.

8

MAKING HER WAY up the garden path, Rafe Salvaggio smiled as she recalled her conversation with Eden. It was good to know they were still able to play after all this time, even though they weren't together.

She wanted Eden.

Rafe laughed out loud. It sounded painful and tragic. Just yesterday, she couldn't bring herself to make any kind of decision. The thought of wanting Eden made her happy, but at the same time, it was heartbreaking. She had been fighting those feelings in her head for so long because she was sick. It looked like she would need to keep fighting them. Until she saw Eden, she hadn't even been sure if those feelings would come back to reality or if it was all just in her mind. The feelings were real, though. What made Rafe sad was knowing she could never act on her feelings. Eden was with Julia and leaving with her tomorrow.

Rafe made it to the large lawn behind the villa where the tents were set up. She could hear a few of the musicians were already up and playing or, more likely, hadn't yet been to sleep. She went to the tented stage area and made rounds, putting chairs back into place, picking up trash and taping down electrical cords. Then she went to check the stage area and the equipment. One of the speakers rattled horribly so she disconnected it and sat it off to the side of the stage. Someone would need to take it into town to have it repaired or replaced for tonight. Finally happy with everything, she went to check the dining tent. It had been cleaned up, and the caterer was already getting things set up to serve the guests breakfast. Rafe gave them a wave then headed to the kitchen inside the villa.

The kitchen was full of activity as Rafe made her way to the long table at the end of the cooking area. Nora and Gabri were both there eating, so she joined them.

"Good morning," said Rafe. She smiled as she sat next to Nora.

Nora turned to Rafe, smiling back. "You're up early and looking happy," she said. She had been worried when Gabri said Rafe didn't want the sleeping pills the last two nights. It was a relief the worry was for nothing. "I take it everything is good out there."

"So far," said Rafe as one of the servers set a cup and saucer in front of her. "Just this," she said with a wave of her hand to her cup. "I already ate." The server poured her coffee then went back into the kitchen chaos. "One of the speakers blew last night. I sat it next to the stage."

"I knew it was going to go," said Gabri. "It didn't sound right last night. I need to take it into town. Hopefully, it can be repaired."

"I can take it if I can get everything done for Nora quickly," offered Rafe. "I'll just need a car."

"We can just send Fausto with instructions," said Gabri as he ate. "He has to take a few people into town anyway."

"Great," said Rafe with a shrug.

Nora watched Rafe sip her coffee. Rafe looked fine today, despite the dark circles around her eyes. She was glad Rafe was doing well. Based on what happened over the last two nights, and what Gabri told her this morning, she had expected her to be a bit more down. Something must have happened between when Gabri was with her last night and this morning.

"So, it looks like the music last night really was healing," said Nora nonchalantly. She knew this would be her only chance to have them both in the same room today, so she made her move to help Eden. "I talked to Eden again last night," Nora said. Rafe snapped her head up, her eyes wide with surprise. "She was disappointed she couldn't see you yesterday. She said she's here because she's in love with you." Rafe looked down into her cup without responding. "So, it means everything is good," said Nora and put her hand on Rafe's arm. "You don't have to worry about how she feels or if she's with the other woman." Nora watched Rafe fidget with her coffee cup and caught the frown Gabri flashed. "Don't worry. I just told her you were busy," she assured both of them. She wondered if this was the time she should reveal the rest of her conversation with Eden.

Rafe sighed and closed her eyes for a moment because everything was not as good as Nora thought. Just because Eden said she loved her didn't mean she wasn't with Julia. She didn't know if she should tell Nora about Julia and their conversation. Everything was already causing so much turmoil, she didn't know if she wanted to add Nora being upset to the equation. She turned her head and smiled weakly at Nora. "Yeah, she told me," said Rafe then looked away again.

Gabri watched and knew Rafe was uncomfortable. He hadn't told Nora everything Rafe said had happened the night of the concert or the real reason he was up so late with her the last two nights. "You don't have to see her," he said ignoring the sharp look from his wife. "We can just ask for Bronte again."

"Maybe." Rafe shifted uncomfortably. "There's a lot to do today, so I don't know if I'll even have time."

"But they only have a brief time left," Nora reminded her. "Eden mentioned their flight home was tomorrow."

Rafe nodded. "I know." She looked across at Gabri. "I don't know what I'm going to do right now. There's just so much to think about," she said and bit her lower lip. "I don't know if I can see her again," she confessed.

"It's okay," said Gabri. "You can tell us when you decide."

Nora looked from one to the other not sure what was happening, but clearly, something was going on that they weren't telling her. "What's going on?" she asked with a frown. "Why don't you know if you can see her? She was very sincere, Rafe. I think you should give her a chance."

Rafe couldn't help her slight smile at Nora's concern. She looked from Nora to Gabri and back again. "I talked to Eden this morning," she said with a slight shrug. She couldn't help her smile at the memory of the conversation. "Bronte does want to see us. I told her I'd call her when I was finished so they could visit."

"You should have told her to just come when she was ready," said Nora, happy Rafe had finally talked to Eden after what happened at the concert.

When they talked yesterday, Eden seemed upset and sounded sincere in how she talked about wanting to spend time with Rafe and talk about their relationship and their daughter. She had not revealed to Eden anything about Rafe and what was happening. She knew both Rafe and Gabri would take it as a betrayal.

"Hey, what time did you talk to her? It's five-thirty in the morning now," Nora said.

"Earlier," Rafe said offhandedly, still smiling. "I'll call her when we're done for the day," she relented under Nora's questioning gaze. "I should get going. The volunteers should be showing up." After sipping the last bit of coffee she went out to start giving assignments for the day.

Nora looked over at Gabri and could tell he wasn't happy. "Don't worry so much," she said and leaned forward to put her hand on his. "Don't you want to see her happy?"

"I do, but what is the price?" he asked with a frown.

"Whatever it is, Rafe seems to be okay with it," she said giving him a serious look. "She said she was inviting her to come. You can only help her when she tells you she needs help. She's in love with her."

"How do you know? She's never told us she is in love with her," he argued, knowing the things Rafe had told him about what Julia had said and the certainty Rafe had that Eden would lie to him to get what she wanted. "Rafe is doing this for the baby and to get along. This is what Eden must understand."

"Gabri," Nora started, and then shook her head in disbelief at his hardness toward Eden. She thought it must be his childhood jealousy or his fear Rafe would get sick again. She knew Rafe was an extraordinarily strong woman who, once she decided what she wanted, would do everything in her power to get it. If Rafe decided she wanted Eden, there was nothing anyone, including Gabri, could do about it. She was sure Rafe would make the decision to be with Eden. Otherwise, she wouldn't fill notebooks with drawings of her. "I'm going to call Eden and tell her to come out whenever she's ready," she declared. "When she gets here, I'll have someone else help with things so they can spend time together."

"Oh, it's okay for you to interfere now?" asked Gabri disgruntled. "You may make Rafe angry for calling her."

"I'm not interfering, and Rafe was going to call her anyway." She smiled at him tolerantly. "I'm helping." She got up and planned to make the call as soon as possible. Then she would find Rafe to tell her.

Gabri watched her leave and threw his hands up. "I will never win," he grumbled.

9

EDEN KINGSLEY COULDN'T wipe the hope-filled smile from her face. She also couldn't go back to sleep after talking with Rafe. Eden had been worried all day yesterday when she couldn't contact Rafe. She was only glad, after everything, Nora had agreed to talk again. Eden wished she hadn't taken Julia's advice and used their first day to rest and get oriented. If she had gone right away, she would have had another day. Nora said Rafe was busy but Eden got the feeling more was wrong. She was sure Julia's argument with Rafe was the reason for the silence.

Julia had been apologetic yesterday and bent over backward to help with Bronte. Julia even went out shopping with Bronte and brought back gifts when Eden wouldn't leave the hotel room. Eden knew Julia was upset she had suggested she leave and was doing things to make herself useful. No matter what she did, though, Eden found it hard to forgive Julia for causing her to lose time with Rafe.

After Bronte woke, Eden ordered room service for breakfast. Eden was glad she had Bronte to focus on. It kept her from thinking about all the nerve-racking things happening. As they waited for the food, Eden watched Bronte find a morning cartoon on her iPad. It was amazing to Eden how easily Bronte picked up on using electronics so quickly.

Rafe sent the iPad not long after she left home. Flynn helped set it up so Bronte could get the emails Rafe sent through Katheryn with videos and photos. Once they showed Bronte a few things, she figured out the rest on her own. Eden was sure Lydia helped a lot too because Bronte would come home with new games to help learn letters and other fun things.

The breakfast trolley was wheeled into the room, and Bronte abandoned her iPad to help uncover the food. The waiter smiled as he pandered to Bronte's every request. Eden couldn't help chuckling at her daughter's antics. The waiter finally had everything to Bronte's satisfaction and left them to their meal. As they ate, Eden listened to her daughter chatter happily.

"Are we gonna play at the big house?" Bronte asked with a mouth covered in Nutella. "More chocolate, please," she said and held out her bread to her mommy.

Eden took the bread and spread more chocolate on it. She watched as Bronte licked the chocolate from the bread. "I don't know," she answered, just as she did all the other times Bronte asked that question. She hoped, with all her heart, they would get to see Rafe again today. "Did you like it there?"

"We sang a song," Bronte said, wiping her sticky hands on her pajama shirt. "I didn't know all the words. Nora said I sing good." She ate for a while then started again. "She's gonna have a baby. It's a boy. When he's borned I can hold him."

"That'll be nice," said Eden with an amused smile. "You have to be gentle with babies."

"I will 'cause babies are tiny," she squeaked and scrunched her face and body to show how tiny babies were, and then she licked more Nutella. "I like Gabri. If I say *corri Gabri,* he'll pull me and Mama on the blanket. He can play the piano. I think I could play 'cause Nora says I'm big." She picked up a piece of fruit from her plate. "Look at this big strawlbarry," she said as she held it up then ate it happily.

Eden put more fruit on Bronte's plate. "Would you like to try some eggs or ham?"

"No, I just like chocolate. Are we gonna see Mama? I want to dance again."

"I don't know if we'll see Mama today." She didn't want to make a promise and not be able to keep it. Rafe said she would let them know after helping Nora. "Did you have fun seeing Mama while we were here?"

"Yes," said Bronte. "She lives in a garden."

"I know." Eden smiled at how Bronte was so taken with where Rafe lived that she had to repeat it a lot. "Maybe we can come back again. Would you like to?"

"We can go tomorrow," the little girl whispered dramatically.

"Well, we have to go on the airplane tomorrow," she explained copying her daughter's dramatics, tussling her hair, and making her giggle.

"Is Mama going with us?"

"I don't know," she said pensively. "I hope so."

"Are you sad?" asked Bronte. "I'm not sad."

"No," Eden said softly, "I'm not sad." Eden kissed her on the cheek. Bronte was really sensitive about whether or not she was happy or sad. She tried to be as positive as she could, but sometimes it was hard, and she couldn't hide her tears. She hoped her conversation with Nora yesterday had helped. She needed to see Rafe again and find a way to convince her to come home. The phone call from Rafe this morning was a good sign. "If Mama has to stay here, we'll come back to see her."

"I want to stay here too," Bronte declared with a smile, fully expecting to get what she wanted. "I can live in the garden with Mama."

"We'll see," she said and kissed Bronte on her chocolate covered cheek, knowing if she told her 'no' it still just meant, to her two-and-a-half-year-old mind, she should ask again later.

Bronte ate more fruit with chocolate and continued. "I wanna draw a picture of the garden for Mama."

"I think it would be nice if you drew a picture for her. We'll get out some paper after we eat."

"I wanna use my markers," she said happily.

"Your markers are at home," Eden reminded her. "We just brought the crayons and some pencils."

"But I need my markers," she insisted as she licked her fingers. "I don't want craowns."

"When we get home, you can use your markers," said Eden patiently. "We'll be riding the airplane home tomorrow. Until then, we only have crayons."

"No, I don't wanna go home," said Bronte with a frown. "You go home and get my markers. I'll stay here with Zia Julia. When you get them, then I can draw."

Eden smiled at Bronte's logic. "Zia Julia is going home with us," she told her. "Home is too far away for me to go get them and bring them back. Why don't you use the crayons for now, then when we get home, you can draw another picture, and we can email it to Mama."

Bronte thought about things as she ate. "Mama has lots of markers," she said with wide eyes. "We can go to her house and get some. She let me use her markers, but I had to be gentle."

"I think we can wait until we get home for markers," Eden told her with a small smile.

"I don't wanna go home!" said Bronte in frustration because she was not getting markers. "I wanna go to Mama's house and use her markers."

"I understand," said Eden trying to calm the situation. "I know you want markers, and it's hard when all you have right now are crayons. I'll tell you what we can do. You can use the crayons now, then you can make another drawing with markers when we get home as a surprise for Mama. And, if we see Mama today, we can ask her about using her markers. We can't use Mama's things unless we ask first. Does that sound fair?"

Bronte thought about the compromise for a moment. "I can call her and ask now," she decided. "Can I use the phone?"

Eden sighed and looked up trying to figure out this new tangle. "We can't call her right now," she said then stopped. The realization that she may not get to see Rafe again hit her. Her hands shook as she took a sip of her orange juice. She felt her stomach lurch and felt sick.

"'Cause she's still sick?" Bronte asked thoughtfully.

"Yes," Eden answered softly. Keeping Rafe's illness from Bronte was hard. She tried, but little ears heard everything. She had never been able to call Rafe, and the only reason Bronte would accept was that Rafe was sick.

"I'll make you a picture too," she said congenially as she licked her fingers.

"Thank you, baby. I'd like one," she said and swallowed the lump in her throat. Eden turned at the light tapping on the door. She could tell by the tentative knock it would be Julia. She steeled herself as she got up to answer the door. Eden was still upset at Julia for arguing with Rafe. She knew Julia only had her best interest in mind, but sometimes, Julia lost control of her temper when it came to Rafe. Julia had become a big part of their lives, and that closeness made Julia overprotective. Eden appreciated that Julia didn't want to see her hurt but arguing with Rafe made the situation worse.

"Hi," she said as the door opened.

"Hello," said Julia with a timid smile. "Are you up for company?"

"Sure," she said. "We're still having breakfast." She led Julia to the table.

"Well, hello there," Julia said to Bronte. "I see you're chocolate coated again." She chuckled as Bronte licked her Nutella bread.

"Can we ride the horses again?" asked Bronte.

Julia took Bronte out for dinner the night before while Eden stayed in by the phone. Once again, the restaurant staff treated Bronte like a princess. They made sure Bronte had every treat she wanted. Julia liked the fact they thought the little girl was hers. Afterward, they spent time playing in the square, stopping only to buy a toy and ride the carousel. They went for gelato then headed back to the hotel so that Bronte could play with her new toy. "If your mommy says it's all right, we can."

"I want to ride the white one again," Bronte informed her.

"I'll think about it," said Eden. She hoped to get a call from Rafe and wanted to keep Bronte close.

"Tell your mum what you said about those horses last night," said Julia with a chuckle.

Bronte cocked her head trying to understand what Zia Julia was asking her to do. "I love them?"

"No, about how they all go in a circle," she hinted. Julia could tell Bronte didn't remember what she said. She looked over at Eden who was waiting expectantly to hear the story. "She rode around a few times. Then, when she got off, she told me she didn't like how they only went in a circle. The way she said it yesterday struck me as funny."

"The horses go round and round and round," said Bronte. "I want to ride one to Mama's house."

"Yes," said Julia clearing her throat, knowing the subject could get touchy. "Well, tell her about how you want them to be ponies."

"All the horses are grown up," said Bronte with a shrug. "I want some baby horses and some baby dragons," she said and made a playful growl.

"It struck me as funny then, but now it doesn't really come off," said Julia with a bit of disappointment. She wanted to show Eden how well she and Bronte got on.

"It sounds like you had a fun time," said Eden as Bronte played with her food. "If you're finished, we need to clean you up so you can have art time."

"I'm done!" Bronte jumped down from her chair. Standing in front of Eden, she allowed her to pull off her chocolate-smeared pajamas.

"Your clothes are on the bed. Let me know if you need help."

"I can do it!" Bronte ran into the bedroom.

Eden couldn't help smiling as she turned to Julia. "Rafe called. She's going to call again when we can go see her."

Julia bit back the harsh words on her tongue. "Fantastic," she said instead.

"I know you're still angry with her," said Eden, "but don't be. Like Nora said, we came here uninvited. We have to be patient."

"Patient?" Julia scoffed. "I think we are beyond that at this point." Hiding her annoyance was difficult. "I don't like how they're treating you. I know I've said it before, but I think you need to hear it again." She could see Eden visibly stiffen her body, and it was heartbreaking.

"I don't need to hear your opinion again about how Rafe is treating me," Eden said softly.

"Okay," Julia conceded. "Just know I care about you and Bronte. I don't want this trip to send you back into despair and depression. It's hard for me to sit by and watch as Rafe and her keeper act like you don't matter and leave you in the dark, pining for Rafe to agree to come home. Something they keep telling you won't happen." The room phone rang, saving Eden from having to argue her position for the moment. Julia watched Eden quickly make her way into the bedroom to answer the call.

Bronte burst out of the bedroom. "Zia Julia, will you help me get out paper?"

"Sure," Julia answered putting on a happy face. She helped Bronte get art supplies from a backpack and set her up at the coffee table. "What are you going to draw?"

"Mama's garden."

"Brilliant." Julia watched Bronte add pen to paper for a moment then decided she needed a cup of tea. She turned on the kettle and then sat again next to Bronte. "You've made a dog's dinner of your shirt."

Bronte looked at Julia in confusion. "I don't have a dog."

"No, your shirt's turned wrong," she explained. "Here," she said pulling Bronte close. She stripped Bronte's shirt off then helped her put it on the right way. "There. Now you're smart."

"Lydia says I'm smart, too. So does Flynn."

"Yes, well, we'll use our own measuring stick, shall we?"

"We can't take sticks in the house," said Bronte turning back to her drawing project.

"Very sad," mumbled Julia. She wished she could shake a stick at a few people. She looked up as Eden came out of the bedroom practically skipping. "Who was it?"

"It was Nora." Eden beamed with delight. "She says Rafe will be finished helping her soon. She's sending a car to pick us up to join them for lunch."

"I want ice cream!" said Bronte excitedly as she danced around her mommy.

"You just had chocolate," said Julia bemused.

"Ice cream, ice cream, ice cream," Bronte chanted happily as she jumped up and down with her mommy and ignoring Zia Julia.

Julia shook her head and smiled watching the two as they celebrated the thought of ice cream.

Her celebration would be when she could tell the world they were hers.

10

AS SHE STRETCHED and yawned, Rafe Salvaggio turned her head toward the clock and checked the time. She had napped for over an hour and a half and hunger had finally won out over the need for sleep. Wearing herself out seemed to be the only way to get sleep lately. Climbing out of the warm bed, she decided to take a shower to help wake herself and not feel so grimy from the work she had done earlier. Dressed in fresh clothes and feeling much better, she headed to the kitchen where she found little to eat. She decided to head up to the villa.

Rafe made her way along the garden path, glad she had the rest of the day free. After a busy morning, it was good to have had some alone time to sleep and regroup. Nora called Eden and asked her to come to the villa whenever convenient. At first, Rafe was a bit put off she didn't get to call her, but in the end, she was glad it was already done because she ended up being terribly busy and had little time to stop and make a phone call.

Maybe seeing Eden again would be okay. They had to get along for Bronte's sake.

Now, waiting for Eden and Bronte to show up was the only challenge. There were lots of other things, easier things to do at the villa until then from walking in the garden to listening to the performers and watching the shows.

Rafe looked up at the sound of a golf cart on the path and couldn't believe her eyes. Eden was behind the wheel and making her way down the path quickly. Rafe stepped to the side of the path as she rolled up.

"They let you have a cart?" Rafe laughed taking in Eden's windblown hair and the glow of her smiling face.

"Nora insisted," Eden said happily. "I brought lunch." She was so excited to see Rafe. When Nora called and offered to send a car, Eden was ecstatic. Waiting had been excruciating. Hearing Rafe's voice in her ear over the phone had brought back memories of the times they talked when Rafe was away on business trips, and they would play and flirt with each other. Rafe could always make love to her no matter how far away she was, but it wasn't until she was home and they were able to touch each other that they were both able to be satisfied. Now, being in Rafe's presence, she could feel the familiar uncontrollable pull again. She needed to be closer to her.

Rafe looked in the back of the cart and saw a food basket from the kitchen. "Where's Bronte?"

"Nora and Gabri have her," she said with a chuckle. "She was getting ice cream and playing with some other kids. Nora said something about recording them all singing a song in the studio. We waited a while for you, but then Nora suggested I bring you some lunch." She smiled at Rafe as a bubbling thrill ran through her.

As Eden stopped talking, Rafe's stomach growled, and they laughed. "Great timing," Rafe said with a grin. "Scoot over, I'll drive." Eden slid over, and Rafe climbed in and drove them back to the cottage. "Wait here," she said and went inside. A few minutes later, she came out with a bundle under her arm that she threw in the back of the cart. She climbed behind the steering wheel again and looked over at Eden. "I'm going to take you to a secret garden where we can have a picnic," she said mysteriously.

"Secret garden," Eden repeated and laughed. "I guess they have everything here."

"We do," said Rafe and drove them down the garden path. Soon, she turned off the path and took them through an un-manicured and wild part of the property. She stopped the cart and sprang out then grabbed the basket and bundle from the back. "We'll walk from here," she said and began walking through the woods.

Eden watched her for a moment in surprise then scrambled out of the cart and followed her. "Do you want me to help carry things?"

Rafe stopped and handed her the bundle. "Be very quiet," she whispered. "We don't want to reveal the garden to anyone." She started walking again, and Eden followed her quietly.

Soon, they came to a green clearing with a small bench, an old broken statue, and a bird bath. Off to the side was a marble structure, once a small chapel now abandoned. Over the years, the forest tried to reclaim it. Rafe stopped in the middle of the clearing and put the basket down then turned to Eden with a satisfied smile.

"Here we are," she said happily and took the bundle from Eden. She unrolled it and laid out the blanket and tossed the pillows over to the side. "Okay, let's eat!"

"What is this place?" Eden asked with amusement.

"It's an old prayer garden," she answered as she unloaded the basket. She wondered if Eden would recognize the garden as the paradise she had painted her into so many years ago. "When they built the villa, they included places for the priest to pray. Many times, each estate had a priest who lived on the property to handle the needs of the owners and the workers who lived and worked on the land. This one was forgotten because the villa was empty for a long time. They didn't expand the garden out this far and just left it forest. Gabri and I found it one summer when we were on break from college."

"It looks pretty taken care of for a secret garden," Eden said in observation as Rafe opened a bottle of wine.

"Yeah, Gabri always took care of it," said Rafe casually as she poured the wine. "We'd come out here all the time when I visited. He'd bring his guitar, and I'd bring my drawing pad or my paints. I think he brings Nora out sometimes now."

"I really like Nora," said Eden as she sat down on the blanket next to Rafe. "She really does rule the roost, doesn't she? She told someone in the kitchen to make a basket, and they jumped for her."

Rafe laughed and nodded in agreement. "She's the boss lady!" Rafe began filling her plate with food. Along with the wine, Nora had the kitchen staff fill the basket with grissini bread, pecorino and mozzarella cheese, olives, prosciutto, cherry tomatoes, strawberries, and grapes. "Gabri says, since Nora came to live with him, everything works better in the villa." She motioned to Eden to fill her plate then began eating. "It was her idea to modernize the kitchen and expand it. She also opened several other rooms in the house so there were more to rent out to tourists. When he wrote to me about it with the costs, he was afraid to tell me and Papa it was her idea because they were just dating then I think. It was just before Papa got too sick to work." She took a sip of her wine. "I knew something was up because of all the details he sent. Anyway, we gave him the money, and it turned out to be a worthwhile investment. Soon, they'll be able to remodel the other half of the villa. Then they can hold bigger events and rent out more rooms."

"Why did they ask you for money? Couldn't he get a loan or something?" Eden asked then began eating.

Rafe shook her head in confusion. "Why should he get a loan?"

"Well, it's just, it's his house and estate. Why would he want to ask your father for the money?" she asked innocently. "Don't get me wrong. I know you and your father have known him for a long time, and now he's letting you live in one of the cottages," she trailed off at Rafe's sudden laughter. "What?"

"Gabri doesn't own the villa," she said forcing herself to stop laughing. "It belonged to my father, they all belonged to him. Now they're mine," she said matter-of-factly but with a smile.

"They? All?"

"Yeah, there are five more, and Gabri runs them. He's run them for my father since the year after he got out of college," Rafe informed her with a smile. "He's done an excellent job, and now he's hired managers who actually make the estates profitable. You met Carisa. She's a tenant with her business but her husband, Frankie, is the manager for that estate."

Eden took in this added information unable to hide her surprise. "Why are you living in the cottage?"

"Because," said Rafe slightly lifting her shoulders, "more privacy and much quieter."

Eden laughed softly. "Julia's going to freak when she finds out. She thinks Gabri is forcing you to live in a shack and all kinds of stuff."

"Julia needs to mind her own business," said Rafe evenly then sipped her wine. "She told me all about how she thinks Gabri is stealing my money and mismanaging me," she said feeling her anger surface. "She's just jealous."

"Jealous?" Eden repeated. She recalled Rafe telling her about the conversation Rafe and Julia had long ago about not dating and just being friends. At the time, when Julia was living with Rafe, Eden had been afraid they had slept together. "Why's she jealous?" Eden asked as she pulled more grapes from the basket.

"She's jealous I gave Gabri my power of attorney instead of giving it to her or her father," she said feeling her annoyance at Julia creep into her voice.

"Oh." Eden chuckled in relief. "I thought maybe it had to do with what you told me about Julia wanting to date you when you were younger."

Rafe hesitated then looked up at Eden with a half-smile. She wondered if Julia had complained to Eden about her hurt feelings and if this was Eden's way of starting to talk about her new feelings for Julia. "Well, she did want to date me in high school, but I turned her down, and I've dealt with her jealousy a lot since then. She can be very possessive and jealous."

Eden laughed. "Right, and so she's been jealous of you all this time."

"It's true!" Rafe grinned not sure if Eden was playing or showing confidence in her relationship with Julia. She decided to play at Julia's expense to see how far Eden would allow her to go. "She's spent her life pining after me and being jealous of all my girlfriends, and anyone else who she thought might be closer to me than her."

"You really are full of yourself, aren't you?" Eden laughed, loving Rafe showing her playful ego again. "She must not be very jealous of me since she helped me get here."

"She's just waiting for you to leave me behind, so she can sweep in and finally have who she wants," said Rafe, knowing Julia had been waiting for Eden this time. She hoped Julia appreciated what she had now. "She's been there for me every time I had a break up just waiting for me to see the light," she teased, wondering if the thought of Julia wanting someone else would upset Eden, or if she had already considered it.

Eden looked into Rafe's sparkling eyes and, though they were filled with humor, she wondered if there was more than a little truth hidden in there somewhere. "I hope you never see the light," she said, wanting to be the only one to make Rafe's eyes sparkle with love again.

Rafe frowned then brushed her hands off and put the empty dishes back in the basket. She wasn't sure what to make of Eden's comment. Did Eden mean she wanted Julia for herself or something else? She decided to just wait to see if Eden would make things clear on her own. "Anyway, I wouldn't date her, and the list of things she gets jealous about could go on forever. Julia and her jealousy, not to mention her 'daddy issues,' has been a pain in my ass for a long time. Sometimes, I don't even know why she wants to be around me."

Eden frowned at the edge in Rafe's voice. "Daddy issues?"

Rafe nodded. "She thinks I take her father's time from her and is always mad about it."

"Julia thinks you take her father's time?" Eden repeated trying to understand what was really happening between Rafe and Julia.

"Yes." Rafe nodded. "Ian and I get along. We have since I was young, and Julia has always been jealous of the time he gives me. Before me, Julia never spent time with her father. He was always working." She frowned at Eden. "My father was out of the country most of the time, but I spent more time with him than Julia spent with her father." She lay back on the blanket. "At least her father was in the same country." She turned her head toward Eden who was looking at her with confusion. Of course, Eden didn't understand. She lived with both parents in one place her whole childhood. "You want to know what I did for her, to help her?"

"Sure," said Eden hesitantly.

"One time, Julia was angry with me. She didn't want to talk or anything. At first, I was mad, and then I decided it was her problem and I didn't care. One day, she suddenly wasn't mad anymore and begged me to hang out again. From then on, I paid attention to when she got mad. I found it was usually after I did something with her father." She glanced over at Eden for a moment. "I used to help him at his office in the summer," she explained. "Then I figured things out. Julia didn't like me spending time with him. So, I made up a game she could play with her father."

"A game?"

Rafe nodded. "Yes. When Julia and I went places together, sometimes I took my camera. I would take a few pictures then we would take one to his office and pin it on the wall."

"Oh," exclaimed Eden with a smile. "I saw those in Ian's office. It looked like you were always in motion. You were blurry in almost all of them."

"Yeah," Rafe confirmed. She was surprised the photos were still there. "I was blurry because I wanted Julia to be who he saw. I would move in the picture or move too soon on purpose. The game was for him to guess where we'd been and what we were doing. Really, I pinned those photos on her father's wall so they would have something to talk about, and they could have time together." Rafe lay silent for a moment as she looked up at the trees above her.

"I think it worked," said Eden. "She and her father are close."

"I also did it so she wouldn't be jealous anymore. She's still jealous, though. And they both hate my papa, and I don't understand why."

Eden knew Julia's thoughts about Ettore Salvaggio. She could only assume Julia's father had the same opinion of him. It was difficult for Eden not to share the same feelings knowing the things she now knew. Both Rafe and Gabri thought the world of Ettore, and she had promised Rafe she would defend him. "It doesn't matter," she said tenderly and ran her fingers gently through Rafe's hair again.

Rafe pulled her head away from Eden's fingers. "It matters. It matters to me!" She frowned angrily at Eden. "Have you kept your promise? When they talked bad about him, did you defend him?" The anger in Rafe's eyes and the set of her jaw told just how much the answer to the question mattered.

"I kept my promise," said Eden softly, "but we didn't ever talk about him, so there was nothing to defend."

Rafe crossed her arms not sure if she believed Eden.

Seeing Rafe was unhappy, Eden felt frustration again at Julia for arguing with Rafe. She knew Julia had been upset, but she also knew they made this trip to Italy to bring Rafe home. Getting into fights and making her angry had made things much harder than they had to be.

"I'm sorry Julia upset you," she said as Rafe scowled and looked away. "I told her arguing with you wasn't helping things. I even told her to go home early so you wouldn't have to worry about her anymore," said Eden calmly.

Rafe looked over at her with surprise and confusion again. "If she's helped you, and you think you need her here, you should tell her to stay with you. Did she already go?"

Eden shook her head slowly. "No. She's still here," she said. "She has helped me. She's been by my side, helping with everything, since you left. I really don't know what I'd have done without her. She's been very good to me... and to Bronte."

Rafe gripped her glass tighter preparing for more of Eden's words of adoration for Julia. "I see," she said so softly Eden almost missed it.

"She's offering me a new job at her father's company," she revealed as Rafe frowned. "I'm not sure about it, though. I don't understand how it'll work, or what I'm supposed to do. Apparently, she's come up with some way to invest in film production or something. It just seems risky to me unless you know what you're doing, and I'm not sure she does."

"Hmph," Rafe rumbled. "Then you should talk to Ian before you make a decision," Rafe advised. "If you want to change jobs then you should. Go into business for yourself or work for a company doing a job you love. Don't do something you feel pressured into doing out of guilt... or something else."

Rafe took a sip of her wine and remembered when she gave Andi almost the exact same advice. "Did I ever tell you about Julia's ex, Andi?"

Eden frowned at the name. She had heard the name but really did not know anything about Julia's ex. "No, I think she was before my time."

"She was," Rafe confirmed with a nod. "Andi, or Andrea as Julia always calls her, dated me for a while. She preferred to be called Andi, but you know Julia. She had to improve Andi to Andrea." Rafe took another sip of wine. "After I broke it off with Andi, it didn't take long for Julia to go after her. They started dating, and they seemed happy. Andi was between jobs because the museum she worked for lost a grant and had to make cutbacks. Julia decided she would create a job for her at Hawthorn Financial."

"It was nice of her to help," said Eden, "Julia's a good person."

"Andi thought so too. Julia had done a lot for her. She let her move into her apartment, paid for most everything so Andi could save as much money as possible, and even took her on trips. Julia romanced her. Andi went along with everything thinking as soon as she got a job, she could return the favor. But soon, they were arguing about everything. Julia pulled the 'I pay for everything' card a lot. Then, when it looked like Andi was going to leave, Julia suddenly created a job at Hawthorn Financial for her. Andi was supposed to be the curator for the company's art. Julia tried convincing her father to start a division in the company to help clients buy art and to let Andi run it. Don't get me wrong, Andi would have done a great job. The problem was, the company had very little art, and it wasn't in Ian's business model. Plus, there are a lot of very experienced companies out there, and it's not an easy business.

"Anyway, it turned out Andi was nothing more than a glorified, and highly paid, coffee and file girl. She couldn't help with much because she didn't know anything about investments and wasn't licensed. She hated the job. Julia, on the other hand, was happy and thought things were great. Whenever Andi tried to tell Julia she was unhappy, Julia waved her off and just ignored it. Finally, Andi came to me." Rafe hesitated a moment. "She found out Julia wanted to pop the question. Andi wanted to break up with Julia and wanted my advice. I told her almost exactly what I told you. She shouldn't stay with anyone out of guilt or let anyone pressure her into an uncomfortable situation."

Rafe licked her lips noting Eden was listening closely. "When Andi asked me how she could leave if she had no job or money, I gave her the name of a woman I knew in France." Rafe shrugged and glanced down into her glass. "Andi made the call. I guess one call was all it took. She broke it off with Julia and moved to France. Of course, there was more to it with the fighting and other drama. In the end, if Julia wouldn't have made Andi feel like she was trapped, things may have been different. Julia still doesn't see what she did wrong. She just thinks Andi picked her work over their relationship."

Eden took in Rafe's words but was not sure why she was being told about Julia's past relationship. "That's really sad. Julia's a good person. It's too bad she doesn't have more confidence someone would stay without being trapped."

Rafe nodded her agreement. "You're right. I hope you don't feel a similar kind of pressure from Julia."

"Oh, no," answered Eden as she smiled. She finally understood Rafe didn't want her to feel like she had to take Julia's job offer. "I'm not being pressured. Like I said, I'm just not sure about what I'd be doing if I took the job there."

"Okay," said Rafe and set her wine glass down. She hoped now Eden would see what kind of person Julia could be when it came to relationships. Then maybe she would decide not to be in one with her.

11

RAFE SALVAGGIO TOOK a deep breath and let it out slowly. She knew Eden's view of her might be tainted now because of the things she said about Julia. Eden kept putting off admitting she was in a relationship with Julia so, technically, she could say anything she wanted. It was a fine line, but she felt Julia had crossed lines made very clear lots of times. "Julia thinks Gabri swooped into my life to save me. She thinks he's taken over my life and is controlling me somehow. I saved myself. It was my choice to contact him. I'm in control and decided who I wanted to help me. Do you want to know why I didn't give Julia or her father my power of attorney?"

"Sure," said Eden feeling Rafe's anger at Julia. She was glad Rafe was sharing her reasons with her, though.

"Julia has always been," she hesitated for a moment, "meretricious."

Eden pulled a look, scrunching her face. "Meretricious? I don't get it."

"Well, it's like she's flashy but without much value," said Rafe with a small shrug.

"Rafe! You're terrible!" Eden rebuked, shocked Rafe would say such a thing about her friend. "Why would you say something like that?" She shook her head in disbelief. "What does being meretricious have to do with giving her or her father your power of attorney?"

"I needed to give it to someone I knew could handle things the way I would handle things," she explained. "Julia has never run a business or owned her own, well, anything. Her father still pays her, and she lives off her trusts. She's never done anything really, except spend money and work for her father when she wants to work. She knows nothing about my father really, except she hated him. So why would I trust her or let her have control of anything?"

"Okay," said Eden as she nodded, "okay, I get it, but what about her father?"

"Ian already handles a lot of my financial accounts," said Rafe with a downward quirk of her lips. "I didn't feel he had the time to commit to me, and he also had a bad history with my father. Plus, Julia has influence over him, and even though he would have been great for the business side, he wouldn't have been any help at all with the personal side. So I couldn't give it to either of them."

Eden looked away from Rafe and down at her hands. What Rafe was saying made sense. If Julia couldn't help with the business side—she stopped her thoughts there. The business side? What business? Then she remembered the estates. She wondered if Rafe's father had more businesses Rafe had been taking care of too. If so, it would mean on top of trying to hold herself together emotionally and mentally, she was also trying to hold together all her financial things and those of her father. Eden sighed and put her face in her hands. She wondered what other burdens Rafe was carrying while she was sick.

"I'm sorry," Eden said softly. "I'm sorry I wasn't helping you with those things."

"You couldn't help," said Rafe waving her off. "You weren't even around for most of it, so..." She shrugged not wanting to think about the pain of Eden leaving to the turmoil caused by Jake and his cult.

Eden felt the cut of the reminder she had left Rafe for Jake and the fallout afterward. She swallowed the last of the wine in her glass allowing its thick warmth to comfort her even though she felt she probably didn't deserve it. She tried to think of what she could say to make things better but no words coming to her seemed good enough.

Rafe picked up the bottle of wine and refilled their glasses then leaned onto one of the pillows and looked over the clearing. "Anyway, after Mexico, I knew I had to make a decision about who I wanted to take care of things if I couldn't. I felt Gabri was the best and only choice at the time." Eden had gone quiet, so Rafe decided to change the subject. "I love it here," she said softly, "it's so peaceful and calm." She lay back and looked up at the canopy above. Sunlight filtered down through the leaves she knew, if they stayed quiet long enough, the birds would start to sing again.

Eden watched Rafe as she lay quietly then moved a pillow next to Rafe's and lay so her head was close to hers. "I miss this, just being with you," she said softly. "I'm glad you wanted to see me today." She listened as Rafe breathed evenly for a while then moved so she could put her arm over her. She let Rafe pull her closer then closed her eyes. She could hear Rafe's heart beat loudly in her chest. She missed being held close by Rafe. She missed her smell and feel of her body against her. She took a deep breath so she wouldn't cry with all the joy she was feeling right now.

Rafe felt Eden's shuddering breath and knew the last six months, plus showing up here, had taken a toll on her. Julia had not kept it a secret how angry she and Eden were about it all. Though the damage to their relationship may never be completely repaired, and Eden would soon be back in America with Julia, there was no doubt in Rafe's mind there would always be a very deep love for Eden in her heart. She pulled her close and kissed her cheek. "I'm glad you came to see me," she whispered.

"Yeah?" Eden breathed keeping her eyes closed and enjoying the sensation of Rafe's kiss on her face.

"Yeah, and I'm glad you brought food. I was really hungry," Rafe said with a light chuckle.

Eden tried not to smile but failed. She opened her eyes and turned her head to say something but stopped when she saw Rafe looking back at her. "I was hungry too," she said then lifted her head and gently kissed her on the lips. "You taste really good," she said and kissed her again.

"Be careful," warned Rafe as she chuckled, liking the game. "If you go too fast, you may get stomach cramps."

Eden sat up and leaned over Rafe. "I'll just have to go very slow then," she said and kissed her slowly.

The familiar brush of Eden's hair falling against her face was all it took, and Rafe pulled her closer as she reeled at the kisses she poured over her face and neck and kissed her deeper. It felt so good, and she didn't want Eden to stop kissing her. "Have you had enough yet," Rafe whispered into her ear playfully.

"Not nearly," Eden said with heated breath. She barely had time to register the sensation as Rafe lifted her, twisting her body so they had switched positions and Rafe was above her. She felt Rafe's warm hands move over her body, melting her in the way it always did, driving her crazy and making it so she couldn't resist her. It was like she magically knew just where and how to touch her. She lost control and let out a low moan of desire. She ran her hands through Rafe's hair and pulled her deeper into their kiss.

It was a long and familiar exploration. Rafe fought herself so she wouldn't start stripping Eden's clothes off. It took a while, but soon, the hot, desire-filled kisses and touches became sweet and soothing. Rafe finally allowed herself to put her hand under Eden's shirt to feel the warm skin of her back. "I've missed you," she said huskily. "It feels so good to hold you."

Eden's head spun, her body ached with desire, and she felt what seemed like an electric shock when Rafe's hand finally ran over her bare skin. *Only Rafe* was the only thought she could process. Rafe was the only one who could ever make her feel this way with just a kiss and a touch. This moment reaffirmed everything for Eden, and it made her even more determined to show Rafe how much she loved her.

"I love you," Eden said between their kisses, "I want you." She reached up and grabbed the edge of Rafe's shirt and began to unbutton it to take it off. She wished she had the strength to rip it off her like Rafe had done to her so many months ago.

Rafe stopped kissing her and pulled away. "Ede, we can't," she said, not moving to make it easy for Eden to get to the buttons down lower.

"We can," Eden said softly and kissed Rafe's neck then reached up and pulled Rafe's face to her kissing her deeply. "I need your touch," she said breathlessly. "I need our connection, and I can feel you need it too." She tried to kiss her again, but Rafe turned her face away. "Don't you want me?"

"Of course, I want you," Rafe said, fighting to control herself while resting her head on Eden's shoulder. "But we can't. Not like this, with so much hanging over us."

"Why?" she asked and ran her hands through Rafe's soft hair. "You love me, you said you did, and I love you too."

"I know," said Rafe and pulled away to lay on her back. "But you have things you want to talk about," she paused wondering why Eden hadn't mentioned Julia yet, "and there are so many unresolved things. There are things I need to talk to you about, too. We can't just do this without being sure."

"I'm sure," said Eden firmly. "I'm very sure. It's one of the things I want to tell you."

Rafe sat up and straightened her clothes. She drank the last of her wine and put the glass in the basket. She didn't know how Eden could say she was sure when she was in a relationship with Julia and supposedly came here to tell her about how she was moving out of the house. This was going nowhere. Rafe couldn't take it anymore. "Maybe we should get back," she said and started to get up.

"Wait," said Eden and pulled her back down gently. "You said you need to talk to me about things. Talk to me now."

Looking at Eden's determined face Rafe suddenly wished she could just stop and think about things again or have Gabri here to help, but it was too late. "Why did you come here?" she asked bluntly.

Eden could see the turmoil on Rafe's face and wanted to take it away. "I came because I love you and someone once told me I have to be brave for *amore* and not wait for everything to just come to me," she said then studied her hands. "This is me being brave and fighting for you."

Rafe gave her a small smile and a short laugh because she was the one who told Eden those words. She genuinely appreciated them, but so much seemed to contradict them. "You say you love me," she paused, "but do you really? Are you sure of your feelings?" she asked. "Even after everything we went through and everything I did and said to you?"

"Yes," she said at once. "I'm completely in love with you."

"Okay," said Rafe and ran her hand over her hair in confusion. This was not what she was expecting, and she didn't understand why Eden was not telling her about Julia. Was she trying to hide her relationship? Was she lying? Did she think she wouldn't find out? "I'm still sick, and I don't think things will be easy for you if you're around me. I'm better but—" She shrugged hoping to give Eden a chance to take things back or tell the truth. When Eden stayed silent, she continued. "Like I've said before, I can't take losing anyone else right now," she said softly, watching her intently. "If you think it might be too hard, or you might want an easier relationship, or to be with someone who's less," she paused, "less difficult to deal with at times, I'll understand. I don't want you to feel trapped or unhappy."

"I don't feel trapped," Eden assured her, not understanding why Rafe would think she would feel trapped. Maybe it was why she told her about Andi and Julia. "I want to be with you."

"Okay," said Rafe as she nodded slowly. Rafe thought Eden sounded sincere and wanted to believe her, but she couldn't forget what Julia said or the fact they were sleeping together. "Why? Why do you want to be with me? I don't think I have much to offer you anymore. I always upset you or make you cry or cause you frustration and anxiety. I'm sure there's someone out there who would be better for you, someone who's well and can focus on you. Someone who can be good to you," she said repeating Eden's words about Julia. *Someone like Julia who you're already with,* she thought sadly. She wished Eden would just get it over with and stop doing whatever it was she was trying to do or prove.

Eden moved in close, kissed Rafe again and then sat back. "I want to be with you because I love you. I've caused you frustration too, but we've worked through it before. We can work through things again. Maybe it's time for me to focus on you like you used to focus on me." She took the last sip of her wine and contemplated Rafe thoughtfully.

Rafe stared up at the forest canopy. She didn't understand how what Eden was saying could ever happen. They would be living a world apart because Eden was going home. Plus, Julia again. She didn't know what she was supposed to do. Was she supposed to go along with Eden's game for the time she had left and pretend things were going to be great? Was she supposed to call her out as a liar and tell her she knew about Julia? They were getting along now, and it was good for her relationship with Bronte. Rafe sighed and frowned as her head began to ache.

"Love isn't everything," she said softly. "You can love someone and still not be meant to be together." She thought about the love she still had for certain people she knew she could never be with again and wondered if Eden would become one of them.

"Please, don't say that," said Eden forcing herself not to cry at Rafe's words. "I know you aren't ready right now, but someday when you are, we can work through things because we're meant to be together. I know we are."

Rocking slightly, Rafe thought about what Eden was trying to tell her, but she wasn't sure what it was. Was she saying they should both work on things, and someday, they could try again? Was Eden saying when she was better, she would leave Julia? Rafe just didn't know, and it was getting hard to think about it all.

Eden waited to see if Rafe would respond, but she just continued to rock and look around at the garden. "I've been thinking a lot about the things you told me about. The things about what happened when you were younger. I'm sorry you had to go through it all. I can see it's still hard for you," said Eden as she thought about what Rafe said about Julia earlier in the morning. "Did you keep things from me because you wanted me to be oblivious, like Julia?"

"No," said Rafe and shook her head as she fidgeted with the edged of the blanket. "No, not at all. I just didn't want you to have doubts about me. I thought what happened didn't matter anymore. I know now I should have told you about the things in my past, from when I was young. I..." Rafe hesitated. "I just couldn't. Then when I tried to tell you, it was too late, and I just made things worse. Everything's always been this big secret, so I thought I had to keep it a secret and make you swear not to tell. My father always worried it would come back to haunt me, and it did. He wanted me to tell you," she revealed.

"He did?" asked Eden, surprised Rafe's father felt she should know their secrets.

"Yes, but I didn't want you to know," Rafe confessed. "I liked how you looked at me, and I didn't want you to change your mind about moving in with me. I'm sorry. I know now keeping everything from you was a betrayal, but I didn't at the time. I really thought it would never matter."

"You didn't betray me, Rafe," said Eden as she reached out and pulled Rafe to herself and hugged her. "You couldn't have known." She kissed the top of her head. "I don't think knowing would have stopped me from being with you."

"If I had told you in the beginning, maybe none of the things that tore us apart would have happened," said Rafe regretfully. "Maybe we would've never been together. I just don't know." Rafe pulled away and saw the tear Eden was wiping away as she took in everything. "I know, even though I might not have betrayed you with the affair," Rafe continued, "I still betrayed you by not telling you about what happened and how it affected me. I'm still the Betrayer," she said softly.

Rafe wondered if Gabri had talked with Hannah yet. The fact Julia had accused her of having an affair with Hannah still weighed heavily on her mind. She didn't want it to be true but knew it was possible because she couldn't remember what happened in New York. Maybe Julia was right and, even though it was hard to accept, maybe Eden would be better off with her. "I'll do whatever you want me to do. I'll stay away. I'll stay in Italy, whatever you say. I just hope you'll let me see Bronte again and you'll let her come back to meet Gabri and Nora's baby."

Eden wondered if Gabri knew Rafe was still calling herself a Betrayer and taking all the responsibility for what had happened on herself.

"I'm the one who should be sorry, and I am," said Eden putting her hand on Rafe's arm. "If I were there for you, it wouldn't have mattered if you told me about your childhood or not. If I hadn't been so blinded by all the mistakes I was making, I may have seen something was wrong. Maybe things would be different now."

"No, I know it all started with me," said Rafe and leaned into her hands. "See, this is why it's so hard. There's just been too much over too much time. I just can't ever seem to outrun my past."

"Rafe," said Eden, pulling Rafe's head up so she could look at her. "You don't have to outrun anything. Not with me. I love you, and no matter what comes up, or what happened in your past, I'm here for you. I promise," she said and kissed her.

It was as though every cell in Eden's body wanted to be part of the kiss. As her body reacted, waves of dizziness crashed over her mind. She deepened the kiss and pushed Rafe back onto the blanket, climbing over Rafe so she could feel her body under hers.

"Love may not be everything, but it's something," Eden said confidently and covered Rafe with more kisses. She felt Rafe's warm hands flow over her body and could feel herself getting wet for her. It was like she was awake again, and Rafe's kiss was the magic cure. "It's something we feel for each other, and it's something, after everything, that wasn't lost. It has to mean something." Eden dug deep for strength. "I think it means we should try again," she said firmly and kissed her again. She moved her kisses down Rafe as she began unbuttoning her shirt from the bottom up this time. She kissed Rafe's stomach grazing her hard abs with her teeth. She loved being close to her and feeling her body. She wanted to kiss every inch of it again and again.

12

RAFE SALVAGGIO HEARD all of Eden's words. She felt Eden's kisses and the touch of her hands as they moved over her body. Eden was doing everything right, and Rafe's body was electrified. She felt Eden's hands move under her shirt and over her breasts and couldn't help the sharp breath she took as her body arched into her touch.

I should stop this.

"Ede," she called softly, but Eden kept kissing her body. It felt good, and she missed her so much, but she knew it was wrong. If she let this happen there was no telling what the fallout would be and how much pain it would cause. She would be hurt, Eden would be hurt, Julia would be hurt, and then there would be chaos again. She didn't understand why Eden wanted to take this risk.

She didn't understand why Eden wanted to betray her and Julia. Or was it she just wanted to give her something, knowing she was taking it away, to hurt her again? Was she still punishing her? She felt Eden's kisses make their way down her body and her hands take hold of the top of her jeans. She realized Eden was trying to undo them to take them down.

This needs to stop.

She felt Eden unzip her jeans and kiss her pelvis bone just above her underwear. Rafe opened her eyes and sat up quickly pushing Eden back. "Stop," she said, grasping Eden's hands. "We can't do this."

Eden tried to push Rafe back down. "Yes, we can," she said through her haze-filled mind. "I love you." She tried to kiss her, but Rafe turned her face away.

"Stop," Rafe said firmly and pushed her back. "What about Julia? She's in love with you. How can you do this to her?"

Eden shook her head in confusion, blinking several times, trying to take in what Rafe was saying. "Julia?"

"I can't take this," said Rafe and got up. She stumbled over to the low wall covered with rose vines, her shirt billowing behind her as she fastened her pants. She fell to her knees and put her head in her hands. She couldn't take any more lies or chaos in her life. She needed to get away from them all. She needed them to just go away and leave her alone.

Eden watched Rafe in shock, still unsure of what had happened. She went over and knelt down beside her. "Rafe, what are you talking about," she asked in dismay.

"Julia! I'm talking about Julia," she said angrily. "She told me you two were together. She said it 'just happened' and she was in love with you!"

Eden was stunned. "What?"

"She said she'd take care of you," said Rafe shakily, just wanting her to stop pretending. "She's in love with you, and I know everything, so stop lying to me!"

"No," said Eden shaking her head, "no, Rafe. I—" she was at a loss. She had no idea what was happening. "Julia is just my friend. She's our friend. That's all," she said and put her hand on Rafe's back.

"Don't touch me!" said Rafe and pulled away. She buttoned her shirt shakily then looked up as Eden started to cry. "All you do is lie to me." Eden shook her head in denial. "Well, someone is lying to me!" Rafe walked away because she needed distance. Sitting down on the bench, Rafe leaned over to catch her breath and calm herself. It was not long before she could feel Eden sitting next to her. "How can you fuck her then come here and try to fuck me too? What the hell do you want? Are you just trying to figure out your feelings again?"

Taken aback by Rafe's harsh words, Eden was stunned for a moment. "I..." she stammered and then her anger took over. "I'm not fucking her!" she said vehemently.

"Then why the hell is she staying in your room?" asked Rafe, not believing her. "Why's she telling me she's in love with you and is sleeping with you? Why would you want to go to work for her father and move out of our house?"

"I don't know why she said those things to you," Eden said bewildered and upset as tears sprang from her eyes. "It's not true, Rafe." She felt like the floor had dropped out from beneath her and wasn't sure why or how. "I don't want to move out of..." she paused, "our house." Eden wiped the tears from her face. Saying 'our house' created a spark of hope in her heart. "She talked to me about moving out of our house, but only because she was upset about how I wasn't able to see you and how she felt I was being treated. She offered a job because I've been worried about getting fired. I've had to take a lot of time off to get myself together and then to come here. She's not staying in my room. She has her own room next door to mine."

Rafe frowned, not sure if she believed her. It sounded wrong when added to what Julia told her and what she overheard. "Please, don't lie to me," she begged her. "I understand if you're with her. I'll stay away, just like I did with Jake. I won't make things hard. Please, just don't," her voice caught, "don't make me think you love me then just take it away. I can't do it again. I can't—"

"I'm not lying," sobbed Eden, unable to help the rain of tears at seeing Rafe's heartache. "I wouldn't lie, especially about this, not after all we've been through," she said hoping Rafe could hear the truth in her voice. Her mind was reeling because she had no idea why Julia would tell Rafe all those things.

"But she told me," said Rafe as she rubbed her head trying to ease the pain. "She's in love with you."

"I don't care what she told you!" Eden said in frustration. "I don't love Julia! I don't love anyone except you! I've always loved you! I only love you!" She fought to calm herself. She felt like she wanted to blow up with anger but knew she shouldn't direct it at the wrong person. She had to hold herself together and regain her ground with Rafe.

She slid off the bench and knelt in front of Rafe, taking her hands and kissing them gently. "I love you," she said softly. "I can tell you may still not trust me, and I know Gabri doesn't trust me, either, but I'm telling you, you can. I don't know why Julia said those things, but I only love you. You can trust me. I'm not going to stop loving you." She kissed her hands again and looked up into Rafe's pain-filled gray-blue eyes. "I'm here because I love you, and

I want you to come back to me," she said as tears dripped off her face and onto Rafe's hands. "I just want us back." She bowed her head onto Rafe's hands and sobbed. "I'm sorry for everything. I'll do anything if you'll take me back, and we can be together again. Please," she whispered desperately and squeezed Rafe's tear-soaked hands.

Looking down at Eden's golden hair as she leaned over her lap, Rafe could feel Eden's warm tears drip onto her hands then quickly cool as they spread out, flooding over them. She could hear Eden speaking but didn't know what to do. Pulling her hands away, she saw Eden's tears glistening on them, making them look unreal. So many tears had flowed over her hands from so many people.

The first tears she remembered were her mother's, but she thought it was just a dream. It seemed real sometimes, the vision of a tear breaking away from her mother's eye. It fell right before she died and ran down her face landing on Rafe's hand. Rafe never told anyone about her vision, and never would. Mostly what she remembered about the day her mother died was being in the hospital crying with her father. His tears flooded all over her, and she thought she would drown. They were different at the funeral. There, they were hot and didn't make it past his cheeks before evaporating. It was like the angels were scooping them up and making sure his wife received the love for her in them.

She remembered Maria's tears when she found her again. Maria thought she had stopped loving her, and she cried and cried when she saw her again. Rafe always wondered if Maria cried when they never saw each other again after Brettito died. Rafe had cried her own tears then but hid them from the world. She remembered all the tears for Brettito. Those of his mother were angry and hateful when they splashed on her as she screamed, blaming her for his death and demanding that she leave. Her own were full of guilt and sorrow. Gabri's tears were still like diamonds when caught in his eyelashes. They got large and heavy before they fell and rolled down his face, leaving wide streaks. His tears were always proud to fall because they were pure and full of empathy and compassion from deep within his soul.

Now her hands were covered with Eden's tears again. They were tears of anger, sorrow, pain, heartache, and betrayal all caused by her. Rafe couldn't remember a time when she had caused Eden to cry tears of joy or happiness or for anything positive or good. She didn't think she had ever moved her to tears with beauty or words of love or with a selfless act. She had only ever driven her to dark tears caused by dark deeds of the Betrayer.

But it didn't matter what deeds caused the tears anymore. What mattered was Rafe had created them, and so many had collected that she felt like she was drowning again. The icy lake was filling up and getting cold again. Rafe squeezed her tear-stained hands into fists then released them. She knew deep in her mind she needed Gabri, but he was too far away.

"I'm sorry," Rafe said softly, knowing she had caused the tears flowing from Eden. She had to give herself distance again. She stood up and walked back over to the blanket and fell to her knees. She wiped her hands on the blanket to get the tears off, but the stain of them wouldn't go away.

Immediately, Eden knew something more was wrong with Rafe than just being upset with their conversation. Fear and guilt ran through her, and she could hear Gabri's voice in her head calling her cruel and selfish. She remembered what the doctor from home had told them to do to help if Rafe was having problems. She had to find a way to take her from the place she was in her mind by changing locations or making some sort of change to engage her mind and put it on a new path.

Eden rushed over to Rafe and ran her hands over her face and shoulders to get her attention. "Rafe," she said shakily. "I'm so sorry." She looked around the clearing trying to think of something she could do or someplace she could move Rafe to help her. "Let's go look at the chapel," she said as she pulled Rafe up. "Come on," she said and led Rafe over the green grass through the clearing.

Rafe knew Eden was trying to help, but it was hard to accept when it felt like she was part of the problem. It seemed like everyone wanted her to believe they were telling her the truth even when their versions of the truth hurt her. She saw the concern on Eden's face, but it didn't stop the memory of having to choose who to believe between her and Jake. She knew now her mistake was to believe anything Jake had said, even though some of the things he had been saying were true. She had been right about him not loving Eden. Now she didn't know if Julia was lying about being in love with Eden. She only knew she didn't want to make the same mistake again, and she didn't want to reopen that wound. The dilemma she found herself in was if she believed Eden, it could mean the now dulled pain of heartache would return. This time, the sharpness may never dull again. "I want to believe you, Ede," she said softly.

"We don't have to talk about it anymore," said Eden as they walked. "I don't blame you for being upset. I'm upset too. We can talk about it later when we have time to process."

Inside, Eden felt like her emotions were in a competition to see which one could obliterate her defenses and burst through her skin. It was painful, and all she wanted to do was go somewhere and cry, but she couldn't right now. She had to think of Rafe.

Eden didn't understand what had happened between Rafe and Julia, but she knew there would have to be a hard discussion as soon as she saw Julia again. Julia's interference was making it impossible to do what Eden came to Italy to do—take Rafe home.

13

EDEN KINGSLEY HELD on to Rafe's arm as they stepped up to the front of the small chapel. "Can you tell me what it says there," she asked as she pointed to the words carved into a marble plaque inset into one of the thicker marble blocks.

Pulling her arm away, Rafe put her hand on the cool marble and felt the smoothed edges of the carved words. Feeling the cool stone helped ground her so she could pull out of her dark thoughts. "It's kind of a motto," Rafe said softly. "It says, *Dio mi guardi da chi studia un libro solo.*"

"What does it mean?" she asked with interest, rubbing her arms to try and ease the pain her emotions were causing.

Rafe frowned as she watched Eden rub her arms, knowing Eden was in pain caused by anxiety. They were both in pain, and Rafe just wanted it all to stop even if it was just for a little while. She wanted to go back to how they were this morning when they were playing on the phone. She wanted to hear Eden's laugh again and not worry about everything else. She didn't want to think about Julia and Eden's denial. She smiled to herself and made the decision that while here in the garden, they would try to play again. "It says, abandon hope all who enter here," said Rafe and tried not to smile.

"What?" Eden exclaimed in confusion. "They put that on a chapel? Did something bad happen here or something?" She groaned and was beside herself because it seemed like she couldn't win. Negative things came up even when she was trying to do something positive.

Rafe couldn't help laughing at her reaction. "No," she kept laughing as Eden still thought she was serious.

"Rafe," she said, finally understanding Rafe was messing with her. "What does it really say?"

"It literally says, 'God, guard me from those who study a single book.' It can also be interpreted as 'fear the man of one book,'" she said with a grin. "I guess the original owner of the estate wasn't very devout." She shrugged. "But this is Florence."

Eden pursed her lips doubtfully. "Is that what it really says?" She wondered why Rafe's mood had suddenly improved but didn't want to say anything to upset her again.

"Yes."

"Hmm, I wonder how he got away with putting something so irreverent on a chapel."

"He was probably the only one for miles around who could read it at the time," said Rafe. "It was probably a good laugh when his friends came around. Florence was always butting heads with the Vatican and the Pope. It may have even been a comment on which book to live by—the accounts book or the bible. Florence, at one time, was the home of super banks and the Florentine florin was coveted by the church who wanted to be in control of all the money and power. It really upset the church that the Medici's had more money and enough power to defy them then buy into the church. Not to mention all the new ideas and art they were financing. I guess putting family members at the head of the church kind of muddled which book was more important at times." She pulled some vines from the side of the chapel. "There's really no way of knowing when the quote was put on the chapel without going to a lot of trouble. It's possible a more modern owner could have added the plaque. It was there when we found it."

Stepping over the threshold, Rafe entered the small chapel. The interior was barren and cave-like with the only light coming through long narrow windows that once may have had stained glass in them. The room was only large enough for a handful of people and the priest. A lot of nature's clutter littered the floor and marble benches.

"When this place was used, there were probably wooden seats with cushions over the cold marble," said Rafe. "The walls were probably covered with tapestries or paintings and the windows were most likely Italian leaded glass. There was definitely an altar here." She pointed at a slight impression in the floor. "But someone either stole it or used it somewhere on the estate, and it hasn't been found." She looked back to make sure Eden had followed, and she wasn't talking to herself. "There was definitely a lot of silver, gold, and jewels in here, too. They really blinged-out their religious décor back then."

"Do you think they had weddings here?" Eden asked as she looked around, not minding at all Rafe going into lecture mode. It was always a sign Rafe was happy when she would want to overshare.

"No, not unless they were secret ones," Rafe joked. "It was probably built just to save face with the Vatican and make sure they didn't get on their bad side," she said as she kicked some leaves aside. "If they were devout, they would have just used it for private devotions, confessions, and other rites with a priest who may have lived on the estate. Sometimes, priests just lived on estates for a few months when they passed through, and other times, they spent their lives there. It depended on the noble who owned the estate and if the Vatican approved."

Eden watched Rafe walk around the chapel running her hands over spots on walls, examining the ceiling, and becoming engrossed in assessing the building. She could see Rafe's mind working as she went from end to end, pacing off dimensions and brushing debris away from the floor to get a better look.

"What do you think?" Eden asked teasingly, infected by Rafe's happy mood. "Will it last another hundred years?"

Looking over her shoulder, Rafe let out a short laugh. "Longer," she said with a smile, "and without any help from me."

This was not the first time she had assessed the little chapel and probably wouldn't be the last. She walked over and looked out of one of the narrow windows.

"I think this place would make a great secret playhouse for Gabri's baby. I could fix it up and put a solar panel on the roof to have a small amount of electricity. There's a good secluded spot over there," she pointed out the window, "where I could put an outbuilding with a composting toilet in case they want to do overnights."

"Sounds amazing," said Eden, but she really thought it sounded like Rafe was creating projects to keep her in Italy.

Seeing Eden wasn't very enthused, she walked over and put her arms around her. "Or I could turn it into a lover's retreat," she said throatily into her ear. "Softness everywhere and a bed right there where the altar was. I'm sure the Vatican would approve."

Eden laughed and shook her head. "Well, it is Florence," she said, repeating Rafe's words.

"It is," she said and kissed Eden softly. She put her head against Eden's. "I'm sorry for what happened. Sometimes I still..."

she paused, "have dark thoughts. Mostly, when I'm feeling a lot of uncertainty and anger about something."

"It's okay." Eden sighed, breathing Rafe in again. "I was having some dark thoughts myself." Pushing thoughts of Julia from her mind, she was determined to stay in a calm place for Rafe.

Rafe chuckled. "Oh, you were? Not my sweet Ede," she teased.

"Yes, your sweet Ede," she said with a smile, loving that Rafe used her nickname while they talked. It meant so much to her.

"Are you completely corrupted now? Did I miss the transformation?" Rafe laughed, glad Eden was playing now too.

"Not completely," said Eden playfully. "I have found myself cussing more and," she raised a brow, "as you've probably been able to tell, I have sex on the brain. I can't stop thinking about sex with you. I may be a sex addict. I may need you to cure me again."

"I can prescribe batteries." Rafe laughed and doubled over at Eden's wide-eyed expression of shock.

"So rude!" said Eden acting offended and playfully slapped Rafe on her arm.

"Now, now! No abusing the *dottore!*" Rafe hummed laughingly as she escaped the playful abuse. She made her way out of the chapel and back into the sun with Eden not far behind.

Eden followed and watched as Rafe threw herself down on the blanket then reclined on one of the pillows and looked up at her. She tried to fight it, but she couldn't stop from hurling herself into her arms and kissing her again. "I love you," Eden heard herself saying, and she felt tears spring out of her eyes. "I'm sorry," she sobbed, "I can't help it. I do, I love you. I only love you."

"Shh," Rafe breathed softly and wiped her tears away. "It's okay. I love you, too." She kissed her sweetly and pulled her close. She took a deep breath, breathing in Eden's satisfying scent and let it out slowly, relaxing as she held her. It felt good to have her arms around her again. She knew Eden was telling her again she didn't love Julia, but it didn't change the fact that Julia had said she loved Eden. Rafe didn't want to think about Julia at the moment, though.

"Rafe," Eden said softly then kissed her neck. "I..." she hesitated, "I want you to come home with me. I can't live without you anymore."

Holding Eden tighter, Rafe knew the playing was over again. It was back to the pain of reality. "Ede..." She sighed and loosened her hug. "I can't."

"Why? We'll be okay. We love each other."

"No," said Rafe shaking her head softly. "I'm sick and may not be able to give you what you need anymore."

"We got through something hard today, and we're doing really good now," Eden reminded her.

"We did," she agreed, "but we're not really good." Rafe wanted to tell her today was not reality. It was just playing while they could, while they didn't have to think about anything else. Now they had to go back to the real world. She couldn't tell her this, though, because she didn't want to hurt her and make her cry again. "Like I said before, there's just too much, and I'm not ready," she said instead.

"If you came home, I'd be there to help you. I want to help you," said Eden and couldn't help herself as she reached out and touched Rafe's face and trailed her fingers down her jaw. "I want to be with you no matter how hard it is. I want us to be a family again."

Rafe kissed her hand then leaned her head back and sighed out her name. "Ede." She hoped Eden would see this was where she needed to be right now. A calm place far away from the chaos in California. She hoped Eden would see their last six months apart was worth it because she was better and getting back in control of her life.

Rafe knew she wasn't ready to go back to America. She also knew Eden was here to convince her to go home now, and she said she wanted to try to stay together. It made things even harder because holding Eden again made Rafe want her more. She wanted to make love to her and keep her close and didn't want anyone else to have her. Rafe's thoughts darkened when she thought of Julia's words and the knowledge, even if Eden denies it, Julia might be trying to pull her knight-in-shining-armor operation on her.

"I know you're still working on getting better and things won't be easy," said Eden softly and kissed Rafe's neck. "It's your turn to be taken care of by me." She rose up so she could look into Rafe's eyes. "The real question is, will you let me take care of you?" She smiled knowing how hard it would be for Rafe. "We may end up causing each other a lot of frustration, but I think knowing we love each other will temper it for us."

Rafe tried to smile but knew she looked grim. She sat up with Eden, and they stayed close. The look on Eden's face told Rafe she was worried, and the grip Eden had on her hand told her she was afraid to let go right then.

"So many things have happened and need to be resolved," Rafe reminded her and pulled her hand away gently. "I haven't been working on any of it or even really thinking about it while I've been here. I guess I was just trying to forget."

Eden sighed in disappointment, missing the warmth of Rafe's hand in hers. She ran her hand through her hair, trying to think of a way to fight Rafe's stubbornness. The situation was difficult because Rafe was right. There were still a lot of things to resolve and Eden knew most of it was her own fault. She knew she had to be careful talking to Rafe. She didn't want to pressure her and upset her again. She knew if she wasn't careful, Gabri would use it to justify not letting her see or talk to Rafe again. She didn't want to witness Rafe lose herself again because of a mistake she made around her.

"You once told me we can't forget because we're human," she said softly. "Maybe trying to forget and keep things locked up inside isn't the best way to handle things. Just like with the secrets." She looked up at Rafe wanting to show her she could be strong for her. "I told you I've been thinking and working in therapy on the things that happened with..." she paused, "with Jake and the Stewards. I intend to keep working on everything. Maybe by the time you're ready to think about them again, I'll have more answers for you."

Rafe put her head into her hands. She didn't want to think about Jake and the Stewards. So many things ran through her mind she had purposely not been thinking about for months. She knew she didn't have any answers for all the questions Eden would probably ask her. She didn't know where she was in reconciling everything that happened with Eden and Jake and the Stewards group. Those things compounded what happened at the school, and it all blended together with the things that happened when she was young with her mother and Brettito. She had a difficult time separating everything and figuring out what was manipulation and lies and what was the truth. She wanted everything to be as easy as Eden tried to make them seem, but it was impossible.

"I've just been working on a few things at a time," Rafe said as she inspected the ground near her feet. "I can't think about everything right now. Sometimes it feels like..." she paused deciding on the right words, "I've stepped outside my life, and when I look back, I wonder how I can get back... or if I should go back. It's like." She hesitated, trying to think of how to explain it. "Like I've stepped out of chaos, and I'm trying to figure out how to make sense of it all, and I really don't know how long it will take."

"I understand," said Eden. Her heart ached knowing Rafe was telling her again she wasn't ready to go home. "I've been working on a lot of things myself. I think you do just have to take the time you need to work things out and feel like you can deal with everything. A lot's happened to both of us." She sighed, wanting to beg her to come home again but stopped herself. "You've been dealing with a lot of painful things for so long."

"Ede," said Rafe, putting her hand on Eden's shoulder, "I'm glad you've been taking care of yourself. You need to keep doing it." *God, why did this have to be so hard*, Rafe thought. "I know it's going to be hard," she hesitated, "for both of us. You need to start thinking about the possibility of letting me go." Eden burst into tears, and Rafe pulled her close. "Ede, I'm sorry. I'm so sorry. I just don't want to hurt you again, and I want you to be happy. I don't know if waiting for me will make you happy. Look at how hard things have been for you. Even though I don't understand what Julia is doing by saying some of the things she said, I think she was telling the truth about how hard things have been for you. Don't hold onto me out of feelings of guilt... or pity."

Eden pulled away from Rafe, hurt etched across her face. "You're not going to talk me out of how I feel about you," said Eden, determined to hold her ground. "No one is going to push me or trick me or convince me my feelings are anything but what I say they are again." She looked into Rafe's eyes and could see her worry and pain. "I've been working on all the questions you asked with Dr. Cathcart," she revealed, "and I realized a lot of the things

I did and said were because of my own insecurities and anxiety. I know you would never do anything to hurt me. My *guilt* over what I had done online, including the cybersex, and the *guilt* I was feeling about not being able to conceive, it turned into *anger,* and I focused it all on you," she said in anguish. "I know it was wrong! It was very wrong, and I'm sorry I hurt you. I'll never blame you or project my mistakes on you again. I'll never be so gullible again to allow some stranger—or Julia or anyone else—to convince me how I should feel. I'm not going to mix up my emotions again and mistake my guilt for anger or mistake guilt or pity for the feelings of love I feel for you! I hope you believe me and will give me the chance to prove myself."

Rafe could see the determination in Eden, and the confidence she showed matched her words. Eden had certainly changed since she last saw her. She still had some of her familiar anxiety, but now she had underlying confidence she could push forward when necessary. She had always thought Eden was beautiful but had never imagined adding more confidence could make her even more beautiful—but it did.

Shaking her head, Rafe just couldn't see how to give Eden what she wanted or be the person Eden thought she wanted. "I'm glad you're doing so well," she said and licked her lips. "But things aren't the same anymore. I don't have anything to offer you or anyone else right now. I think you would be hurting yourself if you wait for me. You've already proven you need more from me than I can give you."

Eden understood Rafe was pushing her away again, even though she just told her she was not going to allow anyone to push her about her feelings anymore. "Rafe, I love you," she said looking into her gray-blue eyes unwaveringly. She moved closer and took her face in her hands and kissed her. "I'm *in* love with you." She kissed her again. "You said you love me, and I know you meant it. That's what you have to offer me. I know what it feels like to be truly loved because of the way you love me. Even with all my mistakes and all the pain I caused, you can still look at me and tell me you love me. I don't think anyone else would be able to love me enough to do that, no one else has ever given me that kind of love. You've already given me the most important thing I needed."

Rafe could see the determination in her eyes and felt a mix of love and sadness. "I love that you think things can be so simple," she said softly and kissed her sweetly. She took a breath and started to get up. "Come on, let's get back. I want to see what Bronte's doing."

14

GABRI DE ANGELES SAT on the wooden bench holding his guitar as he watched Rafe run and play with Bronte and the other children in the garden. He watched as Rafe made sure to include Eden in their play and a few other adults joined in the fun. All the things he and Rafe had talked about the night of the concert ran through his mind as she waved at him. He waved back and set his guitar down as Nora sat next to him, handing him a small plate with a snack.

"Why are you looking so down?" Nora asked as she slid her arm around him.

"I'm still worried," he confessed as he ate some fruit. "I worry about what will happen to her when Eden leaves with the baby."

"She'll be fine," she said reassuringly. "She knows they have to go home, and she can invite them to come back anytime she wants them here."

"She can," he agreed, "but I need to speak with Eden again about a few things. Rafe wants me to make sure she has enough money, and everything is good with the house."

"Do you really think it's why she's here?" Nora asked surprised.

"I don't know," he said holding in his frustration. "Apparently, her friend, Julia," he said with distaste, "said Eden needed money, and she said a lot of other upsetting things. So, Rafe wants me to talk with Eden about them." He had been on the phone for hours looking for Hannah Pierce. Watching over Rafe and his lack of sleep was affecting his mood.

"Just try to be nice and calm when you talk to her," Nora insisted. "Rafe is so happy, and it's a good thing. I told you it was what she needed," she said and smiled knowingly. "Don't do anything to mess things up for the remainder of the time she's here."

Gabri coughed as he choked a bit on his food then stared at Nora with surprise. It seemed to him there had been a large swing of change in Rafe over the last several days. He was unsure if it was a good thing or not, even though it looked like Nora seemed okay with Rafe's current mood. Women, he decided, gay or straight, were beyond him. *I will never understand them,* he thought to himself. He would not let anything push Rafe into sickness again. "I know," said Gabri with a frown. "I only want to do what she asked me to do. I don't want to mess things up."

"Just keep that in mind because they're coming over," she said and nodded toward them.

"Hi," said Rafe happily, "We're going over to the refreshment tent to get drinks and rest before the dinner bell rings. Do you want to come?"

"Sounds great," said Nora as Gabri helped her stand up.

Gabri leaned over to talk to Rafe quietly. "I should talk with Eden now about the things we discussed. I may not have another chance."

"Oh, okay," said Rafe. She looked over at Eden then back at Gabri. "Do you want me to tell her?"

"No," he said, "I'll let her know. Just make sure Nora is okay for me."

"Absolutely," said Rafe as she smiled then picked Bronte up. "Are you thirsty?"

"Yes!" answered Bronte with excitement.

"Let's go get something." Rafe put the little girl back down. "Can you help Nora and hold her hand?"

"Come on, Zia Nora," said Bronte. "I want lemonade!"

Nora laughed as Bronte took her hand to lead her away. "She's so sweet," she said with mirth as Rafe followed closely.

"Eden," Gabri called. "I was wondering if we could talk a moment."

"Sure," said Eden. Seeing Gabri's serious face made the smile leave her own. "What's wrong?"

"Nothing," he said, forcing a smile. "Let's go to my office for some privacy." He motioned her to follow, picked up his guitar, and headed to the villa.

Looking around, Eden saw Rafe had already gone with Nora and Bronte. "Okay," she said softly and followed Gabri. She did everything she could to steel herself for what might be coming. She had a few things she wanted to talk with him about too, so she knew she had to stay calm.

They made it up to Gabri's office, and Eden found herself in the same seat she had been in the first day she came to ask about Rafe.

Gabri placed his guitar against the desk, sat down, and then regarded Eden, trying to figure out where to start. "I know I was upset that you came, but Rafe is happy you and the baby are here. Her wellbeing is my main concern, so if I seemed," he paused, "less than hospitable, I hope you understand."

"I understand," she said softly and clasped her hands together with worry.

"How are things at the California house?" he asked. "Are you able to take care of everything on your own?"

Caught off guard a bit, Eden hesitated. "Things are fine," she answered. "I'm lucky I've had a lot of help from Julia and the others."

Opening a side drawer in his desk Gabri took out his laptop and turned it on. "Yes, Julia," he said under his breath. "Your friend Julia paid for your trip here, didn't she?"

"Most of it, yes," she answered, not sure why he needed to know that information.

"Rafe wants me to make sure you're both repaid," he said as he began to tap on the keyboard. "I am going to write you a check, and it should cover everything. If not, let me know. If it is too much, then put the money aside to help with Bronte."

"You don't have to write one," said Eden wondering if this was some kind of payoff. "I didn't come here for money."

"Well, good," he clipped, "but Rafe insists. So I will write the check, and you do with it what you will." He tapped a button and then the printer engaged and printed a check. "It has also come to Rafe's attention you may need more money to help you live."

"It's come to her attention," Eden repeated confused. "How?"

"Again, your friend Julia, who was full of all kinds of disturbing information," he said trying to quash the building anger inside himself. "So Rafe will be increasing your support to help so you are not 'barely scraping by' as your friend put it."

"I don't want more money," said Eden shaking her head as a flash of anger at Julia ran through her mind. "I'm fine with the agreement we have."

"It's already done," he said concisely and shrugged. "I sent in the new amount to the accountant and the next deposit into your account will show the increase."

Eden could feel herself flush red with anger. "I don't want her money," she insisted. "I want her to come home."

Gabri could not hide the anger in his eyes as he took a moment to calm himself. "No," he said flatly. "She needs to stay here. This is my decision right now."

"I'm going to ask her to come home," she said firmly, not wanting to tell him she had already asked her and was turned down. "If she says yes, you can't keep her here."

"Do you think I don't know why you're really here?" He released a bitter laugh. "I know what you want, and you have been told, in many gentle ways, you won't have it. Rafe is not going back to America at this time. Maybe, when she's much better and ready, she will go."

"You're wrong," said Eden matching his low burning anger. "She misses us and loves us. She wants to be with us. She's doing much better, and she should be at home with her family."

Gabri just stared at her, biting back his words until he could calm himself, remembering what Nora had said about not ruining things for Rafe.

"Why would I send her back into a place where she is still being lied to and accused of things that never happened? You and your friends will do nothing but drive her back into sickness again. You are all selfish and cruel," he said unable to stop himself. "Yes, I am still of the same feeling from the first day you came. Even more now since your so-called friend has hurt Rafe again so terribly."

"Hurt her? What are you talking about?" asked Eden at a loss.

"I'm talking about how your friend came all the way here to again accuse Rafe of having an affair in New York," he said irritably.

"Wha—" started Eden. "I don't understand. Julia was with me when we talked to Lauren. She knows Rafe didn't have an affair with her."

"Yes," said Gabri and sat back in his chair. "She accuses her of having an affair with another. Hannah Pierce."

"Who?" Eden asked unable to stop the elevated pitch in her voice. "I don't know what you're talking about."

"Hannah Pierce is the dancer Rafe and Lauren had dinner with in New York," he reminded her. "She is also someone Rafe dated when she was young. She dated her before she left New York to come to Italy, and then at times when she was in France." He could see Eden was still confused. "You can tell your friend, I spoke with Ms. Pierce, who I found in France, and Rafe did not have an affair with her."

Eden was stunned. She processed the information Gabri gave her but was unsure what to think of the situation. Julia never mentioned anyone else she suspected Rafe of having an affair with in New York.

"Gabri, I didn't know Julia thought there was someone else. She never told me about her. If she had, I swear, I would have told her I didn't think it was true," she insisted.

"I can only hope your words are the truth," he said regaining his calm. "You see why I can't allow her to leave. She must be stronger to deal with these things on her own. You think she's better, and she is, to a point. I just can't take the chance you, or anyone else, will hurt her and cause her to get sick again. If you love her, you will understand this and allow her to get better."

Eden frowned at him then looked down at her hands. "You have to know I would help her," she said softly. "She could get a good doctor at home, and I wouldn't let anyone say or do anything to hurt her."

"You've already proven you can't stop them, and you can't help her like she needs," he said knowing she believed her own words. "What will they do for her there when a situation comes up, and you can't help her? Put her in a hospital? Drug her with pills to make her manageable but don't really help? Do you really want her given something that takes the Rafaella we know away like they did before? At least I have her power of attorney, and they will listen to me. You have nothing to make them listen and no power. I know she is better off here where she can be in her home and not forgotten in a hospital and subject to a system that just expects you to manage things with drugs and never get back to a good life."

"That's not true, Gabri. I know you've only heard the worse stories about the medical system in America, but we have the best medical system in the world. She has insurance and money to get the best. It doesn't mean she'll be in a hospital."

"Maybe," he said but shook his head no, "but I know this system, and this is the one that helped her before. I already have the best care for her here. If she leaves, she'll have to start all over telling another doctor about all the things she wants no one to know about. What do you think that will do?" he asked. "I can tell you it won't help."

Eden thought about her talk earlier with Rafe and the things she had said to her. "You should know she told me she still thinks she's a betrayer," said Eden. She saw his look go dark as his brow wrinkled with his frown. "Not because of New York," she said shakily, "but because she didn't tell me about what happened to her when she was young."

"I know Rafe still feels like she betrayed you," he said and picked up his pen. "But now you know what happened," he said softly, "you know even more than she does." He leaned over to the printer, grabbed the check, and then signed it.

"You've trusted me... and told me so much," Eden said hesitantly. "I need to tell you something else Rafe doesn't remember."

Gabri frowned with concern. "What? What is it?" he demanded.

Eden knew he wasn't going to like what she had to say, but there was no way to tell him without looking bad. He needed to know to have it in her medical file. She knew it could come back to hurt Rafe if she didn't tell him, especially if Rafe came home and the others brought it up. "Well, the first thing is... she had blackouts in therapy."

"Yes, yes, I know," he said and tapped his pen on the desk. "I have all the medical files."

"Oh," said Eden and swallowed down her anxiety. "Well, she had another one," she said softly. "The day before you came to get her... she, I think she had another blackout," she explained. "I was talking to her this morning on the phone, and she doesn't remember what happened that night."

"What happened?" he asked impatiently.

"She was upset about everything from the therapy session," Eden started nervously. "I was trying to help her and get her to talk—" Eden stopped herself because she knew she was glossing over the truth. "We were laying together on the floor of her room. I was telling her I loved her and wanted her." Eden could see Gabri knew she had been pushing Rafe for what she wanted. "At first, I thought things were good. She kissed me back and was talking sweetly. Then she just," she paused, "she just changed. She yelled at me to get away, and the others came in to see what was wrong, and she wanted them to all leave, too. We were all leaving, and I was upset and confused, so I decided not to go. I yelled at her about everything she was doing. She unlocked the back door and went out onto the patio, and I followed her. I begged her to come back, and she suddenly turned around and grabbed me sitting me down in a chair. I thought I was getting through to her when she started kissing me. I thought she was changing her mind and wanted me but... she started hurting me."

She glanced up at Gabri then back down at her hands. "I think she was having a blackout. It was like she couldn't hear me or feel me pushing her away. I was screaming at Rafe to stop when Julia pulled her off me. Rafe kept coming back, grabbing, and hurting me, until Julia pushed her away. Finally, Julia pushed Rafe away one last time, and she left us alone."

She peered up guiltily at Gabri. "The others came outside and asked where Rafe was, and she—" Eden swallowed hard again. "She was at the bottom of the pool." She could see the red anger bloom on Gabri's face, but she continued. "They got her out, and she was fine," she said shakily. "We got her back inside, in her bedroom. I'm not sure what happened, but when I came back into the room, they said Rafe wasn't responding. Julia did something, and Rafe screamed like, like nothing I've ever heard before and woke up. She seemed fine and wanted us all to leave." She swallowed nervously then looked up at Gabri again. "When I talked to Rafe this morning, she said she didn't remember being rough with me... or falling in the pool."

Gabri couldn't keep the pain he felt for Rafe from his eyes. "How can you want to take her away from here?"

"I don't want to be without her," she said determinedly. "I'm in love with her, and I do want the best for her. It's why I told you what happened. She knows I'm in love with her. She's in love with me, too."

"How do you know? She's not talked about being in love. She loves you and Bronte but not like you may think. Has she said she's in love with you?"

"Yes," said Eden, angry he would doubt it. "She's told me several times, including today, she loves me."

Gabri shook his head. "Of course, she loves you, but it doesn't mean she's in love with you. Don't put words in her mouth that she never spoke."

Anger at Gabri boiled up and burned away Eden's anxiety. She would not let him push her away from Rafe or make her have doubts. She had gone through hell to get to this point, and she wouldn't be dissuaded easily. She knew Rafe was in love with her. She could tell from Rafe's kisses to how she touched and looked at her. "She's in love with me, Gabri," she said evenly. "I have no doubts about that fact."

"What proof do you have?" he said, wondering if this were one of the lies Eden would tell to get what she wanted, as Rafe had warned him might happen. "If she is in love with you, then prove it."

Eden stared at him in disbelief. "Prove it?" she repeated and threw up her hands. "What do you want me to do, get her to come and make love to me in front of you?"

"No," scoffed Gabri. "Even sex is not proof of someone being in love."

"Why can't you just see it for yourself in how happy she is to have us here?" she demanded.

"I've seen more pain since you have come than happiness," he said scathingly.

"She's in love with me," Eden insisted. "What, do you want something in writing?"

"Sure, if she puts it in writing I would believe you," he said growing tired of the argument.

Eden couldn't believe he was doing this. She thought they were all getting along. She thought he and Nora were trying to help. Maybe he was just doing this to make her leave angry enough she wouldn't ask Rafe to come home.

"Here is this check," said Gabri, handing her the check. "I'll let Rafe know I gave it to you."

Eden snatched the check and wanted to tear it up and throw it in his face. The only thing stopping her was what he might tell Rafe. She folded it up and tried to put it in her back pocket but felt resistance. She looked up in surprise as she remembered the letter she had put there to keep it close. It was the letter Rafe's mother wrote. She pulled it out and unfolded it and then glared at Gabri.

"Okay! Okay, you want proof in writing? Look at this," she stormed, slapping the letter on the desk in front of him.

Gabri rolled his eyes and examined the letter. He saw it was something Rafe's mother wrote to her. At the bottom was a note in Rafe's handwriting.

I found her, and my heart is settled into a warm space. I like the way she sees me. Her name is Eden, and she is golden like the rays of light from Cyprian the Fair. I wonder if she is the one who takes me there. I'm in love with her, and I think you would love her too. I'm the happiest I have ever been and can't wait to begin our adventure!

He shook his head at her. "This must have been written long ago," he said and handed it back. "It means nothing."

"Then why did she give it to me yesterday?" she asked pointedly and snatched the page back. "She gave me this because she wanted me to have it and because she's still in love with me!"

Gabri glared at her and could not refute she might be right. "If it's true, now all you have to do is prove you really are in love with her." He got up from his desk, grabbed his guitar, and walked out of the office, leaving Eden stunned.

Eden followed him out angrily and fought the tears threatening to fall. She tried following him fast enough to tell him the only person she had to prove anything to was Rafe, but he took the stairs two and three at a time and walked out of the house before she made it halfway down the stairs.

15

AS SHE WALKED out into the garden, Eden Kingsley worked to pull herself together before looking for Rafe and Bronte. Her mind was filled with everything Gabri said, and she didn't know what to do. She wanted to tell Rafe what he had said, but she did not want his words influencing her. She knew Rafe said she was staying in Italy, but she might change her mind, and Gabri didn't know what he was talking about. As far as changing doctors, it was Rafe's decision too. Her anger threatened to erupt again as she thought about Gabri making her prove Rafe loved her and his flippant remark about her having to prove she was in love with Rafe. She wiped her eyes quickly and took another calming breath. She saw Rafe walking toward her, so she forced a smile to her face.

"There you are," said Rafe. She was glad Eden was smiling. It meant everything with Gabri went well. Now they could all have a fun night together. "We have a place saved for you. We can get some food and listen to some music."

"That," she cleared her throat, "that sounds nice." She let Rafe take her hand and pull her along.

As they walked, Rafe saw Eden had a faraway look, and her smile had fallen. She worried since Eden had talked with Gabri, she would want to leave. "Are you okay?"

"I'm fine," she said. "Fine," she repeated. "Gabri gave me a check. You don't need to pay for the trip."

"I want to," she said reassuringly, happy Eden wasn't thinking about leaving yet. "Plus, I don't want Julia to think either of us owe her anything."

"Okay," said Eden, remembering she was angry with Julia too, and now she had even more to be angry about. "You don't need to increase the money you give me every month," she said softly. "I'm fine, really."

Rafe scowled, and the muscles in her jaw tightened. "I've been told you're not doing fine," she said. "I'm sorry I didn't know you were having a difficult time sooner. I don't want you to not have enough to be comfortable and get the things you and Bronte need."

"You know, Julia doesn't know what she's talking about. I know, if I need anything, I can tell Katheryn," she said unable to hide her annoyance.

"For someone who doesn't know what she's talking about, she has a lot to say," said Rafe with an edge in her tone. "Let's not think about her now," she said as they got to the tents. "Let's enjoy the food and the music."

Rafe led Eden into the refreshment tent where they loaded their plates with choices from the catered feast that included everything from *Acquacotta* to *Zabaione*. They filled their glasses with wine then made their way over to the music tent where they found Nora and Gabri helping Bronte with her food. They sat down and enjoyed their dinner to the sound of laughter and music.

Soon, Bronte was up playing with the other children, and Gabri was with Stefano and the other musicians playing music. Everyone else talked and laughed as they drank wine and danced to the music, enjoying the night.

In the middle of a fast set, Gabri rushed over and grabbed Rafe. They danced with abandon, feeling the effects of their wine and the music. Nora and Eden watched the pair between keeping an eye on Bronte.

"They're so beautiful together," Nora said to Eden as she laughed. She saw the same expression on Eden's face she may have had herself the first time she saw Gabri and Rafe dance together. "The first time I saw them dance, I have to admit, I was so jealous, I took Gabri home and let him know he belonged to me!"

Eden blinked clearing her vision and her mind as she heard Nora talking to her. "I've never seen her dance. I mean, I've seen her dance, of course, but not like that, and never with a man."

Eden watched as Rafe allowed Gabri to lead her across the floor, and then he would pull her close then push her into a turn or a spin. They were so graceful together and looked like a perfect couple.

"Gabri said they used to go to clubs and parties together when they were in college," said Nora as she watched them. "Everyone thought they were together and would eventually get married. They both knew it would never happen. Gabri told me stories about how he would go out with two women on his arm, and everyone thought he was what he calls '*machismo*,' but it was just Rafe and her date," she confided with a laugh. "But it didn't hurt Gabri's reputation, and he loved it! I think they both had no problems when it came to getting women into bed." She winked and pointed her chin toward the dance floor. "You should go dance with her."

"What?" asked Eden, her eyes wide with surprise. "I can't dance like that," she said quickly. "Plus, Rafe said we have to be careful here."

It was Nora's turn to look at Eden with confusion. "We're not out on the streets of Rome. This is Florence, and it's always been a more liberal place. Not to mention, this is Rafe's home, and I'm sure everyone here knows she's gay. She doesn't exactly keep it a secret. She told me there were lots of gay people here. If you're uncomfortable, there are lots of men who will dance with you just for the fun of dancing, like Gabri and Rafe."

"No, I'm not uncomfortable. I just thought Rafe always said things were different in Italy, and I didn't want to make a mistake," she said and took a swallow of her wine.

"I guess it's different when you're just here as a tourist. I'm sure it's quite different from Los Angeles," said Nora thoughtfully, knowing there were unfriendly places in America similar to some places in Italy. "But don't worry while you're here at the villa. Have some fun. I'll keep an eye on Bronte."

Eden cast her eyes around the dance floor finding Bronte, who was happily dancing with her friends. Occasionally, she would run to Rafe, who twirled her around, and then she would run to Gabri who did the same. Rafe picked her up, spun around with her, and then brought her over to the table.

"Hello, Mommy," Rafe said playfully. "Are you going to dance with us?"

Eden kissed Bronte on her ruddy cheek. "Are you having fun dancing?"

"I wanna dance more!" yelled Bronte and pulled away from Rafe then ran back to the dance floor.

Rafe picked up her glass of wine to quench her thirst. "How are you two doing?" she asked happily.

"Just fine," said Nora and gave her a wink. "We were just admiring all you have to offer."

Rafe laughed and sipped her wine. "So, which of you will dance with me when Gabri sings?"

"Well, it'll have to be Eden," said Nora with a smile. "I'm not drinking wine and not feeling graceful."

"Wine is sometimes necessary to make you dance gracefully," Rafe teased. "Have you had enough wine to dance?" She held out her hand to Eden. "You have admired me long enough. Now it is time to taste." She pulled Eden up and led her to the dance floor.

Eden couldn't help her smile. She was glad Rafe had come to get her. After her conversation with Gabri she was feeling a lot of anxiety. She felt confined in her mind, and it made it hard to even move on her own. She hated the fact Gabri made her feel so powerless. It was like how she felt around her father when he was angry and discounting everything she would try to say. Feeling

Rafe's warm hands and having her close helped her break out of those feelings

"You've always been a very good dancer," Eden said as they danced to the music, "but I don't think I've ever seen you dance like you did with Gabri. Why didn't you ever dance like this at home?"

"I don't know," she said with a slight shrug. "I guess I never had time to feel relaxed enough and let go."

"You did do that one dance with Julia," she reminded her.

"Yes, but it was a competition, and I had to win," Rafe reminded her with a smile. "And I got to throw her in the pool."

"True." Eden laughed as Rafe pushed her into a spin then pulled her close. "It's been a long time since you've danced with me."

Rafe gave her a quick kiss on the lips as the music changed to a fast, upbeat song. "I'll show you my moves if you show me yours," she challenged playfully. She jumped back and began dancing and showing off her wild, seductive moves.

Eden watched as Rafe danced close to her and swung her hips to the beat of the music. Rafe took her hand and pulled her along until they were caught up in the crowd who had flocked to the dance floor. As Rafe encouraged her, Eden began moving to the fast and stimulating beat of the music. It didn't take long for her to get caught up in Rafe's playfulness, and she danced around Rafe showing herself off and running her hands over Rafe and herself. She danced close to Rafe and looked into her eyes lustfully as she pressed in on her, unable to hide the desire building in her over the past months.

Eden's movements and touches were burning through Rafe, hypnotizing her so she only saw Eden, the woman who she was drawn to, who she could never get enough of, who owned a piece of her soul. She knew it was going to be difficult to let her go again.

As the song ended, they were covered in a fine sweat from their exertions, and Eden clutched Rafe close, breathlessly kissing her as a slow song began. She took hold of Rafe's hands, looked into her eyes, and then slowly, deliberately, placed Rafe's hands on her hips pulling them into an intimate embrace. As they swayed to the music, Eden lifted her face and kissed Rafe again. Rafe had her eyes closed and leaned her head against Eden's, keeping her hands exactly where Eden had placed them.

Eden pulled Rafe closer so they could only sway to the rhythm of the music. She ran her hands over Rafe's hips and up her back. "Rafe," she whispered into her ear, "I love you." She felt Rafe hold her tighter for a moment. When her embrace loosened Eden immediately missed the feel of Rafe's body so close. "I like it when you hold me close," she whispered breathily into her ear.

Rafe's mind was in turmoil. Her desire for the woman who was telling her she wanted her and needed her was at a boil, but her reasoning reminded her she would be gone tomorrow. She hesitantly, carefully, moved her hands over Eden's back pulling her close and into another tender, gentle kiss. "I'm glad I get to hold you again, Ede," she breathed out the words. Rafe pulled back to look deliberately into Eden's eyes for the first time since Eden showed up in Italy. In that moment, she could see the desire and the spark of determination. "You still have beautiful eyes."

Eden could feel herself flush red like she always did when Rafe gave her compliments. The music changed again. An upbeat song began, and everyone launched into dancing to the new beat. She glanced down in surprise as she suddenly felt little arms around her leg and found Bronte wanting to dance. "Hey there, little dancer," said Eden with a laugh, taking Bronte's hands to twirl and dance.

Rafe watched happily as Eden danced with Bronte. "I'm going to get another drink," she called over the music. Eden waved showing she heard. Rafe made her way back over to Nora and sat down next to her exhausted.

"Are you ready for a dance?" She grabbed her glass and took a drink of wine.

"Maybe the next slow one," she said and patted Rafe on the leg. "Looks like you may be very good at slow ones."

"Oh, I am." Rafe grinned. "And I smell good, so it'll be much better than dancing with Gabri."

Nora laughed putting her hand on her pregnant stomach. "I think this baby is dancing right now." She saw Rafe's worried face. "Stop it, I'm fine," she said and put her hand on Rafe's leg again. "I can't wait until next week. He should be here, and I can breathe again and get some rest."

"Wishful thinking," scoffed Rafe then flashed a smile. "But you're lucky. I have experience with newborns, so you might just get a little sleep."

"Have you asked Eden if she'll let Bronte come back?"

"I haven't really asked her, but I've told her I hope she lets her come back."

Nora wondered if Rafe was afraid to ask her. "Well, ask her soon so we can make plans."

Rafe turned her attention to Eden dancing with Bronte. She felt pain in her chest at the thought of them leaving. The music changed to a slow song. "There's our song," said Rafe and held her hand out to Nora. She led her to the dance floor, and they began to dance to the slow song. She leaned close to Nora. "Can I tell you something?"

"Of course." She chuckled, noting Rafe did smell good, and she was an incredibly good slow dancer. She knew just where to put her hands to lead her along effortlessly. She was a bit jealous Rafe knew both how to lead and follow when she danced.

"I'm thinking about asking Eden if she'll stay here," she said arching her brow. She didn't reveal she had already contacted Katheryn. Rafe knew she would have to make assurances to Eden to ease her anxiety about moving to Italy. Eden had survived moves before though. Rafe was certain Eden would agree they both needed to stay in Italy. "What do you think?"

Nora thought about how happy Rafe had been since she came back from lunch with Eden. She knew Rafe and Gabri had been upset over a few things, but Eden wasn't really part of those things as far as she knew. Plus, if Rafe wanted to ask Eden to stay, it proved she loved Eden.

"Are you thinking about asking her now?" she asked, trying to hold in her excitement. "You know, she told me you're all she's been thinking about for months."

Rafe turned Nora to the music and smiled. "Does Gabri know about your new job as couple's counselor?"

"Ha, ha." Nora smirked. "I think you should ask her," she said smugly and smiled. "I can see how much you love her."

Rafe laughed. "Oh, you can?"

"Of course," quipped Nora playfully. "Remember, I'm a sensitive and jealous woman. I see a lot," she teased. "Unless there's some other reason you're so aglow with happiness tonight."

"You don't think it's selfish?" she asked softly her voice tinged with worry.

"Selfish? To want the people you love most with you? I don't think so," she said confidently. "I can see she makes you happy and having her and Bronte here may help you. I think it's wonderful."

"What do you think Gabri will say?"

"Don't worry about him," she said firmly and took a quick look at him playing his guitar. "If he has a problem, I'll deal with him."

Rafe chuckled and believed her. "I'll ask her tonight. She'll have a lot of time to think about it on her trip home."

"Think about it?" Nora asked, shaking her head. "Doesn't she know how much you have to offer? She should say yes right away, like those of us who can't resist you," she teased, and Rafe chuckled in her ear.

"I asked her to come to Italy with me before Gabri showed up in America. She didn't want to come," she revealed. "So..." She shrugged. The song ended, and Gabri waved Nora to the stage.

"Ask her again," she said quickly then went to see what Gabri wanted.

Rafe found Eden sitting down with Bronte and joined them. "Did she wear you out?" she asked happily.

"Completely," said Eden with a smile and handed Bronte her cup. Bronte took a drink and handed it back. "Right now, I'm the official cup holder. I can't set it on the table yet."

"There's a little bit of wine left in the bottle. Would you like some?" Rafe asked and picked up the bottle.

"I think I need to stick with water," she said as Bronte took the cup again. "We'll need to go soon. She'll probably fall asleep in the car."

"Yeah, she's fighting it." Rafe chuckled as she watched Bronte do anything to stay awake. "Did she even have a nap today?"

"I don't think so," she said with a sigh at the fact Bronte rarely took naps anymore. "It's been an exciting day."

"I don't think things will wind down here until the early hours of the morning," said Rafe. "Do you want to let her run until she drops or get her to the car before she has a lack-of-sleep meltdown?"

"I think option two," said Eden not wanting to deal with the meltdown. "I have to get her backpack from the villa and see if she'll go potty before we get in the car. She's had a little problem with bedwetting, so I like to make sure she at least tries before she goes to sleep."

Rafe was surprised at this latest information. "Why is she having a problem?"

Eden looked at Rafe then looked away quickly, feeling guilty. "She's just going through a phase. She's growing and sleeping harder, I guess." She wasn't sure if she should tell Rafe now that Bronte started having the problem right after she left, and it took a long time for Bronte to understand why Rafe wasn't there. Bronte still didn't understand, but she was getting used to the change. She was doing better with the bedwetting, but Eden still wanted to take precautions because it upset Bronte whenever it happened and they had to change pajamas and sheets. "Come on," she said to Bronte. "Let's go for a walk."

Rafe and Eden each took a hand and walked Bronte up to the villa. Rafe ran up and got the backpack while Eden took Bronte to the restroom, and they met outside the kitchen. Rafe drove them down to the garage in the golf cart and let Bronte steer for a while. They made it to the garage, and while Eden put Bronte into her car seat, Rafe looked around for Fausto. She found the keys in the little office and left a note then went back out to the car.

"Looks like I'll be your driver tonight." Rafe shook the keys. "I think the driver may be at the party."

"Great. I get to have you a little longer," Eden said and happily got in the car.

They drove in silence. Eden reached over and held Rafe's hand like she used to do. She was happy Rafe was driving her back to the hotel. She wanted to ask her to come home again and hoped Gabri was wrong.

16

INSIDE PALAZZO VECCHIETTI Hotel, Rafe Salvaggio carried Bronte, and Eden Kingsley managed the car seat as they took the lift up to Eden's room. Bronte had fallen asleep in the car and was so worn out that she didn't wake when Rafe laid the sleeping girl down in her bed. Eden began working on getting the shoes and clothes off the little girl and getting her into her pajamas without waking her. Rafe slipped quietly out of the bedroom to wait in the living room. Sitting on the couch, Rafe examined the hotel room. She appreciated the fact Julia booked a nice hotel for their stay. She hoped the check Gabri gave Eden would cover everything. Rafe was happy she didn't find Julia in the room. It told her Eden was telling the truth and made Rafe's decision about asking Eden to stay even easier.

Leaning her head back, Rafe wondered what was taking so long. She was impatient to talk with Eden about the possibility of her and Bronte staying in Italy. She could imagine them living together again in the villa and all the things they could do and the places they could visit. When she was better, they could even travel to Paris, or Greece, or other countries, and stay for a while.

They could even follow Gabri on one of his tours. She would have to figure out a different place to live. The two-bedroom cottage would work for a while, but they would need something bigger so Bronte could have her own room and she could have an office and studio. Rafe smiled at her thoughts because she was already assuming Eden would be sharing her room.

The bedroom door opened, and Rafe opened her eyes as Eden walk out of the room. She had taken the time to shower and change into her pajamas.

"Hey," said Eden as she sat close to Rafe, "I hope you don't mind, I changed. I just thought I'd take the time to shower tonight so I can sleep in tomorrow if Bronte does."

"I don't mind," said Rafe with a grin, noticing Eden had on the pajama's she described this morning. "Wearing my pajamas again, I see."

Eden glanced down at the pajamas then back up at Rafe. "Yes," she said then leaned in and kissed her. "What are you going to do about it?"

Pulling Eden close, Rafe held her and whispered in her ear, "I think I'll give you a pass tonight, but take care of them for me," she said and kissed Eden again as she ran her hands over her body. It felt so good to hold her close, feel her body, enjoy the taste of her and smell the scent of her skin. She kissed her face and neck then leaned her head against hers. "I hope you had a good day," she said softly.

"Oh, I did," she said suggestively. "Now we can have a good night too." She gazed into Rafe's eyes while running her hands over her, sliding them under Rafe's shirt.

Rafe laughed and grabbed Eden's hands and held them. "Ede, we can't."

"Why?" Eden asked disappointed Rafe had rejected her again. She wanted to make love to her and to be close. She wanted Rafe to feel their connection and the love she had for her.

"You know why," said Rafe and kissed her. "We've talked about it already. I can't do this and then lose you. It's already so hard for me."

Sensing Rafe's dispirited demeanor, Eden felt like this was the time to ask again. She reached up and held Rafe's face then kissed her. "You won't lose me," she said softly. "I want you to come home. I need you to come home. I love you."

"I can't leave yet," Rafe answered. The disappointment crossing Eden's face was immediate. Rafe took Eden's hands and held them gently. "I need to stay here," she paused, "and I don't want to go back right now."

"Why?" Eden asked, hanging her head down recalling all the things Gabri said. "Is it because you love me but..." she hesitated and prepared herself to try not to cry, "you're not in love with me anymore?"

Rafe could feel in the way Eden held her hands so tight that she was afraid of her answer. It made her sad she had done things to make Eden think she was not in love with her.

"No," she whispered and pulled her close and hugged her. "I'm still in love with you. I'll always be in love with you. This isn't about how I feel about you," she said and kissed her to reassure her. "I need to be here. I'm getting better, my doctor is very good, and I can depend on Gabri to help me with everything."

"You can get a good doctor at home, and Gabri can still help you," she reasoned as Rafe released her. She immediately missed the warmth of her. "Then you can be with all your friends and me. We miss you... I miss you."

"I miss you too," she said, wanting to reassure her. "I don't miss Julia and the others. Maybe I miss Jude because she understands me, and Letty. The others just make things so hard. Look at everything that happened before I left. I told you they were just pushing me, and I needed to be away from them."

"I know," said Eden, "but they know not to do those things now. Things will be different, and I'll make sure they don't push you or make things hard."

"You can't be there all the time, and I'm not ready to deal with them right now," she said shaking her head. "I know they won't change. It's who they are."

"How do you know?" Eden asked. "You won't even give them a chance."

"Why do I need to give them a chance? Why do I even need to think about them right now?" Rafe asked, trying to control her frustration. "I have to think about what's best for me right now. Why can't you and everyone else think about me for a change?"

"We do! We are thinking about you," Eden insisted. "You're all we've been thinking about."

"Really?" Rafe scoffed. "Were they thinking about how I was doing and what I was going through? I don't think so," she said, the doubt and frustration clear in her voice. "Maybe they were thinking about you, but they weren't thinking about me at all."

"But how can you even know how they'll be if you don't come home," she asked trying to find a hole in her logic. "You won't answer emails or take calls."

"I tried to deal with all the emails and voicemails," Rafe said and stood up in anger, "but they were all so angry and hurtful. Gabri made me stop reading them and stop listening to the messages. If they were so concerned for me, why would they send them? I'll tell you why—because they don't care about anyone but themselves!"

"That's not true," said Eden softly, not wanting to upset her more. "They were just worried. Letty is your cousin—and she's beside herself with worry because she can't get through to you. She asked me to beg you to call, or email, anything so she can know how you're doing."

"I'll tell Gabri to contact her," said Rafe softly reigning in her feelings. She was sorry about not contacting anyone, but it couldn't be helped.

"They don't want to hear from Gabri," said Eden in frustration. "They want you."

"Well, they can't have me right now!" said Rafe unable to hide her anger. "They'll just have to accept they are not my priority. I have to think about myself and my progress right now."

Eden flinched back at Rafe's anger, her own frustration with everything flaring. "So, do you mean Bronte and I aren't your priority?" she asked, feeling hurt.

Rafe ran her hand over her face in frustration then sat down next to Eden again. She didn't want to argue with Eden and ruin the day they had together. "No," she said softly, "no, it's not what I mean. You and Bronte are my priority. It's why I wanted to make sure you had everything you needed, and why I sent Bronte those gifts and videos."

"You left us behind without a word except for Katheryn coming to move you out of the house," she reminded her. "Don't you even care how everything affected us and how we were feeling?"

"I asked you to come with me. Of course, I care," said Rafe, distressed Eden thought she didn't care.

"I didn't know what was going on when you asked me to go," complained Eden. It was frustrating Rafe seemed not to understand the heartache and pain she left in the wake of leaving them all behind.

"I know you really didn't understand how sick I was." Rafe sighed and leaned back in the couch. "I love you and Bronte, but I really was in no shape to do anything more for you than what I've been doing. I could barely function for a while, and I had to depend on Gabri heavily. If you had talked with me then, you may have never made this trip." She rubbed her head as it began to throb. "I'm sorry Gabri didn't send you the gifts I wanted you to have. Maybe, if he had, you wouldn't think so badly about me." She could see her words weren't enough for Eden.

"I would have made the trip," Eden insisted. "I think most of the blame, from my point of view, is with Gabri." Looking down at her hands, Eden tried to hide her guilt. She hadn't even thought about or opened the gifts Gabri gave her when they talked. "He could have sent us information and kept us in the loop. He could have helped us more with everything concerning you and what you were going through."

"He couldn't," said Rafe leaning back on the couch. "He was dealing with a lot, and he was angry too. I know you don't understand, but he had to live through everything again with me. I'm lucky he had the strength and had Nora to help him. Nora kept us both in check."

Rafe thought if Gabri's mother was alive, she would love Nora, even though she wasn't Italian. Nora was tough and had the Italian spirit in her when it came to taking care of the people she loved. Rafe smiled inside at the memory of Gabri complaining about Nora. He grumbled about how Nora acted just like his mother, but he was still unable to deny her whatever she wanted.

It didn't take long for Gabri to get over his anger and admit how lucky he was to have Nora.

"Nothing he did was meant to hurt you, or anyone," Rafe assured her. "He was just focused on helping me."

"He has helped you," Eden conceded. "Now, I need you to come home. Bronte needs you, too. Please," she begged softly and put her hand on Rafe's leg, "please, come home."

"I still need his help," said Rafe and sat up. She took in the pleading look on Eden's face. Eden's posture screamed she was working to control her anxiety. There was only one way she could give Eden what she wanted.

17

EDEN KINGSLEY WORRIED Rafe was going to become angry and leave, so she wanted to change the subject for a while. She still had no idea what gifts Rafe had given her, and since they were together, she thought she could open them with Rafe like they talked about. She was determined to open the gifts tonight and keep Rafe here while she did.

"You know, I haven't opened the gifts you gave me," she said and stood up. "Let me go get them, and you can watch me open them." She held out her hands, motioning her to stay, and then turned and went into the bedroom. She rushed to the closet, retrieving the gifts she had taken out of Bronte's backpack. With them all in hand, she took them back into the living room. "Here they are," she said and sat them on the coffee table.

Rafe scrutinized the three packages and wondered if it had been a good idea for Gabri to give them all to Eden. Maybe he should have just given her the one she wanted to send for Eden's birthday.

"Which one should I open first?" Eden asked as she sat close to Rafe.

"Your birthday gift," she answered softly.

"Which one is my birthday present?"

"That one," said Rafe and pointed to a small rectangle box.

Eden picked up the gift and unwrapped the paper covering the box. She lifted the lid and looked inside. She then looked up at Rafe in surprise. "It's beautiful," she said softly and took the pendant out of the box by the gold chain. The pendant contained a bloodstone about the size of a quarter. The bloodstone was a very dark green and dappled with bright red inclusions. It was inset into an ornate eighteen karat gold frame encircled with diamonds around the edge. Set into the bloodstone were aquamarine stones in several sizes in a scattered pattern across the stone.

Rafe pointed to the aquamarine stones. "These represent the stars in the sky making the Pisces constellation," she explained. "I thought about a fish, but I wanted something different."

"I love it," Eden said happily. She turned so Rafe could fasten the gold chain. When Rafe finished, Eden turned back around to show Rafe the necklace lying against her chest. "Thank you," she said then kissed her. She loved the feeling of Rafe pulling her close, holding her so tight, and kissing her back.

"You're very welcome. Happy birthday," said Rafe and kept kissing her, the image of the necklace against her skin surrounded by the low neckline of her pajamas in her mind. She was happy Eden liked the necklace. She was even happier she had another reason to kiss her, and they weren't arguing about going home.

As Rafe kissed her, Eden felt the familiar rush of love run through her. She pushed against Rafe as they kissed until she had Rafe leaning back on the couch. "I want to show you how much I love it, and you," she said breathlessly and moved her body against Rafe.

"You do?" Rafe smiled and ran her hands over Eden. She could feel her body reacting to Eden's efforts.

"Yeah," she whispered, "so let me thank you properly." She kissed Rafe deeply then moved her kisses over her face and down her neck.

"Ede," Rafe said softly and held on to her hands. She could feel Eden preparing for rejection. "Ede, stay here with me," she said and kissed her again. "Stay. I want you," her words were stopped by Eden's kiss. She pulled back and looked into her eyes. "I want you to stay here, in Italy, with me."

Eden frowned at Rafe in confusion. "I-I..." she stammered, "Rafe, I can't stay here," she said and pulled her hands away. "We need to go home."

"I can't go back right now," said Rafe softly, "but you can stay. Then I'd be with you and Bronte again. I think having you here would help me... and it would help us."

Eden could feel herself shutting down at the idea of leaving her home and everything she knew. She came here to take Rafe home, not stay in an unfamiliar place. "What about my job, and our friends, and the house, everything? I can't leave everything behind," she said shakily. "I can't," she whispered.

Rafe could see the idea of leaving home was causing Eden discomfort. She knew moving to California for college and leaving behind her parents and her home was one of the hardest things Eden had ever done. Rafe imagined moving to Italy was just as scary for her.

"I know it sounds scary, but I'll be here," Rafe assured her. "I'll do everything I can to help you. So will Nora and Gabri." Eden moved away and sat on the edge of the couch silently in the tell-tale repose she habitually presented when trying to control her anxiety. Rafe reached out and took her hand. "I'll take care of you, I promise. You can see if you can do your job from here, or you can get a different job or, if you want, you can choose not to work while we're here."

Eden came out of her thoughts and shook her head. "I can't quit my job. They won't let me work from here. I have to be at home to do my job." She looked up at Rafe in distress unable to hold back all the worry she felt. "I need my job because of our agreement. Where will I go if things don't work out? You keep saying we have to work on things, and I—" She stopped to rub her head. "I don't want to be here alone if you think things won't work out. No," she shook her head and fought back her tears at the thought of being abandoned here, "no, you have to come home."

"I would never leave you here alone," Rafe assured her softly. "I would make sure you had a place to go, wherever you wanted if things don't work out. I want things to work out, Eden. I think we both do. I love you."

"What about our agreement," Eden asked and was unable to stop her tears of anxiety. "You made us equal, and if I don't have a job, I can't support myself. I can't be equal. I don't think I could get a job here. I don't know how to do anything here, and I can't even speak more than a few words of the language."

"We can make a new agreement for the time we're not living in California, and you may not be able to work," she said hoping to solve the problem. "I'm asking you to stay, so I should take care of you and Bronte. I'll put it in writing, so you'll know you'll be taken care of no matter what happens."

"I don't know," said Eden still filled with uncertainty. "What if I quit and I can never get a job I love again? If I can't keep up with the industry it'll make it even harder to find a job."

"There must be things you could do for your company or another company while you're here," Rafe said knowing Italy had a great film industry. "You won't know, though, until you research and ask. All I'm asking right now is to investigate things. You can take all the time you need, and I'll help in any way I can. If you can't find anything, then think about other things you can do. You said you were helping Abby write a screenplay so maybe you can help others, or maybe you could write your own. You're a great writer," she said with a smile remembering all the people who were so grateful for Eden's help over the years. She just hoped she didn't go to work for Julia. "You have a lot of people you could call who would help you with a project."

Eden's mind was spinning with all the reasons it would be impossible for her to stay in Italy. "What about the house? You can't leave it empty." She couldn't control the worry boring through her. "Are you going to sell it? You worked so hard on it, and I love everything you did for me there. I feel like it's my home, and I love it there."

"I won't sell it," Rafe promised and reassured her with a smile. "I'm glad you love the house. We can rent it out to Letty and Ephraim or someone else until we decide to move back. I'm not asking you to stay here permanently. How long we stay will depend on things like me getting better and if we just decide to stay a while afterward."

"I don't know if they can afford it," said Eden her hands shaking with worry.

"You don't have to worry about them affording it," said Rafe and bit her lip. "If you want them to live there, and they want to live there, we'll work something out."

"What about Abby and Julia? What about Flynn and Jude? What about all our other friends?" she asked, suddenly feeling the bloom of painful pinpricks over her skin. She rubbed her arms to ease the pain. "I don't know anyone here. I'll have to start again." She looked pleadingly at Rafe and wiped a tear. "You know how hard it is for me. I could barely speak to Nora, and she speaks English."

Rafe put her hand on Eden's back and ran it gently up and down and could see she was feeling pain. She knew how hard it was for her when they were first dating. Meeting Abby and the others had been overwhelming for her. It had been strange to Rafe how it was hard for Eden to deal with people on a personal level, but at work, she had few problems. Now she knew Eden dealt with work differently than home. At work, she could focus on the job more than the people. In public, especially around new people and places, she didn't have the buffer work gave her until she could feel more comfortable. "I know it won't be easy for you," said Rafe comfortingly, "but I know you can do it. You're stronger than you give yourself credit for. You've done a lot of things over the past few years proving just how strong you are."

"I wasn't strong," Eden said bitterly. "I was stupid! I know you mean leaving you and moving in with Jake and all the things I did while we were apart. I thought I was handling everything well back then, but I was just tricked and lied to and manipulated. Please," she said desperately, "please, come home."

"Eden," Rafe said softly and stopped, knowing the more backed into a corner Eden felt, the more she would lash out.

"I know I was gone physically, but I was with you in here," Eden said, pointing to her heart. "I know I'll never stop needing you and loving you and feeling you in my heart," she said shakily. "I just can't move so far away. And what about the friends we have?" she asked frantically. "Am I supposed to leave them behind and forget about them?"

"No," Rafe answered quietly. "I would never say you should forget them. I know you love them. I would never stop you from talking to them or even inviting them to come when I'm better."

"It would just be better if you came home," Eden insisted. "It would be easier for both of us."

"No," said Rafe in a calming voice. "This isn't about what's easy or hard. This is about so much more. Plus, my doctor is here. I have to stay so I can get back to being the person you love, and so I can be the person I want to be. I can't if I leave right now."

"Please," Eden sniffed. "I already love you, I do. I don't understand what you mean about being who you want to be. Are you trying to change who you are? I love you the way you are, we all do. I—" She choked and couldn't continue. As she cried, she could feel herself begin to shut down, but she fought against it.

Rafe took a deep breath and let it out slowly. She didn't know how to explain what she didn't fully understand herself yet. After a moment, she continued. "It means I don't want to be a wildling like Abby calls me or the damaged child Gabri knows, or someone to use because they're too afraid to live their own life like Julia or be a victim because of my PTSD, or someone to be pitied because of stories people may hear about me."

Watching Eden try to deal with the distress and discomfort she was in caused a wave of sadness to flow through Rafe. "I just want to be how you saw me when we met. I want to be well and be sure of my own mind again. Mostly, I just want to be seen by you as the one who loves you and not someone who needs your sympathy. I want you to love me again like you used to love me," she said wanting Eden to understand.

Rafe could see Eden was not going to make the decision to stay right now. Either she just didn't want to stay, or her anxiety was making it impossible for her to see staying was the only choice that would work for both. "But I guess it's impossible now," Rafe continued. "It's all ruined. I know it's my fault and I'm sorry. I was selfish. My father warned me things would turn out badly, and he was right. I keep wondering why he left the painting of Maria out. I think it may have been to warn me I should tell you the secrets. I didn't do it until it was too late. Maybe, if I had, I wouldn't need to stay here to get better." She stood up, pushing her hands through her hair and out of her face. "I'm sorry if I upset you."

"Wait," said Eden, clinging to her, not wanting her to leave.

"I don't know what else I can do or offer you right now," said Rafe, annoyed staying in Italy caused Eden so much anxiety and disappointed that Eden had so many things she felt were more important than being with her and her health. Rafe pulled away from Eden then made her way around the coffee table. "You should do what you think is best for you and go home."

"Stop," said Eden frantically. "Don't say that!"

"You know," she said in frustration as she made her way to the door, "maybe Julia should have tried harder to keep you from coming since she's so in love with you. Be sure to tell her I'm not walking away from anything, and this was your choice. I don't want to force you to do anything to upset you or make your life harder."

Anger making her snap from her immobility, Eden stood to follow Rafe thinking how much she would like to throttle Julia. "It wouldn't matter how hard she tried. Julia couldn't have kept me from coming!" Her anger at Julia came out in her words. "If you come home, we can just tell everyone to give you space, including Julia. Please," she pled in desperation.

"No," said Rafe shaking her head. "Dealing with Julia has proven leaving here would be a mistake. Julia is supposed to be my friend, and she's done more damage in one conversation than you can even imagine! For all I know, everything she says is true, and if it is, maybe you're right not to stay."

"Everything she said isn't true!" argued Eden. "You know it! What she said about her and me isn't true," she asserted shakily. "Gabri told me something Julia said to you," she said with a sigh of frustration. "I really had no idea she thought you might have had an affair with someone else. Gabri said it wasn't true because he talked to the woman." She saw Rafe bristle and hunch her shoulders in anger and could tell she was unhappy with the subject.

Rafe turned on Eden with blazing eyes. She was relieved Gabri found out the truth and that Julia was wrong, but angry because, once again, she had been falsely accused and punished.

"It just proves my point," said Rafe angrily. She took a breath to calm herself. She just wanted Eden to understand she needed to stay here to get better. She hoped, when she understood, Eden would agree to move to Italy so that they could be together. "When Julia and the others do things like they did when I was home, and things like Julia has done, accusing me of having an affair, especially when I have no way to know if it's true, I can't deal with it and at the same time work on other things I need to concentrate on. When she accused me of—" She shook her head at the memory. "It felt like my world imploded again. I had no idea if it was true, and all I could think about was, what if it was true?

What would my life be like? What would you and everyone think about me? How would I overcome more pain if it were true? I'm just thankful I have Gabri. I can't go through it all again right now." She stopped and worked to control herself until she could speak calmly again. "I need more time to get to a place where I'm sure I can handle everyone and what they might say or do, especially if they're still angry with me and the whole situation. I need time to get back to being myself a hundred percent." She held back telling Eden that, right now, she didn't think she ever wanted to see anyone from California again. Rafe put her hand on the doorknob knowing she had to leave or become angry again. She didn't want to be angry or in pain anymore.

"Is that what you want me to go home to and try to live with? I can't," Rafe said clenching her jaw. "What about everything you said about wanting to focus on me? Was it all a lie?" She waited for an answer, but Eden was silent as tears ran down her face. "If no one else will think about me, then I have no choice but to think about myself. Is it too much to ask that I choose the place where I feel I can get better? Is it too much to ask that the woman I love, and who says she loves me, stay with me wherever I need to be?" She opened the door and then looked back at Eden. "Maybe it is." She sighed sadly and walked out.

"Rafe!" Eden called and followed her into the hallway, but she was too late because Rafe was already going down the stairs two at a time.

18

AS WAVES OF sickness washed over her, Eden Kingsley felt her life going into another tailspin. She had convinced herself everything was going fine, and everything was going to work out just like she saw it happening in her mind for months. Reality slapped her in the face, and she could hear everyone who had warned her not to get her hopes up saying they told her so.

Rafe was not coming home.

Eden grabbed the back of a chair in the kitchenette and leaned over as she tried to breathe. Her breath wheezed in and out as her anxiety did its best to shut down the airways. Watching Rafe walking away brought back the pain she felt when Gabri took her away six months ago. Knowing Rafe walked away angry at her this time seemed to intensify the pain a hundred-fold.

There was a knock on the door, and Eden knew who was on the other side.

Julia.

Eden rubbed the back of her neck with a shaky hand trying to calm herself. She remembered the things Rafe told her Julia had said, and the accusations. Her anger flared. How Julia and everyone treated Rafe was one of the main reasons Rafe said she couldn't come home. Things could have gone so much faster, and maybe Rafe would have come home if Julia hadn't interfered. It was a certainty she would have been able to spend more time with Rafe. Right now, though, she knew was not about her own anger. It was about Rafe's feelings of guilt and betrayal caused by Julia's defamatory words and lies.

Eden wanted to demand answers from Julia. She wanted to know why she had told Rafe they were sleeping together and that they loved each other. She wanted to know what Julia was thinking, what Julia thought she was going to accomplish. She wanted to set Julia straight about just who she loved in case she was confused somehow. Suddenly, she wanted nothing less than to throttle Julia, but the only way she could do anything was if she let her in the room.

Eden pulled the door open angrily finding Julia's surprised face. "Come in," she forced herself to say.

"I heard arguing," said Julia. "What's happened?"

"Rafe isn't coming home."

"Son of a—" Julia started and stopped herself. "Sorry. I'm sorry she's doing this to you and treating you like this." She should have known things hadn't gone well by the way Eden looked. Her eyes and face were puffy from crying, and she had dark circles under her eyes. Even her posture told the story of hurt and disappointment.

"How she's treating me?" demanded Eden. "She's been sweet and honest. She told me she loves me. Is there something wrong with that?"

"No," said Julia defensively. She took a moment to collect herself. "It's just, you came all this way. She may have been nice to you, but you're still leaving without her. What happened?"

Eden glared at Julia and could not control the anger she felt about what she had done. "Why?" she asked angrily. "Why did you say all those things to her and then accuse her of having an affair again? You've made it impossible for me to convince her to come home!"

Julia was stunned for a moment. "I..." she stammered, "I just wanted her to see what she was doing. When Lauren mentioned Hannah, I knew Rafe had been with her before, and it was possible Rafe was with her again. She could be lying about what she remembers, and I wanted to let her know she wouldn't get away with hurting you again. I didn't say anything to you," she hesitated, "because you were already so upset."

Eden felt her whole body go rigid and her jaw clench. Julia was calling Rafe a liar. Rafe was many things, but she had never been a liar. She spun on her heal and left Julia in her wake as she strode over the tiled floor to the bedroom.

Julia gaped after Eden not sure what she was doing and if she had been dismissed. She threw her arms up in frustration just as Eden returned.

"Just so you know," Eden said angrily, "Gabri contacted the woman, and Rafe didn't sleep with her. He told me when he gave me this." She shoved the check Gabri gave her at Julia.

"I'm glad she didn't, but from where I stood, it was a possibility," Julia insisted and inspected the check.

"He hopes this is enough to cover everything. He said Rafe wanted it, but I think he also meant it as a payoff because it's way too much."

Julia unfolded the check and glanced at Eden in surprise at the amount. "He's definitely mismanaging her money. I still can't believe she's okay with living in a shack behind her friends' mansion."

"He also increased the child support because of whatever you told her," said Eden angrily. She collapsed on the couch tossing the other paper she had pulled from her pants pocket on the coffee table. "Now he thinks I'm just here for the money! How could you do this?"

"I was trying to help you," she tried to explain as she followed.

"Well, you didn't!" Eden said hotly.

Julia didn't know what to say. She just wanted to make sure Rafe understood the position she had left Eden in when she left.

And she wanted Rafe to know she would be taking care of Eden when she did exactly what she was doing to her right now.

"Oh, and the shack is very nice, and the mansion," Eden fumed, "it belongs to Rafe! She's just living in the cottage for privacy! You don't know anything!"

"Well, how am I supposed to know what property she owns in Italy?" Julia said defensively. She frowned at what was around Eden's neck. "What the hell is this?" she asked pointing at her necklace.

Eden put her hand to the necklace. "It's the gift Rafe gave me for my birthday," she said as she felt the coolness of the bloodstone.

"Let me see it," she said taking the pendant in her hand and pulling Eden closer. "Are those real diamonds?"

"I guess." Eden pulled back, and Julia released the pendant. Gripping the pendant, Eden ran a finger over it. "It's a Pisces pendant with my birthstones and the constellation."

"You do realize that thing is twenty-four karat gold and has about thirty very clear looking diamonds," she asked, impressed. "It looks like something custom and must have cost thousands."

"So?" Eden said in exasperation at Julia's changing the subject and her concern with the price of the gift. "After she gave it to me, she asked me to stay."

"In Italy?" Julia asked in surprise. "What is it, some kind of bribe?"

"No, it wasn't a bribe," said Eden annoyed. "I was supposed to get this for my birthday, but Gabri didn't send it. Why do you think she'd have to bribe me to stay?"

"Because Rafe knows how to get her way," she said with certainty. "Did she seduce you too?"

Eden just stared at Julia unsure of what to say for a moment. "What? Why would you ask such a thing?" she asked, affronted for Rafe. "For your information, I was the one trying to seduce her, and it didn't work!" The memory of Rafe's revelation about Julia's claim of love fanned Eden's flame of anger. "Did you tell her you're in love with me?" she asked, standing over her angrily. "Did you say we've been sleeping together?" The shocked look on Julia's face told her it was true. She paced the living room angrily. "How could you?" she fumed as she moved away from Julia and tears burst from her eyes. She thought Julia was her friend, but now it turns out, all this time, Julia had been working against her and causing the problems making Rafe push her away.

"I didn't tell her we were sleeping together," said Julia petulantly, trying to save face though she knew she let Rafe think more happened than truly had.

Eden was at a loss. She didn't know how Julia could think her pathetic denial helped. "Why would you say those things to her?"

This was not how she wanted to tell Eden about her feelings, but she knew she had to take the chance. "Well," she said softly as she stood to face Eden, "I said it because... it's true. I've fallen in love with you." By the incredulous look on Eden's face, she knew she had to explain herself quickly. "I knew she would disappoint you and push you away. I just wanted to let her know I would be there for you. I know you're not ready to move on from Rafe, but I was just hoping, when you are, you'd see how much I love you, and you'd love me back."

"Oh, my god! Oh, my god!" groaned Eden. She stumbled back to the couch and had to sit down. She loved Rafe, and it was not going to change for Julia or for anyone else! How could Julia not know she only loved Rafe? She would only ever love Rafe. It was why they were here, to get Rafe and take her home.

Julia knew she had to make Eden see she was only thinking about what was best for her, unlike Rafe who was being the true Machiavelli causing all the problems by playing with Eden's emotions. "Look at what she's doing to you," she said sitting next to Eden. "First, she avoids you and treats you with insouciance, then she gives you a few hours of her precious time and, in the end, tells you she won't go home."

Eden wiped her tears defiantly. "She'll change her mind. She loves me, she said she loves me."

"Please," Julia said irritably. "She built you up. Gave you false hope. She's refusing to go home. And now she's trying to make you stay here." She got up and paced in front of her agitated. "Can't you see what's happening? She's doing to you the same thing Jake was doing." She knew all about Jake and what he was doing to her because Eden had confided it all to her. Eden had confided a lot of things to her, and it was one of the things that brought them closer. "She's telling you she wants you to leave your home, your job, and the people you care about. The difference between her and Jake is she knows you won't do it. She knows all about your anxieties. She's doing it so you look like the bad guy, and you will feel guilty about it. That's not love!"

"I think you should go," Eden said softly. Julia's words felt like a slap in her face. Jake never really loved her, she knew that, and to equate Rafe with Jake was unfair. The thought of Julia using the information she confided to blast away the hope she would finally be with Rafe again was like cutting her with a knife. She could feel it in her soul that Rafe loved her, no matter what Julia said.

"Eden," Julia said softly and knelt in front of her. "I do love you. And I can take care of you in ways Rafe can't or won't. I won't make you leave your friends or your home. You can even keep your job if you don't want to work at my company. I just want you to be in a place where you feel happy and loved." She wished Eden would look at her, but she kept her head down and her hands over her face. "Please, stop crying. I don't want you to have to cry over her and what she's doing to you anymore." She could see her words didn't have the effect she had hoped, so she tried again. "We've spent so much time together, and it's obvious we make a great team. Bronte and I get along too. Everything I've been doing has been for you... because I love you."

Eden slowly looked up at Julia with red-rimmed eyes brimming with tears. She did not understand how Julia could tell her to stop crying. Her world was crumbling, and she was in pain. Rafe would never say those words to her when she was dealing with her anxiety.

"I'm sorry. I don't love you. I can never love you," Eden whispered because she felt like the wind had been knocked out of her. "I'm in love with Rafe. You know I am." She wiped the tears from her face. "Why? Why would you do this to us? To me?" Julia knew all the problems they had with believing infidelity had broken their relationship and what it took for her and Rafe to find each other again. How Julia could sabotage her was beyond her understanding. Eden just hoped Rafe had believed her when she told her it was not true. Now the thought was in Rafe's mind. Eden knew it meant she would always be working against doubt once they were apart again. Rafe would always worry, and Eden knew she would always have to prove she wasn't with Julia... just like she had to prove she wasn't with Jake.

"I only wanted to help you see the truth," Julia said, desperate for Eden to understand. She took Eden's hands gently. "I know this side of Rafe. I know when it's time for letting go. I've seen it so many times." She shook her head because of her disappointment with Rafe. "I didn't ever think she would do something like this to you. You have to start looking at the reality of things."

Eden snatched her hands away. "Let go?" Those words were the ones Rafe had used to push her away. Nothing was going to push her away again. "No!" she said her anger returning. "I'm never letting go! Even if I have to wait a hundred years for her, I'll never let go!" She stood up and crossed the room to put distance between them. "You're the one who needs to go," she said shakily. "You should just go now. I need you to go."

Julia could see Eden was getting overly upset with the conversation. It was hard to understand Eden's stubbornness when she was trying to protect her. Julia had fallen in love with Eden and, when she confessed it, Rafe hadn't told her to back off or anything. In her mind, it meant Rafe was walking away again.

"Fine," conceded Julia with a slight nod as she walked toward the door. "I'll go. Think about what I said. You don't have to live like this. I promised Rafe I'd take care of you, and I promise you, I'll do anything to make you happy."

19

EDEN KINGSLEY WATCHED numbly as Julia walked out the door. She sat down in one of the chairs at the kitchenette table. It had been shocking to hear Julia confess she was in love with her. She tried to wrap her mind around why Julia told Rafe she was in love with her and they were sleeping together. Even though Julia wanted her to think about being together, Eden didn't have to think about it. She knew she could never be with Julia. Not only because she loved Rafe, but because she felt lied to and manipulated. She had no idea when Julia started developing feelings for her or why she hadn't seen it. She didn't think she encouraged Julia's feelings but was unsure. It wasn't her intent. She loved Rafe. She was only in love with Rafe.

The more she thought about it, the angrier it made her. The motivation behind Julia accusing Rafe of having an affair in New York again and demanding Rafe pay for the trip and increase the child support was clear now. She had kept asking herself, why? Why would Julia get into arguments and say those things to Rafe? What was she trying to accomplish? Julia had to know that telling Rafe those things would hurt their relationship. Eden sighed heavily and shook her head in frustration. Julia had to know it would make Rafe doubt them both and make it harder to convince her to come home. Julia was supposed to be Rafe's friend. Julia was supposed to be a friend to both of them and to help bring Rafe home. It all suddenly made sense. Julia wanted them to fail.

As Eden rubbed her arms to try and soothe herself, the argument with Rafe about Julia popped into her mind. Now she understood why Rafe was saying some of the confusing things she had been saying. Julia had professed her love and her intent to take care of her and Bronte. It was the reason Rafe thought being with Julia was what would make her happy. It was the reason Rafe had been trying to let her go. Rafe did the same thing with Jake, just stayed away, and tried to let her go. The comparison Julia made between Rafe and Jake now made Eden even angrier. There was no comparison. What Jake did was evil and was meant to trick her and hurt her. She couldn't believe Rafe meant to hurt her by asking her to stay. It all felt like just another manipulation, but by Julia this time, to make her want to go home without Rafe.

Eden scrubbed the tears from her face, sorry she ever made Rafe think she would be happy with anyone else.

"Oh, my god, this is so f'd up."

Thinking about having to see Julia again made Eden feel queasy and uncomfortable. She was unsure how to act now or what more to say to Julia. She felt what she already said was enough. By the look on Julia's face, her words may have even been too harsh. Julia was clearly hurt by her words and the rejection. Eden could feel herself becoming overwhelmed with anger and confusion. She considered telling Julia she never wanted to see or hear from her again. She wondered what the girls at home would think when she got home and refused to talk to or see Julia. She wondered if they already knew about Julia's feelings. She knew if Julia couldn't... or wouldn't accept her decision, things would be uncomfortable. If she was lucky, Julia may just back away on her own. It was so hard to think she was on the edge of losing Rafe as well as her friendship with Julia who had helped her so much over the last six months. Now the friendship seemed tainted. It was painful.

Now, instead of taking Rafe home, Eden was on her own and against a wall trying to choose between leaving behind two things that terrified her to leave—her home or Rafe. Leave her home, the friends she made, and the life she knew and had worked hard for since she left her parents, or leave Rafe, the person she was in love with and had been working so hard to hold on to. Stay here in Italy where she knew no one and had to start again or go back to a familiar life, but an empty house.

Feeling sick, Eden rushed to the kitchenette sink and quickly made herself a glass of water. She drank it down in large gulps, hoping to cool down and calm her stomach. She sat the glass down and leaned heavily on the sink trying to breathe and will away the tingling that was running up her legs. She knew the agonizing pain the tingling promised because she had waged war with it in the past.

"Rafe," she sobbed as she sank to the floor, "I need you." She wiped her hands over her face clearing away her tears.

Eden's mind went back to Rafe asking her to stay in Italy as she closed her eyes. Every time she thought about not going back home, pins and needles bloomed over her, and she shook uncontrollably. Rafe said she was strong, but it was not how she felt right now. She felt trapped by her own thoughts and anxieties. She loved Rafe and wanted to be with her, but she just wanted her to come home. She had never considered staying in Italy, and when Rafe asked her to stay, she panicked. Even though Rafe said she should go home, think things through, and look into her options for work, she could think of nothing but what she would be leaving behind if she moved. Her mind found roadblocks at every turn, and most of them were painful. There was just no way she could do it.

None.

Pulling herself up from the floor, Eden made her way to the couch. As she curled up, she saw the two unopened gifts from Rafe lying next to the paper she had tossed there earlier. It was the letter Rafe's mother wrote, and she had saved it from being turned to ash. Eden put her hand to her chest and felt the smooth surface of the necklace Rafe had given her. She wiped her eyes and picked up the letter Rafe's mother had written. Opening it, she read it for what seemed like the hundredth time. She had never thought a lot about Rafe's mother. Having a letter from her made her more real.

Everything Gabri told her about Rafe and what she went through as a child, churned through her mind again. Nothing

Letty had told them was anywhere near the truth about what had happened to Rafe. The truth was Rafe had not only been involved in the horrible incidents leading to the deaths of her mother and her friend, but she had also witnessed their deaths up front and personally. Eden couldn't imagine watching anyone die in front of her, especially not a parent, doubly not a friend riddled with bullets. The thought made her ill.

She wondered if the words Rafe remembered her mother saying outside the school were real. She felt pain for Rafe if they were just something Rafe's mind had created. She wondered if Rafe's mother's real last words were similar to what was in the letter she wrote. Rafe never talked about her mother much, other than the fact she was an American art teacher and had met Ettore when she was in Italy for school. Eden skimmed the letter again and read the part Rafe's mother wrote about meeting him.

If we came to together from two very different continents and overcame challenges like language and traditions and income and the differences in our ages, I know you can overcome any challenges life may put in front of you when it comes to finding love.

Eden thought Rafe's mother, Mary, must have been a very brave woman to have left everything behind for Ettore. Mary must have loved him very much. Eden studied the words Rafe had written to her mother so long ago about her and felt a stabbing in her heart. She was not sure Rafe was right about Mary approving of her.

The two unopened gifts Rafe had given her lay ominously on the table. She needed to distract her mind before the pain returned. She hesitated then quickly picked up the tube and unwrapped it. She pulled the plastic cap from the mouth of the tube and set it aside then pulled out the papers. As she unrolled them, she frowned, not sure what she was seeing. The pages had been torn from a drawing notebook, but the subject of the drawings was confusing.

Some pages were completely covered with black charcoal, and it looked like nothing else. Then, when Eden slanted them, she could see indentations and that some places were darker than others. It looked like portraits had been drawn under the blackness. She had no idea why Rafe would black out her work.

Other pages were filled with faces Eden didn't recognize. They were all looking up into what looked like an inky night sky. She shifted through the charcoal covered pages, getting dark smears on her fingers. She found one that looked like a normal drawing. She saw herself looking out from the page. More darkness surrounded her portrait. Next to her head was a small sideways dome.

Shifting the pages, Eden found what looked like the outline of a man with a flat-ended cylinder of some kind next to him. At the top of the page were a leg and foot all in black. Eden flipped to the next page, and there was a woman's body. Most of the body was either blackened out or seemed to disappear into the background. Behind the body was some sort of cave with stalagmites looking like people or animals and stalactites formed into legs or arms hanging down. The final page looked like some sort of gate. It was very ornate and drawn in incredible detail. Next to it was a person whose face was blacked out.

Eden spread the pages out with a frown. She rearranged the drawings and found when they were put together, they made one larger piece. All the black pages made up the body of a man who was all in dark tones. He surrounded the portrait of Eden.

The cylinder was completed, and now Eden could see it was a bullet moving toward her head. She looked closer at the dark features of the man's face. Her hand flew to her mouth in shock. It was Jake. She never expected to see his face again. She shivered as she remembered the day he came after her and put her in the hospital.

She focused on the drawings again. A woman's hand was reaching toward her portrait. She slid more pages together, and there was Rafe. It was a self-portrait revealed when the pages were aligned. On Rafe's face, there was a look of pain and horror too contorted to be real. Eden shook her head at the disturbing work. Tears formed at the thought that this work, full of darkness and pain, came from Rafe.

Gabri was right not to send it to her. If she had seen this, she would have come sooner. She would have demanded Rafe come home. Julia would have tried to find some way to have her admitted to a hospital in the States.

She was almost too afraid to open the other small box based on the disturbing work she had just seen. She picked it up hesitantly and unwrapped it slowly. She took the lid off and looked inside with confusion. She picked up the object inside and inspected it closely. It was a small chunk of rough rock about the size of a one-euro coin. She checked the box to see if there was a card or note with an explanation. There was none. She had no idea why Rafe would want to send her a rock.

She glanced from the rock to the drawings and saw there was a small incomplete place in the cave Rafe had drawn. She sat the rock in the space. It was a perfect fit. The rock was part of the cave. She contemplated the collection a moment more. Eden still didn't understand what it all meant. She gathered everything, putting it all back in the boxes they had come from. Thoughts of everything Gabri had told her about Rafe dealing with the death of her mother and her friend Brettito ran through her mind. Coupled with that were the secrets Rafe was making her keep about Maria and both of her parents. There was so much.

It was not long before Eden's guilt piled onto the heap of worries. Guilt about Jake and the Stewards, not to mention the incident at the school. It was too much for Eden to hold in her thoughts without crying and feeling empathy for Rafe. It was all so much more than she could have ever imagined. Eden felt she was unprepared to face it all, even with the sessions and help from Dr. Cathcart.

Being in therapy helped remind Eden of the indisputable fact that Rafe was the only person in her life who had gone to the trouble to try to understand her anxiety and help her through the times when she was having problems. Rafe had this way about her that somehow tempered and soothed her anxieties—if she would let her. Sure, there were times when even Rafe couldn't help if things were really bad, but Rafe had been patient at those times too.

Gabri's words rang in her ears, telling her she was selfish and cruel.

It was true. Eden saw it. She was being selfish.

She told Rafe she would focus on her and realized, right now, all she was doing was focusing on her own wants and needs. She could see it would be cruel to make Rafe start her therapy over again, too. It was plain to see Rafe needed to be where she felt she was able to get better, and here in Italy, she had been making progress.

Eden's mind picked up on a pattern making her squeeze her eyes shut suddenly. She wondered if she was the only one who could see the pattern in Rafe's life and the only one who would ever know it was there. She was the only one who knew about Maria, so her reasoning was probably right.

Rafe had lost her mother, her friend, and her girlfriend tragically at a very young age and was still dealing with the trauma. According to Dr. Cathcart, it seemed Rafe started getting sick right after she lost her father. Simultaneously, their relationship had fallen apart. Things got worse after the hostage situation at the school. Things were becoming more severe when Jake and the Stewards were targeting them. Then Flynn had to use his gun to stop Jake. Everything piled up, and Rafe's PTSD came to an ugly head. It seemed Rafe was better now, but really, she was still afraid of more loss, especially the possible loss of Gabri.

It was as though Rafe was waiting for history to repeat itself. Eden realized, when she left Italy tomorrow, if anything happened to Gabri, it wouldn't be good for Rafe. She recalled Gabri and Nora talking about going on tour after Nora had her baby and was able to travel. Eden wondered what Rafe would do when she was all alone.

20

EDEN KINGSLEY FOUGHT the turmoil painfully wreaking havoc in her mind. Her failure to convince Rafe to come home had pressed its way forward again. Gabri had warned her Rafe would not go home, and she didn't want to believe him. Even Julia was doubtful, though now Eden was wary of her motives. It wasn't real to her until Rafe said it and walked out. She knew Rafe was right. Rafe should be able to choose where she sought treatment and her doctor. Eden just wished the place she chose was their home.

The home they lived in was Rafe's, but without her in it, Eden felt alone and vulnerable. Coming home now was not exciting or something she looked forward to because Rafe wasn't there. She had thought, after the first few months, things would start to get better, but she was wrong. After Rafe left, Eden had continued to sleep in her own room. Some nights, though, she felt she had to sleep in Rafe's room to feel closer to her. She walked through the house, and all she could see was what was missing. Even the scent of Rafe had faded, and Eden found herself searching for places where she could feel close to her. Sometimes she found herself sitting out in the art studio off the kitchen remembering all the times she had watched Rafe paint or draw and missing their quiet time together.

Tomorrow, she was going back to the lonely house, which was so empty of Rafe, alone again. No longer in a state of panic, she could really think about what she would be leaving behind in Italy.

Rafe.

Eden knew Rafe didn't want to go home and deal with the interference she felt was caused by their friends. She had seen what Rafe was talking about firsthand, both at home and from Julia here in Italy. Rafe had asked her if she wanted her to go back into that situation, and of course, she didn't want her to be where she wasn't comfortable. She didn't want their friends to upset Rafe and make it hard for her. She wanted them to help and not make Rafe feel like she had to go away.

A sudden barrage of pins and needles burst through her body making it feel like her skin was on fire. She could feel sweat break out on her face and back.

"No, please," she cried in desperation. Sliding from the couch, folding slowly to her knees, and holding onto herself, she tried to will the pain away. She rocked herself on the floor riding out the pain firing at every nerve ending. She clenched her jaw tight to keep herself from crying out but couldn't stop the keening sounds deep inside from escaping. Slowly, the pain eased enough so that Eden was able to relax her tense muscles and lay back on the cool tile floor. When Eden could pick herself up off the floor, she slowly stood and made another glass of water. After finishing the water, she shakily made her way into the bedroom.

She checked on Bronte who was sleeping contently. After gathering her things, she quietly went into the bathroom to get ready for bed. In the mirror, she saw back smudges on her face streaked from tears. The smears had transferred from her hands that were covered in charcoal from Rafe's drawings. As she cleaned her face, she wondered if she would get any sleep tonight.

Before climbing into bed, she took off the necklace Rafe gave her and put it on the nightstand next to her phone. Sliding between the cool sheets, she tried to get comfortable and turn off her mind.

Sleep was impossible. Eden wanted Rafe next to her. She wanted to feel her warm hands on her again. She wanted to be held and to breathe in Rafe's scent and taste her kisses again.

Eden took a deep breath, ran her hand down her body and fought the urge to take care of herself. In her mind, she could see herself making love to Rafe. Kissing her body again and feeling it react under her. This time, though, Rafe wouldn't stop her from taking her pants down.

"Rafe," she groaned in frustration, "you kill me even when you aren't here." She sighed heavily. "I've gotta stop thinking like this and driving myself crazy. I need to sleep." She turned on her side and curled up around her pillow.

Turning her thoughts away from making love to Rafe led her mind back to her troubles. Several times, she felt herself slip into a tormented sleep only to wake suddenly as her anxieties rushed through her subconscious and shot into her sleeping mind. Sometimes, because of the turmoil in her mind, she could feel the beginnings of the pins and needles under her skin and the pain the sensation caused.

She just couldn't get everything she had learned since coming to Italy out of her mind. She took several deep breaths and decided to try to imagine what her conversation would be like if she could talk to Dr. Cathcart about everything Rafe had gone through.

The first thing he would probably point out, she thought, *was Rafe had a lot of loss in her life.* Within a short amount of time, she lost her mother and her friend Brettito. *Then there was Maria,* she reminded herself. *Rafe lost her too.* So there were three people she loved suddenly gone under traumatic circumstances. Then, after living through all that loss, Rafe's father moved her away from her friend Gabri to America.

The image of Rafe looking at her with fear and pain in her eyes telling her she couldn't lose anyone else appeared in Eden's mind. Rafe had been terrified of losing Gabri. With everything Rafe was going through, Eden could empathize with her fear. In the last few years, Rafe had lost her father, gone through their break up, and had to deal with all the uncertainty she had with the adoption. Eden wondered if Rafe considered their break up a loss. She teared up at the thought and could feel the pricking pain begin under her skin.

Through the thrumming pain still pricking at her body, Eden could feel the push and pull in her mind deliberating over Rafe's question about moving to Italy. The thought of leaving her home and everything she knew swirled through her mind. Fear of the unknown created the waves of physical pain rushing through her. She didn't understand why she was in so much pain. She wasn't staying in Italy. She was going home. Everything should be fine. The echo of Julia's words about Rafe emulating what Jake had done when he was trying to convince her to move away reverberated through her mind. She knew it wasn't true. Rafe was nothing like Jake. Rafe loved her. Tears ran down Eden's face as she willed the pain cutting through her to stop.

"She loves me," she whispered as if saying those words would stop the torment.

21

THE NIGHT WAS long for Eden Kingsley. Her dreams were full of images of Rafe. She kept seeing the drawings Rafe gave her and trying to understand what they meant. They were all twisted together with Julia's words and confession of love, her experience in the cemetery, and what she had learned about Rafe since talking with Gabri. Eden would find herself desperately searching all through the darkness for Rafe. When she finally found her, Rafe was looking at her with those gray-blue eyes and asking her to stay. In her dreams, she tried to pull Rafe along with her but Rafe would turn into smoke no matter how many ways she tried to take her home. It was all so crazy and surreal.

The morning seemed to come too soon. Eden lay curled up in bed exhausted, thinking about her dreams and everything that had happened this week. Late at night, she had awakened from her tormented dreams feeling sick and exhausted—physically and emotionally. Her anxiety had gotten so bad, she was sweating from the pain of the itching and burning hives wanting to erupt from her skin. She ended up getting so sick, she lost the contents of her stomach. Fear of being unable to wake and take care of Bronte prevented her from taking a pill to prevent pain and help her sleep. She hadn't been so sick from anxiety since moving from her parents' house to California for school. When she was moving into Rafe's house and dealing with her parents about being gay, she might have gotten even sicker if Rafe hadn't been there to help with everything. Even her time with Jake, though she had been sick a lot, hadn't caused her to actually get so sick that she broke out in night sweats and vomited. *No, I just broke out into hives and had to make trips to the hospital,* she thought. Eden curled up and groaned at the memory of having to spread doxepin cream over hives that had erupted all over her body.

The message being sent by Eden's mind and body was suddenly very clear. Her dreams gave her all the answers to her questions—and they all led to the same conclusion. Eden just wished the delivery methods were not so painful. When she finally accepted the solution and gave up fighting against herself, waves of almost cooling relief spread over her body. With her decision made, she was finally able to fall into a calm sleep for a few short hours.

She had to be with Rafe. She couldn't leave without her. She loved Rafe, and her soul was telling Eden she had to stay.

Eden awoke abruptly. It seemed her body now refused to sleep anymore, even though she needed it. She slowly got her aching body out of bed and into the bathroom. In the mirror, Eden saw the dark circles under her eyes, telling the story of how little sleep she'd had. She ran her hands over her face, wishing she could wash away the dark circles. A shower helped, not only to clean herself up, but it had a calming effect as it warmed her muscles. After showering, Eden was awake but still feeling exhausted while Bronte still slept peacefully. She dressed and put the necklace Rafe had given her back on. She was glad Bronte was sleeping late. Not wanting to wake Bronte, she decided not to worry about drying her hair. Instead, she just combed it out then gathered all her bathroom things together to pack in the suitcase.

Everything had been packed and was ready to go except for a few of Bronte's things when she heard a light tap at the door. Opening the door slowly she saw Julia standing in front of her. "Hi," she said softly, feeling a nervousness she had never experienced before with her.

"Hello," said Julia and stood up straight. "Can I come in?"

"Sure," said Eden, feeling awkward. She moved so Julia could enter. "We have to be quiet. Bronte is still asleep."

"I'm all packed and thought I'd see if you need any help," said Julia as she walked over and sat at the kitchenette table. She had put on her armor of calm and decided she wouldn't talk about her feelings again until things calmed down and they were back at home. Revealing her feelings to Eden while they were in Italy dealing with Rafe had not been her plan. She was hopeful, though, once Eden wasn't in such an emotional state, she would be more receptive. "I hoped we could spend a little time seeing the sights today before we have to leave for our flight. You haven't really seen much of the city."

Eden could feel her face flush red as she turned on the kettle to make tea. She was glad her back was to Julia. "Uh," she cleared her throat, "I'm a little tired." She didn't want to spend any time with Julia. She sat down at the table, determined not to cry or get emotional in front of Julia.

Julia scrutinized the state Eden was in. It was obvious she was not doing well. "Are you going to be okay?" She wanted to hug her like she normally would have, but she didn't want the gesture to be misconstrued.

"I'll be okay," she said softly. "I was up most of the night. I couldn't sleep because I kept thinking about Rafe asking me to stay."

"You shouldn't feel guilty about not staying," Julia said hiding her frustration with Eden. She took a moment to rein back her anger at Rafe for asking such a thing of Eden and toying with her anxieties. "You came here for a week, and she spent less than three days with you. She can't expect you to make a decision about staying or anything else when she's got you wound up in such an emotional state."

Eden got up and walked back over to the counter to get the teacups ready. After choosing teas and adding them to the cups, she poured the hot water over them from the electric kettle. She could tell Julia was still upset and prepared herself for the reaction she might receive because of her decision. She was unsure if Julia would bother to try to understand or accept her reasons, even if she could explain them.

"Actually," Eden hesitated, "I'm staying." The silence after her announcement was unnerving. "I decided last night," she quickly informed her. She just knew if she left Italy, the emptiness she felt when she was at home without Rafe would return. All the things Rafe said, along with the pain in her eyes, told Eden that Rafe needed her too. They needed each other.

Julia finally erupted. "What? You can't stay here!" Julia could not hide her frustration any longer. "Snap decisions never work out."

"I have too." If she left, there was no doubt the pain she felt last night would return. After her long agonizing night, Eden did not feel like it was a snap decision. She was sure if she went against what she felt in her heart was right, the pain would be worse. Then, just like Rafe said, it would be her own fault. She couldn't lose Rafe again. She also knew that any decision she ever made that was pro-Rafe had turned out to be right. It was when she was without her that things went wrong.

"No, actually, you don't!" Julia countered. "Staying would be a mistake. What about how she's treating you? Where are you going to stay? What will her friend Gabri do? When were you going to tell me?"

"I'm telling you now," Eden answered evenly, ignoring everything else Julia spat out at her. "In case you forgot, getting Rafe back is why we're here! You're really pissing me off right now."

"Getting her back," scoffed Julia. "This isn't getting her back. You said you wanted to take her home! It's not the same as you staying. You just can't stay here and leave everything behind. Think about how it will affect your life and Bronte!"

"It's all I've thought about," said Eden as she threw her hands up in frustration. "Every thought came back to Rafe and thinking about her before myself for a change. We've all been doing it. Our thoughtlessness is not helping her or any of us. If we want Rafe to get better and come home, then we have to listen to her and stop trying to do what we think is best. She says she needs to be here, and it's true because she's getting better." She turned her head at the sound of Bronte calling her. "Bronte needs to be with Rafe, and so do I." She knew Julia wouldn't understand. "Rafe said she needed us. So, I'm staying," she said and got up to check on Bronte.

Julia followed Eden into the bedroom. "So, this is it then? What do I tell everyone when I get back?"

"Tell them our family is living in Italy for a while, and we'll see them as soon as we can," she answered and then took Bronte into the bathroom.

Julia shook her head and went back into the living room. This was crazy. They came to bring Rafe home, not so Eden could be delivered to Rafe. If Eden stayed here, it meant either Julia would lose her or Rafe would hurt her even worse. It was fucking criminal how Rafe had such a hold over Eden. It was even worse than the hold she had over Andrea. Julia felt she had to constantly warn Rafe off because she thought Andrea had more than 'just friends' feelings for a long time. She fought the anger caused by the memory of her last argument with Andrea being about Rafe. She retrieved one of the cups of tea Eden had prepared and sat down at the table heavily wrapping her hands around the hot porcelain.

Before she could take a calming sip of tea, there was a knock at the door, and she went to answer it. A breakfast cart was pushed in by a happy hotel worker and placed by the table. Julia began setting things on the table, and as she finished, Bronte came bounding into the room.

"Hi!" said the little girl and hugged Julia.

"Well, hello," said Julia with a smile masking her anger. "Are you hungry?"

"Yes," said Bronte as she nodded. "I want to take off the tops."

"Okay, knees or booster?" she asked as she pulled out a chair. This had become a routine whenever they ate in the room.

"Knees," said Bronte and climbed into the chair and got up on her knees.

Julia put one of the plates in front of Bronte so she could pull the cloche off to reveal the food.

"Ta-da!" sang Bronte as she revealed the food.

Julia sat the plate aside, and they did the other plate with just as much flare. She dished out Bronte's food, and the hungry little girl started eating before she was finished plating. "I think I should get a napkin on you so you don't get your clothes messy." She tied a napkin around Bronte's neck just in time for a little hand to wipe down it. Julia sat down and was finally able to sip her now tepid tea. "I didn't get to see you yesterday. Did you have fun?"

"Yes," she said through a mouthful of food. She held out her piece of bread. "Chocolate."

Julia took the bread as she shook her head and laughed. "Are you sure? We have butter and jam."

Bronte regarded her as if those were the most awful things she had ever heard offered. "No. Chocolate," she insisted.

"Right," said Julia and put some Nutella on the bread and handed it back to her. "Tell me about your day."

"We danced," she said as she licked the chocolate from the bread. "I played with all the kids too."

"Did you?" asked Julia. "Did you get your ice cream?"

"Yes!" exclaimed Bronte brandishing her fork. "I ate it while Mommy went to find Mama."

"Was she lost?"

Bronte laughed as she chewed her bread. "No, she was in the garden." Bronte grinned. "Mommy was happy yesterday," she said in a not so quiet whisper.

Julia sipped her tea wondering if it were true. Both she and Bronte had seen Eden shed a lot of tears. They had made a pact to always help make Eden happy. "I'd say it was a very good day then." She wondered if the reason Eden had decided to stay was that she was just worn down by Rafe. She looked up as Eden came out of the bedroom pulling their suitcases and putting them next to the car seat.

"Okay, I think I have everything," said Eden joining them at the table. "Eat some of your eggs, baby. You have to eat more than chocolate."

"If you put chocolate on them, she'd probably eat them," Julia snickered.

"Don't give her ideas," warned Eden making a plate for herself. "There's plenty if you want some," she offered as she tried to be calm for Bronte's sake.

"I'm good," she said. "I had a scone and coffee already. I'll miss the coffee here." She wished she could convince Eden to come home with her. Since Bronte was awake, negative discussions about Rafe were out of bounds. Eden had made that rule very clear early on.

"I know," agreed Eden. "When I went out with Rafe she got me a desert of mocha gelato combined with hot espresso. It was so good." She moaned at the memory. "It was almost as good as sex," she joked.

"I'll have to try it then," Julia said wryly, hating Eden's acting like nothing was wrong, and Rafe was some angel. There was a knock at the door, and Julia raised a brow as she glanced at Eden.

"I'll get it." Eden answered the door and found a hotel messenger smiling at her.

"I was asked to deliver this to you," he said in accented English handing Eden a large manila envelope.

"Thank you," said Eden softly looking at the envelope. "Wait! Can you get a car for us?"

"Of course, we have several available," he answered helpfully.

"Good, we should be down soon," she said with an appreciative smile.

"I will let the concierge know. You will be taken care of immediately when you arrive at his desk. Have a good day," he said politely and left.

Eden closed the door then while checking the envelope for a name. It was blank. She looked over at Julia with uncertainty. At the table, she used a butter knife to open the envelope. Her hands shook as she took out the contents. "It's from Rafe," she said softly and read the cover letter.

Eden,

I hope you give returning to Italy and staying with me serious thought. Take all the time you need. I hope you'll let Bronte come back soon because now I'll miss her more than ever. I'll miss you, too—I already miss you.

I'm sorry if I upset you on your last day here. As discussed last night, I've enclosed an addendum to our cohabitation agreement. I hope it helps you with your decision.

Whatever you decide, I'll always be here for you and Bronte. Now you have my number so, please, call me anytime you want to talk.

I do love you, and always will. I hope you can understand—I have to stay.

~Rafe

Looking over the other enclosed pages, Eden found Rafe had already signed them. The agreement covered everything Rafe had talked about and more.

"What's she say?" asked Julia softly. Eden handed her the note. "You mean she doesn't know you're staying?" she asked after reading the note. She wondered if there was still time to talk Eden out of staying. It was crazy of Rafe to want Eden and Bronte to stay here. Besides the fact she was practically blackmailing Eden emotionally, Rafe was in no shape to take care of Eden. Italy was fine, except maybe for their plumbing, but Eden was used to how things were in America. She didn't know how Eden thought she was going to help Rafe. Eden would be in an even less desirable position to help Rafe here. She wouldn't be recognized as part of Rafe's family, and they certainly couldn't be open with their relationship. She just couldn't understand why Rafe would talk Eden into this, or do this to her.

"No, she doesn't know," said Eden as she read the addendum. "I'm going to sign this. I need to find a pen." She got up and went to the desk to find a pen. "I need a witness. Will you sign it?" she asked looking back at Julia.

"I'm done," said Bronte suddenly and began pulling the napkin off.

"Let me help," said Julia. She quickly got the napkin off the messy girl without leaving crumbs and chocolate on her or Bronte's clothes. She wiped Bronte's face then let her get down from the table. As Bronte went to get a toy from her backpack, Julia turned to Eden who was waiting for her answer. "Are you sure you want to do this? Italy isn't exactly gay-friendly, and it's a big decision."

Eden felt disappointed Julia wouldn't help her. Though Julia hadn't mentioned the elephant in the room, her confession of love, Eden was sure Julia's reasons for wanting her to leave Italy and Rafe were selfish. "Julia, can't you see what this means? She loves me and wants me here. This proves it." She held up the paperwork. "Rafe had to have had Katheryn make this before last night. She's been trying to find a way to help me stay this whole time. I was just too blind to see anything."

"She could have sent this any time," Julia pointed out, "but she's only giving it to you now. You should take her suggestion and think about it. She's still sick and moving here is a big decision. What if her friend disagrees and you get hurt again when he sends you away? She says you have time to think about it. Why don't you go home, and really think it through? She said you could take all the time you need. You don't have to make a hasty decision."

Walking quickly to the table Eden gathered the letter and put everything back in the envelope. "It's fine," she said shortly not knowing exactly what she would do if Gabri sent her away. She hated Julia for causing her doubts. She pulled the check Gabri gave her from her back pocket. "I'm giving this check back to Gabri," she said as she put it in the envelope with the other paperwork. "I'll give him all my receipts too, so he can repay me the actual amount I've spent. Email me all the receipts for the things you helped with. I'll give everything to him so he can write you a check." Eden wished Julia had supported her instead of working against her and trying to talk her out of staying. She spun on her heal and went to gather the suitcases. "Okay, Bronte, let's go."

"Are we going home," Bronte asked as she went to her mommy carrying her toy.

"Yes, we're going to see Mama and stay at her house in the garden," she said as she opened the door. "Would you like to go?"

"Yes!" Bronte said happily. "Can I play with the kids?"

"Sure," said Eden turning to Julia. "I have to do this." Pulling the luggage and the car seat out of the room, Eden held the door for Bronte. She looked back at Julia. "Have a nice flight home."

Eden wasn't sure what else to say to Julia. It seemed her message was clear. She didn't love Julia. She only loved Rafe. She hoped someday Julia would find someone, but she could tell by the look in her eyes she shouldn't broach the subject again.

Julia followed Eden out and watched her load everything into the lift. "I hope you know what you're doing." She wanted to beg Eden not to go. She wanted her to stop so Rafe wouldn't hurt her again. She wanted to tell Eden she loved her again but knew it would only drive her away faster. Her only hope was after Rafe broke her heart again, Eden would come home to her.

A warm, comforting feeling flowed through Eden as she helped Bronte into the lift. "I think this is the first time in a while I actually do know what I'm doing, and I know," she paused, "I know with everything in me, this is the right thing to do." Ignoring the doubtful look on Julia's face, Eden pushed the button, and the elevator door closed.

The lift carried them down to the lobby. With the help of the concierge, they gathered everything and headed out to the driver who was waiting.

The drive to the villa didn't take long. During the ride, Eden could feel her anxiety building. Even though she was sure about her decision, there were a lot of variables creating doubts and worries creeping into her mind. Pulling up the main driveway, the driver parked near the garage.

The taxi driver helped Eden unload the luggage from the trunk. After Eden got Bronte out of the back seat, the driver took the car seat from the car and put it next to the luggage. Eden thanked the driver for his help, paid him, and then watched him drive away. Leaving the luggage next to the garage, she picked up Bronte's backpack and the envelope Rafe had sent, then took Bronte's hand.

"Let's go find Mama," she said nervously.

Leading Bronte down the garden path toward the villa, they made it to the kitchen entrance of the villa, bypassing it when it was clear Rafe wasn't there. They walked around to the back where all the tents for the festival were set up. Only a few people were in the tents cleaning from the night before and setting up for the events of the day. Smells of breakfast cooking came from the food tent and workers scurried around carrying supplies setting up for breakfast service. Eden didn't find Rafe in any of the tents, so she continued down the path leading to the cottage.

Eden did not know why she felt so nervous. Maybe it was the anticipation of seeing Rafe. Maybe it was the uncertainty of everything and the possibility Julia was right, and she should have gone home and really figured everything out. Maybe it was the fear Rafe would still be angry that she had not agreed to stay right away.

The cottage was in sight when Bronte pulled away to run ahead, and Eden picked up her pace. She was breathless when she caught up to Bronte at the door to the cottage. Pulling herself back together, Eden wiped a light sweat from her brow then knocked on the door.

22

INSIDE THE COTTAGE, Rafe Salvaggio put down her coffee cup at the knock at her door. She hoped whoever it was would just go away. She really wasn't in the mood for company. Figuring it was a volunteer showing up early to work, she ignored it. She just wanted time to herself to deal with a headache from drinking too much last night.

She knew it was not the best choice to drink to forget, but it was the one she made rather than take a pill to sleep. The worst part was that the drinking had not made her forget. It made her feel sad and miserable as she thought about Eden and Bronte leaving.

Gabri grudgingly promised her letter to Eden, and the paperwork Katheryn sent would be delivered this morning. He had been unhappy she hid what she was doing from him, but Nora talked to him as she promised. Rafe could only hope, once Eden got home and had the chance to think about things, she would change her mind. Another knock on the door announced whoever was there was not going away.

With a groan, Rafe pushed her chair back and got up to answer the insistent knocking. Opening the door, she was about to speak harshly then realized who was standing in front of her.

Eden.

"Eden?" Rafe said with confusion. Eden had dark circles under her eyes, and her hair hung close to her head like she had not had time to dry it as she usually did. Eden visibly trembled as she held tight to Bronte's backpack. "Wha—" Rafe started, "uh, are you okay? Did you miss your flight?" She looked down and saw Bronte smiling up at her.

"I have to potty," said the little girl, pushing past Rafe and heading toward the back of the cottage to the restroom.

"Come in," Rafe said quickly opening the door wider so Eden could come inside. "I'll go check on her." She went to the bathroom to help Bronte.

When they came out, Bronte ran to Eden and took her backpack to get out her iPad. "Do you have chocolate?" she asked Rafe.

"Not down here, but I do have some fruit," she answered and went to the kitchen. "Would you like some?"

"No. I just like chocolate," Bronte said as she touched the screen on her iPad and opened a movie. "Are the kids here?"

"Not yet," said Rafe. She came back to the living room where Eden was still standing near the door nervously. "Do you need to sit down?" she asked seeing Eden was pale and still shaking. She watched Eden go to the couch and sit down. Rafe sat down next to her worried. She took her hand gently. "Eden, what's going on?"

Eden could see Rafe was concerned, but at the moment, her anxiety was taking over her mind. She wasn't sure what to say or do. She didn't want to say the wrong thing or say something to make Rafe mad at her for just showing up like this.

"I..." she stammered when she finally found her voice. "I just wanted to say, I'm sorry. I just," she hesitated nervously, "I just panicked. I didn't miss my plane. I changed my mind," she said, speaking quickly. Her plane didn't leave until later in the afternoon. "I want to stay. I'll sign this," she said as she handed Rafe the envelope she had in her hand. "I just don't have a pen or a witness. I thought about you all last night. I couldn't go home. I can't go home without you. I can't live without you anymore. I can't." She forced herself to stop talking and looked into Rafe's gray-blue eyes. "I love you," she said softly swallowing nervously.

Rafe took in everything Eden was saying so quickly. She couldn't help the smile forming on her face. "I love you, too," she said softly as she pulled Eden close and hugged her. "I can't believe you changed your mind."

Relief flooded through Eden's body as Rafe held her, but she couldn't stop shaking. She pulled back as Rafe released her hug, and she couldn't stop her burst of words. "I woke up last night and realized what I was doing," Eden said, desperate for Rafe to understand. "It was the same thing that happened when we were talking about Gabri being our donor. I just had a solution in my mind for so long, and I couldn't let go of it. I didn't want it to happen again. I didn't want to let my anxieties and the hyper-focus I get caught up in be the reason we weren't together. I realized you weren't the one who had to come home," she paused to catch her breath, "because wherever we are can be home for us, as long as we're together and a family. So, I'm sorry. I'm sorry I didn't say yes right away. I'm sorry I didn't come sooner. I'm sorry when you talked to me about coming to Italy that I didn't understand and didn't help you get here."

As Rafe wiped a tear away from Eden's face, she was struck by the surreal feeling of amazement. What she wanted and agonized over was actually happening. She knew she still had a lot to resolve in therapy, and she and Eden had a lot of issues still unsettled, but this moment told her everything could work out for them. She pulled Eden close again and kissed her on her lips then her forehead.

"It's okay," Rafe said softly and kissed her again. She looked into Eden's soft brown eyes and marveled at the golden flecks as they seemed to shimmer like liquid.

"Rafe, I love you," Eden said softly. "I never want to be without you again. Please, don't ever make me try to live without you again." She kissed her again as tears fell and Rafe's arms surrounded her.

As Rafe held Eden close, they clung together quietly. Eden's tears eventually stopped, and her mind and body were able to calm and relax. She was glad Rafe was quiet and not making her talk. She didn't know if she could put her jumbled thoughts into words. She just knew she would never allow herself to think of anyone or anything before Rafe. She would keep her promise to focus on her and always see her as the one who loved her. Everything felt right again.

Bronte glanced up from her iPad at her mommy with concern. Mommy was crying and being held by her mama. Putting her movie aside she went up to them. "Are you sad?" she asked her mommy. "I'm not sad."

Eden pulled away from Rafe and hauled Bronte up to her lap. "I'm not sad anymore," she assured her and gave her a kiss. "I'm very, very happy."

Bronte looked over at her mama. "Are you happy?"

"Yes," said Rafe as she smiled. "Are you?"

"Yes," said Bronte. "We're going to live with you in the garden," she declared.

"Really? Are you sure you don't want to go live in the big house?" Rafe asked with a chuckle.

"No, I like the garden," she said as she wiggled off her mommy's lap. "Are the kids here yet?

"I don't know," said Rafe giving a quick grin to Eden. "Do you want to go look for the kids?"

"Sure." Eden laughed feeling like she would do anything as long as she was with Rafe.

"Well then, let's go!" said Rafe excitedly as she got up and picked up Bronte. "B Girl needs to play with all the kids!" She kissed Bronte as the little girl laughed happily.

Eden stood up and joined in kissing the giggling Bronte then looked up at Rafe. It was like she saw her again for the first time as she smiled and played. Rafe's eyes were sparkling, and she looked so beautiful. Eden reached out and touched Rafe's hair at her temple. "You have some silver here now just like your father had," she said surprised.

"I know," said Rafe as she released Bronte back to her feet. "It was just suddenly there one day."

"It looks good." She laughed and kissed her.

Rafe just smiled and hugged her close. "I love you," she said softly into her ear then pulled away. "Let's go."

They made their way out of the cottage and down the garden path, each holding hands with Bronte. Rafe examined Eden and Bronte with amazement. They were walking as a family again, and she could hardly believe it was real.

23

MAKING HIS WAY through the house quickly, Gabri De Angelis searched for his wife. Nora was supposed to be in her office but, to his ire, she was off probably doing something a pregnant woman should not be doing. He begged Nora to slow down and let him and Rafe handle more things, but she was so stubborn. He caught a glimpse of Nora's blond hair in the midst of a group of guests and headed toward her.

"Nora! Nora, what are you doing?" he asked with concern. He could see by the way she was standing that her back was probably hurting.

Nora smiled at Gabri and his overzealous concern. "Good morning to you, too," she said with a little snark. "Fausto found some luggage by the garage. Did you check someone in or sell a room and not tell me?"

"What? No," answered Gabri confused by what she was asking because she should be resting. "You should be taking it easy and sit down."

"I'll rest later," she assured him. "I need to figure out who's here. We're completely booked so I'll probably have to find them somewhere in town to stay."

"They can do that for themselves," said Gabri disgruntled she was ignoring his concerns.

"Gabri..." Nora sighed and shook her head. "If I booked them then it's my fault. Plus, there was a car seat, so they have at least one child. I can't just kick them out on their own." She ran her hand over his arm consolingly. She knew he was only being overly concerned. "Now, let me do my job, and then I'll go rest. Okay?"

"I will go with you," said Gabri with a firm nod. "Then I will find Rafe, and we will take care of everything."

"Have you seen Rafe this morning?"

"No, but she'll be here."

"How late did you two stay up drinking?" she asked as they walked down the marble hallway toward the back entry. She laughed as Gabri simply blinked at her and said nothing. "Yes, I know."

"She needed to cry," Gabri said to explain why he let Rafe get drunk when he knew she should take it easy on the alcohol with her medication.

"I know," she said softly, entwining her hand with his. Rafe was taking Eden and Bronte leaving hard. It was all up in the air if they would ever be back. She understood why Gabri drank with her as she cried. In all the time she'd known Rafe, she had only seen her cry one other time, and it was when she was very sick. According to Gabri, crying was not something Rafe liked to do, and she resisted doing it if at all possible. Nora just hoped whatever had happened, Rafe wouldn't have to feel so much pain and there would be no more reasons for Gabri to get her drunk so she could cry. "Did you get the papers to Eden like she asked?"

"Yes," he nodded thankful Nora wasn't admonishing him more. They had the conversation several times about how drinking a few glasses of wine and being happy was one thing but drinking so much that Rafe lost control of her emotions was another. Nora had been angry when he wouldn't stop Rafe from getting so drunk she could barely stumble home. He knew though, from all Rafe had told him, she needed to do something to give her an excuse to cry or she would never shed more than a tear or two. He was glad Eden was leaving today so they could go back to the way things were, and Rafe could concentrate on getting better. He knew no matter how well she seemed, she was still having problems and needed to heal.

They stepped out the back door to the sight of workers bustling around serving breakfast and guests enjoying the morning. Nora wanted to check the dining tent and the performance tents to see if the new guest had decided to have breakfast or listen to music before checking in. She wasn't looking forward to telling them they would have to stay elsewhere.

"Are the kids here?" called out a little voice, and Nora felt arms around her legs.

Nora looked down in surprise at the little girl. She looked up from Bronte at Gabri who she felt stiffen beside her. She followed his eye-line and saw Rafe with a big smile leading Eden toward them. "Oh, wow," Nora said, almost laughing. She stopped herself because she could tell Gabri wasn't happy. "Now we know who belongs to the luggage we found." Looking down at Bronte, she smiled. "I think all the kids are eating breakfast. Are you hungry?"

"Why is she still here?" Gabri hissed under his breath.

"Do you have chocolate?" Bronte asked Nora despite the fact she had already eaten.

"Oh, I think the cook can come up with some," she assured her. She put her hand on Gabri. "Be nice." She watched Gabri choke back some words as he looked from Bronte back to her. "I'll take Bronte to get something to eat. You go talk to them." She peered at him sternly. "Remember, she loves her."

Gabri puffed out his chest to state his opinion on the matter, but the look Nora gave him when she cocked her head stopped him. "Fine," he said, clenching his teeth and deflating. As Nora led Bronte away, Gabri headed over to intercept Rafe and Eden. "Be nice," he mumbled to himself. "That woman should be nice and go home." He didn't like Rafe's emotions being played with like a yo-yo by this woman.

Rafe saw Gabri coming toward her, and her smile got bigger. "We have a surprise today, Gabri! Eden and Bronte are staying in Italia!"

.

24

JULIA HAWTHORN GLANCED at the time on her phone and then checked her flight itinerary again. There was still plenty of time before the driver would come to take her to the airport. Reclining on the hotel room couch, she felt deserted and discontented. She was unhappy at the turn of events. There had been no warning, let alone expectation, Eden would stay in Italy. Julia could only hope Gabri would send Eden away, and she would be waiting at the airport. If Eden actually stayed in Italy, Julia knew there would be no going back to the way things were. She realized, with a groan, she may have lost her chance with Eden and had unquestionably lost any hint of a possibility with Rafe.

How am I going to explain this to my father? Julia knew, if asked, Rafe would tell him why they were no longer friends. Julia's father told her to just be friends with Eden, but she wanted more. She always wanted and needed more. Julia didn't understand why she could never have what she wanted and felt she needed—deserved. She was better than any of the girls Rafe dated. She was certainly better than Rafe could ever be for Eden, and the others, too—including Andrea. All she wanted, she told herself, was someone to love and care about who felt the same.

Snapping herself out of her pensive state, Julia punched in the code on her iPad and brought up FaceTime. She decided she should warn everyone at home what was happening. Even with the time difference she knew Abby would be available. She chose Abby's number and waited as it connected.

"Hey, stranger!" Abby said with a laugh. "I hope you remembered my shoe size is an eight!"

Julia rolled her eyes because Abby had no idea what the European sizes were. "Don't worry. I got several pairs of Italian shoes in your size as promised."

"Good! So, I guess you're flying out today?"

"Yes," said Julia. "Later today."

"To bad you'll be on a plane. I'm getting ready to go see King Princess tonight. Lucky me! I love interviews with hot lesbians!"

"Lucky you," said Julia drolly with an uncontrollable roll of her eyes. Now she had Abby on the line and suddenly felt reluctant to tell her what was happening. Seeing and hearing Abby reminded Julia about Abby's habit of sharing information with everyone and anyone.

"Why are you calling?" asked Abby. It was weird Julia had called and was suddenly so silent. "Is everything okay?"

"Oh, sure... Everything's fine," Julia lied, regretting she had made the call. "I just wanted to let you know there's been a change in plans," she said, thinking quickly. "I'm going to visit Mother in England... and Eden has decided to stay in Italy for a bit longer." Julia knew she couldn't face everyone back home, especially if Eden decided to tell them everything that had happened. She doubted Rafe would speak to anyone because, well, it was Rafe, and she wasn't speaking to anyone from home at the moment.

"What?" Abby screeched. "Why?"

"Don't worry," said Julia, dryly. "I'll ship your shoes along with everyone else's requests and gifts."

"That's not why I asked," said Abby, a bit offended. "I mean, did Eden and Rafe make up? Is Rafe okay? How long are you and Eden going to stay over there?" Abby stopped herself from asking the thousand other questions running through her mind.

Julia hesitated because she did not actually know if Eden and Rafe actually had made up, or if it even mattered. Gabri may send her away before she even got to see Rafe. "Well, actually," she started, "I don't know if Eden will be on the plane home or not today." She saw the confusion on Abby's animated face. "She decided just this morning to go ask Rafe and Gabri if they would let her and Bronte stay," she continued. "The trip hasn't really been much of a success. So, if Gabri says no, she may be back tomorrow, or in a few days if she misses the plane today."

"What the hell, Julia?" exclaimed Abby. "Are you just leaving Eden and Bronte to fend for themselves?"

"Not at all," Julia snapped. "This isn't my doing at all. This is what Eden wants. I tried talking to her, but she's told me to bugger off. I've been practically on my own this entire trip," she complained. "I decided, since now I'm traveling alone, I'd go see Mother," she finished huffily.

Abby was silent trying to process the information. "Well, crap! Why wasn't the trip a success? What happened?"

Julia quirked her lips in annoyance, not wanting to get into the ugly details. "All I can really say is things are up in the air and Eden is taking a risk. This whole trip has been emotionally draining. Rafe is still as stubborn as ever, and Eden seems to have gone off the rails. I advised her to go home before making such a big decision about trying to stay, but she wouldn't listen. Now Eden is upset with me, and Rafe is still mad at the world. I barely spoke to Rafe. From what little was said between us, I know Rafe isn't coming home and doesn't want to see any of us. I'm exhausted, and I want to go on a more relaxing trip to recharge. Hence, a stop to see Mother in England." She hoped Abby was satisfied with her answer. She didn't feel like she was lying, just not giving certain details.

Abby furrowed her brows in confusion. "So, no one is coming home?"

"Possibly."

"Fuck."

"Well, I need to ring off," said Julia. "I need to make more travel arrangements. I'll call you again when I have more time," she said. "Bye." She disconnected quickly. Really, Julia decided, she would call Abby and the others again after she thought through everything a bit more. She may even wait to see if Eden calls to inform everyone about what happened between them and her confession of love. If Rafe sends Eden home, there may be, in time, an opportunity to salvage things. If Eden talks Gabri into letting her stay, then maybe Eden will just forget about everything.

Julia checked the time again. Since she told Abby she was going to England, she needed to make arrangements. First and foremost, she had to call her mother. Mother didn't like surprises interrupting her social calendar. Julia braced herself and selected her mother's FaceTime icon.

"Darling, how are you?" asked Päivi Hawthorn in her perfectly paid-for British accent.

"I'm fine, Mother," answered Julia. As always her manner turned docile as soon as she saw the woman's face. "I'm in Italy and thinking of you. I thought I'd pop over for a visit."

"Oh, Julia! Must you speak so crudely?" She gave a closer look at her daughter through the screen. "What are you wearing?" she asked with pompous revulsion.

Julia looked down at herself. "Just traveling clothes," she answered and knew immediately by the disapproving look something was wrong with her answer.

"Well, if you're coming to visit, you need to change," said Mrs. Hawthorn. "I won't have you seen in such an ensemble. My image!"

It took everything in Julia not to roll her eyes at her mother. Päivi Hawthorn used to be known as Päivi Holm a rising star, according to herself, in the modeling world. The narrative was, Päivi gave up the fast-paced world of fashion to marry Ian Hawthorn and start a family. Julia saw all the fashion magazine clippings and photographs of her mother in the 1970s when she was quasi-famous. It was never discussed, but Julia imagined Päivi was probably one of those girls brought to New York where competition was fierce and promises were broken. It didn't stop her from marrying well and becoming a society sweetheart among the elite in both America and Europe, though.

"I'm only going on a plane," said Julia. "Then I'll be in a car until I get to your flat."

"Haven't you heard, dear? They have CCTV everywhere here. You don't want to be caught on camera not looking your best."

"CCTV?" Julia bit the inside of her mouth to keep from saying more. "Isn't that just for criminals?"

"CCTV footage shows up everywhere, dear. You never know who's watching. So change into something appropriate," commanded Mrs. Hawthorn. "Oh, I know! Go to Massimo! I'll call and let him know you're coming. He can do your hair and get you properly clothed, too."

"Where is Massimo?"

"Milan, of course, darling."

"I'm in Florence."

"Well, take the train, dear. Your ensemble is fine for Italian rail travel. You'll be there in a couple of hours. I'll arrange for Massimo to collect you. Just send me your arrival time."

"Well, I wanted to go to the airport first," said Julia. She wanted to be there if Eden was sent home.

"Whatever for?"

"I came here with Eden to see Rafe," said Julia and it was all she got out.

"Rafe? Again with *that women*. Are you still raising her child? You should be raising your own by now, Julia. Whatever happened to your fiancée?"

"She wasn't my fiancée," Julia reminded her. She never got the chance to ask Andrea to marry her.

"Well, you're not getting any younger," quipped Mrs. Hawthorn. "That engagement was almost ten years ago. I thought you would have been married by now. You've already come into your majority, and once you marry, you'll get the rest of your trust. I hope you don't plan to be unmarried at forty! I mean really, you can actually marry a woman now, so I don't know what's taking you so long."

Julia clenched her fist and her jaw. "I told you, Mother, I haven't found anyone I want to marry." *Or who wants to marry me,* she thought.

"Yes, yes. Well, do you still have to marry a woman? Karen Cholmondeley has a son, Albie, he's single and available."

"Albie? He has no chin!" complained Julia. "In any case, yes, it must be a woman."

"When you have money, looks matter less," she said haughtily, "and he has money. Well, no matter, I thought you were dating the woman with the child," said Mrs. Hawthorn. "There have been so many women I get confused."

"I've just been helping Eden," she said with a frown. She hadn't told her parents about her hopes for a relationship with Eden. Her parents knowing how she felt about Rafe was enough. "There haven't been that many women. Besides, I'm fine alone," insisted Julia.

"I suppose you are, dear. You've always been a solitary child. You take after me," she said with a self-satisfied smile. "Friends and lovers make life enjoyable, but we just can't allow them to hold us down."

Julia blinked in astonishment. Did her mother just admit to having affairs? "But you have Daddy, right?" she asked warily.

"Of course! Oh, you know what I mean. You're an adult now. Your father and I understand each other. It's what makes our relationship work."

Julia didn't understand. Now she wondered if her father had affairs. Surely not. Not Ian Hawthorn. Julia shut down those thoughts. She couldn't deal with her parents love life along with everything else she was going through at the moment.

"I'd like someone to be more than a friend or a temporary lover," Julia said softly. "I thought Andrea would be the woman I married. It turned out even she chose a job over me."

"Oh, don't start feeling sorry for yourself. You're rich and beautiful. You can have anyone."

"Yet, you're bargaining me out to Albie Cholmondeley?

"He gets your beauty, and you get his money," reasoned Mrs. Hawthorn. "There have been worse marriage arrangements."

Julia bit her lip to keep herself from asking if it was the arrangement her mother and father had made. "I don't need more money, Mother. I would rather marry for love."

"Such a romantic," Mrs. Hawthorns said wistfully. "Look around, Julia. Even your friend Rafe understands money lasts longer than love sometimes."

"What are you talking about?"

"I'm just saying, she was lucky. She still has all her money. She didn't marry her lover, and their relationship ended before she inherited from her father. If she had married, *that woman* would not only have the child but half her money too. Rafe is lucky she wasn't taken to court for palimony. Ettore was a ruthless businessman, but he failed to make sure his daughter and his wealth were protected by insisting on a legal agreement between them, especially when they decided to have a child."

"I suppose," said Julia. She had never thought about the agreement between Rafe and Eden.

"I have little doubt the woman wants to go back to Rafe because of the money. I never really cared for Rafe, but I know you did. If I had known just how much money she would inherit, I might have been more... encouraging."

"More encouraging? Mother, my feelings for Rafe had nothing to do with her money. Besides, how do you know how much money she has?"

"I have my sources," she said mysteriously. "It's clear you suffer from *la douleur exquise.*[7] But over who, I'm unsure," appraised Mrs. Hawthorn. "Rafe, or Rafe's lover, maybe." She smiled tolerantly. "I know you, dear. You wouldn't be accompanying *that woman* on a trip to Italy if there wasn't something in it for you. There is where you take after your father."

Julia fought to hide her anger. "What's that supposed to mean?"

"It only means you and your father have been similarly captivated by Rafe for years. The reasons why may be different, but the attachment is clear."

"What are you saying?" Julia sputtered. Did her father have *feelings* for Rafe?

Mrs. Hawthorn waved her delicate hand as if to brush aside Julia's concern. "I mean you both only wanted Rafe around to use

---

[7] The 'exquisite pain' that one feels from unrequited love.

her in some way. Your father wanted her to be his little spy, and you want her to be your little pet. I was hopeful when you were considering asking Andrea to marry. 1 was surprised you didn't move to France when Andrea moved away all those years ago. I'm glad your father was able to keep you away from her."

"I never wanted Rafe to be my pet," Julia insisted. She wasn't sure about her father's intent. "As far as Andrea goes, I chose not to go to France on my own," Julia contended. Though really, she decided to stay after speaking with Rafe. She made a mistake again of thinking they might begin a relationship. If she had *la douleur exquise* for anyone, it would have been Rafe.

"Of course, dear." Mrs. Hawthorn was getting bored with the conversation about Rafe and adolescent fantasy love. It was one she had many times with her daughter over the years. "As I've said many times, stop making such emotional decisions. You're a brilliant child. Use the rational mind you have and determine a mate on facts, not feelings."

"You mean base my choice on how much money they have?" Julia wanted to throw the iPad across the room. She had money all her life, and no matter how much she spent, it couldn't love her back. She didn't think it was too much to ask to have someone to love her back.

"Well, money is a factor," concurred Mrs. Hawthorn.

"Money can't love me!" hissed Julia unable to hide her anger.

"True. Although it can take care of every other need," said Mrs. Hawthorn. "Love is either an illusion or an enigma. When you have money and power, you can create an illusion and solve any mystery."

Julia rubbed the bridge of her nose, pushing away the anger headache she always got when talking with her mother. "I don't know what to say to that," Julia said throwing her hands up. "I have to go. My car will be here soon," she lied. She had to end the conversation.

"Don't forget to see Massimo and change your ensemble, darling. Ta!"

Julia stared at the black screen of the iPad. She wished she had never called her mother. She wished she hadn't told Abby she was going to England. This whole trip was a mistake. Trying to be with Eden was a mistake. Her feelings for Rafe had always been a mistake too, but she couldn't help having them.

Julia put her head in her hands, and her silver hair fell forward. *Will I always be alone? Will I end up being unhappy until I die?* "Thanks for nothing, Mum!" she growled. She knew Mother hated it when she called her mum, and it was her own private rebellion. "I should have gone to France. I should have ignored father and Rafe. Rafe always ignores me," Julia mumbled to herself. She wondered if Andrea was in a relationship. It seemed like it had been a lifetime since she last saw her. She could still hear Rafe's words. She wondered if it was true and Andrea felt manipulated and trapped. Julia didn't understand why she would feel trapped or manipulated. She did everything for her. She let her move into her apartment, got her a job at the firm and tried to give her everything.

Julia pulled up the photo app on the iPad and swiped through the photographs until she found the ones she had kept of her and Andrea. They looked happy. They looked in love. She swiped and saw a photo of the three of them—herself, Andrea and Rafe. Rafe was looking away from the camera while she and Andrea smiled for the picture. It was rare when Rafe stood still for a photo back then. She swiped again and saw Rafe and Eden and herself. Rafe was looking at Eden. At least Rafe seemed like part of the picture. Rafe and Eden looked happy. Julia thought they looked as happy as she and Andrea had looked. She realized, even if Eden were sent home by Gabri, in reality, a relationship with Eden wouldn't turn out like the relationship in her dreams. She guessed her mother was right, in her own way, about love being an illusion. It seemed she had even tricked herself in order to grasp a chance at love.

Julia swiped back to look at the photos of Andrea again. She wondered if Andrea was happy. It was hard to accept Andrea being happy without her, with someone else. She let everyone convince her it was for the best but Julia never really felt right about letting her go. She followed Rafe's advice and gave Andrea space, but she never came back or called. Julia switched apps and looked Andrea up online. She had followed Andrea's professional career and knew she was still in France. She was at a different museum with a more prestigious title to go with the impressive art collections she curated.

There had been photos over the years of Andrea with other people and each time Julia saw one, she could feel her heart break again a little. It was a lot like the feeling she got when Rafe started seeing someone new. Julia read about the new exhibit Andrea was opening. It sounded like there would be a lot of wealthy socialites attending. *Maybe I should attend,* thought Julia. It would be nice to see Andrea again. Maybe after all these years, they could talk. Maybe Andrea could tell her if Rafe was right about her feeling trapped and manipulated. It might even give Julia some closure so she could move on now since everything would be different back in California.

Julia smiled at the photo of Andrea. "I'm going to France," she said to herself. Saying it out loud felt good. "But first, I'm going to see Massimo." She smiled wickedly. Her mother was paying after all.

25

MOST OF THE morning, Gabri De Angeles worked to hide his frustration and concern about the current situation. He took extra steps to keep an eye on Rafe most of the day, worrying about a repeat of last night. To get Rafe relaxed enough to release her feelings and be able to sleep, he had let her drink too much last night. Luckily, Nora was not angry about it like last time when she, cited every reason why he should not have let her drink from medication conflict to stupidity. He felt there was no other more immediate option to help her. He thought Eden was leaving and everything would finally settle. He had wanted to get Rafe through the night, and then he could get her back on track.

Most of the week, Rafe fluctuated from happy down into almost a fugue state at its worst. Her mood swings made Gabri worry. Such large swings would lead Rafe into a downward spiral, and Gabri would do whatever it took to balance her. Though her normal doctor's appointment was a week away, he made an emergency home appointment for Monday. He already had a lot to tell the doctor when she arrived and now he would have to explain the presence of Eden.

Eden had shown up unannounced again. This time, she claimed to be staying, but Gabri had doubts about her telling the truth—and about it being a good idea. His frustration came from feeling like he was damned if he made her go, but damned if he allowed her to stay. His concern centered on the certainty, no matter what happened, Rafe would be affected. Rafe hadn't been doing well since the traumatic contact with Eden and her friend Julia. He could see her slipping back into sickness.

"I can see you're worrying," said Nora as she sat next to Gabri. She followed his eye-line to Rafe who played with Bronte as Eden watched. Nora couldn't hide her delight and almost cried tears of joy over Eden staying. It gave her hope Rafe now had a real chance to be happy again. "Look at me," she said. "I'm such a romantic I'm almost crying."

Gabri frowned as he saw her eyes fill with tears. "You should feel worry, not romantic," he said gruffly. "She's not ready."

"It is very sudden," she said putting her hand on his leg. "But it's what she wanted."

"Come on, Nora!" Gabri flailed his arms in disgust as he spoke. "You saw her last night. All this push and pull is making her spiral and lose the progress she's made. What if Eden changes her mind in the morning? In a week, a month?" he asked, exasperated.

Nora watched Rafe for a moment. "I understand," she said softly, "but Eden is her family, and Bronte is her daughter."

"So, that's your excuse for witnessing the paperwork, showing Eden around, and acting all supportive?" he asked unable to hide his frustration.

"Rafe needs them," she said with a calming tone. "I'm being supportive because it's the right thing to do." Gabri scoffed and crossed his arms. "I know Rafe has had troubles since they came," Nora continued. "And I know she may have another setback, but having Eden and Bronte here may be what she needs to make real forward progress. It's better than drinking until she passes out." Gabri furrowed his brow at the admonishment. "She can't live in limbo, letting you handle everything forever. From what you've told me, that's not who she is. She needs to get control of her life again. She has to deal with her relationships sometime. And whether things work out or not, Eden will always be part of her life. Our lives, too. So we need to support whatever relationship grows between them and hope for the best."

"But why now?" Gabri complained. "They weren't really in a relationship when I found Rafe. Why couldn't Eden have waited until Rafe was well and ready?"

Nora nudged Gabri with her shoulder. "Hey, it may not have been perfect, but they did have a relationship," she corrected him. "It's never going to be a perfect time. The longer they're apart, the less likely they'll reconcile. I don't think Rafe will ever really be well until things between her and Eden are resolved. Remember her worries and the drawings in her notebooks."

Gabri leaned into his wife, his unspoken apology. "I know you're trying to help and you think you understand." He saw her frown. "Okay, you understand a lot, just not everything. I can't have Eden undermining Rafe's progress and challenging me when it comes to my decisions concerning Rafe."

"Explain it to her then," Nora suggested. "Let her know where the boundaries lay. Just remember, no matter what either of you want, Rafe has the right to take control of herself and her life."

"I know," said Gabri. "I'm not going to stop her from taking her life back. I'm trying to help her. Now Eden is already trying to influence Rafe. She wants her to go back to America, change doctors, and push her back into a relationship she may not be able to handle."

Gabri tensed as he remembered the nightmares Rafe had and the pain Rafe had gone through trying to make them stop. Eden had a starring role in most of them, and it was the main reason he had been angry about her arrival in Italy. He blamed Eden and her friend for the setback he felt Rafe was having. He blamed them for everything… *everything*… including finding Rafe had ransacked the cottage and had destroyed her artwork, as well as for the pain of last night. Finding out Rafe, according to Eden, had a blackout episode while in America also upset him. He worried Eden would push Rafe into another blackout. He wondered if she already had and hid it to keep from being sent away or to keep control of Rafe. He suspected Eden's real reason for staying was to have more time to convince Rafe to return to America.

"Stop brooding," said Nora as she rubbed his shoulder. She leaned over and kissed his cheek. "Talk to her."

Still feeling the sensation from Nora's kiss on his cheek, Gabri nodded. He knew she had a point, and he should take her advice. He would talk to Eden. He would make sure she understood what was expected of her if she stayed. Gabri kissed Nora on the lips then stood and made his way toward Eden.

26

EDEN KINGLSEY WATCHED as Rafe Salvaggio and Bronte played a game with the other children on the large lawn. She couldn't help smiling at their antics. The children were yelling something in Italian at a girl ahead of them. When she answered back, the kids moved toward her while imitating an animal walk. Rafe was helping Bronte by showing her what to do. Eden wasn't sure what they were saying, so she had to try not to think about her inability to communicate with most of the people around her.

"They are playing *Regina, Regina Bella*," said a smooth Italian accented voice making Eden jump in surprise. "Sorry. Didn't mean to scare you."

"I'm okay," said Eden and smiled weakly at Gabri. She quickly looked away wanting to see Rafe again and calm herself.

"Regina, Regina bella, quanti passi devo fare per arrivare al tuo castello con la fede, con l'anello, con la punta del coltello?" the children shouted.

"They said 'Queen, beautiful Queen, how many steps do I have to take to get to your castle—with the faith, with the ring, with the tip of the knife?' and now the Queen will tell them how many steps to take and what animal they will be," said Gabri. "Oh, five steps, and they must hop like a frog!" He chuckled as he watched the children play. "I think we should talk again," he said, not taking his eyes away from the game. He heard Eden take a sharp breath, but she remained silent. "Come. Let's take a walk." He took her arm gently and felt Eden stiffen. He moved forward and led her down the garden path. Rafe waved at them, and they both waved back.

Eden prepared herself for Gabri's words. She could tell from the moment she saw him this morning that he wasn't happy. She took a quick, desperate look back at Rafe. "What did you want to talk about?" she asked nervously.

"My Rafaella, of course," he said with a knowing look and a slight shrug.

Eden could feel the jealousy surge through her at his possessive words. Gabri calling Rafe 'my Rafaella' reminded her of when Gabri took Rafe away. Her face flushed in anger.

"How long do you plan to stay?" Gabri asked.

Eden swallowed her anger. She wouldn't let him control her emotions no matter how much he reminded her of how her father spoke to her. "For as long as she'll have me. I told you... I love her."

"Yes," he said with a nod, "you did tell me." They continued down the path. "If you are staying, you need to know my rules."

"Your rules?"

"Yes," he confirmed. "I am in charge of Rafaella. I am in charge of her medical, financial, and most of her personal business. If you are here to challenge me, you should go home now."

To Eden, his words weren't only possessive but a threat. There was no doubt Gabri could send her away if he wanted. He could probably even convince Rafe it was for the best. To stay, Eden knew she would have to accept Gabri's position no matter how much she disliked it.

"I'm not here to challenge you," Eden uttered softly.

"Based on some of the things you've said to me, it seems you are. I've made every effort to explain the situation, yet here you are again. You have disrupted Rafe's progress, and along with your friend, you have caused her a lot of pain."

"I didn't know about the things Julia had said to her," she said holding in her frustration at Gabri as well as Julia. "Rafe knows—"

"It doesn't matter what Rafe knows," he interrupted. "What matters now is how things will be handled in the future. I will not allow you, or anyone else, to put her through hell again. I don't want to witness Rafe in the pain she was in last night, or like she was when I first brought her home, again." He could see Eden's body tense defensively. "Releasing the pain so it does not overwhelm her is not easy," he continued. "Nora does not agree with my methods, but she does not truly understand Rafe."

"Methods?" asked Eden in confusion.

Gabri nodded. "Last night, I encourage Rafe to drink until she lost the tight control she keeps over her emotions," he hesitated but decided to continue, "and she finally cried. It's probably why she seems a bit better today. Rafe rarely cried after her mother's death. I only remember her crying a few times after Brettito. She told me I cried enough for both of us." He gave a slight smile at the memory of Rafe trying to tease him in order to take attention from herself. He wondered how many times, if ever, Rafe cried over Eden before coming to Italy. "But last night, with my help, she was able to cry for you again. So, tell me... how long will you stay? A week? A month? I need to let Rafe's doctor know so we can prepare to repair the damage."

Eden felt the effect of his accusation as if it here a punch to her gut. "I'm not going to leave her again," Eden said through clenched teeth.

Gabri gave her a doubtful look and kept walking. "You know, Rafaella told me everything."

"What do you mean?"

"She told me all about you," he said and raised an eyebrow. "You have a history of leaving her and of cheating on her," he reminded her. Eden opened her mouth to protest, but Gabri cut her off. "Knowing this history about you means I don't trust you, no matter how much Rafe and Nora think it's okay if you stay."

"You don't know everything," she said, her voice hoarse from holding in her anger.

"I know enough."

Eden ran her hand over the back of her neck. Though the day was mild, she had broken out into a light sweat. She knew it was more from the turmoil inside her body than the weather or the exertion of their walk. "We..." she started then sighed. "We both made mistakes," she finally said.

"No," said Gabri. "You made mistakes. Rafaella was sick. She couldn't make good decisions because of her illness. You, on the other hand, knew what you were doing."

"I know you think that's true," said Eden, "and I know it may be hard for you to believe, but I was having problems too. I've been getting professional help. I can see now what I did wrong and know how to deal with my problems better. I can't go back in time. All I can do is hope Rafe can see how much I'm trying and how much I love her."

"There is no need to provide excuses to me." Gabri noted the flush in Eden's skin and knew she was angry. Her anger was the least of his concern. From what he knew of Eden, and Rafe's other California friends, he was not at all impressed.

He recalled the first time he met Eden. He had agreed to travel with Rafe back to her home to meet the woman she loved and had agreed to be the father of her child. As he told Nora, he thought Rafe would have the baby.

When they walked into Rafe's house, it was filled with people. Most of them seemed to be Rafe's friends based on the introductions. They looked through the house for Eden and found her near the kitchen. Rafe introduced him, and Eden barely said a word. She was silent and cold—taciturn. She had no *appassionata,* no passionate song came from her presence. He was not impressed. Rafe was a song of passion and deserved an equally passionate song to accompany her.

Throughout the ordeal of going to the cryobank, and being subjected to tests and questions, he could tell Eden was hesitant... reluctant. He had been sure she did not approve of him as a donor. He spoke about it recently with Rafe and found he was right.

In Gabri's opinion, things would have been better if Rafe were the birth mother of Bronte. At least then he could have the baby here for Rafe all the time. Now his only option was to deal with Eden. He had to make Eden understand her place, yet balance the need for Rafe to maintain her relationship with Bronte. He was not finding it an easy task. Eden's decision to stay could make all Rafe's months of hard work fall apart. To prevent this, Eden would have to yield to him until Rafe was ready to take back power of attorney, and her life.

"I know you never approved of me as Rafe's choice for a donor," he revealed. "But the die is cast. I have many options if you make things hard."

Eden clenched her fists as she took in his words. She knew they were another threat. Bronte was his biological child, and he could make things hard for her. A flash of doubt surged through her about her decision to stay. Jake's words, Julia's words, and now his threat rang loud in her mind. As they turned a corner on the path, she could see Rafe playing with Bronte and the other children.

"Rafe would never..." She stopped herself, remembering Rafe was not in charge of anything at the moment. "I'm not here to make things hard," she said firmly. "I just want our life back. I love her and want to have our family together again." She watched as Gabri raised his eyebrows in doubt. Eden quickly grasped at the memories from her session with Dr. Cathcart and the techniques for fighting the anxiety building in her. It was clearer now than ever that the doctor's advice was something she now had to apply to her life immediately. She could no longer afford to allow her anxieties to run her life. She couldn't use her anxieties as an excuse to let herself, or others, take away the life she wanted to have with Rafe.

"I can tell you don't like me," Eden continued, "but you don't know me. Not really. You don't know how hard this is for me. Moving away from everything I know, being in an unfamiliar place. I just keep reminding myself Rafe is my familiar place. I need to be wherever she is." Gabri frowned but before he could speak, she resumed. "I know you think I'm adding to Rafe's burden. That's not what I'm doing," she insisted. "Yes, I'm using Rafe as an anchor point so I can manage my anxieties. It doesn't mean I'm going to put any burdens on her. I hope by focusing on her, I can help us both. Being with her means I can feel assured by her presence, and she can know I'm here for her, to help, and love her. I want to make her life better, just like she's made my life better. I want... I need you to believe me. I love my daughter, and I love Rafe, deeply. I'm doing my best to bring my family back together. I know Rafe wants this. I want this. We want it for ourselves, but especially for Bronte."

Gabri took in the look of determination on Eden's face. *So she does have passion in her blood*, he thought. Turning away he saw Nora looking at him expectantly. Instinctively, he knew what Nora would tell him. She would want to give Eden a chance. He turned his head toward Rafe who was happily playing with Bronte. He glanced back at Eden and hoped the passion he saw was only a fraction of what Rafe saw in her. If he was wrong, it could be disastrous. As Ettore would say, 'every situation can be an opportunity as long as nothing is done that can't be undone later.' The problem, Gabri found, was sometimes, undoing things could lead to misfortune unless all the variables were thought of in advance. Determining those variables was never easy.

"You know, when Rafaella and I were young, her father, Ettore, depended on Brettito and me to take care of Rafe after her mother died. We saw how sick Rafe was and were honored to help. We all loved her in our own ways." He flashed a smile though it did not hide the sadness in his eyes. "Then Brettito... Well, then there was only Ettore and me to take care of Rafe who was sick again. His decision to take her away to Milano was hard for me to understand, but I still got to see her. I didn't know what to do with myself when he took her to America." He looked down at the path as they walked. "Oh, they came back. Ettore brought Rafe back all the time for short visits. The first time they came, I could tell she was different, but she was better. She was still my best friend, and still loved me, and that was the most important thing to me. We spent all our time together when she came, and I kept her too busy to think about the past." He glanced at Eden quickly and saw he had her attention. "We were worried when she came back for college, but she was fine. She has always been smart and driven. Did you know Ettore did not want her to attend college in Italy?"

"No."

"Yes, well, he wanted her to stay in New York."

"Julia told me he sent her to Italy because she got in trouble in school."

Gabri chuckled. "I'm sure she probably did get in trouble. She hated the American school because she thought it was behind academically compared to what she would be doing in Italy. She was right." He kicked a pebble off the path. "She attended college in Italy because she went behind Ettore's back and applied. She got recommendation letters from all of his biggest clients. So, he really had no choice but to let her go or lose face. He was angry with her for a while, but she ended up making him very proud."

"Why are you telling me this?" Eden knew there had to be a point to his story.

"I'm telling you this because what Ettore did was the right thing. He took her away from the places and things that could hurt her and keep her from getting better. He was right to do it, and I am right for keeping Rafe here. Do you understand?"

"You think keeping her away from everything in California will help her, like taking her to America did?"

Gabri nodded, glad she understood. "Yes. I think time and distance will be a great help to her."

"So...," Eden hesitated. "You think time away from Bronte and me is what's best for her?" Eden shook her head and swallowed her anxiety. "I think you're wrong," she said defiantly. "You are wrong."

"I know," he said.

"What?"

"I'm wrong, but I'm right," he answered. "Nora believes you should stay. She thinks it will be good for Rafe. I worry you will bring... discontent to her. I do see how happy Rafe is now, and I believe Nora sees things in a way I can't because I'm too close to the problem. So I will agree to you staying under the condition you will not try to convince her to go back to California. I know I'm right to keep her away from there for now. Someday, like when she was young, she can take short trips. Or maybe, with you here, she will be in a place to take her life back, and I won't have control over this decision."

Eden took in his words with a feeling of disbelief. "I..." she stammered, "I can live with that."

"Good," said Gabri. "We will be partners like me and Ettore used to be, yes? You will be the old me. You will tell me what you see and hear. You keep her secrets and help keep her mind with us." They turned a corner, and Rafe and the children were in view again. "She is already doing very well, except for some recent issues. All of that is behind us, yes?"

"Yes," Eden agreed. "This is what I hoped for. I want to be together and love each other again."

"Be careful of your expectations," he warned. "Even after all these years, the Rafe I knew when I was twelve has never returned. This is not an easy path, and it is long."

27

RAFE SALVAGGIO CARRIED the sleeping Bronte into the cottage. Every time she looked up and saw Bronte and Eden, it was like a dream. She thought she had lost them again but now they were here, in Italy, in her house, and Eden had agreed to stay. She couldn't help wondering if she would wake up and the dream would end. It was still hard to wrap her mind around the fact Eden showed up this morning and said she was staying in Italy with her. The fact she made the decision so fast was both incredible and surreal. She understood how hard the decision to stay must have been for Eden and the suffering her chronic anxiety caused when making such a huge change. She wondered if, when her anxieties caught up to her, Eden would decide moving so far away from everything she knew was a mistake.

Last night, she thought Eden would go home and think about everything first. It was why she gave her the paperwork. She had hoped it would help but knew it was a decision Eden had to make for herself. All the doubt and anger she had last night while drinking with Gabri had turned into hope, astonishment, and a healthy amount of guilt knowing what Eden was going through with her anxiety issues.

Eden closed the door behind them quietly so it wouldn't wake Bronte. It had been a full day playing in what was now officially her new home, and Bronte had been having too much fun for a nap. Bronte happily told Gabri and Nora, and whoever else would listen, she was going to live in the garden. The rest of the day was full of playing, dancing and eating with the other kids. As Rafe held the sleeping girl, Eden took Bronte's shoes off then pulled the blanket down on the small bed in the room Rafe had been using as a studio office.

"I guess I'll have to move all my things out of here," Rafe said softly and laid Bronte in the bed. Eden smiled back at her with beautiful shining eyes. "I'm glad she had a good day."

"Me too," Eden whispered as she tucked Bronte into bed with a gentle kiss on her cheek.

"I hope she doesn't think it's going to be like this all the time," Rafe said with concern.

"What, you're not going to throw festivals year round?"

"First, Gabri is throwing it, and second, no... it's too exhausting."

"I think she'll be fine just having you around," Eden assured her.

"I can't wait to take her to all the places I went with my mamma. I'll show her everything."

Though glad she made the decision to stay, Eden still felt terrified. She had waves of doubt and anxiety about not knowing exactly what her future held in a foreign country. She had to force herself to stop thinking about what she had done. Focusing on the look of happiness on Rafe's face throughout the day helped. It was something she had been afraid she would never see again. Gabri's words worried her. She hoped, though, since she and Rafe were together again, everything would get better for them both.

Once Bronte was settled, they closed the door, leaving a small gap so they could hear if she woke in the night. Rafe left Eden to unpack a few things from her luggage someone had brought down from the villa and went to take a shower and change into clean clothes. Helping Gabri throughout the day with everything from crawling under the stage to retrieve sheet music to organizing and helping the trash brigade to keep the grounds clean was dirty work. After she showered and dressed, she came out to find Eden waiting on her.

"I'm next," said Eden, smiling as she passed Rafe on her way into the bathroom. "I hope you left some hot water for me."

Rafe chuckled quietly. "I think you'll be fine."

Turning on her heel, Rafe walked back into the bedroom to get the pills she had forgotten. She was met with the sight of Eden pulling her shirt over her head getting ready for her shower. Eden's blond hair fell onto her bare neck and shoulders. Rafe could see the slight curve of her breast just before her arms went down to her sides. A rush for Eden ran through her, and she forgot the reason she came into the room. Before Rafe could look away, Eden turned around and caught her gaze.

"Sorry," Rafe said softly, feeling guilty and wary at the same time. She wondered if it was too much to be happy that Eden was here. She wondered if it was fair to want more from Eden than she could give back.

Eden chuckled at the fact Rafe seemed hesitant. Rafe had never been one to not take what she wanted when she wanted it. "Did you forget something?" she asked, hoping Rafe would take her in her arms.

"Uhm." Rafe cleared her throat, her mind had gone blank. "No."

"Oh, okay. Well, I should take my shower," said Eden even though she wanted the awkward moment to become something intimate. "The water's running." Gabri's words kept echoing through her mind and the ache to have Rafe close was fringed with the guilt of wanting something more and knowing right now she might be demanding too much from Rafe.

Rafe nodded as the clear signs of disappointment flickered over Eden's face. "Oh, okay," she said as Eden turned away.

After watching Eden close the bathroom door, Rafe went into the kitchen. She noticed what was on the kitchen table. The message saying Eden was welcome from Nora and Gabri was clear. Rafe couldn't stop the smile on her face. Nora had sent down wine and a nice supply of food, even chocolate for Bronte. Rafe got out some glasses and opened the bottle of wine. She gathered everything and took it all outside and set it on the small table on the side of the cottage. After pouring herself a glass of wine, Rafe sat on the bench to relax and wait for Eden.

Eden was here.

Throughout the day, it seemed Eden was becoming more at peace with her decision. Eden began talking more and smiling. She looked less worried and more like she was enjoying herself. It was going to be a big change from living in California for Eden. Rafe was determined to help Eden feel like this was her home in order to keep her and Bronte here.

Rafe glanced up at the sound of the door closing. "Hey," she said softly.

Eden sat down next to Rafe taking the glass of wine she was offered. "Thank you," she said taking a sip then putting her glass on the table.

"I still can't believe you're here," said Rafe as she took in the beautiful woman next to her in the moonlight.

"I know," said Eden shakily. It had taken everything in her to hold herself together today. The only thing keeping her from shutting down was seeing Rafe and keeping track of Bronte.

Rafe took Eden's hand hoping it would help calm her worries. "I think you'll like it here. I know having you here makes me very happy."

Eden swallowed nervously. "I'm actually really terrified. I feel very out of balance and—" She stopped a moment. "I don't know how to describe everything."

Rafe sat her wine glass down. "Come here," she said and pulled Eden to her and wrapped her arms around her.

"I think Gabri's angry, and I don't know how to deal with him. Nora seems nice, but I can tell she's being cautious…" Eden sighed and couldn't finish. She sat quietly for a while focusing on Rafe's heartbeat to help calm herself. "I believe you when you say you love me, and I heard everything you said to reassure me, but I… I'm still processing what I've done."

Rafe held Eden and ran her hand consolingly over her but didn't speak. She knew there was nothing she could say to make the processing Eden had to do easier. Every time she held her like this, she wished she could take away her anxieties so she could be happy again. She knew from experience, with time, tenderness, and patience, Eden would come out of her anxiety and see things were going to be good again.

"Let's have some wine, look at the stars, and listen to the music," Rafe said softly as she released Eden and reached for their wine glasses. She handed Eden's glass to her, and they took a sip at the same time. "You look beautiful in the moonlight," said Rafe with a wink and watched her blush.

"Thank you," she said softly and sat back with her wine. "So do you."

Eden tried to enjoy the sight of the stars above them, but the blackness of the sky only reminded her of the drawings Rafe had done. She didn't understand them and didn't know if she should.

She also did not know why Rafe had given her the rock. She was unsure why those things were on her mind. Maybe to stop her from thinking about the fact she wasn't on the flight home with Julia.

She turned to Rafe. "Can I ask you a question?"

"You just did," Rafe teased, then realized Eden was not ready to be teased. "Yes."

"I opened the other presents you gave me." She heard Rafe sigh as she shifted on the bench. "What did the drawings mean? They were so," she hesitated, "dark."

Rafe's good humor left her. She sat her wine glass back down wishing she had taken those gifts back. "I was sick," she explained softly. "I wish you hadn't seen them." She wiped her hand over her eyes to brush away those dark memories. "I think we should burn the drawings. I think holding onto them will only remind us of all the bad things that happened. I want to move past it all."

"Did Gabri see them? Is it why he didn't send them?"

"I don't know," said Rafe with a frown. "I doubt it. He just didn't want to contact you and give you a reason to come before I was ready."

"Maybe we should keep them and show them to your doctor. Maybe it will help."

"She has reams of drawings." Rafe groaned. "It's part of my therapy. It's a way to get things out of my mind and show her what I'm thinking and dreaming. She doesn't need more drawings," she insisted tersely. "The images in those drawings aren't real to me anymore. I swear I'm getting better."

Rafe could tell, by becoming upset, she was making Eden anxious. She took a moment to calm herself. "I would never lie to you about how sick I was or how I'm doing now. I'm better, and I want you here. I know, when I was sick, I pushed you away, and you have every right to know why and what was happening with me. Right now, I just want to enjoy this moment with you." She hoped Eden would just let it go for now.

"What about the rock?" Eden asked shakily. "It seemed like it went with the drawings."

Rafe leaned forward and shook her head. Eden was not going to let it go. "It did," she said softly. "Do you remember the night you helped me with my nightmare?"

"Yes," she answered softly. It was one of the scariest nights of her life and the first time she had a real idea of how sick Rafe had been. She was sure, if she knew then what she did now, things would have been different.

"You said I told you to go into the grotto with Maria." She watched as Eden nodded. "The rock is from the grotto," said Rafe. Surprise was clear on Eden's face. "I think, at the time, I took it so I would have something real. I thought if I sent it to you, you'd know the grotto was a real place. I thought you'd understand when you got the drawings and the rock, and you would know you should go there to be safe. I know. It makes no sense. I was sick. Please, just know I'm better, and I don't think those things anymore."

"So," she wavered, "you defaced a national monument? Is this part of your criminal behavior Julia and Abby are always trying to warn me about?"

Rafe turned her head toward Eden with a rankled look. "I didn't deface anything," she said, unable to hide her annoyance at Abby and Julia. Even distance didn't stop them from talking about her and saying negative things. "They don't know everything, and you shouldn't listen to them." She could see Eden wanted more of an explanation. "Fine, if you must know, it fell from the ceiling and onto my notebook while I was drawing. It fell, and I traced around it. Then, I just closed my notebook over it and kept it. I thought I needed to send it to you." Rafe could feel her emotions burning inside. At the time, she thought it was a gift from the goddess Ceres to help keep Eden safe. It had almost been heartbreaking to finally understand it was only a coincidence, an anomaly, a result of gravity, and had nothing to do with her life at all. "I was sick, I wasn't thinking right." She turned away from Eden's eyes.

Eden took in Rafe's words remembering her experiences with Rafe and all the things Gabri told her and the drawings he showed her. She nodded her head knowing Rafe was telling the truth. It was just hard to fathom her being so sick. "I believe you," she said and took Rafe's hand. She smiled as Rafe scowled. "It looks like we really do need each other."

"We do," Rafe said and pulled her close. "I'm sorry it all upset you. It's not what I intended."

"You wanted me to be safe," she said and put her hand on her face gently. "You never stopped thinking about me." She kissed her lightly and felt the warmth for Rafe run through her. "I never stopped thinking about you, either." She kissed Rafe again and leaned into her. They sat together under the stars and forgot everything except that they were finally together again.

28

EDEN KINGSLEY FELT Rafe's warm hand in hers. Rafe leaned against her and kissed the top of her head just like she had so many times before. Rafe's touch was comforting. Eden remembered talking with Rafe about needing to feel safe. At the time, she had forgotten just how safe she felt with Rafe. Now, though, she knew all those insecurities and fears were a combination of her chronic anxiety and manipulation by the Stewards. She was completely aware of her own part in the events leading to their break up. She was grateful Rafe wanted her back and was determined to do everything in her power to make things right.

The most pressing thing she felt they needed to address was Julia and the things she said to Rafe. She had to make sure Rafe knew the truth. "I'm sorry about what Julia did to you, to us," said Eden. It was still painfully inexplicable that Julia had ever thought she would leave Rafe for her. Eden had no idea what made Julia think she was in love with her and believe she would return the feelings. "She lied. I didn't know she had feelings for me, and we certainly never slept together. It was shocking that she would hurt me... us, like she did. I really thought she was my friend."

Rafe shrugged and scoffed. "She's done it before. I wasn't surprised." She was determined to get out her next words without showing the pain they caused. "If you change your mind... and think you want her, I'll understand. Just don't come to me asking for help getting out of the relationship. Maybe we shouldn't be friends, either, so when you break up, Julia can't accuse you of fucking me as part of your reason for leaving her."

"What?" Eden said, shocked at Rafe's suggestion. "I won't change my mind about her. I only love you," she said firmly. She frowned trying to figure out why Rafe would say those things to her when she just told her she had no feelings for Julia—at all. "Are you talking about, Andi, the girl Julia dated?"

"Yes," said Rafe scornfully. "Julia accused Andi of sleeping with me when Andi told her she wanted to break up. It never happened. I told you why she left."

Eden nodded remembering the conversation. "She felt trapped."

"Right," confirmed Rafe. "Still fucking jealous after all these years," she mumbled.

"I'm sorry," said Eden, not sure what more she could say.

"Why? None of it matters anyway. I was betraying her the whole time, so maybe I deserved everything she did to me." Rafe regarded Eden with a frown. "Maybe it's why no one was surprised when I betrayed you."

"But you didn't betray me," Eden reminded her.

Rafe let out a mocking laugh. "I did, though. I'm still doing it, and you just don't understand anything."

"No."

"Yes." Rafe nodded sharply.

Eden fought the urge to argue. She knew it would solve nothing and could make the situation worse. She was brought back to the moment by Rafe who was pouring more wine. "Thank you," she said as Rafe handed her a glass. "I should probably call everyone back home tomorrow. I know they would love to hear from you. They miss you."

"No one misses the Betrayer," said Rafe evenly.

"You haven't betrayed them."

"I have," said Rafe in frustration because Eden was arguing. She began counting all those she had betrayed on her fingers. "My mamma, Papa, Maria, Brettito, Gabri, Letty, Julia, you, all my friends, everyone!" Eden was shaking her head no. "Yes," Rafe said firmly, "and it all started with my first kiss, leading to so many secrets and lies."

Rubbing her temples, Eden tried not to show her surprise the list of people Rafe thought she betrayed had grown. She wondered if it was a new thing, or if Gabri knew. "How did you betray everyone, Rafe?" asked Eden. "I don't understand. Letty? Your friends?" She already knew Rafe's reasons for listing the others had to do mostly with what happened with Maria when she was younger.

Rafe frowned in disbelief that Eden couldn't see it. It was so obvious. "They're all so angry because I walked away and haven't contacted them. I betrayed their trust and friendship."

"They love you. They're worried and upset," Eden explained.

"Yes, exactly, because I betrayed them." Rafe looked out into the night hating that it brought darkness, not only into the world but into her mind no matter how hard she fought.

"Rafe..." Eden sighed and shook her head. "What about Letty? As for Julia, I think she did the betraying from my view of things." She frowned remembering the things Julia said to Rafe. Eden felt sabotaged by Julia as well as betrayed.

"Letty," Rafe said softly, thinking about how much Letty turned out to look like her mother. "She was so nice to me, and I told her so many lies and kept so many secrets from her. I don't understand why she hates my papa." She remembered when Letty announced she was heading off to Hollywood to be a star. "Letty thinks she left New York because she got a big break on her own. I don't think she ever realized that I used to talk about her all the time to my papa. Whenever he showed buildings to a client who wanted to rent space to shoot films, he repeated the stories I told him about Letty. One day, one of those clients called Letty and offered her a job in California," she revealed hanging her head. She never told Letty what her papa had done because she did not want to take away Letty's feeling of achievement. Letty really was a great actress. "It doesn't matter now." She noticed the surprise on Eden's face. "Don't look so surprised. My papa was a good man."

"I know," she said softly but still had a hard time hiding her surprise. Knowing what she knew now about Ettore, she wondered if he somehow purposely sent Letty away to get her out of Rafe's life.

"Letty tells everyone I left New York to get away from him." Rafe frowned and tried to rub away the pain at her temple. "I chose California for our new offices because Letty's father died, and I thought she was all alone. When I got there, I found out she was dating Ephraim. I thought I was doing something for her, but I was gone so long from her life, I knew nothing about her. Then she got married, and I helped them get the place for the bistro because all I could do was give her money. She didn't need anything else from me, just like she didn't need anything more from Papa."

"Letty loves you," Eden insisted. "You give her more than money. You're her family."

"Am I?" Rafe rubbed her hand over her face. She never told Letty about being sick, and neither did her papa. If she was family, then it was true she had betrayed her.

"Yes," Eden said and put her hand on Rafe.

Rafe didn't feel like Eden's assurance was helpful. It just made her even guiltier of her transgressions. "Julia knows I betrayed her. She'll tell you I did and probably already has," said Rafe tersely.

Eden sipped her wine wondering what everyone back home would think when they found out about what Julia had done. Eden wasn't sure if she wanted to tell them but knew any continued friendship with Julia would be difficult. She could at least, hopefully, put Rafe's mind to rest. "She told me a lot about you," she confessed. "Mostly it was about when you two were younger. I'm sure, if she thought you had anything to do with Andi, I would have heard about it. Julia never really talked about her ex to me, though."

"She's still in France."

"Who? Oh, Andi?"

"Yes. I talked to her when I was working at the Conservatory. I wanted to plan a student trip but never got the chance."

Eden wasn't sure what to say. She knew Rafe had really connected with a lot of the students and faculty from the Conservatory. "When did she move to France?"

"Not long after I first met you. Before I introduced you to everyone." Rafe couldn't help the slight smile at the memories.

Eden yawned and saw the expression on Rafe's face. "What are you thinking about?"

"Us," said Rafe and pulled Eden into a gentle hug. "I was thinking about the very first time I saw you."

Eden smiled and pulled away to see her face. "Really?" Rafe grunted an acknowledgment, and Eden leaned into her. She was glad the conversation had become less stressful, and Rafe seemed more relaxed. "What made you decide to have more than one brunch with me? I must have talked your ear off."

"You were beautiful," Rafe whispered. "You still are."

Memories of their first actual conversation flooded into Rafe's mind. Eden talked about everything from her childhood on a farm to her medical issues. It was interesting to Rafe how Eden felt comfortable speaking about the suffering she went through with her chronic anxiety. The fact Eden didn't keep it a secret had been fascinating. Rafe wasn't used to anyone sharing information about their mental illnesses. In her world, those things always had to be hidden.

Along with the physical attraction Rafe felt for Eden, at the time, it felt like there was another likeness between them—their lifelong fight to be seen as normal. The difference was how they handled their issues. Eden made people aware, and somehow, it helped her deal with people and caused people to have patience. Also, though, Rafe saw what she considered pity from people toward Eden. For Eden, it seemed, pity was okay to accept from others. This was a difficult concept for Rafe to accept. She still didn't want to be pitied by anyone. Because Eden was so pitied and understood pity differently, any pity from Eden would be much worse, in her mind, than pity from anyone else. Besides, Rafe knew Eden didn't understand the similarity. Back then, she didn't want her secrets known if they would change Eden's feelings.

"I liked the way you talked to me," Rafe said softly. "You made me feel... privileged."

"Privileged?" Eden let out a soft laugh. "I was nervously rambling about anything popping into my head so I wouldn't completely shut down," she admitted. "I thought it was more likely you were suffering in silence."

"I guess I thought it meant you liked me."

"I did like you," said Eden. "I mean, you know, in a friend way. I didn't like you the other way until..."

"Until, you jumped my bones," Rafe wise-cracked with a grin.

"I wouldn't call it that," Eden complained. "It was more," she hesitated, "like an uncontrolled fall into a new amazing reality."

"Uncontrolled?"

"Okay, maybe not totally uncontrolled. I just knew I couldn't stop it. I didn't want to stop it. We were starting a new life then. We're starting a new life again now."

Rafe took in her words, and a flash of terror ran through her. It was true. They were starting a new life, one where Eden knew all her secrets. She quickly swallowed the last of her wine to wet her dry throat. "You ready to go in?"

"Sure," Eden said sleepily and sat up. She took the last sip of her wine then stood and stretched.

Rafe couldn't take her eyes off Eden as she stretched. She fought down the discomfort, working to convince herself there was no need to worry. She stood up and hugged Eden then kissed her on her lips, face, and then her neck. "Let's go," she said as she released her and gathered the wine glasses.

Eden followed Rafe inside. She was starting to feel better. The comfort of Rafe's arms around her and feeling her kisses again had helped. She had been reflecting about the events over the last week, specifically her time with Rafe. The drawings, the visit to the cemetery and how Julia's words affected Rafe. She didn't want to do anything to mess things up or do anything that might cause Rafe to be sick or upset or have a setback. She was determined to focus on her and do everything Gabri, and the doctor said would help her.

Rafe walked into the kitchen to put the wine glasses in the sink, and Eden headed over to the couch and began taking off the cushions so she could pull out the sofa bed. Rafe entered the living room and watched Eden for a moment. "What are you doing?" Rafe asked in confusion.

"Oh, I thought I'd pull out the bed before I get too tired. Does it already have sheets and blankets?"

Rafe stared at her for a moment when she suddenly understood. She realized Eden wanted to sleep on the pull-out bed and not in hers. Eden must think they needed to sleep in separate beds because of the cohabitation agreement. Maybe it was some other reason, Rafe just didn't know. She was a bit hurt, but she didn't want to make Eden's decision to stay here harder. She hesitated. "I'll get you a blanket." She went into her bedroom to find an extra blanket.

When Rafe returned to the living room, the pull-out bed was extended, and the room was turned into a makeshift bedroom. Rafe quirked a small smile when she saw what Eden was wearing. She put her arms around her waist from behind and pulled her close. "I think these are mine," she said, pulling playfully on the pajamas.

Eden leaned back into Rafe and turned her head so she could kiss her. "They are." She slid her arms around Rafe's neck as she turned her body. "They're very comfy." She stretched up on her toes and kissed Rafe again.

Rafe pulled away and looked into Eden's eyes. "I've missed you," she said breathlessly as she caressed her face and lips and brushed her hair away from her eyes.

Eden melted under her gaze and knew she had no choice but to follow her anywhere. "Oh, god, I've missed you too," she breathed and dove back into their kiss. It felt so good to be held by Rafe again. To be able to kiss her and smell her and touch her was all she had been dreaming of for so many months. She pulled her kisses away and nuzzled her face into Rafe's neck. "I don't want to do anything that'll make getting better hard for you," she said softly. "Maybe we should take things slow. You know, until we can talk about," she hesitated, "everything." She looked up into Rafe's gray-blue eyes. "I can wait. I love you," she said and then released Rafe to give her the promised space.

Rafe wasn't sure what to think. It seemed Eden had been so willing last night to be with her, and now she was throwing up a wall between them. The only reason she could fathom was Eden was still processing.

She knew Eden was right, there were a lot of things to talk about, so she nodded her head. "Okay," she said quietly. "Okay, well, goodnight." She kissed Eden gently again pulling her close and running her hands over the pajamas separating her from touching her warm skin. God, she wanted to touch her so much.

"Goodnight," Eden answered when they pulled away from their kiss. She watched Rafe walk slowly into her bedroom then climbed into the pull-out bed. She closed her eyes and wished she would have asked Rafe to hold her for a while.

29

WAKING SUDDENLY FROM her nightmare, Rafe Salvaggio sat up covered in a fine sheen of sweat. Her body shook as she leaned forward putting her head in her hands. She groaned, understanding her nightmare may have come not only from the stress she had been under lately but because she forgot to take her pills. As she wiped her eyes to help focus, she realized she had fallen asleep in her clothes again. She frowned, remembering she kept them on in case Gabri called needing help with the guests in the middle of the night.

Unsteady, she moved to the edge of the bed. Reaching into her nightstand, she pulled out a few pill packets, hoping one was blue. Not bothering with a light, she headed quietly toward the kitchen. As Rafe passed through the living room, a form moved in the dark. Startled, her breath caught in her chest.

Then she remembered.

Eden.

Relief flooded through her.

In the kitchen, she flipped on the light near the sink. Looking at the pill packets in her hand she saw she had grabbed a blue packet. She made a glass of water and took her pills then leaned over the sink, shivering as her body cooled, pushing her nightmare from her mind. She hated the feeling of waking up after a dark dream and not being able to control her shaking body or muddled thoughts. She hated not being in control of herself.

Sitting at the table, Rafe opened her drawing pad and picked up her pencil. Her hand moved quickly as she drew the images from her dream as her therapist had suggested. She didn't mind drawing them but hated looking at them and talking about them. She hated some of the images her mind could conjure up, and her hand could record so easily. As images formed on the paper, Rafe knew these drawings would have to burn. She looked up from her work and turned when she heard a shuffling behind her.

"Are you okay?" asked Eden softly.

"I didn't mean to wake you," said Rafe, closing the drawing pad. She couldn't control the shiver running through her body. "I'm fine. I just forgot to take my pills." She was determined to work harder since Eden was here.

Eden put her arms around Rafe. "You're shivering." She ran her eyes over Rafe for a moment. "You're still dressed?"

"Yeah, in case Gabri calls."

"I don't think he's going to call tonight," she said softly. "Let's get you back to bed." She pulled Rafe into the bedroom. As Rafe sat down on the bed, Eden ran her hand over Rafe's face and through her dark hair. "So do you want to change clothes or at least take off your jeans?"

"No."

Eden kissed Rafe and whispered to her, "I was worried when I saw you up," she said as she rubbed her hands over Rafe to warm her and calm her shivering.

"Don't worry," said Rafe softly. "I'll be okay."

"Did you have a bad dream?" asked Eden hesitantly wondering if she would always have to ask about her bad dreams. "Are you still having them?"

Rafe nodded her head in answer. "Sometimes. This one was probably just from not taking my pills." She looked up at Eden not wanting to tell her she had been having problems all week. Eden knew. She had to know. She was there when it happened. At least she thought she was there. "It seems so unreal."

"It's real," Eden whispered and kissed her forehead. "I'm real, and I love you." She knew the stress she had been under over the last few days was affecting Rafe, probably more than missing the pills. It was a big change for them both.

Rafe gaped at Eden. She wondered if she had said her thoughts out loud or if Eden was reading her mind.

Eden sat on the bed and held Rafe until she stopped shivering and had relaxed. "It's real," she repeated.

"Okay," whispered Rafe as she nuzzled further into Eden and felt warmth begin to flow through her again.

Rafe found it difficult to close her eyes. She didn't want to go back into the dark dreams she had just left. She didn't want to lose control and let the darkness she knew was in her mind take over again. Everything had been so good today, but from the depth of her mind, torment and worries surfaced when she tried to sleep just like she knew it would. She felt Eden kiss her face, and she lifted her lips toward her ear. "I just," she sighed into Eden's ear, "I don't want to go into the dark place again. I just need you to keep me here," she said.

"Always," Eden whispered and kissed her gently. "I'll keep you always."

Rafe could feel the icy hand of despair claw at her heart, and a chill ran over her skin. They were supposed to be starting over, but now Eden knew about all the blood on her hands. She didn't know how, or even if, Eden could really love her now. She was suddenly terrified, realizing she didn't know who she should be with Eden anymore.

As the moonlight shined through the window and into Rafe's gray-blue eyes, Eden saw them fill with uncertainty. It seemed Rafe was looking through her in a kind of trance. Without breaking eye contact, she took Rafe's face in her hands. "Hey," she said softly, and Rafe seemed surprised she was so close, "are you okay?"

Rafe just gazed at her silently.

"Let me help you," said Eden as she pulled Rafe up from the bed and began undressing her.

Eden knew Rafe said she didn't want to change her clothes, but she wanted her to be more comfortable. Even if Gabri called, Rafe was in no condition to go anywhere. Rafe didn't stop Eden as she removed her shirt revealing her braless body covered with goosebumps. Reaching down, Eden unfastened Rafe's jeans and pushed them over her hips and down her legs as far as she could, reeling at the closeness.

It was hard to be so close and not be able to have her. Eden kissed the hollow of Rafe's neck and felt her shiver again. Rafe's gray-blue eyes were searching for something.

Eden quickly stripped out of her pajamas then took Rafe's hand. "Come here," she said. Climbing into Rafe's bed, Eden gently pulled Rafe along. Rafe kicked her jeans from her legs and lay back in the bed beside Eden. Holding Rafe close and feeling the familiar sensation as their skin connected, Eden worried maybe Gabri was right, and she had pushed Rafe too fast already. "It's okay, we can just hold each other for a while," she said gently as she covered them both with the blanket.

Rafe leaned into Eden's shoulder fighting her emotions. Squeezing her eyes, she blinked away a tear before it could escape and slide down her cheek.

Eden ran her hand over Rafe's dark hair and kissed her head softly. "What's wrong, babe? Let me help you. Please, talk to me." Talking with Gabri and convincing him to let her be included with what was going on with Rafe's doctor was her first priority for tomorrow. She could now see how important the deal Gabri had offered her would be in helping Rafe. She would make sure she kept up her end of the partnership.

Rafe rolled on to her back and wiped her hands down her face. "I just," she whispered, "I just don't want to trick you into being here or being with me."

"Trick me?" Eden repeated with a small smile and climbed up so she could look into Rafe's face. "It was my decision to be here. You didn't do anything to trick me."

"No, no," mumbled Rafe as she rubbed her face and looked away so she wouldn't have to see the light go out in Eden's eyes again. "That's not what I'm talking about." She sighed in frustration as she sat up and put her head in her hands. "I just don't think you really understand."

"Understand?" said Eden as she sat up and put her hand on Rafe's warm back. "What don't I understand, babe?"

"I'm doing it again." Rafe laughed to prevent a sob. "I wanted you here so bad. I asked Nora if I was selfish. I shouldn't have asked you to stay."

Eden stammered in shock. "I don't understand. Rafe, what are you talking about?"

Rafe turned with pain and desperation in her eyes. "I know Gabri told you things. Letty and Julia told you things too," she said through her teeth trying not to yell. "And now you know what no one else knows—what I told you in the cemetery," she hissed out as she leaned close to Eden. "What will you do when you realize what it all means? Will we really be able to start over? How long will I have before you leave? How will you ever be able to look at me again? How will you be able to love me?"

"Wha— Rafe, what are you talking about?" Eden watched Rafe shake her head and clutch her hair and wondered if she was having a break and if she should get Gabri. "Listen to me," Eden said as she crawled in front of Rafe and took her face in her hands. "Nothing anyone has told me would make me not want to look at you or not love you or make me want to leave."

"It's because you don't understand yet," Rafe said softly, swallowing the sadness wanting to ooze out of her.

Anxiety was threading its way through Eden's body, and she worked to shut it down. She had no idea what to do. The fear of making things worse crept upon her, and she could feel it pricking at her skin.

Eden moved close to Rafe and held her hand. "What don't I understand?"

As Rafe rocked forward and nodded, she noticed the light bead of sweat along Eden's hairline and knew she was nervous. *Good*, she thought, *she should be nervous. Eden has no idea who she was sitting naked in bed with right now.*

"You don't understand anything. You don't understand what all the secrets mean. You don't understand who I am, what I am," Rafe said shakily. "I'm afraid of what will happen when you understand."

"What do you think will happen?" Eden asked softly. Everything Gabri and Rafe had told her was running through her mind. There were so many versions—so many secrets within secrets. "Babe," she said as she stroked Rafe's hair, "you should tell me what the secrets mean. I'm sure I already know who you are. You're the love of my life. The person I can't live without," she kissed her forehead then her eyelids. "I love you."

"For how long?"

"Rafe..." Eden sighed trying to understand why she was asking such a question.

"Until you understand," Rafe whispered and pulled away from her. She looked down at her hands then held them up for Eden to see. "All the secrets and all the deaths start and end with me. Their blood is on my hands. My hands," she repeated and held them out for Eden to see as if the blood might still be there somehow. "My father and Gabri thought they knew the truth, but now you know the real reason I'm guilty. Did you forget what I told you? Can you see who I am now?"

"I didn't forget," said Eden as she took Rafe's hands. "You're not responsible for their deaths. They were accidents and out of your control." She kissed the back of her hands. "I'm sorry you had to see those things."

With a scowl, Rafe snatched her hands away. *She should not be kissing bloodstained hands*, she thought angrily. "I am *Traditoré*," she said harshly. "I am the Betrayer. I've betrayed you and everyone in my life!" she said in frustration because Eden didn't understand. Rafe reached out and brushed the warm tears falling down Eden's face. "Don't cry for me!" she growled, smearing the tears from her fingertips angrily on the sheets. "Cry for yourself! If you cry for the Betrayer, your tears will turn to ice and be sent to hell before they hit the ground because the earth does not want those tears to taint it!"

Wiping her tears away the best she could, Eden remembered the drawings Gabri had shown her. They were self-portraits Rafe made when she was young in different stages of being encased in ice or being pulled under icy water. "No, you haven't betrayed anyone," she said softly.

Spinning through Rafe's mind were all the fractured moments leading to all her betrayals. She could see clearly where everything started. "I should never have made a bargain with a *zingara*. I should have run away and never let her kiss me. I had to know," said Rafe said softly. "I just don't know how to find redemption as the *Traditoré* when I can't change who I am. I don't want to change." Rafe took in Eden's sad and confused face. "Is it selfish... to want to be me?"

"No," said Eden softly. "I love who you are. You were just a child who was hurt terribly, and no one was listening to your cries for help, except maybe Gabri, and he was just a kid too." Eden wondered if she could convince Rafe to talk to her doctor about Maria if the doctor would keep it from Gabri. Since Gabri was power of attorney, she doubted the doctor would keep the promise.

Hearing Eden say Gabri's name filled Rafe with dread and guilt. He couldn't find out about Maria. "No," Rafe shook her head slowly, "you're not listening. I've betrayed him most of all! You brought the school bag! You read the letter! You know!" She looked at Eden wildly and fought her panic. "You can't tell him."

"I won't," Eden promised seeing her distressing. "It's okay, you burned that part of the letter, remember?"

"Yeah," Rafe nodded, "and I got rid of the school bag." She saw Eden's confusion. "I filled it with rocks and threw it in the *Arno*," she said and licked her lips nervously. "Now we're safe."

Rafe's gray-blue eyes seemed to vibrate in their sockets and Eden had to look away. Eden felt like she couldn't breathe because she was weighed down by the remorse of bringing the bag and upsetting Rafe. She didn't know it would hurt her. Gabri had warned her Rafe still wasn't well and needed more time to get better. He begged her not to push Rafe and pressure her, and now Rafe was paying the price for her mistake in not listening to him.

It was too late now. Rafe knew, no matter what anyone said, there was no way to change things or go back in time. She couldn't stop the unraveling of her life. She couldn't give Eden what she wanted. She couldn't give her what she needed. She couldn't live with another lie or secret. "I can't give you what you want," said Rafe.

"What is it you think I want?"

"Forgiveness. I can't give you something impossible to give. It's a promise I can't keep." Rafe rubbed her temples trying to keep the pain at bay.

"Rafe, I don't understand."

"Don't you?" she asked skeptically. "Don't you see? Forgiveness is a lie, a promise no one can keep. Even you can't keep it. You said you forgive me, but you kept punishing me." She licked her lips. "Are you going to keep punishing me? Will you use everything I've told you, and everyone else has told you, to punish me more? I can't take it if that's why you're here."

Eden's jaw dropped as she shook her head. "No," she forced out. "That's not why I'm here." Her chin quivered as she fought back the mixed emotions rushing through her. She was here to help and love Rafe, and that meant putting her own fears and anxieties aside.

There was no doubt in Rafe's mind Eden was beginning to understand now. Eden was starting to see who she was and couldn't look at her anymore. "Do you want me to tell Gabri to buy you a ticket home?" she asked softly.

"No!" Eden burst angrily into tears. "I don't want to punish you. I don't want to hurt you! I'm here because I love you!"

"It's okay," whispered Rafe as she pulled Eden close to comfort her. "It's hard when you start to understand. I'm sorry I'm not who you thought I was. I can't ask you to love me now that you know what I've done. I didn't mean to trick you. I just liked the way you looked at me and wanted you to love me."

"I want us to keep each other safe and love each other."

"How can we? I still have secrets, and you still can't trust me."

"I can trust you. You don't have to tell me all your secrets. If you need to, you can just tell Gabri. I love you, Rafe. I don't need to know any of your secrets to know I love you."

"But you need to know them to save yourself. You can't depend on me. Don't worry. I'll tell Gabri to pay you whatever you need."

"I don't want your money."

"But it's all I have now," Rafe said softly. "Money and secrets."

"Really, Rafe, I don't need to know. Maybe it's better this way. I don't want you or Gabri believing I'm here for anything other than you."

Flinging the blanket back Rafe got out of bed and began dressing.

"Where are you going?" asked Eden.

"I need to think," said Rafe. "And so do you. I'll understand if you want to go." Rafe watched the tears run down Eden's face and knew they were filled with pity. She was sure Eden would leave again. "I can't take it again if you leave me without saying goodbye," said Rafe softly allowing only a single tear to escape. "Please, don't take her and not tell me you're going again."

Eden couldn't stop her own tears from falling in empathy for Rafe. "I won't leave you, babe." She pulled Rafe to her and kissed her face and lips. "I don't ever want to be apart from you, and I won't ever take Bronte away again, I promise." A sharp wave of guilt cut through her, and she was determined to find a way to give her more than just words. Right now, they had to get through tonight.

Pulling away, Rafe ran her hand over her face. "It's okay," she said. "I'll understand. Just let me say goodbye before you go."

Rafe walked out of the bedroom, and seconds later, Eden heard the front door click closed. She jumped out of bed and ran to the living room. Flinging open the door, she caught sight of Rafe walking up the path toward the villa and the music tents. She looked back inside the house and knew she couldn't leave. Bronte was asleep in the other room and couldn't be left alone.

Eden closed the door, found her bag, and took out her phone. She went into the kitchen so she wouldn't wake Bronte. On the table, she saw Rafe's drawing pad and opened it. There was a drawing of a young girl she assumed was Maria, but she looked melted and surreal. Rafe had been dreaming about Maria.

Eden knew Rafe wouldn't talk with her therapist about Maria or what happened while they were in the cemetery. The only person Rafe was willing to talk to about those things right now was her if she could get her to talk clearly and coherently.

Holding onto Rafe's secret about Maria was going to be hard. She just hoped she could take whatever punishment Gabri would rain down on her if he thought she was the reason things went badly tonight. Gabri said they were partners when it came to helping Rafe but knew any betrayal to Rafe about Maria would be disastrous to their fragile relationship.

She took a calming breath and dialed Gabri.

30

MUSIC AND LAUGHTER filled the mild evening air as Nora De Angelis carefully made her way up the path to the villa. Her desire to stay up all night to make music and sing with her friends had been tempered by the need to take a relaxing bath and get some much-needed sleep. Her ankles were swollen, her back ached, and the child she was carrying seemed to be overstimulated by the music echoing through her body. They both needed downtime from all the excitement of the day.

The sound of footsteps behind her startled Nora, and she looked back quickly. "Rafe? You scared me," she said quickly and calmed her breathing. "What are you doing up here? Did you forget something?"

"Sorry." Rafe stepped close to Nora and took her arm. "Let me help you. It looks like you're having a tough time tonight."

"Thanks, my back is killing me," she confirmed as she leaned heavily on Rafe, and they walked up the path. "You still haven't told me why you're up here. Is everything okay with Eden and Bronte?"

Rafe clenched her jaw tightly. She berated herself for walking to the villa instead of to one of the tents where she could get lost in the crowd and music. The noise, though, was what drove her away from the tents. It, combined with the noise in her head, was more than she could take. "They're fine," she assured her.

Nora could tell something was wrong but knew enough not to push Rafe. She hoped Eden hadn't changed her mind about staying. She bit her lip in self-punishment because she knew at least part of her reasoning was selfish. After the baby was born, and the doctor gave the okay, they would be leaving on an extended trip promoting the new music. Leaving Rafe behind had been a worry for both Nora and Gabri. It was still a worry, but Nora felt better about it since Eden was here and could help watch over Rafe.

"Did Gabri call you to do something?"

"No," said Rafe, volunteering nothing more.

"Well, I'm glad you're here. You can help me up the stairs so I can take a long soak tonight." Nora decided not to ask any more questions as they made their way inside.

It had been a relief having Rafe's help powering up the stairs after the long day. Now Nora needed her long-awaited bath.

As she turned off the water to the tub, she thought she heard a thump, like something had fallen somewhere in the house. She went to the bedroom door and looked out into the hallway. No one was there, but she heard more noise coming from Gabri's office. Thinking Gabri had come in early, she went to ask him to join her in the warm bath.

As Nora pushed open the door, she gasped in surprise. "Rafe?" She looked around the room at the open drawers and cabinets. "What are you doing?"

"Where are they?"

"What?"

"Where are they? The pills," Rafe demanded. "I need them tonight."

Nora took in Rafe's drawn face and the dark circles around her eyes. She had seen this sudden change in Rafe before, and it wasn't good. "Let me call Gabri," she said quickly as she backed out of the room. She rushed to the bedroom to get her mobile phone and called Gabri.

"You need to come up," she said when Gabri answered.

"I'm looking for Rafe. Eden called me."

"She's here," Nora informed him. "She's searching for her pills and looks bad again."

"*Merda*! I'll be right there. Keep her there."

The connection broke, and Nora rushed back to the office to find Rafe sitting at Gabri's desk with her head down.

"Rafe," she whispered cautiously. "Gabri's coming."

Rafe lifted her head but said nothing.

"Did something happen? Is this about Eden being here?"

"I can't take care of her," Rafe said hoarsely. "I can't..."

"You only have to take care of you," Nora reminded her. "Eden can take care of herself and Bronte."

"No," Rafe argued. "You don't understand. I've always taken care of her and now... now I can't. When she understands everything, she'll leave." The desperation of Rafe's face was highlighted by the dark circles around her eyes. "Can I stay here until she leaves? I can't watch her leave again. I'll sleep in here on the couch. I just need a pill tonight."

Nora edged her way toward Rafe and was relieved when Rafe allowed her to touch her then put her arms around her. "You can stay here if you want to," she assured her. "I don't think Eden's going to leave. She told me she's still in love with you. Eden can take care of herself. Remember, she's been taking care of herself and Bronte for the last six months. She's here because she hopes showing how much she loves you will help you."

Rafe pulled away and leaned on the desk putting her head on her arms. Images of Eden flickered through her mind morphing with memories of her past, and she just wanted everything to stop. She needed it all to stop so she could think. If she took the pill, it would all stop and then maybe she could think. The longer she was awake, the more crowded her mind would become, and the path it could lead her down terrified her.

"I can't do this," she whispered. "My father was right. I should have listened." Rafe lifted her head and pounded her fist on the desk menacingly. She wanted the noise in her head to stop. "I need Gabri! I need those pills!"

Shocked, Nora backed away. "Okay," she said softly. "I'll get him." She reached behind her for the doorknob. Griping it firmly she spun and rushed out the door.

In the hallway, Nora took a shaky breath and put a protective hand on her enlarged stomach. It had been a long time since Rafe had such an outburst. She had never had one in her presence. Footsteps announced Gabri's imminent arrival and relief flooded through Nora.

"Where is she?" asked Gabri.

"In here," she said indicating his office. "She says she wants you and her pills." Nora hesitated. "Come with me." She led him to the bedroom for privacy. Inside, she sat on the bed to relieve her back. "She's talking about not being able to take care of Eden and Bronte," she continued, noting the frown and furrowed brow on her husband. "I know you don't like me involved when things like this happened, but I'm warning you... you better not go in there agreeing with her about Eden and doing whatever she says to make her happy."

"What do you mean?" asked Gabri feeling affronted.

"Oh, you know what I mean," she pressed. "If you let her talk you into making Eden leave, it will be a huge mistake."

"If she's causing more problems for Rafe, maybe she should leave."

"Gabri," Nora said with a clenched jaw. Sometimes he was so frustrating she wanted to scream. "You know if Eden leaves again, Rafe may never recover, and frankly, she may never want to. She may spend the rest of her life in that damn cottage alone and living in the past. She's saying she thinks her father was right again. We've already had this discussion."

"I know," said Gabri holding his hands up in surrender. "You think we should have told her the truth all those years ago. We didn't, and now it will just do more harm than good. You have no idea what the truth is, and you may think differently if you did."

"Then you should tell me. I know you told Eden." Nora knew she was right when Gabri didn't deny her words. "Fine," she said when he didn't offer to tell her the truth about Rafe's past. "Don't tell me. But listen to me when I tell you, if you make Eden leave, it will be a mistake. I've never seen her so happy, Gabri. I know she's not happy right now, but just knowing she can be happy has to be proof Eden needs to stay."

Gabri could not hide the doubt on his face. "If she decides to leave, I won't stop her. I know Rafe will be hurt, but she will get through it again with our help."

"That's part of the problem, Gabri! Are we canceling the tour? Are we stopping our lives too? I know it sounds selfish, but would Rafe want us to do this to her and to ourselves? For all we know, this is temporary. In a day, a week, a month she may realize making Eden leave was a mistake. Then what? Will she blame you? Herself? Can you live with that?" She could see Gabri wasn't happy with her, but she had to go on. "Listen, just give this situation a chance. Don't make a decision that could affect all of our lives based on one bad night."

"So, you think I made a bad decision bringing Rafe into our life?" Gabri was hurt and getting upset with Nora.

"No," said Nora in frustration. "No, no, I think you did the right thing. This is different, though. This time, you won't be rescuing her to help her get better. This time, you will be taking away the things she needs to live again. Love and her family."

"I'm her family," insisted Gabri.

"I know," said Nora gently. "I know you love her, but she needs more than you can give her alone. She built a life despite everything that happened to her, and then it was ripped away. Now she has a chance to get it back. It's like a lost piece of herself, and she can't really be whole without it. Please, Gabri. Listen to me. Don't do what I'm sure she will ask you to do. Do anything else. Give her the pill and tell her you'll talk in the morning. Delay until she's thinking clearly again. Please. For Eden and Bronte. For us. For Rafe."

"I should have given her a pill last night," said Gabri with a sigh. "I know she hasn't slept well since the concert. I can see it in every movement even though she tries to hide it."

"Maybe that's all this is," said Nora wanting to hang on to any reason to keep the love Rafe needs close. "Maybe lack of sleep and the stress from the week has caught up with her. Maybe she really just needs sleep and time to clear her head."

Gabri nodded and hoped Nora was right. The only way to tell was to see Rafe for himself. "Maybe," he said. "Go relax in your bath and let me talk to her."

"Okay." Nora hugged Gabri then made her way back to her bath hoping Gabri really listened and would take her advice to heart.

Gabri retrieved Rafe's pills from his dresser then made his way back to the office. Opening the door slowly, he was struck by the chaos of open drawers and cabinets. He glanced toward the file cabinet and was relieved to see it was still closed and locked. The papers Ettore sent him about Rafe and her medical history were there, and he didn't know how Rafe would take seeing everything—seeing the truth—after all this time.

Rafe sat up. "Gabri?"

"I'm here." He crossed to the desk.

"I need a pill."

"Tell me what happened, *Eroina*. Come, let's move to the couch."

Gabri helped Rafe up, and they sat together on the couch. Gabri held her close like so many times before while Rafe said all the things Nora had predicted. Finally, Gabri gave her a pill and hoped Nora's instincts were right. He made no promises about Eden and stayed with Rafe until the pill pulled her into a deep sleep.

31

EDEN KINGSLEY WAS able to focus and not allow herself to become overwhelmed by her anxiety and her choice to stay in Italy with the help of calls to Dr. Cathcart and Nora's kind support. Taking care of Bronte and dealing with her job and the fallout of her decision to stay in Italy, especially with her friends back home, kept her mind busy the last few days. The thought of losing her job and what it gave her had been a huge cause of stress for her. At work, she got to do what she loved and had a buffer allowing her to deal with people, even if it was just on a professional level. It also made it so she could stay in Rafe's house and in the home they had made together. Eden didn't know anything about how it worked in Italy. She didn't speak the language, and she knew no one who she could call about working here. She didn't even know if she could legally work. The things she didn't know were overwhelming. To distract herself, Eden put herself into work mode researching her job options in American companies she could do while in Italy. The project helped keep her emotions at a safe distance from the fears causing her anxieties.

Incredibly, after researching industry needs, and several calls to people she networked and freelanced with in California to talk about working from Italy, Eden found she had more options than she would have imagined. There were even possibilities within the company where she currently worked. It was hard, but she got through explaining the circumstances. She asked them to consider keeping her as an employee and worked with them to define what she would do for the company from Italy. Eden was happy she had done her research and was able to make some good arguments and suggestions. In the end, she still would have to wait for an answer. She pitched herself to a lot of companies, and there were a lot of rejections, but a few companies were interested in hiring her and had actually wanted to offer her opportunities. They were putting together employment packages and would email them to her early next week. She had actually laughed out loud at the realization Rafe was right. It really was possible she could work from anywhere, and there was a great film industry in Italy. It was now just a question of if there was a job opening that she felt qualified to do and wanted. The fact other offers were coming was encouraging and calmed her worries about her job.

Barely seeing Rafe since her first night at the cottage turned out the biggest challenge for Eden. Rafe made excuses about needing to help Gabri with the festival breakdown as her reasons for not spending a lot of time with Eden and Bronte. She said nothing about why she wouldn't sleep in her own bed. Eden knew her real reasons, though. Gabri and Nora let her know Rafe was having issues again and her doctor had been visiting to help. Gabri explained that the stress and lack of sleep, along with missing daily meds, had caused Rafe serious problems. Eden felt guilty knowing her visit and Julia's cruelty were also part of the problem.

Fortunately, there were still guests with children at the villa, and Bronte was having the time of her life and picking up Italian quickly. Each morning, Bronte woke up with the same questions. *Are the kids still here? Will Mama draw with them today? Will Gabri sing?*

Eden was glad Rafe made sure to spend special time with Bronte. Watching them from afar was hard. Eden did her best to be positive and upbeat for both Rafe and Bronte. What little time Eden did get to spend with Rafe was usually in a group and very cordial, but Nora assured her it was just temporary. Eden hoped Nora was right.

Eden looked over at Bronte who never got around to changing her clothes after breakfast and was still in her pajamas. She had her colored pencils out again and several pieces of paper around her and was drawing on another as she bobbed her head to the music that played softly in the background. Bronte loved what she and Flynn called her brain music. Eden got up and found the letter Rafe's mother had written and then took it back to the couch. The letter had become something like a talisman that helped calm Eden when she read it. It reassured her not only of Rafe's love but the wise words of Rafe's mother expressed the kind of love she wanted to give to both Rafe and Bronte. She leaned back and remembered Rafe's confession about not being able to lose someone again and realized Rafe may be staying away because she still thought she would leave. It was painful. A wave of guilt ran through her because she knew it was her first refusal to move to Italy that was partly to blame. Eden hoped by seeing her and Bronte every day it would reassure Rafe that they were staying.

Her thoughts were interrupted by a little body crawling up on the couch beside her. A small pudgy hand thrust a piece of paper in front of her eyes.

"Is this good?" asked Bronte as she laid her head on Eden's arm.

Eden took the drawing and gathered Bronte to her. "I think it's good," she said and kissed her head. "I see a house and people dancing. Can you tell me about it?"

"It's Mama and me," she said as she pointed at the figures in the drawing. "And that's you," she pointed, "and Gabri and Nora, and those are the kids singing. That one's Nikki. She's a big girl, but she's nice."

"Nikki? I don't think I've met her," said Eden amazed at how fast Bronte was able to make friends.

"She helped all the kids get cookies," Bronte said helpfully. "I think I'd like a cookie."

"You would?" Eden laughed as she hugged her. "Don't you think you've had enough sweets this morning?"

"I didn't have a cookie," she answered as she crawled up on her mommy to sit in her lap. Eden moved the drawing and the letter she was holding so Bronte could get comfortable. "You could have one too," she offered with a toothy grin.

"I would rather have a snuggle," said Eden and hugged and snuggled Bronte making the little girl laugh. She gave Bronte a shower of mommy kisses. "I love you, sweet girl."

"I love you," said Bronte with a giggle. She looked down with a little frown. "The paper is pokin' me."

"Oh, I'm sorry, baby," said Eden and moved the paper. "Better?" Bronte nodded her head and tried to pluck the paper from her hand. "Careful, I want to keep this safe," she said and moved the letter away from Bronte's hands.

"What is it?"

"It's a letter."

"Is it to me?"

"No," said Eden smiling down on her daughter. "It's to your mama from her mamma."

"Oh," said Bronte and sat up. "Does her mamma live here too?"

"No," said Eden then stopped. "Well, she used to. Her mamma died when she was little, and she left this letter for her."

Bronte frowned at the letter with concern. "Oh, no... Her mamma died?"

"Yes," said Eden softly, "but she had her papa."

Bronte looked up at her for a moment taking in the information. "Like Nemo? His mama died, and he just has a papa."

"Yes," Eden nodded, "like Nemo."

"But Nemo has Dora now," Bronte informed her. "She's funny. I like her."

"She is funny," Eden agreed as she started to fold the letter.

"What do the words say?"

"Well," said Eden as she unfolded the letter again, "they say her mamma loves her and is proud of her. And they say her mamma hopes she finds someone to love her."

"I love her," said Bronte with a nod and a smile.

Eden smiled back. "So do I."

"Where's her papa?"

"Well, her papa died too," she explained.

"And your daddy died," said the little girl.

"Yes. A long time ago." Eden was unsure about what to tell Bronte about her parents, and why her mother wasn't around, so she said as little as possible at the moment.

Bronte reached out and picked the necklace up from Eden's chest. "This is pretty." She put it to her cheek. "It's warm," she said as she rubbed it against her face.

"I think it's pretty too," said Eden, glad about the subject change. "Mama gave it to me for my birthday."

"Oh, it's a present!" Bronte grinned. "I like presents." She examined the necklace closely and rubbed her fingers over the gems. "Can I wear it?" she asked innocently.

Eden chuckled knowing how much Bronte loved wearing jewelry. "Well, this is 'big girl' jewelry," she explained. "So, when you're a big girl, then you can wear it if you want."

"I'm big," she insisted. "I'm gonna be three." She held up her fingers to emphasize her age.

"Yes, you're gonna be pretty big soon," Eden agreed. "But you have to be even bigger. Then you can wear it."

"Oh," Bronte said in disappointment. She put the bloodstone to her lips. "I love it," she said and kissed it then placed it gently back on her mommy's chest.

"I love it too."

"Mama gave me a present too," Bronte announced.

"She did? What was it?"

Bronte bounced up and down excitedly. "A baby kitty!"

"A baby kitty? Really?"

"Yeah, the mommy cat lives with the cars," she informed her mommy. "It's gonna have babies, and I can have one!"

Eden fought the frown wanting to appear on her face. She didn't understand why Rafe would promise Bronte a kitten if it would be wild and she wouldn't be able to really have it. Of course, she knew it was possible Bronte was interpreting things the way she wanted them to go, so Eden held those thoughts to herself. "A kitten sounds exciting."

"Mama said we have to catch one," she said clasping her hands together. "If we can't catch it, then it has to live with its mommy, but it's still mine."

Eden laughed softly. "Oh, I see." Rafe saved herself with that deal. "It sounds like Mama loves you a lot to help you get a kitten."

"Yeah," Bronte nodded her agreement. "She loves you too 'cuz she got you this necklace," she said as she ran her fingers over the bloodstone again.

Eden put her hand over Bronte's' small hand. "I think you're right," she said fighting her tears threatening at the sweetness of her daughter's words and the innocent truth in them.

"Can I have a cookie now?" Bronte asked sweetly.

Eden couldn't help smiling at her ability to not be sidetracked for too long about treats. "I know something much better and sweeter than a cookie."

"What?" asked Bronte with big round eyes.

"An apple. I think we have one in the kitchen too. Would you like me to cut one up for you?"

"Okay," Bronte agreed and climbed down from her mommy's lap.

In the kitchen, Eden got the apple from the fruit basket and the knife from the block. "Do you remember the Italian word for apple," she asked Bronte as she cut the fruit.

"No," said Bronte as she climbed on to a chair and leaned on the table.

"It's *mela*. Can you say it?"

"*Mela*," Bronte repeated.

"Very good. It was the first Italian word your mama taught me. She was painting my picture, and I was holding an apple, and she taught me how to say it. She said saying it in Italian would put me in the mood to be painted." She smiled at the memory.

"Did you eat the apple?"

Eden laughed. "No." She set the apple slices in front of Bronte then sat at the table with her. "I just held it." She watched as Bronte ate an apple slice. "Are you finished drawing for now?"

"Mmhmm," she nodded and chewed her apple.

"Well, then you need to pick everything up off the floor so we don't step on anything. Then, if you'd like, you can get out your toys and play for a while.'

"Can I watch a movie?"

"Oh, I think we should save the movies for after dinner. We could go outside and play. You have to put on some outside clothes, though."

A knock on the door interrupted the negotiations.

Nora poked her head inside. "Good morning!"

"Good morning, come in. We're just negotiating entertainment options."

"I want a movie," said Bronte.

"But a movie is not an option right now," answered Eden as Bronte pouted.

"I know," said Nora. "The kids are in the music tent singing. They will be having lunch in a little while too."

Bronte perked up. "Can I have chocolate?"

"I'm sure there will be chocolate and maybe even some *cornetto* with all kinds of other good things." She knew Bronte loved the croissants with all the sweet fillings. "How about if I take you to join them."

Bronte thought about her options. "Is Nikki still here?"

"Yes," Nora assured her. "She likes singing too, and I'll bet she even likes cornetto."

Bronte ignored the mention of singing. "Do they have the chocolate ones?"

"The only way to know for sure is to go and check with the cook," said Nora.

Bronte turned to her mommy, eyes wide with expectation. "Can I go?"

Eden laughed. "Sure, but you have to change out of your pajama's first."

"Okay!" Bronte jumped down from the table and ran toward the bedroom.

"Choices are on the bed! Let me know if you need help!"

"I can do it!" Bronte yelled back.

"She dresses herself?" asked Nora a bit surprised.

"It's hit and miss," said Eden. "Some days, she does it all on her own, others it's a cry-fest." Eden smiled at Nora's impressed face. "It's worse when I don't lay clothes out. Then who knows what she'll leave the house in. Her choices are interesting, to say the least. One day, she ended up leaving the house in a t-shirt that was too small and a tutu. At least I convinced her to wear shorts with the outfit. I sent a change of clothes, just in case, but she wore it all day and was a hit at day school. Julia picked her up that day, and I think she was offended by the outfit." Eden couldn't help but laugh at the memory. It still made her sad they may never be able to have Julia in their lives again. Bronte missed her.

Nora joined her laughter as she sat at the kitchen table. "I guess you're wondering why I'm here." She saw Eden steel herself for bad news. "I think you should go talk with Rafe today." The look of surprise on Eden's face made Nora smile. "I know for a fact she's going down to the secret garden to draw, and she only had coffee for breakfast. Gabri told her to take the day off since the only things left to do is break down the food tent and the last music tent later today. We have plenty of help and don't really need her to be there."

"Does she want to talk?" Eden asked hesitantly.

"I think she'd be open to you. She was doing really well last night and this morning. She watches you and Bronte all the time," she revealed. "You did the right thing by staying and giving her a chance to get through everything."

"I need help!" Bronte made her way into the room with her shirt half on and an arm in the wrong hole.

Eden quickly helped before Bronte's frustration had turned to tears. "There you go. Now, get the brush and the detangling spray, and I'll give you a pony. It's on the bed." She turned back to Nora as Bronte ran on her errand. "I don't want to do anything wrong. I don't want to upset Rafe or Gabri."

"Don't worry about Gabri," said Nora with a wave of her hand. "You just worry about showing Rafe you're still here and you love her. She needs you, Eden."

Eden blushed at the sincerity of Nora's words. "I need her too."

"So, you go talk with Rafe, and I'll take Bronte up for breakfast with the kids. I'll even leave the golf cart so you can get over there earlier. I've got the energy to spare this morning, and it feels like a great day for a walk."

Bronte burst into the room with the hair supplies. After Eden gave her a ponytail and helped her with her shoes, Bronte ran up the path toward the breakfast tent with Nora following at a swift waddle. Once they were gone, Eden went back to the couch and made sure the letter Rafe's mother wrote was safely folded and put away.

32

AN UNDERCURRENT OF anxiety and excitement charged through Eden Kingsley giving her nerves a tingle. She rushed getting dressed to take advantage of the opportunity that Nora had provided to see Rafe. She put her hair up in a loose ponytail and threw on a lightweight shark-bite dress she could wear with her slip-on sandals. She emptied her makeup bag and decided to go with only lip gloss so she could get out the door faster. Stepping outside, Eden laughed when she found Nora had included a picnic basket in the golf cart, complete with a blanket.

"She really is working for us," she said to herself. Gratitude filled Eden, and she hoped she could think of a way to repay Nora's kindness.

After a bumpy ride in the golf cart, Eden made it to the head of the path leading to Rafe. It was tricky to locate the path, but as soon as she discovered Rafe's golf cart, she knew she had taken the right turn. She parked her golf cart next to the one Rafe had used. Carrying the basket and blanket, Eden was glad she wouldn't have far to go. Focusing on following the subtle walking path helped keep Eden from being nervous about showing up unannounced.

The path opened up to a lush grassy clearing, and Eden found Rafe sitting on the bench with a notebook in her lap. It looked as if Rafe was waiting. *Of course, she's waiting*, thought Eden. She *could probably hear me crashing through the woods.*

"Hi," said Eden as she approached. She sat the basket and blanket beside the bench relieved to be free of the weight.

Rafe nodded but didn't return the greeting. She watched as Eden sat down beside her and wondered why she was there. For the last few days, Rafe worried Eden would want to talk, and she was afraid it would be to say goodbye. By avoiding Eden and spending as much time as she could with Bronte, fearing each moment may be the last, Rafe hoped to spare herself more heartache.

"Nora said you were here and sent a food basket with me," Eden explained.

"I see," said Rafe. Now she understood. Nora had talked with Rafe last night about Eden, and now Nora was 'helping.' Rafe watched as Eden fidgeted nervously. "I hope she didn't make you carry your basket all the way down here."

"Oh, no," said Eden with a nervous smile. "She let me have a golf cart. It looks like a parking lot at the start of the walking trail."

Rafe laughed softly. "We may have to change the name from secret garden to hidden garden."

"Or to the little park in the woods."

They sat in silence for a moment.

Eden looked down at the basket. "Let's see what Nora sent," she said suddenly. "Why don't you spread out the blanket?"

Together, they arranged the picnic lunch Nora had sent. Nora loaded the basket with pastries, fruit, cheese and even a few savory sandwich selections with pancetta and prosciutto. Eden found not only wine but a bottle of prosecco and real dishes inside the basket. Now Eden knew why the basket was so heavy.

Eden slipped off her shoes and sat on the blanket next to the basket. She pulled out the plates and glasses while Rafe opened containers and poured the wine. When everything was ready, they filled their plates and took a moment to enjoy the bounty provided by Nora.

"Nora went all out," Eden said, unable to hide the humor in her tone.

Rafe popped a piece of savory pastry in her mouth then licked her fingers. "She probably just told the chef to make a basket. They go over the top for her all the time because she's so bossy," Rafe teased.

Eden chuckled, but she believed Rafe. Over the last few days, she got to see Nora in action. She admired the way Nora handled everything from kids with skinned knees to directing volunteers. Eden also noticed how Nora and Rafe made a good team.

"I'm glad you're doing better," said Eden. It was good to see Rafe working on projects again. It was rare that Rafe was idle, and Eden knew keeping busy was something that made Rafe happy.

"I guess you're here to have the conversation we never finished," said Rafe, wondering if the conversation would end with Eden going back to America.

"Only if you're ready. I have some questions."

Rafe nodded. She wasn't sure she was ready but knew she couldn't avoid Eden forever. She did not want to avoid Eden. She just didn't want to be out of control around her. "Okay, what do you want to know?"

Eden put her fork down and dug deep to calm herself. "Well, are we, you know, are we going to be okay?"

"I hope so."

"Me too." Eden took a chance and put her hand on top of Rafe's.

"You mean... you're staying?" Rafe asked cautiously.

"Yeah." Eden nodded. "I'm staying. I've not thought once about leaving. Not until you come with me anyway."

Rafe closed her eyes and rubbed her hand over her face. "Thank you," she said softly.

"I love you, Rafe. I know we have a lot of things to work out, but I believe you when you say you hope we'll be okay. It's what I want more than anything."

"I'm sorry I didn't tell you how sick I still was when you came to see me."

"It's okay," Eden assured her. "You never have to apologize for being sick. Gabri tried to tell me, but I wanted to be with you so badly that I didn't want to believe him. I guess I thought once you knew I still loved you and saw Bronte, you would want to come home. I thought I could take you home and help you, but now I know it was a mistake. I know this is where you need to be. I get it now."

Determination showed in Eden's face and body language. Rafe wished they could just hang on and stay in the moment, but she knew Eden had questions and she deserved answers. She could only hope the answers didn't make Eden change her mind.

"What else did you want to ask?" Rafe dreaded the questions to come. She fumbled a bit as she put more food on her plate.

"Well, you're still talking about betraying everyone," Eden began. "I guess I still don't understand why you think that. I know you still have... we have, secrets, but I don't see betrayal. I see you trying to cope with a lot of loss."

"You just don't know everything involved, the history of it all. I've betrayed everyone."

"Tell me then," said Eden. "I want to be here for you and help you. I want you to feel like you can tell me anything and know I'll be here."

"We're starting over, right?"

"Yeah," Eden confirmed softly. "I'll always be here to help you."

It was hard to figure out where to start because the history was so long. It was difficult for Rafe, after so many years of keeping her illness a secret, to go against her father's directives and allow others to know about everything. She understood his reasons for encouraging her to make an exception for Eden before he died, but it didn't make the task easier to follow through. Rafe knew what she had to do, and it terrified her. "I'm not like my father," she said, her voice low and heavy.

Eden shook her head in confusion. "Like your father?"

"Everyone here," she said motioning around her with her hand. "Everyone he knew in Italy thought he was a great man— even Gabri."

"I know," said Eden.

Rafe let her lips slip into a slight smile. She was glad Eden agreed. Her smile faded quickly. "If he did something to upset people here," she explained, "he only had to make some kind of offering or restitution, and all was forgotten. He paid for education, funerals, provided jobs, invested in land and businesses—in people, the community and even the church. Those are the things they remember about him here."

After refilling the wine glasses, Rafe continued. "In America, nothing he did mattered. Americans are so quick to offer forgiveness but never follow through. Did you know only one person ever mentioned my father's contributions to the arts to me? It was Clarice Biggalow, my boss at the Conservatory. Her mention of him was one of the main reasons I took the job there. The only thing anyone else who knew my father in America remembered were things that made them angry. They didn't like his attitude or the fact he got the better end of a lot of business deals. I heard them whispering how glad they were he was dead. Even Ian Hawthorn hated him and shut him out. Neither he nor

Julia came to his funeral. I thought they would at least come to support me. They didn't come, though, and then you..." she shook her head unable to finish the train of thought. "They all made business personal. When Papa understood there were hard feelings, he tried to get their forgiveness, by donating or doing something good for his workers or the community. Instead of forgiving him, they said he was trying to pay people off. Their forgiveness was never given like it was here in Italy. I didn't understand for a long time why there was such a difference. Then I realized, no one really knew what forgiveness was and, even if they did, it was impossible for anyone to give. Maybe because Italy has practiced a certain type of forgiveness longer than America that it seems to work here. Underneath, even in Italy, forgiveness is just a concept no one actually comprehends." The frown on Eden's face told Rafe she didn't understand and probably never would. "Do you know what finally made me understand forgiveness was a lie?"

Eden shook her head, almost afraid to speak. "No."

"It was when I realized everyone who wanted forgiveness had to pay for it. Not always with money, but in some way, it was always paid for. I recognized there's no reason to waste time or money on a faulty concept. So I don't. For my father, I think it was a habit. One I could never fall into. One I was determined not to fall into and let it be used to hurt me."

"Not everyone feels that way about forgiveness," said Eden.

"I'm not like you and the others," Rafe interrupted. "I won't be caught in that trap that creates another lie and more secrets."

"But if we can't forgive, what do we do?" asked Eden.

"We just have to apologize and live every day remembering to prove our apology was sincere. When we accept an apology, we have to prove we accepted it by not hurting or punishing each other with the things that were already apologized for. We can't forgive and forget, and we shouldn't. We should remember what we are apologizing for and remember what things we've accepted apologies for too. Then learn from what happened and try to not repeat our mistakes. It only works, though, if you can keep the promise made when the apologies are extended and accepted."

Eden burned to argue and share her thoughts on forgiveness. She was taught it was important to be able to forgive. Forgiveness was not a bribe or something to be considered secularly. It was an internal process, a private spiritual experience between two people that can be healing when bestowed and received. Even her therapist discussed how important forgiveness was in having a healthy outlook and relationships. Instead, she held back her opinion knowing this was not the time or place. Right now, she just needed Rafe to feel safe. Safe. There was that word again. She wondered if Rafe had ever felt safe with her. She had been worried all this time about her own safety and had never given a thought to Rafe's need to feel safe too.

Adjusting her skirt, Eden lifted to her knees so she could face Rafe, determined to give Rafe the apology she seemed to be asking for even though she felt like she had already been apologizing for everything. She bowed her head for a moment then looked directly into Rafe's gray-blue eyes.

"I realize I've caused you a lot of heartache and pain. I've caused it for both of us, and Bronte too. I know I've made a lot of bad decisions. I've hurt you. I didn't know how much at times because on all my—" She waved her free hand to her head, "I don't know—craziness. I just kept getting stuck, and I couldn't find my way. I'm not stuck anymore. I know I belong with you no matter where we live. I just want to be with you. Be happy. Together. I hope you can accept my apology. I'm not perfect but—" Eden started to take a breath to continue as Rafe began to laugh softly. "What? I'm not finished. Am I doing it wrong?"

"No," said Rafe as she smiled up at Eden. "You're not doing anything wrong." She sat her glass down and took Eden's other hand. "You're not the one who needs to apologize. You've already apologized, and I already accepted and know you mean it. I'm the one who needs to apologize."

"You? What for? I'm the one who left. I'm the one who made it so the Stewards could infiltrate our life. I'm the one..."

"Stop," Rafe interrupted. "I know what happened. I know what we both did wrong."

Eden felt Rafe's hands begin to shake. She watched as Rafe's jaw clenched and her body began to visibly shake as her pallor faded into a fear gray. Worry surged through Eden. "Are you okay? You don't have to do this now."

"No- No, I do," said Rafe, her voice shaking. It wasn't just an apology she had to give to Eden. She had to give her real trust too. The fear of Eden telling her secrets again, especially to Gabri, made her mouth dry. For so long, only her father and Gabri had held her trust. Gabri had never used what he knew against her... Her father may have by leaving out the painting in New York, but she was not sure of the real reason he had the painting of Maria displayed. Then there was what Eden had done...

Rafe worked to control her physical reaction to what she was about to do. Finally, she looked up at Eden. "I'm the one who owes the apology," she began. "I've never apologized for the things I've done... not listening to my father and telling you about my childhood trauma. Not giving you a chance when we first met to choose being in a relationship with someone... someone with my problems." Rafe was determined to do this right. To give Eden back the stolen opportunity to make a choice about being in a relationship. She wanted Eden to be armed with the truth and all the information she needed to make the decision. Even if it's too late, she knew Eden deserved to know the truth. "I have had PTSD for a long time. I didn't even understand for a long time what was wrong because I was so young. Then I was in control for so long, I didn't think it mattered anymore. I didn't understand why my papa had changed his mind and wanted me to tell you about my illness. So I was conflicted. But that doesn't matter now. Lately, though, as you and everyone else now know, things haven't been good. Right now, I'm not in control of much. My life is mostly controlled by Gabri and a bunch of lawyers.

"When we met, I didn't tell you because I was afraid I'd lose you, so I never trusted you with the truth. If I had trusted you, let you in, maybe you would have still loved me. But at the time, I didn't feel like I could take the risk. Because you didn't know, I couldn't get help when I didn't know I needed it. So my life fell apart because I lost control and did not trust anyone around me with the secret of my illness."

Eden could see how hard speaking about her past was for Rafe. It was so rare to see a tear on Rafe's face Eden could feel the empathy inside her wanting to cry with Rafe. Gabri said sometimes Rafe needed to cry so Eden didn't want to say or do anything to make her feel like she should stop.

"It's okay," she said softly.

"Let me... Let me get through this," said Rafe wiping her watery eyes. "I can't tell you I'll be better because the reality is... I will always have PTSD. I can only hope, with time and care, I'll get control of my life again. Right now, I gave Gabri control because I didn't feel like I had anyone else I could trust."

Eden understood the distrust and was unsure if Rafe was wrong. Eden had been controlled by the Stewards, Jake and then

Julia who stepped in and tried to take control of Rafe via Eden to make decisions about Rafe's medical care. If Rafe had put Eden in control, there was a good chance Julia could have influenced any decisions Eden made.

"Maybe you were right not to trust me. Look at how easy I was to control."

"No. If I had trusted you, then you would have known what to do and who to call if something happened. You would have known to call Gabri." Rafe licked her dry lips. "So, now, I want you to know the truth, and I want to give you my trust. I just hope you can accept my apology and will love me despite everything I've done to deceive you and hurt you."

Eden wasn't sure how to react. It was unexpected. Eden realized how important this was to Rafe. She wiped the tear from Rafe's face. "I think, if you'd have told me everything when we first met, I'd have made the same decision. I was in love with you... I still am. I'm not changing my mind if you think that might happen. I love you." She reached out and pulled Rafe into a hug and kissed her wet cheeks. It was so surreal to hold Rafe as she cried. Usually, it was the other way around. A burning desire to protect Rafe rushed over her. She never wanted to let her go.

33

WITH RELIEF AND gratitude flowing through her, Rafe Salvaggio pulled away from Eden. She grabbed a napkin and wiped the tears from her face. "Sorry for getting so emotional," she said hoarsely.

"I don't think I've ever seen you really cry," said Eden gently. "I think that may be one of the signs you really do trust me."

Rafe huffed out a short laugh. "Maybe. Or I'm just too tired and weak to control myself."

Eden smiled knowing Rafe was trying to control the narrative. "Well, I'm here for you whenever you're weak and tired." She refilled Rafe's glass and put more food on her plate passing it to her. "We'll get through everything together. You can tell me about your history whenever you're ready. We have time."

Rafe considered Eden's words and knew she was sincere. "I know there are things I don't remember," Rafe revealed softly, "but there are other things I'll never be able to forget." A bitter laugh escaped. "I always thought it was so strange the only secret I didn't keep was the one so many were living with. I told the world I was gay just to have one less secret to keep." She wiped her hand over her face then picked up her wine. After a couple of sips, she continued. "I worried for a long time that someone would figure out my secrets, especially my father."

Rafe's mouth had gone dry, so she forced herself to swallow and then wet her mouth again with wine. "Before I met you, I learned he knew. He knew all along who I was. He kept my secrets. Do you think he kept them because he loved me or because they were too terrible for others to know?" She could see Eden didn't have an answer. "I loved him," she said softly.

"I know," said Eden. She filled her mouth with a bite of food, doing her best to hold back her opinion of Ettore. She couldn't help wonder if she had talked about him in therapy and if the doctor saw the damage Ettore had caused Rafe. "He was protecting you," she finally managed. She wanted to believe it was true, for Rafe's sake.

Rafe set her plate aside unable to eat more. She leaned back against the bench and looked out over the secret garden. Eden was finally here and didn't realize it was the place Rafe used in her portrait so many years ago. She wanted to bring Eden so many times, but it never worked out for one reason or another. It used to be an escape from the world and was filled with fond memories of Rafe and Gabri working to clear it and then enjoying the fruits of their labor. Now it had turned into the confessional it was once used for in the past.

"Maria's kiss changed my life," Rafe confessed. "After she kissed me, I had to find out more. It was a challenge I couldn't resist. I haven't resisted it from that day. I know who I was then, and I know who I am now. I only wish I knew then how much I would lose by keeping secrets. It all seemed to happen so fast. It was hard to think back then, and it's been hard again over the past few years. Sometimes they all come back to haunt me."

The image of Brettito and the last smile he ever had for her floated before Rafe's eyes. "After Brettito, when I was able to leave the house again, I couldn't find Maria," she said remembering the desperation she had felt at the time. "I couldn't find any of them. My mother and my friend were dead, Maria had disappeared, and I was alone in my grief for them all. They were all gone, and I never got to say goodbye. My world was not a good one," she said her voice cracking. "I created that world, though I didn't understand at the time."

Eden wiped her hand over her eyes willing herself to keep herself together and not let her emotions take control. "You think all of those things happened because you're gay?"

"No, no," said Rafe, "because of my pride. My selfishness," she explained. "Can't you see it now?"

"Your pride? No, Rafe, I don't understand."

In frustration, Rafe ran her hands through her hair and gripped it tightly. Pressing her fists against her head, she fought to focus her mind. She knew the only way to be sure of anything was to make Eden understand. "My father was right," she choked out. "It's always been about me and what I want. I wanted Maria, and they all died. I wanted to keep my secrets, and you almost died." She let out a manic laugh. "I believed Jake," she revealed. "I believed him because of my own pride," she said with watery eyes. "Just another way I betrayed you, another reason you may never trust me again."

Eden shook her head in denial of Rafe's words. She knew what Jake was almost the whole time. Rafe did not. "I can't blame you for believing him over me," said Eden. "That's completely my fault. You did everything right. You are trustworthy, Rafe. If I'd have remembered you were, and told you everything I was hiding, things would have been so very different. You had no reason not to believe him. I'm the one who betrayed you, who lost faith in you, who lost myself and handled everything so selfishly. I'm sorry. Please, don't—"

Rafe laughed, cutting off Eden's words of remorse. She laughed because Eden believed the things she was saying. That anything she did was the source of the chaos that had followed Rafe for her entire life. Rafe knew Eden was not at fault. The fault was her own pride and unwillingness to share, and her audacity to take what and who she wanted—from Maria all the way to Eden.

"Jake knew a lot about me," said Rafe. She wondered how much she should divulge about her visits with Jake, especially the one in the hospital.

"I'm sorry," whispered Eden. Rafe's comment felt like an accusation. Jake had used the things she confided to hurt Rafe. She did not know if the guilt for her actions would ever go away.

"He even knew about some of the things I was keeping from you." The confusion on Eden's face confirmed Jake never told her what he knew. "The money. It's not even really mine."

"What do you mean?"

"It's my fathers," she revealed. "It's his money. Well, his and the Salvaggio family money. I'm the only one left now, except for Bronte." She scratched her head. "I guess that means you need to know about it."

"I love you, not your money."

"But I come with the money. Do you want to know how much?"

Eden groaned. She really didn't care how much. She felt trapped. If she asked, she could be accused of being greedy, and if she didn't ask she could be accused of not accepting all of Rafe. It was strange and frustrating at the same time. "I'm guessing it's millions. Ettore was a smart businessman," she said hoping to talk more about Ettore than the money.

Rafe blew out a short laugh. "Billions," she whispered. "He was a great businessman."

"B—," she started, but Eden couldn't say the word. Rafe nodded, encouraging her. "Billions?"

"Not all in cash," she explained. "Investments, real estate, and other things. He liked to diversify. It was always his lecture to Gabri and me. Diversify and be innovative."

Eden's mouth gaped open, but she closed it as soon as she realized. She didn't know why she was so surprised. Rafe had always had money, so had her father. Eden just never understood how much Ettore Salvaggio was worth. Eden wrinkled her brow. She wondered if she ever really knew how much money Rafe made with her business. Rafe tried to get her to take care of the finances, but at the time, she was dealing with hormones and anxiety. Money was never something she worried about until later when she felt she needed her autonomy. Now that she had that autonomy, how much money Rafe had mattered even less. Eden wanted Rafe because she loved her, not her money.

Rafe watched as Eden drained her wine glass and wrapped her mind around the implications of what having so much money might mean. "I'm going to put some aside for Gabri's son."

"Money?"

"Yes. I want to make sure he has the same opportunities as Bronte."

"I think that's a very sweet idea. Nora and Gabri will appreciate it too."

Rafe nodded, glad Eden agreed. "There's something else," said Rafe. "A secret I don't think I can keep."

Eden looked over at Rafe in surprise. Another secret. She wondered how many more Rafe had. "Do you want to tell me?" she asked cautiously.

"I have to tell you."

"You can tell Gabri."

"No. Well, yes... It's kind of about him... and Bronte."

Eden sat up in concern. Crazy thoughts flashed through her mind. Thoughts like, did Gabri have something bad in his family history that could affect Bronte? Were Rafe and Gabri going to fight her for custody? Or was it something worse she couldn't think of? "What is it?" She did her best to hide her anxiety.

"In my dreams," Rafe began, "I sometimes see Bronte with her hands bound in shackles. I think it's because I'm keeping a secret. We all are." She saw the concern wash over Eden's face. "I can't keep the fact that Gabri is her father a secret," she revealed. "Especially now that Gabri's son will be here soon. He'll be her half-brother. I need her to know who her family is," she said as Eden just stared at her. "Gabri and I were only children, and it's lonely. Knowing she's not alone could be good for her. We haven't talked about more children, and right now, it's not even on the table. I just... I just think telling her will help me too. It's one less thing I have to work so hard keeping a secret."

Eden opened her mouth to speak then closed it. She was stunned. It definitely wasn't what she expected to hear. "I think," she began cautiously, "I think telling her is okay. I think, when she's old enough and starts asking questions, we should tell her the truth."

"Are you sure?" asked Rafe, surprised that Eden agreed so easily. "I'll understand if you need more time to think about it."

"I'm sure," said Eden as she nodded. "If Bronte knowing that Gabri is her father will help you, then it's something I can get on board with." She hesitated, hoping she was making the right decision. "I admit I worry about how confusing things might become. I mean, we never planned or talked about having Gabri in her life other than as a family friend. You're right, though. It is important that she knows, especially since we're living here now. She loves Gabri and will know the baby, so it makes sense," she said, trying to convince herself everything would be fine. Gabri said he would make it hard for her if she hadn't agreed to his terms. She wondered if he knew about Rafe wanting to tell Bronte about him. "Does Gabri know?"

"No," answered Rafe with a shake of her head. "I wanted to ask you first. I thought it could be a nice surprise for him if you agreed."

Eden couldn't think of a good reason not to tell Bronte the truth except for her own anxieties and fears. "Well then, when she's ready... we'll tell her."

Relief flowed through Rafe. She took Eden's hand and squeezed it. "Thank you."

34

BREAKING CONTACT GENTLY, Eden Kingsley moved away from Rafe and busied herself with putting dishes and food back inside the picnic basket. The mood was still heavy, and she wanted to find a more positive line of conversation. She didn't want to push Rafe like she had the other night, sending her into a tailspin. She wanted to be a support to Rafe and not be the detriment Gabri worried she would be. Eden understood that she had to be there for Rafe just like Rafe had been there for her all these years. She saw the way Rafe relaxed her body in relief when she agreed not to keep Gabri a secret from Bronte. She wanted Rafe to stay relaxed and feel she had control in her life again.

Moving aside the apples in the picnic basket, Eden pulled out the bottle of prosecco that was wrapped in a cold towel. She held the bottle out to Rafe. "Can you open this? We should probably drink it while it's still a little chilled."

"Sure." Rafe took the bottle and then unwrapped the towel from the bottle using it to guard the cork as she unbound the cage then twisted the bottle until the cork eased out with a soft pop. Eden had already pulled the champagne glasses from their place in the basket and was holding them out for Rafe to fill. Propping the bottle against the basket, Rafe took her glass and tipped it toward Eden. "*Cent' anni,*" she said their glasses making a sharp clink as they came together.

They sipped the sweet prosecco and Eden smiled at Rafe. "I thought you'd say '*salud.*' I know it means health. What was your toast?"

"Did you come for private language lessons?" asked Rafe with a wink.

"I don't think I need language lessons to get my message to you," said Eden with an arch of her brow. "Tell me what you said. I may want to use it."

Rafe chuckled. "It just means 'hundred years,'" she explained. "It's a short version of '*cento di questi giorni*' which means 'may you have a hundred years of these days.'"

Hope filled Eden that Rafe felt today was a good day. "I like it... I hope we have a hundred years of good days like this too." She sipped from her glass as she watched Rafe. She couldn't help looking at her lips and wanting to be close to her again. She pulled herself out of the daydream and looked out at the garden. "Maybe I should pose for you," she said wistfully. "I mean, you have your paper and pencil. Plus, we're in the garden you've painted me in before. Maybe you can do a different angle."

"You recognize this place?" Rafe was surprised. She didn't think Eden had recognized the garden.

"Last time I was here, I thought it looked familiar. Then I realized I recognized the little chapel from the painting." She smiled slyly. "So, is this paradise?"

Rafe was so pleased she couldn't hide her smile. "Yes, this is paradise. I'm glad you found it."

"Me too," said Eden. She reached in the basket and grabbed an apple. Standing, she placed herself in front of Rafe and then struck a pose similar to the one Rafe had painted her in years ago. "Is this how you want me?"

The image of Eden in front of Rafe brought back feelings and memories of when they first met. She wondered if it was Eden's plan. With an artist's eye, Rafe studied Eden. Her feet were bare in the soft green grass. The dress she wore was summer white and draped down with points that hit her mid-calf then zigged up to an opposite point at her thigh then zagged down again. Rafe liked the way it showed off Eden's toned legs. The dress gathered at Eden's waist, and pleats ran up, forming a loosely fitted top held with thin straps over her shoulders. Taking her hand off her hip, Eden reached up and pulled the tie from her hair and then used her fingers to comb it out. Her hair was shorter than the first time Rafe had painted her. Her skin was the same. Sun-kissed and glowing. Her lips were still perfect too.

Eden shined the apple on her dress then waited, holding out the shining deep red apple in offering. Rafe stood quickly, and Eden stayed still in anticipation. She could feel Rafe's gaze taking her in and couldn't wait to feel her gentle touch as she directed her pose.

Rafe stepped closer. Their eyes met.

Rafe could see the welcoming light in Eden's hazel eyes. The light she felt had been lost to her for so long. Memories flashed through her mind of fighting her dark dreams, of things that had happened, of things people had said that pulled and pushed them apart. She wanted so desperately for the hurt and anger, stirred by the dark chaos of all the secrets and lies haunting her life, to be locked away and buried. She knew, though, that now it would never be a possibility. Eden knew everything, and Rafe had agreed not to keep her past or her illness a secret. She promised to trust Eden.

Being together couldn't be the result of manipulation or seduction. It had to be a controlled choice by them both. This was starting over, and Rafe knew, for herself, if they chose to move forward, the level of intimacy and love would rival anything she had known or shared with anyone in her life. Eden was the only woman Rafe had revealed not only her troubled past but the weaknesses that made her the most vulnerable. At this moment, Eden would finally be privy not only to the depths of pain and guilt in her life but also the true depth of love Rafe could feel when freed from the shackles of her secrets.

Rafe grasped Eden's wrist, pulling her hand and the apple close then took a bite of the apple.

"What are you doing?" Eden asked with a laugh.

Rafe sucked in the juice of the apple, chewing slowly as she gave Eden an easy smile. She swallowed then licked her lips. "What I wanted to do the first time you posed like this for me," she answered still holding Eden's wrist. She pulled again, and the apple fell out of Eden's hand dropping to the ground forgotten. Rafe slipped her other hand around Eden's waist and held her close. Leaning her head against Eden's, lowering her face to capture those perfect lips she had been missing, she kissed Eden gently. "I couldn't resist," she purred.

Eden slid her arms around Rafe's neck. "You've been doing really well at resisting me," she said softly with a slight pout. Rafe kissed her again and ran her hand down her back. "I don't know how much more of your resisting I can take."

Rafe laughed softly wanting to kiss Eden's pout away. "I don't want to resist you anymore. If I start resisting you again, call my doctor," she said breathlessly, "because it means I really am sick again."

Eden pulled Rafe's face close to taste her lips again. Sharing the taste of the sweet apple on Rafe's lips and feeling her body pressed against her as she ran her hands running through her dark hair fanned the flame that had been impatiently awaiting this moment.

As Rafe's warm hands ran over her body, Eden became aware of the fact her dress was now loose. Rafe had pulled down the zipper and was gently pulling the top of the dress forward. Eden's hands went to her chest protectively. The unexpected exposure shocked her. She wasn't expecting anything to happen out in the open. She thought they would go to the cottage where it was private. Blushing, Eden remembered just a few days ago when she had tried to unbutton Rafe's shirt. Then she was desperate, thoughtless, and frantic. Now everything was different. She looked up into Rafe's eyes and saw the questions they asked. Rafe was asking if she trusted her. Rafe wasn't desperate or frantic, she was thoughtful and loving. Rafe was asking if they could make love at this moment.

Slowly, Eden reached out and touched Rafe's shirt. She ran her hands over the buttons and then answered Rafe's question by opening the first button. She had been afraid for so long that Rafe would never give her this trust or this chance again to show her how much she loved her. Her hands shook as she continued to unbutton Rafe's shirt.

When Eden finished unbuttoning her shirt, Rafe wrapped her arms around her, pulled her close and kissed her. She finished unzipping Eden's dress, pushing the top down her arms until the dress hung loosely at Eden's hips.

The familiar feeling of Eden's skin under her hands made Rafe's mind reel. The sensation was the same, but she knew, this time, the difference was that the trust was mutual between them, and they were both aware of what was being given.

Eden felt her dress slide down her legs. Looking down, she saw the stark white glow against the green of the grass. Stepping out of the material, Eden followed Rafe as she pulled her down onto the blanket. She felt Rafe's hands touching her nearly naked body intimately again for the first time in so long. Her skin tingled as the flame inside her grew with each kiss and stroke from Rafe's warm hands. Eden reached out, wanting to feel Rafe's body, but was pressed back onto the blanket. Rafe moved her hands down Eden's thighs following each touch with a sensual kiss as she moved to her calf and then to her ankle. Tenderly, Rafe kissed Eden's foot. From there, Eden felt Rafe methodically using her tongue and kisses to baptize Eden's entire body. Eden couldn't help the feeling that Rafe was symbolically washing away the mistakes of the past and creating a new beginning at the same time. She felt what her heart told her was Rafe's forgiveness even though she knew Rafe would deny it was forgiveness.

Rafe explored and reclaimed what Eden willingly offered. With her hands and fingertips, kneading Eden's skin and muscles, Rafe left the echo of her touch, her scent, and her prints as proof Eden belonged to Rafe again. Eden could feel the love Rafe was giving and the ache in her soul to give it back and surrender herself completely. Eden's every muscle and nerve were alight from the sensations caused by Rafe's assertion of her claim over her body. Her body had never been touched so thoroughly or aggressively, and as Rafe made her way to the hollow of her neck and kissed her there, Eden closed her eyes, her heart racing from Rafe's attention. As Rafe touched her, she recognized the rising heat in Rafe's hands, and the tenderness she had longed for was being shown to her once again.

It didn't matter that they were outside in a secret garden in Italy that Rafe called Paradise. It only mattered that Rafe knew Eden was willing to give anything to have their life back. She thought that meant waiting for Rafe to be ready for sex, but now she knew it meant being willing to evolve into the woman and partner Rafe needed, that they both needed, to handle the rest of their lives together.

Eden understood now that she could no longer be just a bystander who let life drag her along and depended on others, especially Rafe, to take control. She needed to be in control sometimes too. She needed to stand up for Rafe and be her champion. She also knew now that she could give up control without giving up herself. Right now, she knew Rafe felt out of control in her life, and that feeling of control was something she could give to Rafe like no one else could. It all came down to trust. Not just the trust she gave to Rafe, but the trust she gave herself that had been so hard to find because of the self-doubt and anxieties that led her away from Rafe. So many months of living without Rafe and dealing with her own inner demons had made her stronger and more aware of what was truly important. Family. Love. Rafe.

Pushing the shirt from Rafe's shoulders, Eden knew she didn't have to hold back her desire anymore. In a frenzy, Eden fell on Rafe and crashed into her lips. Her mind felt light as waves of dizziness washed over her. Thoughts, doubts, worries were all pulled away as the tsunami of desire devastated the walls they had built, all inhibitions lost as their remaining clothes were shed. Eden pulled Rafe closer, needing to satisfy her craving. Taking control, she slid between Rafe's legs. She felt Rafe's warm hands on her ass and the slight lift of her hips in acceptance. Feeling her body against Rafe's lissome form was like finding home again. Rafe knew her, knew her body the same as she knew Rafe's. The connection between them was one no other lover could replicate. Unable—unwilling to stop herself, Eden let instinct take over.

Rafe had felt a confusing intensity when she looked into Eden's golden eyes. The feeling was invasive, causing a feeling of vulnerability at the same time. Then, as Eden crashed her kiss into her lips, she knew what she had seen. She had suddenly glimpsed that part of Eden she thought she had lost forever. It was the light that had appeared to glow inside Eden the first time they made love. The light Rafe thought had died. It was something Rafe never thought would return—the part Eden had been holding back. The part of Eden that had disappeared long ago before she left the house the first time. Before the accusations, punishments, and pain. Rafe could never pinpoint when that light had left Eden's eyes. She was certain it was sometime after the excitement of making a family but before all the uncertainty and anger that overtook Eden. Rafe had been waiting for that part of Eden to look upon her again with desire and love. Eden had tried to hide the truth that the light was gone by using that primal, instinctual savant to convince Rafe that the passionate soul inside Eden that knew no limits to the love it doled out to a lucky few was still burning for her. But no matter how much Eden wanted Rafe to believe that light was still there when they made love, she knew it was gone. No matter how much of a savant Eden was when it came to causing Rafe's body to feel pleasure in the end, it was just sex—not making love.

Under the leaf-filtered sunlight, sent down by the goddess of love, Rafe found her again. Eden's hair and skin glowed in the golden light as it poured over her and burned from her eyes. Rafe had found the love she had lost in the woman she would finally have a second chance to love.

"*La mia luce dorata*," she whispered. This time, there would be no secrets separating them, no doubts or fear. Their love had survived the labyrinthine path that led them to this moment. Rafe surrendered to the light, and the primal passion Eden was bestowing. Her heart finally filled with the knowledge that they would be together forever and the awareness their affection would again be defined as making love.

Eden had trailed her hand down Rafe's body and between her legs where she found the dizzying measure of how much Rafe wanted her. "You feel so good," she moaned in appreciation. The sensation stirred her desire, making her head spin as she ran her fingers over Rafe's soft hairs teasing and titillating her. She could feel the warm dripping wetness flowing from herself as she moved against Rafe's clit. Eden could tell Rafe's body was aching for release just as much as hers. The words Rafe moaned sent tingling waves down Eden's body straight to her clit. She knew it wouldn't take a lot more than those words for Rafe to make her come. It never really did when it was Rafe. Rafe pressed her hips up, demanding, pleading for Eden not to stop. She fought to hold on as they found their rhythm, the susurration of skin against skin mingled with their heavy breathing. Eden knew Rafe was close. Rafe pushed her hips up and pulled Eden's head down into a deep hot kiss as her body shook with release. The flood of warmth set

Eden off, and she burst with a deep guttural sound escaping her throat.

For a moment, they lay against each other, breathing heavily, neither wanting to move and break the connection. Their earlier desperation had morphed into a languid easy undulation against each other as they kissed. With a firm embrace, Rafe overturned Eden, pressing her against the blanket and kissing her gently.

Eden pushed Rafe's dark curls from her face, running her hands through them. She smiled as Rafe's expressive gray-blue eyes looked down on her. Right now, they said, 'I desire you.' They also sparked with the love Eden had been fighting to get back for so long. Her throat tightened preparing to utter words of love, but before she could speak, Rafe began moving her kisses down.

Rafe trailed her kisses over Eden's breast, claiming the texture and taste as her own again. She made her way down, trying not to hurry through the anticipation of tasting Eden. Rafe's first sweet taste made Eden cry out, curl forward, and reach down to hold Rafe's head in place. Rafe waited, her breath flowing over Eden until she could feel Eden calm and relax. Dipping her head, Rafe slid her tongue over Eden again. As Eden continued to hold on loosely to her head, Rafe claimed what was hers.

Soon, Eden relaxed enough to lay back again letting Rafe have her way. She knew Eden was now very sensitive, so she gently sucked and licked, careful not to spend too much time on the swollen and sensitive clit. Eden began to squirm. Rafe slipped her tongue inside her with a swirl. She flattened her tongue against her, trailing a long lick up through her and over her clit. Eden grasped the soft green grass as she cried out. Rafe grinned as Eden's hips rose and she could see the need trickle out of her.

Eden felt Rafe's fingers scoop up the fluid between her legs as she lubricated them. She knew what was coming and the thought of Rafe's long fingers inside her made her spill out more for Rafe. Opening her legs, Eden pushed her hips up in anticipation as Rafe's finger slid into her and got closer to where she needed them.

Rafe kissed Eden's clit then pushed her fingers into her and stroked her from top to bottom, teasing her with just the tip of her finger inside. Eden moaned in frustration and pushed herself up so Rafe could press deeper. Rafe stopped her fingers on Eden's clit and pressed into it and massaged it as Eden pushed down against her hand.

"In me," Eden whispered breathlessly.

Rafe heard her whisper, and she moved her fingers back through Eden, covering them with more of her slick essence. Gently sliding her fingers into Eden just a little at a time, she put a little more in with each stroke. Eden moved into Rafe's stokes wanting more of her inside her, and as Rafe continued her slow entrance, Eden broke out into a light sweat. Rafe dropped her head down, licking the salty liquid from Eden's body, creating multiple sensations to help Eden last.

Finally, Rafe's fingers were deep inside Eden, exploring and touching Eden's soft silky walls. Eden moaned in appreciation as they moved in unison. Rafe built up her speed, and Eden matched her as she stroked and filled her. Rafe found her undoing and beckoned it to come forth. She felt it swell and grow inside Eden. When it was finally at full attention, Rafe struck it and felt Eden's body shake as she arched and cried out at the sensation. Rafe quickened her pace now because Eden was approaching the edge. She put her tongue on Eden's sensitive nerves, circled it, and pressed into it as her fingers continued their rhythm inside her.

With every stroke, Eden knew she was growing closer. She could feel herself clenching onto Rafe as she moved in and out of her, striking deeper each time. Rafe's tongue flicked faster against her clit, and Eden didn't know which sensation would make her come first. Her senses inundated by the touches deep inside her body to the colors behind her eyes, Eden's breathing quickened. She felt the echo of Rafe's moan against her clit as those long fingers plunged in and curled.

The echo of her climax filled the garden as she spilled out onto Rafe, clenching and releasing her over and over. She quivered and reeled at the electric sensation still tingling through her body. Rafe didn't stop, and Eden felt the torrent gush out of her again and take with it all reason and thought. Her body throbbed under Rafe's control, and Eden couldn't even hear her own screams of pleasure or the calls of Rafe's name. She arched her back but couldn't move away from the excruciating pleasure.

Rafe held her. Rafe was in control. This was exactly what she wanted. What she needed. Rafe's swirling tongue stopped only to be replaced with a vortex of suction and tongue that pulled and pressed her clit at the same time. Rafe's fingers pushed up inside again, and the combination caused Eden to tremble uncontrollably. She knew Rafe wouldn't stop now. She didn't want her to stop. Her body surrendered to Rafe.

Eden shattered.

Slowly, gently, Rafe pulled out and away, then climbed up Eden's body, leaving only slight traces of saliva as she kissed Eden's trembling body. She kissed Eden's neck and jaw on her way to her ear and, finally, her lips.

When Eden was finally able to pull herself back together, the first thing she recognized was Rafe. Her love. Her lover. Her paradise.

Eden turned her head and quickly wiped away the tear that had formed. It was not a tear of sadness. It was a tear of euphoria because her soul was back in the place where it was meant to be and had been missing. Rafe slid her arm under her pulling her up still kissing and touching her and kissed away the next tear that fell.

"Are you okay?" Rafe whispered with concern.

Eden opened her eyes and reached out to touch Rafe's face. All the emotion and sensation that had taken over her mind and body made it impossible for her to speak. She pulled Rafe close and inhaled her scent, creating sparks running through her mind, waking all the reasons why she wanted her and needed her.

With adoration, Rafe set her eyes on Eden's flushed face. "You're so beautiful," she purred softly.

Eden recovered control of her body and pulled Rafe close with the last of her strength and kissed her hungrily, tasting herself on Rafe's lips. "I love you," breathed Eden and couldn't stop the tears. "I'm sorry. I'm just so happy to have this feeling back," she said as her body shook as she still felt the rapture of her orgasm. "I don't know how you do it."

"Well, you helped," said Rafe with an arch of her brow.

"No," Eden kissed her. "I don't know how to describe it. You do something, and it makes me feel helpless, but my soul can't be without it." She kissed Rafe again. "Then you make me feel so full of love, it spills out of me sometimes, and I can't help crying."

Rafe smiled and chuckled a bit. "It's just because you love me."

"I do. I'm so in love with you," she agreed vehemently and kissed Rafe deeply.

"I love you, Ede," Rafe whispered and returned her kisses passionately. Rafe looked deeply into Eden's golden-brown eyes marveling at the golden specks and the flame of light growing larger as she watched. "I'm glad I didn't resist."

"Me, too," whispered Eden and lost herself in their kiss again.

Soon, their kisses became gentle and loving again as they reaffirmed their connection and touched gently and lovingly. Eden fell asleep in Rafe's arms, both emotionally and physically exhausted. Rafe gently kissed Eden's eyelids and her face, watching as Eden moaned and sighed in her sleep. "I'm glad you decided to stay with me." For so long, Rafe had been afraid of jumping back into the fire and chaos of love that had led to so much pain. She had been sure confessing just how much she loved Eden would lead to more pain–or worse Eden's death. For the first time in a long time she felt like she was starting to get better and take back control of her life. She finally allowed herself to take the first step back into the love that her fears had led her to avoid. It was more than a step. It was more of a leap back into love. "I've jumped again," she confessed softly. She was relieved when only a calm warmth filled her. She pulled Eden closer and joined her in much-needed slumber.

For the first time in months, Rafe didn't dream. A cool breeze caressed her body, and mechanical music filled her ears. Opening her eyes with a frown, Rafe found that Eden was still sleeping in her arms. The mechanical music continued, and her mind came alert as she realized it was her phone. She had no idea how long they lay naked and exposed.

Sitting up, Rafe grabbed her phone off the bench. "Pronto."

"Rafe!" Gabri's voice came through the phone. "Where are you? The baby is coming! The doctor is on the way!"

Rafe jumped to her feet. "Now?"

"Now!" confirmed Gabri. "Hurry!"

"I'm on my way!" She hung up the phone as Eden sat up in confusion. "The baby's coming!" She began grabbing their clothes and quickly dressing.

"What?" Eden asked in puzzlement then snapped awake as she understood. "The baby!" She caught the clothes Rafe tossed her way and dressed quickly. She began gathering the basket and blanket.

"Leave it," said Rafe as she motioned for Eden to follow.

Eden stumbled through the woods after Rafe. "We can't go up there like this," she insisted. "Our clothes are a mess, and we probably smell like sex!"

Rafe laughed because it seemed like such a small, simple problem for a change. "We have time. We can stop at the cottage. The doctor is still on her way!"

They jumped in one of the golf carts and sped up the path toward the cottage where they could get ready to meet Gabri's son.

35

THE PAST THREE months had gone by quickly for Rafe Salvaggio. Gabri's son had been born happy and healthy. Bronte was in a preschool where she was learning Italian very quickly and making new friends. Rafe had called in some favors and was able to have better internet and phone lines run to the cottage so Eden could work remotely and video conference for her new job. Rafe was impressed that, within a few weeks, Eden had a great job with a company allowing her to work from Italy. It was a much better job than she had before, and it even paid more.

Rafe was so impressed with Eden, it inspired her to get in contact with her old company *Eroina Conservazione e Design* and, with Gabri's help and blessing, was in the process of buying back the name and taking on some special projects while they were in Italy.

Rafe's therapy continued to help her progress, and Eden being close to her at night and knowing she loved her was helping her more than anything else could.

Eden met with Rafe's therapist and, with Gabri's help, was doing everything she could to be part of Rafe's support system. She had even found a therapist for herself and worked with Dr. Cathcart to make the transition to a new doctor and felt particularly good about how things were going. She and Gabri had resolved their differences with the help of Nora and Rafe.

Now Eden felt like she was part of a bigger family again and was at ease with where she was and the people around her. She did miss all their friends in California, but she had been able to keep in touch and hoped there would be visits soon.

Eden was finally able to begin talking to Rafe about everything that had been happening over the last few years. She was so happy Katheryn, and the FBI had the group that targeted them on the run and got them on a watch list, so others would be less likely to be targeted the way they were.

Both Rafe and Eden now understood communication, no matter how hard, was the best defense against anything that might affect their relationship in the future.

It was a beautiful Saturday afternoon. The plan for the day was to spend time in the secret garden and have a day of getting out in the fresh air. Time just relaxing together had become important because Gabri and Nora would be leaving on tour soon and beginning a stressful time of travel and work.

Bronte was sitting next to Gabri on the park bench. She held the mandolin Gabri bought her while he played his guitar. Nora sat nearby on a blanket holding the baby. As Rafe and Eden stepped into the garden and approached, Nora smiled at what she saw. Eden was glowing and holding tightly to Rafe. Nora knew they must have made love before making their way to the garden. She looked over at Gabri and planned the same thing with him later.

Rafe and Eden sat down next to Nora to listen to Gabri and Bronte play. Nora offered Eden the baby. Eden took him, happy because she couldn't resist holding a baby.

Bronte noticed her mommy holding the baby and stopped playing to go look at him too. "I like Zen," she said and patted the baby's leg gently. At the moment, Bronte had shortened his name from Zenzo.

"He's beautiful, isn't he?" said Eden softly. "Do you want to hold him? Sit down," she said after Bronte nodded her head yes. When Bronte was sitting down, Eden put him in her lap.

Rafe moved to sit next to Gabri on the bench. She leaned against him as they watched Eden and Nora with their children. "Look at them," she said with a smile. "I think Cyprian the Fair has blessed us with love and beauty.

"They are beautiful," said Gabri, moved to tears that he forced not to appear. He regained control of himself and turned to Rafe. "I don't think I told you I am sorry for being wrong."

"Wrong?" Rafe said, looking at Gabri in confusion.

"Yes." Gabri nodded. "About Eden. I can see you're happier now that she's here, and you're doing much better."

Rafe smiled at Gabri. "She is my path into the light," she said and winked.

"And Nora is mine!" Gabri laughed at her reference to Cyprian the Fair also known as Venus the goddess of love. He took a deep breath and took in the good life they were now living. "We are very lucky to have received our true loves."

"We are," said Rafe and looked with wonder at the family they had created. "You're lucky Nora agreed to name your son after your father." There had been some very heated discussions about the baby's name.

"It's tradition," insisted Gabri. "The firstborn is named for his grandfather." He put down his guitar and leaned back on the bench to stretch his back.

"It's not *her* tradition," Rafe reminded him with a laugh. "Plus, you wanted to name him after St. George. I didn't know you were still influenced by our childhood games." Rafe remembered all the times they pretended to be St. George and fought dragons. She looked over at Gabri who was grinning.

"I got my way on his name too, but I'm not sure she knows." He chuckled because his son's name was Zenzo Joris De Angelis. Joris was another name for George.

"She knows," Rafe assured him joining his laugh. "I think she feels like it was a good compromise. Plus, now she has naming rights for the next baby."

"The next," Gabri choked and went a bit pale as Rafe laughed and clapped him on the back playfully.

After letting her mommy take Zenzo back, Bronte walked over and climbed up into Gabri's lap and hugged him. "I like your baby," she said happily. "Nora is his mama," she said and then looked to Rafe. "You're my mama."

"Right," said Rafe with amusement glancing at Gabri.

"That's my mommy," Bronte said pointing at Eden. She looked back at Gabri. "You're Zen's papa?"

"Yes," said Gabri. "Very good."

Bronte frowned and thought for a bit. "The baby doesn't have a mommy," she said with concern.

"No," said Gabri, "he just has a mama and a papa."

"But he needs a mommy," Bronte insisted.

"Well, his mama is his mommy too," Gabri explained.

"I don't have a papa," she said sadly with a dramatic frown.

Rafe and Gabri glanced at each other in surprise. Though it had been on Rafe's mind a lot, she and Gabri had not talked about what to say about this to Bronte. They never thought they would be living this close or that Bronte would ask questions so soon. The memory of Death holding Bronte and the golden shackles around her wrist flashed through her mind. She knew the golden shackles represented secrets, and now she knew what secret put the golden shackles on Bronte in her dreams. She and Eden had talked about telling Bronte. They agreed to tell her when she began asking questions. It seemed to Rafe that time had come. She knew she had to tell Bronte the truth about who her father was so it wouldn't be a secret between them anymore. Rafe looked over at Eden, who was holding the baby and talking to Nora, then back at Gabri. "I think we should just tell her the truth now since she's asking."

Gabri's eye went wide in surprise. "Are you sure?" Encouraged by Rafe's nod, he turned and smiled at Bronte. "You do have a papa. I'm your papa, too," he said softly pointing to himself.

Bronte studied him and took in the information. "Yay!" She laughed happily. "I have a papa too!" She hugged Gabri then reached for Rafe who pulled her to her lap. "If Gabri is my papa then Mommy must be Zen's mommy too!" she said in her toddler logic.

Rafe and Gabri sat silently again not knowing exactly how to untangle from the situation. "I've got this," said Rafe. She turned to Bronte. "Nora is Zenzo's mama, and you call her Nora. Your mommy's name is Eden, and that's what Zenzo will call her. So you will have a mama, a mommy, a papa, and a Nora. The baby will have a mama, a papa, an Eden, and a Rafe," she explained.

"But he needs a mommy," Bronte insisted. "I'll go ask Mommy," she decided. Jumping from Rafe's lap, she went back over to Nora and Eden.

Gabri grimaced at Rafe. "We have a complicated family."

Rafe nodded. "Yes, but none of our babies will be lonely only children like we were. They'll always have us and each other."

"You don't think Nora will want another baby very soon, do you?" he asked warily.

"I don't know," said Rafe with a casual shrug. "Eden gave me a mothers ring with three spaces in it, so I'm pretty sure it means she wants two more. Do you know how many Nora wants?"

Gabri's eyes went wide, and he went a little paler as he shook his head no. "That would mean I'd have four or five," he put his hand to his head, "or even more children."

Rafe laughed at the look on his face. "Don't get ahead of yourself. Who said we'd be using you as the donor again?"

"Why wouldn't you?" Gabri demanded, offended. "I make beautiful babies."

Rafe laughed harder and then pushed him over a bit playfully. "You know, Papa," she said nodding toward the children, "now that we're all family, we can never do anything to make anyone feel threatened or unwelcome."

Gabri looked down at his hands guiltily. "She told you?" Rafe nodded, confirming that Eden had informed her about Gabri's intimidating words about making things hard when it came to

Bronte. "I just wanted to make sure she didn't hurt you," he said softly.

"I know," said Rafe, patting him on the leg gently. "You don't have to worry about that anymore, though. We can all be happy together now. Plus, if you really think we should use your gift again, you'll need to reassure her."

"She will know," he promised. "Do you think she will ever be able to accept and love me too?"

"I think she wants too," said Rafe. "She agreed to tell Bronte you are her father." She chuckled at the surprise on Gabri's face. "I better go see if I can rescue Nora and Eden from Bronte," she said and went to see how the conversation was going. She sat down next to Eden who was holding Bronte. "So, did Bronte tell you Gabri is her papa?"

"Yes," she said and gave Rafe a look. She had not been prepared to say anything yet, though she knew Bronte had been asking questions. She knew Rafe would have to tell her sooner or later. Eden just thought it might be later. "It was a surprising revelation. Apparently, I may be Zenzo's mommy too."

"Yes," Nora added, "we're still in negotiations."

Rafe laughed and pulled Bronte to her. "You know what I think is a good idea? I think we should let Zenzo grow up. Then we can talk to him about it. Okay?"

"Okay," Bronte agreed happily. She jumped up and ran to play with the kittens stalking each other playfully at the edge of the garden.

"Good save," Nora said with an appreciative laugh.

"I think you need to go save Gabri now," said Rafe with a mischievous grin. "He just realized you may want more children."

"Oh, I do," said Nora and chuckled as she gathered the baby and went to sit with Gabri.

Happily, Rafe crawled around behind Eden and pulled her back against her. She kissed her on her shoulder and neck. "I can't wait to have you alone again," she purred.

Eden felt a tingling sensation run through her body at Rafe's words as the memory of what they had been doing earlier clouded her mind. She relaxed and enjoyed the feel of her kisses and rested with her back against Rafe as they watched Bronte together.

"Should we get her a puppy?" asked Rafe.

Eden rubbed Rafe's leg. "What's making you think about getting a puppy? You think with Nora and Gabri gone, she might get lonely?"

Rafe shifted and hesitated. "No," she said softly. "I've just been thinking about what you told me about your dream life. I think it included a puppy and a white fence."

"Oh," Eden said dragging out the vowel. "Well, those things aren't my dreams anymore." She turned and gave Rafe a sweet kiss.

Seeing Rafe happy again made Eden feel so good, and seeing her family together and spending time together, just the three of them, was better than any dream she may have grown up with. This was true love. Real love. She knew they had a ways to go and more things to resolve, but she also knew they would make it together.

Eden leaned her head back and looked up at Rafe. "Can I tell you something?" she asked softly.

"Yes," Rafe said as she kissed the top of Eden's head, "tell me, *mia dolce*."

Eden smiled at hearing Rafe softly call her *mia dolce*—my sweet—again. "I love you, and I want to be with you forever," Eden said and held Rafe's hand to her stomach.

"Forever," said Rafe and smiled at Eden's words. "Forever's a long time."

"A very long time," Eden nodded against Rafe.

Rafe kissed Eden's neck and whispered in her ear, "I have something for you in my left pocket."

"Your left," Eden's voice caught at the sensation Rafe caused in her, "pocket?" she repeated.

"Yes," said Rafe with her mouth still close to Eden's ear.

"What is it?" asked Eden as he turned her head and smiled up at Rafe. "Will you give it to me?"

Rafe gave her a playful smile then leaned back on her elbows, "You can have it, but you have to reach into my pocket to get it."

"Rafe," Eden groaned, "you better not be playing some kind of joke on me," she said as she remembered all the silly tricks Rafe and Gabri had taught Bronte. She was still recovering from some of them—specifically the spiders and mice. She would put up with it forever though to see Rafe happy.

Rafe chuckled and pulled her back. "I'm not playing a joke on you. If you don't want it," she let the sentence trail off and shrugged.

Eden felt Rafe shrug, and she leaned her head back against her again and chuckled. "I want it." She reached back and slipped her fingers into Rafe's left pocket. She pulled out a small flat box and sat up as she held it in front of herself and opened it. Inside were the rings they wore when they were together—one Eden had taken off when she left the second time, and the other Rafe had taken off—Eden couldn't remember when. She wondered how Rafe got them here because her things from home hadn't made it yet. "How did you get these?"

"I had Letty send them to me when they were sorting your things for shipping here and to storage," she said. She sat up and pulled Eden back so she would lean into her again. "I had her ship them separately so they'd get here faster."

Eden contemplated the rings and felt their warmth in her hands. "Rafe." Eden sighed. "This," she hesitated, "this isn't what I want." She felt Rafe stiffen behind her and her body trembled slightly. "I'm sorry," she said softly, "but I've been having these feelings," she admitted as she laid her head back on to Rafe. "I want something else." She leaned forward and turned to look into Rafe's hurting gray-blue eyes. "I've been working through things and thinking about this a lot." She paused, "I don't want to make another mistake." She watched Rafe swallow and look away. "I don't want you to think I'm just doing or saying something without thinking about it, without knowing I'm serious. I want you to know I'm taking this, us..." She touched Rafe's face and turned her head so she could look into her eyes. "And our family very seriously." She paused and beheld the woman she loved. She knew everything was right. She took a breath. "I want a real wedding."

"You," Rafe stammered, "a... but..." She was speechless.

Eden smiled then leaned over and kissed Rafe. "I want to be Eden Kingsley-Salvaggio," she said and kissed her again. "Then we can all claim the Salvaggio pride." She kissed her again. "And make sure everyone knows," she kissed her again, "this wildling is off limits." She smiled and looked into her eyes.

Rafe gathered herself from the emotions swirling inside her from Eden's words and kisses. "What about all the stuff you said about heterosexual archetypes and not wanting to be conformist? You said marriage wasn't for you."

"I changed my mind," Eden said with a shrug, imitating Rafe. "I want a wedding. I want to make an honest woman of you. I want us," she said with certainty, "to be legally married. I know it won't be right away," she added quickly and a bit nervously. "I know we'll have to figure out if we want to go back to California or somewhere else for the wedding. I know it'll mean a prenup rivaling anything I've ever seen before, but I'll sign it. I'll sign anything you want. I love you, and I trust you. I don't ever want to be without you again."

"You want to be Eden Kingsley-Salvaggio?" asked Rafe bewildered and still not convinced.

"Well, just Eden Salvaggio after a while," said Eden as she nodded her confirmation. "I've already emailed Katheryn about starting the paperwork to change my name," she said casually. "The day you marry me, it'll be filed."

"You want to change your name?" Rafe asked dismayed. "To Eden Salvaggio?"

"Well," Eden began happily, "I'll keep it hyphenated for a while, but eventually, yes." She nodded. "Just Eden Salvaggio."

Rafe shook her head, "I don't understand."

"So you don't want me to claim any of the Salvaggio pride?" Eden laughed at Rafe's reaction. "I've decided when they talk about Salvaggio's Paradise, they'll be talking about both of us." It had taken her a long time, but she understood now the love behind being called Salvaggio's Paradise and wanted to add her own love for Rafe to that designation.

"You want to marry me and take my name?" asked Rafe again to make sure it was real.

Nora walked up with the baby just in time to overhear Rafe. What she heard as a marriage proposal. "Oh my god!" she exclaimed happily. "You're getting married?"

"I haven't agreed to anything yet," Rafe mumbled annoyed.

Nora saw the look of confusion on Rafe's face, but the beaming smile on Eden's. After spending time with Eden, she knew now why Rafe loved her. After working through her shyness, Eden was very kind and genuine. Once she understood Eden's chronic anxiety, Nora was able to tell the difference between her shyness and discomfort on a higher level. Now that Eden was comfortable and surer of her footing, it was like she was a new person. She was bright, cheerful, and completely in love with Rafe.

"Well, I guess I'll just go back over there and let you two figure things out then," she said winking at Eden playfully then walking away with the baby.

Eden saw the uncertainty in Rafe's demeanor. "Well, now it's official," Eden said with a cheeky smile. "You have to marry me," she declared. "Nora is probably telling Gabri."

Rafe frowned as she watched Nora sit beside Gabri. "Eden, this is very serious," Rafe said as she looked searchingly into her eyes. "Can I think about it?"

"Think about it?" asked Eden, momentarily stung. Then she saw Rafe trying to hide her smile. "No," she said firmly, smiling back, "you can't think about it. I'm marrying you. I want to open our champagne and whatever else you may have in storage. We're getting married and inviting everyone we know because when we get married, it's going to be a big celebration." She saw Rafe raise her eyebrows. "Really big!" Eden grinned.

Rafe couldn't help smiling back at Eden and the light of love glowing from her eyes. "We're getting married," she said in awe, trying to wrap her mind around the idea because it was something she never thought would happen for them.

Eden nodded and couldn't stop her grin. "Yes, I love you, and I want to be with you forever... and you're mine." She looked lovingly into her eyes. "You're *my* paradise."

Rafe reached out and pulled Eden close, catching her in a deep and loving kiss, one that was theirs to share with each other forever.

"I want kisses too!" Bronte shouted as she flew into her parents' arms.

Rafe hugged Bronte tight and kissed her, and then released her to Eden, who the toddler promptly kissed. Rafe laughed—her heart full at the vision before her. She kissed them both again. "We all get kisses in paradise!"

NOTES

Translations: For translations of Italian, French and Spanish use: www.Babblefish.com

The chapters in this book were arranged with the intent of saving paper. This chapter style saved 18 pages. Original Total Book Pages 332 — Final Pages 314.

♫♪♫
Music mentioned in this book.

No financial incentive was given for the mention of the following artists in this work. The author is a fan and felt mentioning them worked in the story. For the use of their name, credit is given, and links to their work are below.

Enjoy!

King Princess

Website: https://kingprincessmusic.com/
Facebook: https://www.facebook.com/KingPrincess69/
Instagram: https://www.instagram.com/kingprincess69/
iTunes: https://itunes.apple.com/us/artist/king-princess/1349968534
Twitter: https://twitter.com/KingPrincess69
YouTube: Subscribe to King Princess

ABOUT THE AUTHOR

C.L. CATTANO LIVES in the Midwestern U.S. with her partner and their dog somewhere between the city and the forest. With a joy for traveling, she and her partner have visited many countries and have a love for meeting people and learning about the places they visit. When possible, she likes to include references in her work about the things she has learned, the places she has been and people she has met while on her travels and in her everyday life.

Cattano has a variety of creative interests including, but not limited to, creating fine art, writing, photography, and supporting women in the arts. She considers herself a 'Jack of All Trades' dabbling in what she terms the 'whimsies of her soul' that pull her toward happiness and fulfillment.

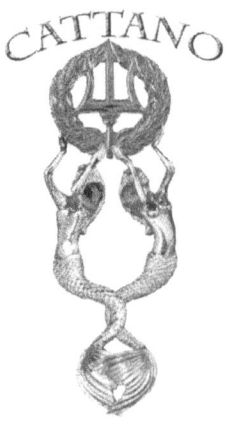

OTHER BOOKS
By C. L. Cattano

Cursed Hearts is a love story transcending time and gender. Two souls, separated by a gift from a bored demon on All Hallows Eve, have been searching through time for each other and have been incarnated as both men and women.

Over time, the gift became a curse and a game for the demons. Connected by the power of love, the two souls have finally met again, and now they must fight for a life together.

Will love prevail? Will they finally be able to live together again for a lifetime? They have one night to figure out the riddle and get it right to break the curse.

NOTE: 18+ Lesbian Romance. Some light erotic moments.

Salvaggio's Light Series

It takes true love to survive secrets, lies, and betrayals from within and without.

Get ready to settle into this epic contemporary drama-filled romance entwined comedy, lust, danger, thrills, regret, tragedy, suspense, and love.

Check out the Salvaggio's Light Facebook page to join in the discussions and fun! www.facebook.com/pg/SalvaggiosLight

Join the CL Cattano Mailing List www.clcattano.com

I love getting fan mail, and you can contact me at clc@clcattano.com

REQUEST FOR REVIEW

Thank you for reading **Salvaggio's Light** — *An Epic Contemporary Romance Serial.*

I hope you enjoyed book ten, **Frenzied Love**, and will consider leaving an honest review. It only takes a few minutes, so I encourage you to go now and leave a review!

Need help writing a review?
Try the Random Review Generator by A. E. Radley!
It's Free!

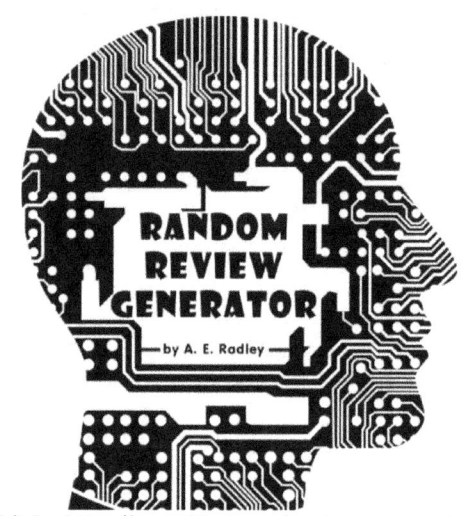

Link: http://aeradley.com/review-generator/